W9-AMU-609

August 2016

Dear Reader,

My career as a novelist started with a rented typewriter, a manual one because the cost of an electric was prohibitive. We were a one-income family, and I was a stay-at-home mom with four youngsters. I put the typewriter on the kitchen table and moved it for mealtimes, and whenever I could, I pounded away on those keys, dreaming one day of selling a novel. *Starlight* was the first book I wrote. And no, it didn't sell—well, not right away. The story was good, but the writing was, in a word, pitiful. I went on to write three additional books on that same typewriter. In fact, I wrote eight books on that rent-to-own manual until the *S* key gave out. Through pure stubbornness (a family trait!) I refused to give up on my dream and eventually I sold. *Starlight* got a complete rewrite and became my first published book. Even now, all these years later, I still believe it's a good story.

I refreshed *Promise Me Forever* for this volume and was surprised at the growth I'd made as a writer between these two books. I wrote it in 1985, which was also fairly early in my writing career. By the way, the bird in the story, Ugly Arnie, is real. My two sons rescued him and he was the most cantankerous, ungrateful creature you can imagine. I used a bit of literary license to soften him up a bit.

My hope is that you'll enjoy both romances. I always love hearing from my readers. I can guarantee that I read every letter and every entry that goes through my website. You can reach me through Facebook or my website at www.debbiemacomber.com. My mailing address is P.O. Box 1458, Port Orchard, WA 98366.

Thank you for your ongoing support of me and my books.

Warmest regards,

Debbie Macomber

Praise for the novels of #1 *New York Times* bestselling author Debbie Macomber

"Macomber is a skilled storyteller."

—*Publishers Weekly*

"It's easy to see why Macomber is a perennial favorite: she writes great books."

—*RomanceJunkies.com*

"Macomber spins another pure-from-the-heart romance giddy with love and warm laughter..."

—*Bookpage* on *The Snow Bride*

"Debbie Macomber writes characters who are as warm and funny as your best friends."

—*New York Times* bestselling author Susan Wiggs

"Macomber's storytelling sometimes yields a tear, at other times a smile."

—*Newport News, VA Daily Press*

"When God created Eve, he must have asked Debbie Macomber for advice because no one does female characters any better than this author."

—*Bookbrowser Reviews* on *16 Lighthouse Road*

"Debbie Macomber is one of the most reliable, versatile romance authors around. Whether she's writing light-hearted romps or more serious relationship books, her novels are always engaging stories that accurately capture the foibles of real-life men and women with warmth and humor."

—*Milwaukee Journal Sentinel*

"Popular romance author Debbie Macomber has a gift for evoking the emotions that are at the heart of the genre's popularity."

—*Publishers Weekly*

DEBBIE MACOMBER

On a Clear Day

MIRA®

If you purchased this book without a cover you should be aware that this book is stolen property. It was reported as "unsold and destroyed" to the publisher, and neither the author nor the publisher has received any payment for this "stripped book."

ISBN-13: 978-0-373-60321-3

On a Clear Day

Copyright © 2014 by Harlequin Books S.A.

The publisher acknowledges the copyright holder of the individual works as follows:

Starlight
Copyright © 1983 by Debbie Macomber

Promise Me Forever
Copyright © 1985 by Debbie Macomber

All rights reserved. Except for use in any review, the reproduction or utilization of this work in whole or in part in any form by any electronic, mechanical or other means, now known or hereinafter invented, including xerography, photocopying and recording, or in any information storage or retrieval system, is forbidden without the written permission of the publisher, Harlequin Enterprises Limited, 225 Duncan Mill Road, Don Mills, Ontario, Canada, M3B 3K9.

This is a work of fiction. Names, characters, places and incidents are either the product of the author's imagination or are used fictitiously, and any resemblance to actual persons, living or dead, business establishments, events or locales is entirely coincidental.

This edition published by arrangement with Harlequin Books S.A.

For questions and comments about the quality of this book, please contact us at CustomerService@Harlequin.com.

® and TM are trademarks of the publisher. Trademarks indicated with ® are registered in the United States Patent and Trademark Office, the Canadian Intellectual Property Office and in other countries.

Recycling programs for this product may not exist in your area.

Printed in U.S.A.

www.Harlequin.com

For all wounded heroes,
injured birds and children with big hearts.

Midnight Sons
VOLUME 1
  (*Brides for Brothers* and
  The Marriage Risk)
VOLUME 2
  (*Daddy's Little Helper* and
  Because of the Baby)
VOLUME 3
  (*Falling for Him,
  Ending in Marriage* and
  Midnight Sons and Daughters)

This Matter of Marriage
Montana
Thursdays at Eight
Between Friends
Changing Habits
Married in Seattle
  (*First Comes Marriage* and
  Wanted: Perfect Partner)
Right Next Door
  (*Father's Day* and
  The Courtship of Carol Sommars)
Wyoming Brides
  (*Denim and Diamonds* and
  The Wyoming Kid)
Fairy Tale Weddings
  (*Cindy and the Prince* and
  Some Kind of Wonderful)
The Man You'll Marry
  (*The First Man You Meet* and
  The Man You'll Marry)
Orchard Valley Grooms
  (*Valerie* and *Stephanie*)
Orchard Valley Brides
  (*Norah* and *Lone Star Lovin'*)
The Sooner the Better
An Engagement in Seattle
  (*Groom Wanted* and
  Bride Wanted)
Out of the Rain
  (*Marriage Wanted* and
  Laughter in the Rain)
Learning to Love
  (*Sugar and Spice* and
  Love by Degree)

You...Again
  (*Baby Blessed* and
  Yesterday Once More)
The Unexpected Husband
  (*Jury of His Peers* and
  Any Sunday)
Three Brides, No Groom
Love in Plain Sight
  (*Love 'n' Marriage* and
  Almost an Angel)
I Left My Heart
  (*A Friend or Two* and
  No Competition)
Marriage Between Friends
  (*White Lace and Promises*
  and *Friends...And Then Some*)
A Man's Heart
  (*The Way to a Man's Heart*
  and *Hasty Wedding*)
North to Alaska
  (*That Wintry Feeling* and
  Borrowed Dreams)
On a Clear Day
  (*Starlight* and
  Promise Me Forever)
To Love and Protect
  (*Shadow Chasing* and
  For All My Tomorrows)
Home in Seattle
  (*The Playboy and the Widow*
  and *Fallen Angel*)
Together Again
  (*The Trouble with Caasi* and
  Reflections of Yesterday)
The Reluctant Groom
  (*All Things Considered*
  and *Almost Paradise*)
A Real Prince
  (*The Bachelor Prince*
  and *Yesterday's Hero*)
Private Paradise
  (in *That Summer Place*)

*Debbie Macomber's
  Cedar Cove Cookbook*
*Debbie Macomber's
  Christmas Cookbook*

CONTENTS

STARLIGHT

One

Karen had dreaded the party for weeks. Her father was sure to use it as another opportunity to find her a husband. She almost cringed at the thought of what lay before her—a succession of eligible men, abrupt introductions, and pointed questions. Yet she loved her godparents and wouldn't offend them by not attending their annual Christmas party.

"Are you ready, lass?" Matthew McAlister let himself into her apartment without the courtesy of knocking.

"Honestly, Dad, one of these days you're going to walk in here and find me stark naked," Karen admonished with a sigh.

Matthew chuckled.

Karen laughed, too, for it was difficult to maintain an injured air when her father was in this mood.

Stepping back to survey Karen, Matthew's eyes lit up in appreciation. "My heart swells with pride at the sight of you, lass," he said in a strong Scottish brogue.

Karen forced herself to smile. His speech always began the same way. After admiring her beauty, he

would recount the days he'd courted her mother and
their marriage when Madeline was nineteen. From there
he'd reiterate his growing desire for grandchildren, most
particularly a granddaughter. It was always the same,
to the point that Karen could have mouthed the words
along with him.

"Dad," she interrupted, "we'd better go. Snoqualmie
Falls is a forty-five-minute drive."

Surprisingly, Matthew insisted Karen drive. She did
so willingly, but glanced apprehensively at her father.
He looked tired and a bit ashen.

"Are you feeling okay, Dad?" she asked, hiding the
concern in her voice.

"Of course I am." He rallied somewhat. "I'm just
saving myself for the grand affair. Certain demands
are made of a widower these days, and the ladies are
expecting a good time."

They were greeted at the large rented hall with soft
Christmas music. The room was lavishly decorated
with hundreds of large, glittering snowflakes suspended
from the ceiling. The reflective glow of the turning
flakes cast the dimly lit room into a winter wonderland.

The hall was already crowded. Several others had arrived and were milling around, chatting in small groups
and sipping champagne.

Evan Forsyth raised a welcoming hand when he saw
Matthew and Karen enter, and walked purposefully toward them. The two men clasped hands with the enthusiasm of many years of devoted friendship.

Her father and Evan had been friends since their
school days, and although they held separate stations
in life, their friendship had never wavered. Evan Forsyth was the president of the University of Washington

at Tacoma, an honored and respected man, while Matthew McAlister was a small-businessman dealing in plumbing supplies. For as long as Karen could remember, her father and godfather had played chess every Thursday night.

The annual party had begun many years before, when Karen and her sister, Judy, were small. Evan and Milly Forsyth invited a few intimate friends into their home to share the joy of the holiday season. Over the years, as Evan's position became prominent, the size of the affair had grown to include business friends and faculty members. This year, the party was so large the Forsyths had rented a hall, their spacious home no longer large enough to hold the growing number of guests.

"Welcome, welcome," Evan said and smiled warmly. His wife, Milly, followed close behind and embraced Karen fondly.

"I'm so pleased you could make it, my dear."

Evan leisurely surveyed Karen, noting how the red velvet gown molded to the slender curves of her womanly figure.

"I swear you get prettier every year, Karen," he said with a hug.

"And I swear your tongue grows smoother every year."

Evan chuckled with delight while Milly tucked an arm around Karen's waist to give her a slight hug. "He's right, dear. You look radiant. And your gown suits you beautifully."

Karen returned the hug and smiled. "It should, considering what I paid for it."

Karen had gasped when the salesclerk had told her the price, and disregarded the woman's complimentary words as an effective sales pitch. But now she willingly conceded that the effect of the simple but elegant style had been worth the price.

The four chatted until social obligations demanded the Forsyths' attention. After sampling several of the hors d'oeuvres and speaking with acquaintances, Karen and her father watched as the floor was cleared to make room for dancing.

Matthew surveyed the crowd while gently directing Karen as they danced the first waltz. His eyes glowed with amusement as he remarked, "There are several available men here. Take advantage of the opportunity to snare yourself a husband."

Karen stiffened and pulled away from her father.

Almost angrily, Matthew continued, "I can't understand what's the matter with men today. You're lovely, Karen."

"Dad, please..." A note of helplessness entered her voice. Karen was so weary of this argument. A thousand times she'd explained that the problem wasn't with men; it was with her. So many of the men she'd dated over the years were self-centered and egotistical, seeking easy conquests and one-night stands. It was almost to the point that she'd rather not date at all. Her natural good looks and vivacious personality invited the attention. But Karen had yet to discover what it was about herself that attracted the least-desirable males.

"I'm perfectly content with my life as it is." Karen sighed with impatience, tilting her chin defiantly.

"But I want grandchildren..."

"You have grandchildren," Karen reminded him coolly. "What do you call James and Carter?"

"I want a granddaughter." Matthew flashed her a disputatious look.

"Dad," Karen pleaded, "let's not argue tonight. You have grandchildren, and more than likely you'll have your precious granddaughter." Karen didn't know how much more she could endure. Matthew had applied constant pressure on her to marry for the past six months. The argument had nearly ruined their close relationship. Unable to endure his interference with her life, Karen had moved into her own apartment. It was a move long overdue. It'd been convenient to live at home and easy to rationalize her father's need for her after her mother's death. Much to her chagrin, Matthew sold their home and moved into an apartment in the same building as Karen. If anything, matters had gotten worse.

As they continued to waltz across the room, Karen caught sight of Mabel Jackson, an aging widow who'd made no effort to disguise her attraction to Matthew. *Turnabout is fair play,* she mused, and giggled devilishly.

"Do you find something amusing, lass?" Matthew asked curiously.

"No. Excuse me, Dad. I see someone I'd like to talk to." Cleverly, she wove her way through the thick couples toward the widow.

"Mrs. Jackson, you look lovely tonight," Karen greeted sweetly.

Mabel Jackson ignored the greeting and craned her long neck to stare into the dancing figures.

"Is your father here?" she asked with obvious interest.

"He sure is. In fact, it was my father who commented

on how radiant you look. Dad said he'd never seen anyone more lovely."

"He did?" The woman beamed and smoothed the
hairs of her lopsided wig.

"You know, Mrs. Jackson, my father is a lonely man.
He'd never admit it, of course, but Dad needs a woman.
A real woman." Karen stared into the crowd, unable to
meet the widow's triumphant gaze.

Mabel Jackson positively glowed. "My dear child,
I'm so glad we've had this little talk. Leave your father to me."

Karen smiled broadly and felt that even if she ended
up disinherited, the taste of revenge was indeed sweet.

In a matter of minutes, several men were vying for
Karen's attention. She danced with a number of partners, young and old, her infectious laughter ringing
through the hall as she surrendered to a swelling tide
of triumph. Not once was she interrupted by her father's forcing what he considered eligible men on her.
An hour later, she managed to catch Matthew's eye and
winked wickedly as he waltzed by in the arms of Mabel
Jackson. Matthew cast her a look that threatened bodily
harm, and Karen burst into helpless giggles.

A moment later, she caught sight of her father's
angry stride as he wove through the crowd toward her.
Wishing to avoid the taste of his Scottish temper, she
hastily sought an escape. A curtained glass door leading to a balcony caught her attention. Unnoticed, she
quietly slipped into the dark, leaving her father perplexed by her sudden disappearance.

Peering through the sheer curtain, Karen waited impatiently for Matthew to abandon his search.

"I beg your pardon," came a deep voice from behind her as she backed into a solid form.

"Oh! Excuse me." She fumbled and quickly straightened. "I didn't realize there was anyone out here."

"Obviously," came the clipped reply as he stared into the dark. Karen watched him for a few minutes, but he made no effort to meet her gaze.

"Would you mind sharing your hideaway for a minute?" she asked sweetly, and deliberately blinked her long, curling lashes at his impassive expression. Men were usually quick to respond to her expressive brown eyes.

"Suit yourself," he retorted unenthusiastically, and continued to stare into the night.

Undaunted by his lack of welcome, Karen joined him at the railing and searched the sky to discover what was so fascinating. The night was cold, crisp, and clear; the stars shone with a brilliant intensity.

"Leave it to my godfather to order a star display for the night of his party," Karen murmured. Her gaze returned to the stranger's face and swept his appearance. He wore a trim-fitting, dark wool suit that hugged his slim hips and long legs. The harsh contours of his face remained blank under her examination.

"Look!" Karen exclaimed, pointing her finger to the sky and counting the stars. "It's Perseus. I can't remember when I've seen the constellation stand out so clearly. You do see it, don't you?"

"No, I'm afraid I don't," he remarked dryly.

"Sure you do. Just look a little to your left," she persisted.

"Listen," he snapped impatiently, "whatever your name may be—"

"Karen McAlister," she interrupted, "and you're...?"

"Randall Prescott," he replied in a voice that spoke plainly of trepidation.

"Well, look again. It's up there plain as day." She pointed to it again for his benefit. "Really, it's very clear, if you'll just look..."

"Mrs. McAlister..."

"Miss," Karen informed him cheerfully.

"Miss McAlister..." he tried again.

"Please call me Karen."

Drawing in a breath as if to hold on to his limited patience, he began again. "Karen... Miss McAlister... whatever it is you wish to be called, I cannot view your precious Perseus, and I shall never view it. I'm blind!"

Karen felt the full impact of shock. After a moment of startled silence, she blurted out, "Oh, dear, Mr. Prescott, I do apologize."

"Randall," he interrupted.

"I had no idea, Randall. I..."

"Please call me Rand," he taunted softly.

"All right, Rand," she replied, a smile evident in her voice, "but please accept my apology."

"An apology is unnecessary; my blindness cannot be attributed to your faults," he countered stiffly.

"No, of course not, but I was being obtuse."

He turned toward her then, allowing for the first time a clear view of his rugged features. He certainly didn't fit her image of what a blind man might look like. His face was boldly defined, almost ruthless. There was a magnetic quality about his dark brown eyes that captured her gaze.

"I don't suppose you came out here without your

coat to view the stars?" he asked roughly, as if aware of her eyes studying him.

"How do you know I'm not wearing a coat?" she asked. Was this unnerving man playing her for a fool?

A sardonic smile touched the corners of his mouth. "I don't. But I suspect the slight quiver in your voice is from a chill."

Karen suddenly realized she was cold. Snoqualmie Falls was only a few minutes from the summit of Snoqualmie Pass, over the Cascades. The bitter December wind bit into her.

"Why are you hiding?" he asked, more gently. "Is someone bothering you?"

"Oh, heavens, no!" she quickly assured him, but paused. "Well, yes and no. I routed a persistent widow toward my father and was sure to taste his anger had I remained inside."

Rand smiled at her predicament, his roguish features relaxing his expression. "I'm sure the whole incident has been forgiven. You can't stay here. You'll freeze."

It was clearly a dismissal, and Karen felt strangely disappointed. She wanted to stay and learn more about this enigmatic stranger. He was the first man to really interest her in a long while. She hovered in the doorway, hoping to find an excuse to remain, but found none.

"Are you coming, too?"

"Later," he replied indifferently, and appeared bored with her company.

Karen could only leave. "Then perhaps we'll meet again," she said softly.

"It's unlikely," he mumbled, as if he hadn't intended her to hear. She watched as he returned to the railing.

Karen didn't immediately see her father once she'd

entered the warmth of the large reception hall. Mrs. Jackson was standing near the orchestra, waving her hand impatiently in an attempt to gain the conductor's attention.

"Here you are."

The voice startled Karen, and she jerked around to see her godfather. "Uncle Evan." She placed a trembling hand over her heart to dramatize her fright. "You're worse than a thief in the night."

Evan Forsyth's eyes twinkled. "Your father's looking for you."

Karen lowered her gaze, a little ashamed of her ploy. As much as Matthew irritated her, she loved him and realized he had only her best interests at heart.

"I suppose he's still angry?" she asked.

"Let's put it this way," Evan said, chuckling. "He hasn't had a free second since you spoke with Mabel. He's hiding in the men's room. I think we'd better dance before he decides it's safe to return."

"Oh, dear, I'm in for it now," she mumbled as her godfather led her to the dance floor. It was a waltz, which gave her the opportunity to speak. "I'm afraid I made a blunder with one of your guests."

Evan's eyes rounded, feigning shock. "You seem to be making a night of it, my dear. Want to talk about it?" His position with the university and in the community made him a ready listener to the troubles of others.

Karen felt uneasy. "I'm afraid I literally bumped into Randall Prescott—"

"Ah," Evan interrupted her. "I imagine he was rude. He tends to be the prickly sort. Damn good professor, though, the finest. We offer the best business program in the state due to him. Prescott could teach anywhere.

The university is lucky to have him." He hesitated, his thick brows knitting his forehead. "Was Cora with him?"

"Cora? No. Who's she?" It hadn't occurred to Karen that Rand was married. The thought deflated her.

"That's unusual. Rand rarely attends any social functions without her."

"Is Cora his wife?" Karen hoped to hide any telltale inflection of curiosity from her voice.

"No, she's a business associate. They've collaborated together, books and the like."

Karen felt herself relax, an excitement flowing through her limbs.

Sensing her interest, Evan felt obliged to add, "I wouldn't discourage you, Karen, but Randall Prescott is a bit of a cynic. A difficult man to get to know. He's independent and proud, highly defensive of his blindness. He's not your normal chivalrous hero…tread carefully."

"Who says I'm interested?" Karen asked defensively.

Evan chuckled. "Karen, I've known you all your life. Certainly I know you well enough to recognize that gleam in your eye."

Several minutes later, Karen saw Rand sitting unobtrusively in the rear of the hall. She had been waiting for his appearance, silently searching faces. Now she wondered how to gain his attention. In answer to her problem, the orchestra conductor turned to face his audience and announced the first ladies' choice of the evening.

Mabel Jackson, with a satisfied smirk, made a beeline for Matthew, who had recently reappeared. Karen groaned in sympathy and walked toward the back of the reception room and the mystifying Randall Prescott.

Without introduction or preamble, she curtsied. "May I have the pleasure of this dance?"

Rand sat up abruptly and stiffened. "Miss McAlister?"

"Karen," she corrected impishly.

"All right, *Karen*. Let's not go through that again." A smile threatened the stiff line of his mouth.

He hesitated so long, Karen grew uncomfortable. "You did hear them mention it was ladies' choice, didn't you?"

He held his shoulders stiff and formal. "I'm honored, but no." His mouth remained inflexible.

Karen would have been surprised if he'd accepted. "Well, that's fine; my feet are beginning to ache, anyway. New shoes," she explained before taking the seat beside him.

If he was surprised, he didn't show it. "Have a seat," he offered sarcastically.

Karen ignored his derision. "Thank you, I have."

Apparently, he felt no inclination to speak, and Karen was courteous enough not to press. After a dance or two, she discovered that she was completely content to sit with him, not talking, if he wished. She hummed and watched the dancers as they waltzed through the wintry scene. She could almost see Rand relax his guard and accept her company.

"Aren't the decorations magnificent?" she asked thoughtlessly, then gasped, recognizing her blunder. How stupid could she be? "If my new shoes are tight, I needn't worry," she apologized. "After they've been in my mouth a couple of times, they'll fit fine. That was stupid. Please excuse me," she added soberly.

"Don't worry," he assured her, almost enjoying her

discomfort. "It's a common mistake. Describe the decorations, will you?"

It was a pleasure to narrate the lovely scene portrayed by the dangling snowflakes. With her natural flair for theatrics, she described the hall in graphic detail. In afterthought, she added interesting tidbits she knew about some of its occupants.

"It's almost impossible to tell when Uncle Evan is angry or upset, but he has a telltale twitch in his upper lip. If you see it move, watch out. And then there's Clayton Dunbar, a distant relative of the Forsyths. He's about as subtle as a garden serpent and has the sincerity of a used-car salesman. He marks his conquests on his bedpost to brag to his friends."

"Do I detect a note of mockery?"

"No use hiding the fact that I detest the man. He's about as obvious as a Sherman tank." It was unlike Karen to be catty, and she immediately felt guilty. Besides, was she being any less obvious about her interest in Rand? "That's unfair. I'm sure Clayton has several good qualities...somewhere."

Rand gave a hearty laugh. "You're apt at describing others. How would you depict yourself?"

"I couldn't," she protested automatically. "How do you picture me?"

"You have an intriguing voice." He paused, thinking. "But I'm not referring to the tone quality. You possess an unshakable resolve. I doubt that you've ever failed in any pursuit. You're upbeat, cheerful."

"Heavens," Karen said dryly, "you make me sound like a high school cheerleader."

"Definitely not high school. You must be all of nineteen, maybe twenty."

Karen laughed lightly. "I'm a whole world away from high school or college. I'm twenty-three."

Rand grinned, then added, "You must be five-seven, five-eight at the most."

Impressed, Karen lifted her brows expressively. "Five-seven."

"Long dark hair and metallic-blue eyes."

"Short dark curls, equally dark eyes."

A hand cupped the back of her neck; his fingers twisted the pliable curls. Karen was too startled by the sudden action to protest. Her heart rate soared as a languorous warmth spread from her neck.

He chuckled softly and said, "Yes, short, but soft and inviting. Your eyes must be expressive, promising." He relaxed against his chair, the dim light illuminating his strongly defined features. Again, Karen experienced the full impact of his masculinity.

"That's not quite right, but I'm not going to disillusion you with the truth." She laughed because she'd always thought her dark eyes, the color of bitter chocolate, were plain. Rand made them sound exciting and enticing.

"Give me your hand," he said suddenly. When she complied, his fingers gently examined hers. "You're not a secretary, or your fingertips wouldn't be this smooth. Nor do you walk with the crisp purpose of a nurse."

"That's a chauvinistic attitude. All women aren't secretaries or nurses. I'm not a teacher, either."

"Aha!" He laughed again. "You're employed in a man's field."

Karen smiled at his novel methods of deducing her occupation, but the smile died quickly as she spied

Clayton Dunbar eyeing her from the edge of the dance floor. She stiffened instinctively, her reluctance obvious.

"Is something wrong?" Rand questioned.

"My wicked past is about to catch up with me. Dad's revenge is here." Karen had dated Clayton only once and spent the entire evening fighting off his sexual advances. She hadn't told her father for fear of offending the Forsyths; now she recognized her error.

"Karen, baby, it's good to see you. I see you've been waiting for me. Let's dance."

Karen's mind whirled, searching for a plausible excuse to refuse as she stood.

Suddenly, Rand rose beside Karen, his imposing frame dwarfing Clayton's. "Excuse me," he said stiffly, "but you'll have to wait your turn. This dance is mine."

In his eagerness to corner Karen, Clayton hadn't noticed her formidable companion. His smug expression instantly turned to that of a deprived child.

Karen's mood lightened immediately. Placing her hand in Rand's, she led the way to the dance floor. With a devilish gleam, she turned back and smiled cheerfully. "Ta-ta, Clayton."

Rand took the lead, guiding her firmly but cautiously through the array of dancers. The dance floor was unfamiliar territory, but his movements were made skillfully and with confidence. He held her lightly, and a warmth flowed through her.

"How are we doing?" he questioned.

"Fine," she assured him. "You don't like to dance, do you?" He so obviously didn't, Karen wondered what had made him offer.

"Let's just say I have an easy enough time making a fool of myself without doing it purposely."

Impulsively, Karen raised her head and gently laid her lips against the rough line of his jaw. "Thank you," she whispered softly.

He drew her slightly closer, and her mind whirled in a confused mixture of emotions. Surely she hadn't imbibed that much champagne. A glass or two, three at the most. Why should this one man affect her like this?

"I didn't want to let you go," he whispered into her hair, as if admitting to a fault, his voice low and husky.

"I didn't want to go, either." She sighed and rested her head against the velvety texture of his suit jacket.

His fingers spread across the small of her back, molding her slender figure against him. The beat of his heart sounded in her ear, telling her he was as affected by their closeness as she. Slowly, his hand stroked the back of her neck, his fingers entwining with her hair.

It wasn't necessary to talk. Karen hummed the melody as the musicians played, but the tune was inaudible compared to the glorious song her heart was singing. Somehow she'd always known it would be like this. Matthew had claimed he met Madeline and decided to marry her all in the space of one day's time. Karen had secretly scoffed. Choosing a life partner wasn't something one did after only a few hours' acquaintance. Now Karen realized her father had spoken the truth. Just as he had known, she knew now. She didn't love Rand; not yet. That would come later. But Karen had never been more certain of anything in her life. It was crazy, unorthodox.

"You're smiling, aren't you?" Rand asked after some time.

Karen had a difficult time finding her voice or thinking coherently. When she did answer, her voice was weak and low. "Yes, I am. How...how did you know?"

"I just do. I can feel it."

Karen didn't want to talk, afraid words would diminish the wonder of this enchanted evening. Instead, she surrendered to the tide of contentment that engulfed them both.

He squeezed her, and his strong hand cut into her waist, arching her even closer, as if he feared letting her go. "This is insane." His lips touched the crown of her hair, his breath stirring her short curls. But he didn't loosen his hold, nor did he give an indication of wanting to let her go.

Evan interrupted them with the news that Matthew was ready to leave. "He's waiting for you at the front entrance," Evan told Karen.

Reluctantly, Karen withdrew from Rand's arms.

"Dad and I rode together," she explained unnecessarily.

"Stay," Rand murmured. "I'll take you home."

"Fine, fine." Evan gave Karen a boyish wink. "I'm pleased you two are enjoying yourselves."

Slowly, Karen led the way off the dance floor, giving Rand time to reorient himself.

"I'll only be a minute." She left Rand beside the chairs they'd shared before dancing and hurried to meet Matthew. Without bothering to explain, she gave her father a peck on the cheek and told him she had a ride home and would talk to him in the morning. Leaving Matthew looking slightly perplexed, Karen rushed to the main part of the reception hall and Rand.

But Rand was nowhere to be seen. For an instant, panic filled her until comprehension came. This time she was wise enough to seek her coat before venturing into the cold.

Opening the glass door of the balcony, she saw him standing at the railing as before. He didn't turn toward her, although she was sure he'd heard the door open.

"Rand," she whispered, suddenly nervous.

He turned to her then, his face a mask of indecision and inner turmoil. Karen yearned to run to his arms and kiss away his misgivings, to assure him that this unfathomable feeling between them was right and good. But she was frozen, overcome by her own apprehensions.

"Rand, please," she pleaded, "don't shut me out."

At the sound of her trembling voice, Rand's hard features softened, and he opened his arms to her.

Hesitatingly, she came, sliding her hands around his middle. "I know it's crazy. I don't understand it, either," she admitted, her voice low and faltering.

"I've never experienced anything like this." His voice was a strange mixture of anger and wonder.

Karen wanted to assure him this phenomenon was as much a mystery to her. "Me either, never."

"Oh, what the hell," he groaned out before his mouth crushed down upon hers in a kiss that was both fierce and hungry. His arms, folded tightly around her, relaxed as the kiss continued. Their reaction shocked them both. It was as if a charge of lightning had arced between them, jolting them. They broke apart abruptly, and Karen's breath came in uneven gasps. Had she been less unnerved, she might have noticed Rand's breathing was just as uneven.

Gently, Rand pulled her back into his arms, as if he needed to further test this sensation. This time, his kiss was tender and sweet, his mouth settling firmly over hers, drawing from Karen her very soul. When he finished, she was trembling and weak.

"Dear heaven," he moaned into her hair, "what's happening?"

Karen laid her head against his shoulder. "It's an enchanted evening, and you're the gallant Perseus," she whispered a little breathlessly, still caught in the wonder of his kiss.

"I'm hardly the gallant one," Rand said with a hint of sarcasm. "It's more like a bewitched Perseus held captive by the charms of the Lady Andromeda." His finger and thumb stroked her chin sensuously.

Mentally, Karen recalled the mythological tale. "Perseus rescued Andromeda, remember? She was doomed without him." Breaking from his hold, Karen examined the sky. "Rand, Andromeda's there." Excitement crept into her voice as she needlessly pointed to the heavens.

Rand's arms surrounded her again. "Of course Andromeda's there. Perseus needs her," he murmured, as if admitting to his own lacking. "It's been said she's very beautiful. May I examine her?"

Karen didn't understand his meaning until his fingertips began gently caressing the contours of her face, causing her to blush. Her eyelashes fluttered downward in confusion.

"Not only soft and delicate but very, very lovely." His husky voice was filled with reverence. Tucking a hand beneath her chin, he lifted her face while his mouth made an unhurried descent to claim her lips. Again, Karen's mind whirled to a new height of sensual awareness.

"I can see a distinct advantage to your blindness,"

Karen mumbled once the rapid beat of her heart stilled. "I'm no raving beauty."

Her hands, pressing against his back, could feel his corded muscles tense. It was wrong to mention his handicap. "I shouldn't have said that," she began haltingly, uncertain. Her teeth bit into her bottom lip as if she wanted to bite back the thoughtless words. "I have much to learn, Rand. I guess I'm afraid of making another stupid blunder."

"That was a compliment," he said stiffly. "You spoke to me as you would any other companion. You didn't attempt to rescue me or fall into the traps others do. People tend to think that because I'm blind I must also be mentally retarded. Nothing on God's earth irritates me more. Treat me as you would any other man."

"Why are you so angry?" Karen asked, attempting to hide the hurt in her voice.

Rand forcefully released his breath before a smile lifted the corners of his mouth. "I guess I do tend to stand on a soapbox every now and then. What I'm trying to say is that I don't want to be treated like a blind man."

"That won't be difficult for me. I have a hard time remembering. You move with confidence and show none of the outward signs. I thought the blind used white canes or Seeing Eye dogs."

"I have partial vision," he explained, and his mouth returned to an inflexible line. "A bad case of the measles as a child ruined my vision, and it's grown steadily worse over the years."

"Then you can see some things?" she questioned.

"Very little. Soon it will be as you mentioned—the white cane or the dog."

With infinite tenderness, Karen's hands cupped his jaw to bring his face downward so she could very gently kiss each closed eye.

Rand groaned and pulled her tightly against him, his breathing ragged. "Oh, Karen," he murmured, holding her fiercely.

"Andromeda," she corrected with a smile.

They danced in each other's arms until there was no more music. They spoke little, embraced by the marvel of the night, creating their own world on a starlit balcony.

Rand was met outside the hall by a lanky, older man who stared curiously when he saw Karen was with Rand.

"Carl." Rand's grip tightened around Karen's waist. "I'd like you to meet the Lady Andromeda."

Without the slightest hesitation, the man grinned, showing crooked teeth but a ready, warm smile. "Pleased, I'm sure," he greeted her formally.

"I'm pleased, too, Carl. But to set the record straight, the name is Karen."

Carl grinned again and opened the back door of the car for them. "Where to?" he asked cheerfully as he started the engine.

"Karen," Rand whispered, "your address."

"Oh, of course." She supplied the information and leaned against the back of the seat until Rand's arm cupped her shoulder, drawing her close to his side. They rode in silence, bathed in a rare kind of contentment.

Sooner than Karen wanted, Carl arrived at her apartment complex. Rand walked her to her door.

Gently, her hand stroked his face. "Thank you for the lovely, enchanted evening, Perseus."

Rand's kiss was tender and fierce all at the same time. Karen clung to him and moaned as the dizzy weakness spread through her limbs. A smile tugged at the corners of her lips, and she closed her eyes, surrendering to the charge of emotion Rand wrought in her.

Again, his mouth parted hers with a kiss as searing as it was devastating. "Goodbye, my lady," he murmured, and pressed his lips against her fragrant hair.

Karen opened the apartment door and floated inside, her heart singing a glorious melody.

Two

Karen woke to the smell and sounds of perking coffee. Reluctantly, she rose, looping the tie of her velour bathrobe around her slender waist. Stifling a yawn, she sauntered from her bedroom; the aroma of the coffee guided her into the small kitchen. She took a mug from the cupboard and poured herself a cup, ignoring the fact that the coffeepot was still perking.

"Ye shouldn't be doing that." A foggy voice broke through her consciousness. "You'll get grounds in your cup."

Surprise snapped Karen's eyes open. "Dad! What are you doing here?"

An injured look narrowed the faded hazel eyes. "'Tis a fine greeting for your father."

Karen lowered herself into the large overstuffed chair opposite Matthew. "Dad, as much as I love you, I must insist you stop entering my apartment like this." She schooled her expression against the pleading puppy-dog look her father gave her.

"Forgive an old man's curiosity." He lowered his gaze, suddenly looking lost and aged beyond his years.

"All right, Dad, you're forgiven. Gosh, you look awful."

His mouth deepened into slanted grooves of amusement. "Too many dances with a demanding widow." The look he cast her sent Karen into helpless giggles.

"Serves you right, old man."

"You're the bane of my life, you wicked child," he teased lovingly. "Now, tell me about the fellow you met last night. Do you like him?"

Self-consciously, Karen centered her attention on the steaming mug cradled between her hands. "Very much."

When she didn't volunteer any further information, Matthew probed again. "Well, go on. What's his name? When will you be seeing him again?"

"Dad, honestly." Karen stood abruptly, her fluid movements displaying a subtle grace. "Did you suddenly join the FBI? I don't like being interrogated. When will you realize I'm not your little girl anymore?" She didn't mean to sound so angry.

"Lass," Matthew pleaded, "you'll always be my little girl."

Karen's mouth thinned defensively until she realized her father's silver head had possessed only a salting of gray three years ago. He was aging right before her eyes. So much had changed in both their lives since her mother's death. Matthew had lost more than his wife and best friend. In the months that followed Madeline's unexpected death, Matthew's appreciation for life, his aspirations, even his personality had altered dramatically. Seeing her father now would have shocked someone who had known him three years before.

Shrugging in a gesture of defeat, Karen lowered

herself into the chair and said, "His name is Randall Prescott; he's a professor at the university. I like him, Dad, better than anyone I've met." She paused, watching Matthew's reaction. "Rand is blind."

Matthew's eyes clouded with uncertainty. "Blind." His tongue tasted the word as if he found it unpleasant. "Lass, are you sure of your feelings?"

"I'm not sure of anything," Karen murmured dryly. "All I know is that I found him to be the most intriguing man I've ever met. Something happened last night, to Rand and me." She was quick to include herself.

"Something unusual. I can't even put it into words. It was almost as if our spirits communicated." She gave a short, embarrassed laugh. "I know that sounds crazy. Rand is tender and sensitive, but I don't think he exposes that side of his nature often. I... I think I was privileged to see that in him. And, Dad, he listens."

Matthew nodded. "I understand the blind often have an extremely good sense of hearing."

"Not hearing," she corrected. "He listens. He's not so caught in his own ego that he felt the need to impress me. He was interested in me as a person, my thoughts, opinions. That's listening, and there's a world of difference."

Matthew was studying Karen when she raised her eyes to his. "Yes, lass, that there is."

"Maybe it was the music or the champagne; I don't know." Her mind whirled with the memory of the electricity that had sparked between them.

"I think the lad was responding to the sensitive chord in you, Karen. Do you remember as a child you were always the one to rescue lost or injured animals? And several people, too, as I recall."

"Oh, Dad, I'm not rescuing Rand. For one thing, he doesn't need it. He's independent and proud. You've got to promise me you won't tell him about those things. He'd think I'm making a charity case of him. He'd hate that."

Matthew's eyes showed understanding. "I won't say a word," he assured her. "A man needs his pride."

Karen relaxed against the back cushion of the chair and sighed gratefully. "Thanks, Dad."

"As for Rand being blind, I would wish a sighted man for you, but that's my own selfishness. You're twenty-three now, and if you aren't an able judge of character, your mother and I have failed. I trust that in you, Karen. Your mother and I taught you well."

An overflowing love for her parents warmed Karen. "That you did, Dad. That you did."

Karen watched the phone all day, almost willing it to ring. She needed Rand to call just to confirm that last night had been as real to him as it was to her, and that the night hadn't been a romantic dream she'd conjured up with the moonlight. When he didn't, she couldn't contain her disappointment.

The next morning, Karen met her friend Audrey in a small coffee shop for their midmorning break. Both girls were employed by Tacoma's largest cable television service. Karen was the supervisor for the data processing department. Audrey had also been a candidate for the position but was relieved when Karen had it. Of the two, Karen had been the natural choice, having displayed tact, discretion, and forethought in a multitude of situations. Hiring a female supervisor had been only a token gesture by the company toward equal rights. Karen had stepped into a cesspool of resentment from her male counterparts. But it wasn't long before she grudgingly won their respect. She was good at her job and knew it.

"Do you realize I only have fourteen more days to finish my Christmas shopping?" Audrey announced as she set her cup opposite Karen's on the small table.

"Luckily, I did mine weeks ago," Karen said without meaning to sound like the methodical, organized soul she was. "I guess it helps when things have to be mailed."

"You'd have had it finished, anyway." Audrey sighed jealously. "I don't suppose I could interest you in fighting the crowds with me tonight? I thought we might have dinner out."

"Not tonight. Sorry, Audrey. I'm expecting a phone call."

"Someone I know?" Audrey quizzed with unleashed curiosity.

"No," Karen said pointedly.

Rand dominated her thoughts. Was he experiencing doubts about their evening? Had he decided this thing between them was the result of too much wine and music? Karen could only venture a guess at his musings. She had never longed to hear from someone so badly. Randall Prescott had her feeling very much like a schoolgirl praying that special boy would ask her to the prom. The melodious song in her heart was now replaced by an aching void of unanswered questions.

The phone was ringing when she let herself into the apartment that night. Karen dropped her purse and rushed to answer it, her heartbeat accelerating wildly. It was a carpet-cleaning salesman with a pitch for steam-cleaning her rugs. She definitely wasn't interested.

Audrey was at Karen's desk first thing the next morning. "Did you get your important phone call?" she asked before adding another pile of papers to Karen's workload.

"No, I'm afraid not." She tried to sound nonchalant and didn't bother to look up from her paperwork.

"I don't think you have much to worry about," Audrey said kindly. "He'll phone; only a blind man would be immune to your charms." Shock held Karen rigid. "I'll bet he phones tonight."

But Audrey was wrong. Rand didn't contact Karen that night or the next.

Friday night, Matthew was in Karen's apartment, waiting for her.

"Dad!" she admonished irritably. "The next time this happens, I'm going to have my lock changed."

"As soon as ye know why I'm here, you'll be singing my praises."

Feigning indifference, Karen hung her coat in the closet and went into the kitchen to make coffee.

"Don't you want to know what I found out about Randall Prescott?"

"Not particularly," she lied with an ease she didn't feel. Walking into her bedroom, she examined the contents of her closet.

"Karen, lass." Matthew followed her, his voice full of exasperation. "Hold still a minute. I want to talk to you."

"Sorry, Dad, I haven't got time now. I've got a date."

Matthew's puzzled features relaxed. "Ah, you're meeting Rand again."

"Not Rand." She pulled a crisp taffeta blouse and black velvet skirt from the closet, laying the outfit across her bed. "Jim Malloy is picking me up in an hour."

"Jim Malloy? What happened to Randall Prescott?"

Her throat muscles were so tight Karen could barely speak. "I... I decided not to see him again. You were right about my feelings for him. Randall Prescott is just another lost kitten I wanted to rescue." She hesitated, then added, "Maybe it was a latent Florence Nightingale complex."

For several minutes, Matthew said nothing. "All right, Karen, you have to decide what you think is best."

"I have," she mumbled, returning to the kitchen to take the coffeepot from the burner. "Help yourself to coffee if you like. I've got to shower."

Scratching his head, Matthew watched Karen head for the bathroom. "Women," he mumbled. "They'll be a mystery to me on my dying day."

Karen had dated Jim Malloy before. He was what she considered a safe date. He was friendly without being pushy, considerate without being condescending. Jim's only problem was that Karen found him unforgivably boring. A hundred times during the dinner and movie, Karen wished she could change her feelings. What was she waiting for? Jim may not be a knight in shining armor, but he was nice. She was being stupid, she told herself as he politely escorted her to her apartment. Meekly, she submitted to his kiss. But it was hardly a kiss at all, more a brushing of lips.

Frustrated with herself, Karen opened her mouth slightly to deepen the contact, then moaned in disappointment. Why couldn't she feel what she had in Rand's arms? Why was she left with this void, this aching feeling at the touch of another man?

Jim reacted urgently to her initiative, crushing her against him. His hands fumbled with the opening of her coat, seeking her breasts.

Karen jerked away. "Stop it," she demanded. Her shoulders heaved with emotion, finding his touch repulsive.

"Come on. What am I supposed to think with a come-on like that?" His eyes were glazed with passion. "Let's go inside, talk this out." He pulled her back into his arms, his lips nuzzling her neck.

Again, Karen fought him. "No," she said sternly. "Not tonight. Not ever."

His dark, beady eyes filled with contempt. "You're nothing but a tease. Do you get your jollies by turning men on and then—"

"I think you'd better leave," Karen interrupted him, her voice steady and cold. Placing her apartment key between her middle and index fingers so its steel edge could inflict harm if necessary, she stared directly into his anger-filled eyes.

Jim didn't ignore the warning. "All right," he spat viciously, "have it your way." He left in a hot temper, and Karen heard the squeal of his tires as he pulled from the parking lot.

After letting herself into the apartment, Karen leaned heavily against the closed door. What was the matter with her? A feeling of desperation encompassed her. She had led Jim to believe she wanted more than a good-night kiss and couldn't blame him for his reaction. For a fleeting second, she almost hated Rand.

"Damn you," she whispered harshly, and sat in the still apartment, staring into the darkness. She didn't move for a long while.

The next week passed with intolerable slowness, although Karen made an effort to keep busy. But each time the phone rang, her heart would beat expectantly. Each time, she tasted bitter disappointment.

Five days before Christmas, Karen received a long-distance call from her sister in Texas.

"Judy?" she asked with surprise. "Is everything okay?" With a limited budget, Judy rarely phoned unless it was important.

"I've got news too good for a mere letter," she began.

"You're pregnant?" Karen guessed immediately. "Well, for heaven's sake, have a girl this time, would you? Dad is driving me crazy for a granddaughter."

"Would you kindly shut up?" Judy chided with a laugh. "I'm not pregnant! I'm calling because Mike's being transferred to McChord."

"McChord Air Force Base?" Karen asked in disbelief. "In Tacoma?"

"Yes, silly."

"Oh, Judy, I'm so glad. You don't know how Dad and I've missed you."

"How is Dad?"

"Wait and see. I swear he's getting crazier by the day. Everything's changed since Mom died, especially Dad."

"I know." Judy sobered. "Even his letters are getting weird. There's a bit of bad news, too. Mike's being stationed in Thailand for a year."

"Judy, no." Karen's voice filled with sympathy. Her

sister and husband had been separated before. It was a miserable time for them both.

"I guess I should be used to it by now. But at least this time I'll be by family."

"I'm so glad you're coming home." Karen tried to disguise the unhappiness in her voice.

"You don't sound right. What's wrong?" Judy and Karen were too close to hide anything from each other. Judy quickly detected the tiniest voice inflection and knew immediately things were not well with her sister.

Karen hesitated. How could she possibly explain? "I can't talk now. I'll tell you everything later. I promise," she said in a long, uneven breath.

"Count on it, sis," Judy said softly.

Judy's news was just the tonic needed to brighten Karen's Christmas. The news did a world of good for Matthew, too, Karen noted as they traveled to the Forsyths' on Christmas afternoon. Matthew seemed happier than Karen could remember since her mother's death.

At first Karen was a bit uneasy at her uncle's, fearing he would mention Randall Prescott, but the day passed comfortably, with no allusion to him or the party.

Everything moved very quickly after Christmas. Within a week, Judy and her family had arrived and moved into government housing. Mike, an aircraft mechanic, was due to fly out Monday afternoon, and he worked around the clock to settle his family before departing.

Karen volunteered to keep the boys Saturday night so the couple could spend the evening alone.

"Are you sure about this?" Judy questioned hesitantly. "James and Carter can be a handful."

"Of course I'm sure. I've been looking forward to this all week. If I were you, I'd make the most of my generous offer." She batted her eyelashes seductively and watched her sister blush.

"I know, but—"

"No buts. Dad and I've got everything planned. We're going to have a great time, aren't we, boys?" Immediately, the two lively youngsters flew into the room, bounding with energy.

"Will you buy me a squirt gun, Aunt Karen?" six-year-old Carter asked.

"Carter," Judy warned in disapproval.

"We'll see." Karen affectionately ruffled the top of his blond head. "Get your sleeping bags loaded into my car. I'll be there in a minute." She placed her empty coffee mug in the kitchen sink and gathered her coat and purse. "Dad and I've got everything arranged. I'm taking the boys to a movie this afternoon, and then we're picking up Dad at the chess club. He's playing in that tournament this weekend," she explained needlessly. "From there we're going to have Chinese food."

Judy walked down the steps with her. "The boys will love it." Her expression softened. "Mike and I appreciate this more than you know."

Karen gave her sister an affectionate hug. "The pleasure's mine."

Judy laughed slyly. "Tell me that tomorrow afternoon; then I'll believe you."

"Come on, Aunt Karen. We're ready," the boys called from her compact Dodge, having rolled down the window.

"See what I mean?" Judy said.

The movie was a Western comedy the boys ate their

way through. After three bags of popcorn, two soft drinks, and a candy bar each, Karen wondered where they'd put the meal she'd planned for later.

"When's dinner?" James asked on the way to the parking lot.

"Dinner?" Karen gasped, then laughed, shaking her head at her nephew. "I can see I'm going to need groceries before we pick up your grandpa."

They made a quick trip to the neighborhood market, buying breakfast items and a few between-meals snacks, just in case the boys got hungry during the night, they told her.

Twenty minutes later, they arrived at the chess club. James and Carter looked around, curiously watching the players sitting at the long tables. Although the club was filled to capacity with nearly a hundred occupants, the noise level was surprisingly low. Glancing about the room, Karen easily caught sight of her father. He sat at one of the tables, intently involved in his game. She pointed him out to the boys and explained why they must be quiet and wait patiently. They sat in the back of the room, watching as each of the players made his move, then hit the clock, setting the other player's timer. The boys asked a couple of questions, but otherwise were content to sit and watch.

Briefly surveying the room again, Karen's attention moved to a table with three players. Instinctively, she stiffened, her emotions muddled and confused. "Rand." She spoke his name softly, her voice barely above a whisper. James and Carter glanced at her questioningly, but she didn't notice.

Rand lifted his head briefly, as though he'd heard, paused, then returned his attention to the game. But it wasn't possible for him to have heard her at this distance. His back, facing her, was held rigid and determined.

Drawing a deep breath, Karen's first reaction was anger and resentment. Yet there was a flooding relief, an elation just in seeing him again, even from a distance.

Karen continued to watch him for several moves with wry amusement. If he couldn't see the chessboard, how could he participate? It was soon evident Rand didn't use the board; the figures were moved for him on command by the third party. The entire game was played in his mind.

She experienced a twinge of pride when he won the match. Her gaze followed him as he left the table and sauntered toward her.

"I'll be right back," she instructed her nephews. "Stay here."

She met Rand at the other side of the room. "Hello," she said evenly.

He showed no surprise, his face a proud mask. "Karen." He nodded in recognition.

"I didn't know if you'd remember me." She was being untruthful. He may not have contacted her, but he darn well hadn't forgotten her. She would have staked her life's savings on the fact.

"I remember you."

"I realize this is slightly out of the ordinary," she began haltingly, "but I'd like to know what I did wrong."

His brows drew together in a frown of confusion. "Wrong?" He repeated the word. "You did nothing wrong."

Of their own volition, her eyes were drawn to his

face. It was unfair that he should have this much effect on her after all this time. For a moment, Karen thought he wanted to reach out and touch her, but he clenched his fist and held it stiffly at his side.

"Is it Cora?" At least she thought that was the name her godfather had mentioned.

Surprise flickered briefly over his expression.

"Uncle Evan mentioned her the night of the party," Karen explained shakily. "He said you usually attend social functions with her, and I thought there…there may be some romantic involvement."

His mouth thinned with impatience. "No, this has nothing to do with Cora."

"If I didn't do anything to offend you and…and if there's not another woman involved, I'd like to know what I did wrong."

He paused long enough to take his coat from the rack and slip it on. Pulling the gloves from the pocket, he clenched them tightly in one hand.

"My godfather also said you were a professor."

"What did you think I did? Sold pencils on street corners?" The tightening muscles of his jaw were the only evidence of anger.

"No, of course not." Oh, dear, she was making a horrible mess of this. She inhaled deeply, hoping to calm herself and clear her thinking. "Listen, I'm going about this in the worst possible way. Could we start again?"

Ignoring her plea, he stepped outside, allowing the door to close before she could follow.

As childish as it seemed, Karen was tempted to stomp her foot and scream. Instead, she swallowed her anger and opened the door, stepping into the dark afternoon.

He had gone only a couple of feet. Karen allowed the door to shut before approaching him. "Rand," she said softly, "it doesn't matter to me that you're blind."

His posture remained rigid and uncompromising until Karen could tolerate it no longer. Without questioning the wisdom of her action, she placed a hand on his arm.

"Randall Prescott, would you kindly listen to me? If you had perfect twenty-twenty vision or if you were as blind as a bat, I'd still find you the most captivating man I've ever met."

His mouth twisted into a cynical smile that told her he didn't believe a word she'd said.

"It doesn't make any difference," she stressed again, quickly losing patience.

"Of course it makes a difference," he shouted angrily, startling Karen. He caught her shoulder in a tight grip. "Blast you, Karen. Blast you for being here. Blast you for—what the hell?"

Icy water hit Karen in the face. She gasped before being hit again. "James… Carter…stop it right now."

The two boys magically appeared and lowered their weapons. "I told you we'd get in trouble," Carter said righteously.

James ignored him. "I'm sorry, Aunt Karen. I didn't mean to squirt you. I was aiming at him." He pointed a finger at Rand. "You moved in my way."

Rand handed his handkerchief to Karen. "You didn't mention you were related to the Dalton Brothers." A mere hint of a smile lifted the corners of his mouth.

Karen accepted the cloth and wiped the water from her face. "These are my nephews, James and Carter Turner."

"He was holding your shoulder real mean," James explained, hoping to vindicate his actions. "He looked like he was mad at you." Rand's imposing figure was enough to give the stoutest of men second thoughts. As far as Karen was concerned, the boys deserved a medal for bravery.

"You both owe Dr. Prescott an apology." Her voice was stern, but she worked hard to suppress a smile. Rand's face and shirt were soaked, and, feeling guilty, she returned his handkerchief.

"You're the one who got Aunt Karen in the face," Carter shouted angrily at his brother. "Now I bet we don't get dinner in the restaurant."

"It's all right, boys." A smile relaxed Rand's taut features. "You were right to protect your aunt."

"You're not mad?" James asked hesitatingly.

Rand allayed his fears. "No, but I want you to know I'd never do anything to hurt Karen."

Carter was obviously pleased with the turn of events and was quick to make peace. "I like her real well. She took us to the movie and let us eat all the popcorn we wanted and—"

"If you'd never hurt my aunt Karen, how come you were holding her shoulder like that?" James was not as easily appeased as his younger brother.

Rand didn't get the opportunity to answer, for Matthew burst upon the scene and demanded, "Where have ye been? I've been ready for five minutes. If it hadn't been for your purse, Karen, I wouldn't have known ye were even here."

"My purse!" Karen cried in dismay. She'd completely forgotten it in her eagerness to speak to Rand.

Her father handed the leather bag to Karen, who distractedly checked its contents for anything missing.

"I took the keys, so the boys and me will be leaving ye now."

"Dad?" she asked, her face a puzzled frown. What was he talking about? She was having dinner with him and the boys; it was what they'd planned. "I thought all of us were having dinner."

"Ye need to be discussing things with Rand," he said, dismissing her lightly. "Are ye hungry, boys?" he asked, grinning devilishly at Karen.

The boys gave a chorus of cheers, and with a hearty shout ran to Karen's car.

"Damn good game, Prescott. I demand a rematch."

Karen's attention swiveled to Rand, searching his face. "Did you have a match with my father this afternoon?" Karen could only imagine the things Matthew had been telling Rand. Indignantly, she turned her attention to Matthew to discover he had already left. Her small car purred as the engine came to life.

"Dad," she shouted angrily. "What about me?" Her full mouth compressed angrily as Matthew passed her in the street and gave her a friendly wave goodbye.

"I think he's abandoned you to my care." Rand's frown showed her he was none too pleased with her company.

"Well, don't look so thrilled," she snapped.

Silence followed until Rand began to chuckle, but the sound of his amusement did little to soothe Karen's ruffled feelings.

"This isn't funny," she insisted.

"Yes, it is." Rand broke into full rumbling laughter that shook his shoulders.

He continued laughing. "The fact is, I haven't found anything this funny in years." He contained himself somewhat. "Is it always like this with your family?"

"Sometimes it's worse," Karen stated dryly.

His amusement relaxed to soft chuckles. "Since Matthew's seen fit to throw us together, let's find someplace to talk."

Karen's spirits soared. This was what she'd originally wanted, to be with Rand. All at once, she wanted to kiss her interfering, meddling father.

They discovered a café several blocks from the chess club, and Rand ordered them coffee.

The silence stretched between them until Karen found her hands were trembling. Nervously, she clenched them together in her lap.

"Coffee hits the spot," she said with a false cheerfulness that sounded awkward even to her own ears.

Rand looked away. "Listen, Karen," he breathed forcefully, "I don't need to tell you I enjoyed meeting you at the Forsyths' party." He paused, his jaw tightening. "I thought you got my message when I didn't contact you afterward."

Karen gave a short, sarcastic laugh. "I got it, all right. I just don't happen to like it."

Rand placed his coffee cup on the table, and Karen noted how tightly he was clenching it. "Do you always get what you like?"

"No," she said lightly, "but not from lack of trying."

"I find this all flattering, but—"

"Flattering?" she interrupted.

"Very flattering," he said firmly. "But, Karen, you're young and pretty, and I won't have you wasting your time—"

"On a blind man?" she interrupted him again. "Squandering my youth and beauty—is that it?"

"Yes," he retorted angrily.

"Honestly, Rand, the next thing you'll be telling me is that I deserve a whole man or something equally stupid."

"That's exactly what I'm saying."

Karen nearly choked on her coffee. "I can't believe this," she said, keeping her voice level. "And even with this ridiculous attitude, don't you think I should be the one to decide? It's my life. I can squander it if I want." She ended with a short, nervous laugh.

"Not necessarily," Rand replied with a twinge of bitterness. "If you aren't going to use common sense, I must."

"What do you mean?" she demanded. "I've got terrific common sense."

Rand leaned against the back of the red booth. "You seem to be disregarding the fact that I don't want you, nor do I need you."

"I know that," she countered swiftly. She glanced down at her coffee, relieved he couldn't see the hurt in her eyes. "All I know is that I've never experienced anything more beautiful than that night with you. I don't even know how to explain myself. But you can't deny it, Rand. You felt it, too." She paused and waited for him to comment, but he didn't. "It might have been some crazy kind of magic that touched us that night—the Christmas spirit of love and goodwill. I can only guess." She hesitated. His mouth had become the thin, hard line she recognized. Her back stiffened. Rand could say what he liked; instinct told her he would lie. She'd backed him into a defensive corner, and he'd say anything to block her from his life. She simply wasn't going to let him.

Suddenly, something changed in his posture. He relaxed somewhat; his mouth softened enough for her to realize he was remembering. The enchantment of the party touched him again, or perhaps he was as weary of the argument as she.

With his resolve weakening, Karen quickly seized the opportunity. "I remember you once told me you wished to be treated like a sighted person. Well, I think you should know that if you could see me, you'd notice I'm half starved."

His mouth twisted into a fleeting smile. "Is that a hint?"

"No, it's a blatant attempt to con you into taking me to dinner." A full smile wrinkling the corners of his eyes told her she'd succeeded. "But before we do anything, I think we need to make an agreement."

A dark brow lifted itself expressively. "Such as?"

"We need a trial period to test our feelings. Everything was so crazy that night—the stars, the music, the moonlight."

"The champagne," Rand added dryly.

She nodded before realizing he couldn't see her acknowledgment.

"I guess I need to know if what I felt was real or some romantic dream." She hesitated before adding, "There would be no obligation on either side. Are you willing to do that?"

A veiled look came over him, one so transient and brief that Karen wondered if she'd imagined it. Then Karen knew. In that fleeting second, she knew. For all his resolve, for all his determination, he wanted her.

He desired her more than she dreamed possible. At the same time, he hesitated; the flint hardness of his will and years of hard-wrought self-control warred with the tumult of his desires.

"No obligation on either side?" he questioned.

"None."

He ran a weary hand over his face, then slouched forward. "All right, Karen."

Three

"I've never known you to be particularly proper about this sort of thing," Judy said with straight pins between her teeth. "If I were you, I'd contact *him*. Turn," she directed.

Karen was standing atop her coffee table while Judy secured pins in the hem of the wild-rose-colored dress. "I think with any other man I would. But not Rand… I've done as much as I dare." It'd been two long weeks since their meeting at the chess club. Two of the longest weeks of Karen's life. A hundred times she was convinced she'd never hear from Rand again. Not even the gentle caress of his hand against her cheek when he'd dropped her off at her apartment or the promise he'd phone had been enough to dispel her insecurities. Karen had been so confident after that night. They'd eaten sandwiches at the café and drunk several more cups of coffee. They'd talked for what seemed only a short time but was actually hours. Karen told him of her childhood and friends, the pain of her mother's death— things she'd never shared with anyone else. Rand could not see her with his eyes, perhaps, but he could read her as if they'd known each other for years. Several times he paused and asked, "That's not all, is it?" or, "What were your feelings?" Karen had bared her soul to him as she hadn't with any other human. He listened intently when she spoke of her worries over Matthew and the changes in him since Madeline's death. He didn't offer advice, only listened with a knowing look that engendered confidence.

That evening, Karen learned bits and pieces of Rand's life, too. His mother lived in New York and worked for the state insurance commissioner's office. His father had died when he was eleven; Rand was an only child.

"Okay, let me stand back and see if this is even." Judy broke into Karen's thoughts. A warm smile formed. "This dress is going to be lovely. I'm proud of it." The vibrant jacquard material was being hand-crafted for Karen as a birthday gift from her sister. "I'm sure if Rand could see you now, he'd be knocking the phone off the hook."

Karen didn't bother to correct Judy by saying Rand would never "see" her or the dress.

Judy's hand went to her chin as she continued to study Karen. "I don't think I've ever realized how much you resemble Mom. You've got her tilted nose and those warm, dark eyes. You're as beautiful as she was."

Karen had always been referred to as the "pretty" McAlister daughter. Judy was far from ugly, but her nose was a trifle too large, her mouth too full. But in the things that mattered, Judy Turner was the most beautiful woman Karen knew. "A lot of good a cute nose does me!" She smiled gently. "You've got the talent, while I'm stuck with two left hands. I could never sew anything this lovely."

"Sure you could." Judy dismissed her lack of confidence with a short shake of her head. "You'd better change. I imagine Dad's thoroughly tired of showing my boys chess moves."

Karen was in the bedroom when the phone rang. "I'll get it," Judy called. Karen stopped dressing, her pants zipper half-closed. Her heart beat expectantly, as it always did when the phone rang.

"No, this is her sister, Judy," Karen heard her sister say. "Yes, I am," Judy added. "I heard you three had quite an introduction. Let me apologize again for the boys." She laughed. "Just a minute. I'll get Karen."

Judy burst through the bedroom door. "It's him… It's him."

Karen released the breath she'd unconsciously been holding. A flooding sense of relief came over her until her knees trembled.

"Well, aren't you going to answer it?" Judy whispered fiercely.

"Yes…yes," she said again, hoping her voice sounded composed and confident, knowing it didn't. Slowly, to calm her nerves, Karen walked into the living room and picked up the phone. "Hello, Rand," she said softly.

"Karen"—his voice was curt—"how are you?"

"Fine, thank you." She was, now that he'd phoned. "And you?"

"Good." An awkward silence followed. "The Tacoma Actors Guild is putting on a play at the Pantages Thursday night. Would you like to go?"

"Yes, I would," she said with an eagerness that betrayed her.

"Wouldn't you like to know the name of the play?" he chided softly.

Karen silently berated herself. Why did she have to appear so anxious? "All right, if you feel it's important." Suddenly, she wanted to laugh. What did it matter if he knew how eager she was to see him? If she'd answered him in a completely monotone voice, he would have guessed her feelings, anyway. "What time should I be ready?"

Rand paused. "I'll be coming directly from the school and will probably be at your place around seven-fifteen. The play's at eight; that should give us plenty of time."

"I'll be ready." Karen felt like singing; she wanted to laugh and dance all at the same moment.

When he spoke, she could hear the smile in his voice. "I'll see you then. Bye for now."

"Bye." Karen replaced the receiver and glanced at her sister's curious face. Driven by a happiness she couldn't contain, Karen flung her arms around Judy. "How soon did you say my new dress would be ready?"

For the second time, Karen smoothed a wrinkle from her skirt. Nervous fingers toyed with the deeply veed neckline of the bodice, examining again the velvet ribbon, lace, and pearls of the ornate trim. The skill and patience it had taken to string each pearl between the delicate lace and ribbon brought a sense of awe to Karen. The dress was far more than a simple birthday gift; it was a labor of love.

Karen was ready early, absurdly so. Rand wasn't due for another twenty minutes, and already she had checked her appearance ten times in the hallway mir-

ror. Careful attention had been paid to her makeup, although she seldom wore much, preferring the natural
look. Styling her hair had taken the major part of an
hour. If anyone had known she was going to such trouble for someone who could never see her, they would
have thought she was crazy.

When Rand's knock came, Karen nearly jumped
from her chair. Releasing a deep sigh of tension, she
paused long enough to calm herself.

"Hello, Rand," she greeted cheerfully.

He moved into her apartment, and again Karen was
struck by his basic masculine appeal. His face possessed character and strength.

"Karen," he said, his voice formal, "are you ready,
or do you need a few extra minutes?"

"I'm ready." They were acting like awkward strangers meeting for the first time on a blind date. The anal-
ogy nearly sent her into nervous giggles. "Would…
would you like something to drink before we go?"

Rand shifted; everything about him seemed controlled. "Thank you, no. The taxi's waiting."

Their conversation in the cab was so polite and
stilted that Karen wanted to scream in frustration. This
evening would never work with Rand's attitude. His
formal greeting, the stiff conversation, indicated that
although he was complying with his part of the agreement, he regretted it.

The seats for the play were among the best. The op-
pressive silence stretched between them while the theater began filling. Suddenly, Karen turned toward Rand
and said the most ridiculous thing that came to mind.

"The rain in Spain stays mainly in the plain."

He relaxed. "The rain?" He arched a curious brow.

"That's right," she assured him coolly. "It stays mainly in the plain."

Against his will, Karen noted his eyes deepened into smiling grooves. "What makes you say that?" He was completely earnest.

"I could see what was coming. First you'd ask me if I was comfortable, and then we'd discuss the weather. It was either say something totally ridiculous or scream."

Amusement softened his expression. "I'm eternally grateful you didn't scream."

"You're most welcome. Now, are you going to enjoy the evening, or do I have to create a scene?"

For a moment, Karen thought Rand was going to laugh. "My mother warned me about women like you."

"I'm sure she did," she said resolutely after a pause. She shifted forward slightly. "Would you mind helping me with my coat? If I don't take it off now, I'll roast later."

His hand lingered as it cupped her shoulder in the briefest of contacts before following the sleeve and holding it stationary while she withdrew her arm.

"Thank you," she said softly.

His mouth moved into a lazy smile as he relaxed against the plush seat. "You're welcome." Tentatively, his hand sought hers, gently folding her slim one in his.

Karen settled into her seat, too. It was almost impossible to describe what a simple thing like holding hands with Rand did to her. Even a dictionary, Karen decided, couldn't define the pleasure she found in his company.

"Tell me about the play. It has the most curious title—*Deadly Vintage*." An aura of anticipation and excitement touched Karen, who enjoyed live performances above all else.

"A friend of mine wrote it," Rand began. "I think you'll find the plot intriguing. I won't spoil it for you by discussing details." He finished just as the curtain rose.

Rand was right; the plot was excellent, and the cast held the audience's full attention. The story revolved around a young man facing financial ruin, struggling against all odds to keep his business and family together. Karen felt herself tense as one complication after another fell upon the young man's shoulders. Right before the intermission, a second, older man was introduced, who promised to help the young man.

Karen sighed gratefully. "Things were beginning to look a little bleak there for a minute," she said to Rand.

He squeezed her hand and murmured cryptically, "Things aren't always what they appear."

"Oh, no?" She slouched against the back of her seat. "I thought you said you wouldn't ruin the story for me."

Amusement glittered from his dark eyes. "I wouldn't dream of it."

A sick feeling knotted Karen's stomach as the second part of the play unfolded. The older man agreed to pay all the younger man's debts on one condition. The young man must agree to have dinner with the older man. Sometime during the course of the meal, the young man would be offered wine. But the wine contained a deadly poison. No physical pressure would be applied to the man to drink the wine. If he chose to drink, it would be of his own free will. The man hesitantly agreed, but told the rich man he had much to live for and had no intention of drinking the wine. The older man amicably agreed that that was exactly as he wished it. Later, the young man learned this same agreement had been made many times over with others in the same financial difficulties. They, too, had agreed to the dinner with no intention of drinking the deadly vintage. In every instance, the men drank the wine and died.

The characterization of the rich man was portrayed superbly. The overwhelming force of his personality, his power of persuasion, had Karen sitting on the edge of her seat, wishing there was some way she could intervene and help the younger man. The play ended just as the wine was offered.

"That's it?" Karen gasped as the final curtain closed. "It can't possibly end there. What happened?" She turned anxiously to Rand. "What happened?" she demanded again.

"My dear Karen, I have no more idea than you."

The cast was called for three curtain calls, after which the theater began emptying. "Are you ready?" Rand questioned.

"No...not yet," Karen said stubbornly. Again and again, certain phrases and scenes played in her mind.

Rand shifted impatiently. "Karen," he said finally, "no one's coming to add a postscript. This is it."

"He didn't accept the wine," she said more forcefully than she meant. She stood and reached for her coat.

"Is that so?" He was mocking her.

"Yes. If you examined the evidence, you'd realize it, too," she defended herself.

"It seems to me you're searching for a satisfactory conclusion. That sensitive female nature of yours insists upon a happy ending."

"Honestly, Rand, my sensitive female nature, as you call it, has nothing to do with this. What do you think he did?"

Karen had the curious sensation Rand was watching her, not with his eyes, of course, but with his other senses.

"I'm not sure," he said thoughtfully. "Why don't we go somewhere and discuss it? Have you had dinner?"

Karen hadn't; her nerves had been a jumbled mess most of the day, and although she hadn't eaten since lunch, she wasn't the least bit hungry.

"No, as a matter of fact, I haven't." Karen smiled to herself. She may not have much of an appetite, but she wasn't about to refuse an invitation from Rand.

Karen ordered a shrimp salad and coffee while Rand had apple pie. "Are you sure you wouldn't care for a glass of wine?" he teased after the waiter had taken the menu.

"Hardly!" She didn't bother to disguise her amusement. This was how she'd prayed their evening would be—a teasing banter between them without the steel-wall facade Rand had erected earlier. They discussed the play in detail; Karen argued her view while Rand, with clearheaded logic, proved exactly the opposite, that the younger man had drunk the wine.

"Now I don't know what to believe." Irrationally, she was almost angry with him. The matter had been settled in her own mind, and he had completely shattered her confidence. "I was perfectly content before."

Rand grinned that crooked little smile she'd seen only at rare times when he was especially pleased about something. Using some of the same rationale she'd used, Rand proceeded to prove that indeed the man had not drunk the wine.

Karen was astonished as she listened to him. Everything he said seemed perfectly sensible, sound, and reasonable, yet only a few minutes before he'd taken the opposing viewpoint.

"Remind me never to argue with you," she muttered.

"I've had more time to think about it, is all. And if past evidence is anything to go by, you hold your own in any argument. I certainly never intended to see you again, and look at us now."

Karen's eyes widened in hurt astonishment.

"I'd better phone Carl," Rand added after checking his watch. It was one made specially for the blind, and Karen was curious as to how it worked. "It's nearly midnight, and you're a working girl."

"Not tomorrow I'm not," she answered absently, trying to catch a glimpse of his wrist again.

"Is there some holiday I don't know about?" he asked, a teasing glint in his eye.

"Not a holiday, exactly." She placed her coffee cup on the china saucer. "It's my birthday, and the cable company gives their employees the day off with pay. Rather a nice gesture, I think."

"Your birthday?" His expression turned serious, as if he'd made a social blunder. "You should have said something."

Karen gave a tiny laugh. "I just did."

"You're twenty-four?" It wasn't really a question, and Karen didn't bother to answer. "There are twelve years between us. I'm far too old for you, Karen."

"My goodness, at thirty-six you must be sitting around just waiting to collect Social Security," she said with a mocking laugh.

She watched as he rubbed a weary hand across his forehead. "See what I mean? You effectively smash any argument I have against the two of us. Rather well, I might add."

While he phoned Carl, Karen excused herself to go to the ladies' room. She took longer than necessary, checking her appearance and applying fresh lip gloss and combing her hair. She felt so different with Rand and wondered if that tingling awareness between them affected her looks. Although she studied her reflection for several moments, she decided she looked exactly the same. Repressing a sigh of disappointment, she joined him.

"Carl is meeting me at your place in about twenty minutes," he told her in the foyer of the restaurant. "I have a cab waiting."

"That's fine," she agreed. "We'll have time for coffee."

Karen rested her head against his shoulder as they rode to her apartment. She could feel the roughness of his breath against her hair.

Once inside her apartment, Karen had no more desire for coffee than she had had for dinner. She hung up both their coats, suddenly feeling uneasy. "Make yourself at home. I'll get the coffee going."

As she turned toward the kitchen, Rand's arm caught hers, drawing her back. "I don't want coffee," he murmured, pulling her close to him.

Without hesitation, Karen accepted his embrace, lifting her face to meet his kiss. It began sweet and gentle but deepened as he parted her mouth. The surge of passion that sprang between them was like a wind-driven wildfire. Her arms slid around his neck, her fingers wending through his hair.

His own hands were molding her hips and back

against the contours of his body. It was a devastating kiss that left Karen as powerless as a newborn baby. It was very much like coming home after a long absence. They hadn't kissed since the night of the Christmas party, and Karen discovered that the magnetic attraction between them had only been enhanced by lapsed time.

Ripples of desire continued as Rand nibbled the sensitive cord of her neck. "Happy birthday, my lovely Andromeda," he whispered huskily.

"When I was a little girl," she began, her voice soft and trembling, "my mother insisted upon giving me kisses to count my birthday instead of spankings."

Karen could feel Rand's smile against her temple. "I'm afraid I haven't the restraint to kiss you twenty-four times without falling prey to other temptations."

Their lips met again in a fiery kiss that fused them together. Karen clung to him as the only solid form in a reeling world. When the kiss ended, she buried her face against his chest while he continued to rain soft kisses on her hair.

"Are you busy tomorrow?" he questioned, his voice no more even than her breathing.

"No," she lied skillfully. Evan Forsyth had invited her and her sister to lunch. Judy and the boys were preparing a birthday dinner for her that evening with Matthew. But nothing mattered, not friends, not family. Nothing save Rand.

"Can I see you, then?"

"Yes." She gloried in the eagerness of his request.

"Could you come to the campus—say, around eleven? I've got a class at nine-thirty."

Karen was too full of happiness to speak. He wanted

to see her again soon. They wouldn't be separated for weeks, as had been the past pattern. "Yes, fine," she murmured, seeking the intimate taste of his mouth upon hers again.

A light tap, then the doorbell, interrupted them. "That'll be Carl," Rand murmured thickly, continuing to hold her shoulders.

Involuntarily, Karen swayed toward him, not wishing to break the contact. Gently, he kissed her lightly one last time. "Until tomorrow," he said, and paused. "My coat?"

"Oh, sorry." She fumbled awkwardly and withdrew it from the closet. Before she could add another word, he was gone.

The doorbell chimed impatiently several times the next morning at about nine-thirty. Karen rushed to answer it, her bathrobe knotted tightly about her waist.

"Dad," she exclaimed, letting him in. "What are you doing here? You're supposed to be working."

"'Tis a fine greeting for the man responsible for ye being here," he scolded her lovingly. "I've come to wish ye a happy birthday." He sauntered through the apartment to the kitchen and poured himself a cup of coffee.

"Did ye notice I rang the bell?" he said as he pulled a chair from the kitchen table and sat.

"I'm real proud of you, Dad, real proud." Her voice hinted sarcasm, but her lips negated any scorn by curving upward in a gentle smile. "Why aren't you at work?" she quizzed again.

Matthew deposited a second spoonful of sugar into his mug before answering. "I didn't feel like working," he told her indifferently. "A man needs an excuse to take a day off every now and then. And what better excuse than my lass's birthday?"

Karen poured herself a cup and sat opposite him at the tiny round table. She would have argued, but Matthew looked pale and drawn; perhaps a day's vacation was a good idea.

"Twenty-four years," he said with the glazed look that crossed his face when he was thinking of her mother. "Ye realize, when your mother was twenty-four, she was married, had Judy, and was pregnant with you."

Karen sighed heavily. She'd hoped to avoid another one of her father's tirades about her single status. "I know that, Dad."

"You're far behind her, lass. Even Judy had James and Carter before she was twenty-four."

Karen stood abruptly and emptied her coffee in the kitchen sink. "I know that, too," she said with a tight rein on her temper.

"There's not much time remaining before people will begin thinking of you as unmarriageable. I'd hate to see ye an old maid."

Karen's eyes ballooned angrily. "That's ridiculous," she spat impatiently. With storm clouds gathering, hands on her hips, Karen squarely faced her father. "Why is it you and I can't have a decent conversation anymore? You're constantly bugging me about getting married, and I'm not about to jump into a relationship to satisfy your whims. It's getting to the point I don't even like being around you anymore. Would you kindly lay off?" she said forcefully.

Her father's sad eyes met Karen's fiery gaze, and once again she noted that her father looked like a man well past his prime, a man without purpose. Taking

deep breaths to control her temper, she offered him a
weak smile. "I love you, Dad. Let's not argue, especially today. Okay?"

"Okay, lass." He responded to her smile with one
of his own. "How was the date with Rand last night?"

Telltale emotions flickered across her face. "Wonderful. In fact, I'm meeting him this morning." Pointedly, she checked her wristwatch.

"I thought you were having lunch with Evan. He
seems to have invited the whole family except me." If
Matthew was hinting for an invitation, Karen wasn't
going to issue one. Both girls were aware that although
the lunch had been planned to correspond with Kar-
en's birthday, the purpose was to discuss Matthew. The
change in his personality over the past months had not
gone unnoticed by his friends, and Evan was as worried as Karen and Judy.

"I am having lunch with Evan, but I'm meeting Rand
first. That's why I've got to get moving."

"All right, lass, I'll see you tonight."

After surveying her wardrobe carefully, Karen chose
designer jeans and a forest-green velour top. Since it
was raining, she chose fashionable knee-high leather
boots.

At precisely eleven, she entered Rand's office building.

"May I help you?" his assistant, an elderly gray-
haired woman, inquired politely.

"I'm Karen McAlister. I have an appointment with
Dr. Prescott."

The woman scanned the appointment schedule.
"Yes, Dr. Prescott mentioned you this morning." There

was a hint of censure in her tone, and Karen wondered what inconvenience their meeting was causing.

"Follow me, please." The cool smile displayed an efficient assistant's welcome. She paused outside the door. "Dr. Prescott's on the phone, but he's asked that you be shown in immediately. Would you like a cup of coffee while you're waiting?"

Politely, Karen declined. With her jittery nerves, she wasn't beyond dumping the contents across Rand's desk. She entered the office quietly so as not to disturb him. He gave no indication that he noticed her arrival, his full concentration directed at the person on the other end of the line. From the conversation, Karen assumed it was either his agent or his publisher.

She stood awkwardly in the middle of his office for several minutes, not wishing to sit, yet equally unwilling to feel like a child being disciplined. Her gaze swept the walls, resting on the degrees and certificates decorating the office. As she read their contents, her discomfort grew. On further investigation, she found Rand was the recipient of several prestigious awards. There was even a picture of him with the president of the United States. Nothing could have made her more aware of how separate their worlds were. A knot grew in the pit of her stomach as she read the contents of each framed accomplishment.

His achievements were astonishing, and Karen experienced a budding respect for the obstacles he'd overcome. She doubted there was any situation or crisis Rand couldn't surmount with patience and persistence. But her admiration did little to quell her uneasiness.

No wonder Rand questioned their relationship.

Depression, heavier than any yoke, weighted her

shoulders. She actually felt her body droop under its burden. There could be no basis for a meaningful relationship between them.

Dismally, she moved to the picture window overlooking Commencement Bay. Oyster-gray clouds met murky waters in a thin overcast. Only a few brave souls weathered the promise of rain, their sailboats slicing through the water. Yet Karen was blind to the picturesque beauty that lay before her.

"I'm sorry, Karen." Rand stood. "I didn't mean to be so long."

"No problem," she murmured abjectly, refusing to face him.

As soon as she spoke, Rand came to stand behind her. His hands rested lightly on her shoulders, drawing her against him. Gently, his lips touched her hair.

Karen suppressed an overwhelming urge to turn and bury herself in his arms. Instead, she stared at the world outside the window, feeling wretched and small.

"You're angry?" he asked, his tone suggesting surprise.

"I'm not," she murmured unhappily.

"Obviously something is troubling you."

Inhaling deeply, she faltered over the words. "I… I know why you asked me here today. It's shown me without words why you haven't wanted to see me again. I don't blame you. I understand now."

The grasp on her shoulders tightened, and, using his strength, he turned her to face him. "Just what are you implying?"

"I'm saying that I've never fully realized how important you are. You're a respected professor, a noted author…a man of unquestionable financial insight. Do you realize I'm not so very different from the woman who ushered me into your office? Basically, I'm a nobody."

"A nobody?" He openly scoffed. "If that's the case, you've managed to wreak havoc on my life in short order." His expression didn't alter. "Do you really believe I invited you here to impress you with our differences?"

A lump rose in her throat, and she swallowed hard. It was ironic that she would argue with him without relenting a whit and then accept defeat after ten minutes in his office without a spoken word.

"Yes." Her voice trembled slightly.

"It was never my intention to see you after the Christmas party," he said deliberately.

"I'm aware of that."

"I said goodbye to you that night, and I meant it. But no woman has ever affected me the way you have, Karen. I'm not a romantic. The relationships I've had with women have been for the express purpose of satisfying a basic human need. That night with you shattered every preconceived idea I have regarding love and romance. You were gentle, sweet, and warm, more like the mythological Andromeda than a mere human. I knew then what could never be."

"I'm hardly a goddess," she interrupted with dry sarcasm.

He began again, his voice fervent. "I'm almost totally blind. I have no intention of maintaining a personal relationship with any woman. Not now, not ever. Even the attraction I feel for you will not convince me differently. You're special, Karen, and you deserve the best...certainly not a blind man."

Immediately, she bristled, but before she could say

anything, Rand continued, "Maybe it's best we end this testing time now. That choice is yours, but I won't have you believing you're not good enough for me."

"Then why did you ask me here?" Her voice nearly failed her.

His features softened as the intensity left his face. "For this." He withdrew a jeweler's box from his pocket.

Hesitantly, Karen accepted the small case.

"It's not wrapped, but happy birthday, anyway."

Karen almost gasped when she lifted the lid. A lovely gold locket rested on a bed of purple velvet. It was old, but not an antique; the jeweler's box and style were outdated, but the locket was obviously new.

"It's beautiful," she whispered, lifting the heart-shaped locket from the case to examine it more fully.

"Can you get it on okay? I doubt that I'll be much use."

"I think so." The chain clasped effortlessly as the locket fell naturally into place between her breasts. Karen longed to ask if the jewelry had been his mother's, but if it had any special significance, he wasn't telling her.

"Thank you, Rand. I'll treasure it always."

Softly, his hand caressed her cheek. As if it were suddenly too much restraint to keep her from his arms, he pulled her to him, hugging her fiercely. "Happy birthday," he whispered huskily.

His assistant's buzzer interrupted them, and Rand responded to the intrusion with a clear, crisp voice. The words were in a cloud as Karen gradually returned to the present.

"I've got to leave for a meeting," Rand told her reluctantly. "I'll phone you at the end of the week."

Karen smiled, her eyes dancing. "It seems I'm doomed to sit by my phone waiting for you to call."

Chuckling at her teasing sarcasm, he reached for his coat. "All right, how about dinner on Saturday? I'd like you to meet Cora Dibner. I believe Evan Forsyth's mentioned her."

Karen's spirits descended rapidly; she had no desire to meet the woman, but wondered what claim Cora had on Rand.

They walked from the building together, exchanging the teasing banter they both enjoyed. Halfway down the wide cement walkway, Rand stopped abruptly. "My book," he said with a shock. "I've left it in the office." He chuckled. "I've left my office a thousand times in the past seven years, and this is the first time I've forgotten my book. See what you do to me?"

Karen smiled, and her heartbeat raced with a new happiness.

"I'll have to go back. Karen McAlister, you'll be the downfall of me yet."

She watched as Rand progressed through the throng of students. "I hope I am," she said to no one in particular.

Four

Karen enjoyed her birthday lunch. The fettuccine complemented a lighthearted celebration, but it didn't take Evan long to come to the point of their meeting. He noted the changes in Matthew's personality, voiced his concern, and suggested the root of the problem was loneliness. Matthew needed to remarry, Evan concluded. Karen could feel the tiny hairs at the back of her neck bristle. No woman, however wonderful, could ever replace her mother. Selfishly, she did not wish to see her father marry someone else.

But the more they discussed the situation, the more both Judy and Karen were forced to acknowledge that perhaps Evan was right. It would take a readjustment in their thinking, but both were willing to make the effort as long as it helped Matthew—anything to change his present attitude.

Anxiously, Karen longed for the weekend and the dinner date with Rand. Her curiosity regarding Cora Dibner was keen; only when she had met Rand's associate could she evaluate the extent of their relationship.

With each passing day, Karen discovered that Rand

was coming to occupy more and more of her thoughts. Even the little things in life like shopping and cooking brought him to mind. While preparing a meal, she found herself questioning his likes and dislikes. When dressing, she wondered how he'd feel about a certain outfit she was planning to wear. Seldom did Karen consciously think of him as blind. Accepting his lack of sight was very much like accepting Judy's too-large nose. After a while, it became unnoticeable, a part of her person that was unconsciously overlooked.

When Rand phoned late and unexpectedly Wednesday night, Karen was reading and ready for bed.

"Karen?" A hint of doubt entered his husky voice.

"Were you expecting someone else to answer?" she teased.

He chuckled, his voice rich and low; the sound of his amusement contained an element of music. "No. I'm sorry to be phoning so late."

"That's fine. I was reading." He could phone any time he wanted, Karen yearned to tell him, but to admit that would be revealing too much.

"I'm afraid I'm going to have to cancel our dinner date Saturday night." The regret in his voice communicated his own disappointment.

"Oh…" She sighed in frustration and absently fingered the gold locket he'd given her. Karen wore it continually, as if wearing it would result in some wonderful magic. She'd been so impatient to see Rand again, and the throbbing happiness she experienced just hearing his voice vanished with his announcement. It seemed their whole relationship was a series of setbacks.

"Karen, I'm phoning from Washington, D.C. I won't be back before Sunday."

"Washington, D.C." she gasped, and quickly glanced at the kitchen clock. "It must be two a.m."

"After two," he murmured tightly. "I've been tied up in one of those dreadful meetings that last forever and solve nothing." He sounded both tired and frustrated. "I suppose I should have phoned tomorrow night, but I needed to hear your voice."

Karen's spirits soared. The need to talk to her was something he admitted grudgingly, as if she were becoming a weakness he couldn't overcome.

"I'm glad you did call," she whispered softly. "I like to hear your voice, too, but I'm sorry to miss meeting Cora." Karen flushed guiltily; her curiosity regarding his business associate had little to do with friendly overtures.

"You'll meet her," Rand assured her, then paused for a moment. "I've been invited to a wedding reception sometime next week. Would you like to attend with me? Cora will be there," he added, as if she needed an incentive.

"Yes, I'd enjoy that." Rand could issue an invitation to a funeral and she'd still experience a thrill of anticipation.

"I'll let you know what day and time later."

"That'll be fine. I don't have anything special planned for next week." She paused, then began hesitantly, "Would you like a kitten?"

"A what?" he asked in disbelief.

"A cat." She giggled. "My two crazy nephews brought home six kittens yesterday. Judy sent them to the store for a loaf of bread, and some lady was sitting outside the store with a box of kittens. The boys couldn't believe the cats were *free* and took all six.

After all, they considered six free cats to be quite a bargain. By the time Judy returned to the store with the boys and the cats, the lady was long gone. In fact, Judy and I spent the evening posting 'free kitten' signs around the neighborhood."

"Those two rascals," Rand said, chuckling. "I suppose all six are females?"

"Do you have anything against females?" Karen asked with mock indignation.

"Not of late," he murmured with a chuckle. "All right, I'll take one regardless of sex."

"Judy thanks you, kind sir."

"Go ahead and choose one for me; I'll have Carl contact you to make the arrangements to pick it up. You can name it for me if you want."

"I'd like that." Already her mind was buzzing with several possibilities.

"I suppose I'd better let you get some sleep." His voice was warm and husky, creating in Karen anything but the desire to slumber.

"I suppose," she whispered on a sigh.

"Good night, my sweet Andromeda."

"Good night, Rand." She replaced the receiver and leaned back in the chair to savor every word of their conversation.

Karen met Carl Friday afternoon at Judy's. By the time he arrived, Karen still hadn't decided among the three remaining kittens. All were equally adorable, with feisty personalities and soft, cuddly fur. Carl stood by silently, refusing to be drawn into the decision making. In the end, James helped her choose the calico.

"The reason no one wants her is because she's female," James declared, "but I think she's the best one."

"Well, that settles it," Karen said matter-of-factly. "Little calico, you're the one." She lifted the multicolored kitten from the box, examining her face carefully. "She's lovely. Thank you, James."

A hint of a smile touched Carl's wrinkled features. "Mr. Rand said you'd be choosing a female. Have you picked out the name?"

"Not yet," she said, frowning thoughtfully, "but I'm working on it."

"I like Super Pooper, because she's the one…"

"Carter, that's quite enough," Judy snapped, looking a bit abashed.

"Yes, Mom." The youngster's enthusiasm was immediately quelled, but his eyes sparked mischief.

Carl happened to catch Karen's eye, and she noted the difficulty with which he restrained his laughter.

The boys enthusiastically helped Carl load the kitten into the carrier he'd brought. Both made their farewells as if they were seeing their only sister depart to an unknown world.

"Such dramatics," Judy whispered with a sigh.

"Is Tuesday evening at seven convenient?" Carl questioned as Judy and Karen walked him to the car, obviously referring to the wedding reception Rand had mentioned.

"That'll be fine. Thanks, Carl…for everything." She gave him a pleasant smile and waved as he pulled from the driveway.

On Tuesday evening, Karen was once again meticulous with every detail of her appearance. She chose a white taffeta puffed-sleeve blouse with a coordinating burgundy tiered skirt. The striking contrast of the two colors highlighted the dark, rich tones of her hair and winter complexion. Her face glowed radiantly with a light application of cosmetics, and her eyes were clear and sparkling. Although an emerald brooch was pinned to the neck of her blouse and she wore matching earrings, Rand's locket remained in place beneath the taffeta.

She looked and felt lovely, but again discovered her confidence slipping. Her stomach twisted with butterflies as she waited for Rand, not knowing how he would greet her. The gruff exterior he'd displayed at their first two meetings after the Christmas party was gradually wearing away. After her visit to his office and their telephone conversation, she knew he was mellowing. Intuitively, she recognized Rand was withholding part of himself, the part she'd witnessed the night of the party. Unexplainably, the barriers had been lowered that wonderful evening, and, with a heavy sigh, she wondered how long it would take to bring them to that point again.

Aside from the brief visit to his office, she recognized his game. Rand had purposely planned that all their times together involved others: the play, the wedding reception—even the dinner date he'd been forced to cancel had been arranged with Cora Dibner. It didn't matter; he could avoid being alone with her for only so long.

As before, Rand arrived promptly, and Karen was surprised to note that he came by taxi and Carl hadn't driven. Her heart raced with excitement. He was tall, strong, and handsome enough to be any maiden's dream.

"I'm early," he explained as Karen took his coat. "The reception isn't until eight."

"I don't mind. Would you like something while we're waiting?" She took the hanger from the closet.

"You wouldn't believe what I want," he murmured almost inaudibly, rubbing a weary hand across his face.

"Pardon?" She stopped, her hand suspended in mid-air.

"Nothing...it wasn't important." He stood awkwardly in her tiny entryway, suddenly looking unsure.

"The most comfortable chair is to your left," she said lightly, hoping he wouldn't find her directions a form of rescue.

He smiled gratefully. "Thanks." He located the large overstuffed chair and sat down.

"Would you like something to drink?" Nervously, she placed a strand of hair behind her ear. She didn't keep a large supply of beverages on hand and could only hope she had what he wanted.

"Coffee, if you have it."

"I do."

"Why the sigh of relief?"

"What?" Although halfway to her kitchen, Karen turned back toward him.

"You sighed like you were afraid I'd ask for a Smith and Currens."

"I did?" she asked blankly. "I didn't even realize it."

"Don't worry. Blind men rarely drink anything stronger than coffee," he remarked.

Waving her hands excitedly, Karen marched to his chair and sat on the ottoman. "There, you did it again." Her voice was high-spirited. "I was trying to explain to Dad about your ability to listen."

"I don't have any unusual listening ability," he contradicted her.

"Of course you do," she said dramatically. "Do you remember when I bumped into you on the balcony the night of the party?"

"I'm unlikely to forget it." He smiled rakishly.

"You knew right away I didn't have my coat because my voice trembled."

Rand straightened, his posture suddenly defensive and stiff. "In case you weren't aware of it, nature often compensates for the lack of one sense by enhancing another. I've been told my hearing is extraordinary."

"Honestly, Rand." She shifted irritably. "That's what Dad said. One would think you of all people would know the difference between hearing and listening."

A frown creased his brow. "I don't understand what you're saying."

Exasperated, Karen expelled her breath unevenly. "Okay. The other day in your office you apologized for being on the phone so long. I told you I didn't mind, but immediately you detected there was something wrong—"

"My dear Karen, it was obvious you were upset; your voice was low and tight—"

"But that's it," she interrupted. "I've used that same tone of voice a hundred times, and no one has ever guessed my feelings. You did because you *listen*. I mean really *listen*. That's so rare, Rand. It's probably the most appealing thing about you."

"You mean my dashing good looks don't faze you?" he teased.

"Well, not entirely." Her long, thick lashes fluttered downward in a disconcerted movement. "The other day, I invited Dad to dinner. He gets home earlier than me, so I asked him to come to my apartment, take the casserole from the fridge at five o'clock, and put it in a three-fifty-degree oven. Dad put it in at five hundred degrees at three-thirty. Needless to say, we went out for hamburgers. If I'd given you the same instructions, I have no doubt they would've been followed explicitly."

Again, he dismissed her theory. "People misunderstand one another all the time. My ability to hear or listen or whatever," he said a little impatiently, "is a figment of your imagination."

Karen studied him, the tiny crow's-feet that appeared at the corners of his eyes, the salting of gray hairs at his temple. The deep-colored eyes stared back at her, but how much he could see, Karen could only guess.

"All right, Randall Prescott"—she gave in graciously—"you're right. The whole thing is a wild, unreasonable assumption." She should have known better. With his defensive attitude, it was unlikely he'd admit to anything that set him apart or made him different.

"Did you say something about coffee?" he reminded her gently.

"Oh, sorry." She apologized quickly and stood, returning to the kitchen.

Both cups were full and steaming when she returned and sat opposite Rand.

"By the way, have you come up with a name for the cat?"

"Yes," she told him uncertainly, "but I'm not sure you'll like it."

He arched a curious brow. "Well?"

"Everyone knows a cat is supposed to have nine lives, but did you also know there are said to be nine heavens, nine regions of hell, nine heads of the hydra, nine muses, nine crosses, nine orders of angels, nine worthies…and…"

"A cat-o'-nine-tails," Rand injected smoothly.

"Right"—she laughed nervously—"and seeing how there are so many nines in the world and all, I thought I'd name her Number Nine." She shifted in an anxious movement. "What do you think?"

"My birthday is October ninth."

"See, all the more reason," she said, laughing lightly.

"I don't suppose this decision has anything to do with the fact that we met December the ninth?"

"Absolutely nothing," she lied smoothly, then giggled because it was so obvious she was lying. She should have known better than to try to outwit Rand. He was too perceptive, too astute.

He gave her a full smile that did crazy things to her heartbeat. "I knew you'd come up with some connection to our first meeting."

Suddenly, they were both quiet, each entangled in the memories of that night. Perhaps it was a time Rand would as soon forget. Perhaps it was even an embarrassment to him now. But for Karen it was more an assignment with destiny. She smiled secretly to herself; Rand would laugh if he could hear her thoughts. Yet more and more she had come to think of their meeting as preordained and as irrevocable as uttered vows.

Rand spoke first. "I think Number Nine, although a bit unusual, will be a fine name."

They talked for a while longer, laughing over the antics of James and Carter with the comfortable ease of friends. More than once Karen found herself thinking that Rand would make a wonderful father. Picturing

Rand with children did funny things to her stomach. The mental image of him holding a child, their child, was more intoxicating than any wine. Karen quickly reined in her imagination. Taking their relationship any further than the moment was a dangerous pitfall she was going to avoid.

The taxi delivered them to the Elks Lodge, where the reception was being held. With Rand's arm placed gently around her waist, they entered the crowded room. At Rand's request, Karen signed the guest book for them both.

Seeing so many people put Karen on edge; meeting a roomful of strangers wasn't her idea of a romantic evening.

"Why so tense?" Rand whispered after the first couple of introductions.

"I'm sorry," she said, surprised at how tight her voice sounded. "I'm a little ill at ease when I don't know anyone. Does it show that much?"

"Only to me." A suggestion of a smile touched his eyes, as if he were suddenly aware he'd almost admitted his listening ability was more astute than others. "I'm not particularly fond of these affairs myself."

"Rand!" A tall, attractive blonde propelled her way through several people to greet him with an affectionate hug. "You made it, after all."

Hastily, Karen removed her hand from Rand's arm as the woman stepped forward.

"Aren't you going to introduce us?" she questioned, eyeing Karen resentfully. She was older than Karen, perhaps thirty, and carried herself proudly, confidently. Her metallic-blue eyes were piercing.

"Cora"—Rand's voice was warm and friendly—"I'd

like you to meet Karen McAlister. Karen, this is Cora Dibner."

"Pleased, I'm sure," Cora said, but her look belied any pleasure.

Karen's heart beat painfully; she had hoped to be friends with Rand's associate. He spoke of Cora so often—often enough for her to suspect their relationship went beyond business interests. Now that they'd met, there was no denying the jealousy in Cora's eyes. Or that she was in love with Rand.

"I'm pleased, too." Karen smiled in return and nodded, as worthy opponents often do when facing each other.

A glimmer of respect entered Cora's eyes. "Are you one of Rand's students?" Her voice remained friendly, but the whiplike flicker of her gaze cut into Karen.

Involuntarily, Karen stiffened. This woman was after blood in their first round. Cora must have known Rand was uneasy with their age difference. She laughed lightly, giving the impression such a question was ridiculous.

"Hardly. Are you?"

"You wouldn't believe the things he's taught me."

The mocking words hit Karen with the impact of a hammer pounding a nail. Were Rand and Cora lovers? A sickening knot twisted her stomach until she thought she might be sick.

Rand cleared his throat in embarrassment. "Yes… well, I think it's probably time Karen and I went through the reception line. If you'll excuse us, Cora."

"Of course." Cora's smile, directed at Karen, was full of malice. "Nice meeting you, *Carol*." She purposely used the wrong name as a means of telling Karen she wasn't worried. Her grip on Rand was secure; she had nothing to fear from Karen.

"You, too, *Nora,*" Karen said in kind, her eyes narrowing. "I hope we meet again."

Rand frowned. "Cora seems to be out of sorts tonight." He dismissed his associate's behavior. Karen wanted to cry because making excuses for Cora's behavior showed he cared.

"We all have off days." She swallowed tightly. "Would you mind if we had something to drink before going through the reception line?"

"I think we could both use something," Rand said.

Two glasses of champagne clouded the encounter with Cora. Another glass and Karen saw the whole incident as comical. Rand was distracted by friends and didn't notice how many times her glass was refilled. But Karen, held protectively to his side, was always introduced and included in the conversation. Another half glass and her former nervousness dissipated; her smile was friendly, her laughter quick, and her eyes sparkled.

"We better do the honors while we can," Rand suggested after a while. "Are there many people left in the reception line?"

"Hardly any," she told him, and had the crazy desire to giggle. Rand honestly believed people really listened. She'd show him.

Rand introduced her to the first person in the reception line, one of the ushers, a brother-in-law of the groom's. Bravely, Karen looked him directly in the eye and smiled sweetly. "I'm very pleased to meet you," she said, shaking his hand. Although her eyes never left his face, she added impishly, "The elephants are loose."

Rand's arm stiffened its hold around her waist, biting into her tender flesh.

"How do you do?" the usher responded politely to her warm smile. "I'm so glad you could come."

"I am, too." Her eyes sparked with mischief. "I am, too," she repeated.

Before proceeding farther, Rand's low voice growled in warning, "Karen, what are you doing?"

She laughed saucily. "I thought you said people listen," she whispered back. "I'm just proving a point."

Undaunted by Rand's tight grip around her waist, she made the same obscure announcement to the next member of the wedding party. Again, nothing was said or noticed. Apparently, wild elephants on the loose were not of interest to the entire wedding party. The only one to add anything to Karen's ridiculous statement was the last woman in the line, who proudly boasted she was the one who introduced the wedding couple.

They'd gone no more than three paces from the line, just out of earshot, when Rand demanded in a low snarl, "Just how many glasses of champagne have you had?"

Karen had to stop abruptly in order to think, causing Rand to bump into her. She would have stumbled forward if not for his grip. "Three." She hiccupped loudly. "Oops, sorry. No, I think it was four." *Could it have been five?* she mused; she'd lost count.

"I'm getting you out of here." The words were muted, and for a moment Karen wondered if she'd heard him correctly.

"Gee, I was just beginning to have some fun." She hiccupped again.

"Karen, don't say another word," he warned.

Her lips moved to protest, but somehow the words couldn't get past her tongue.

"Promise me you won't say a word to anyone."

She hiccupped again. "How can I promise you that when I'm not supposed to talk?" She shot a quick glance at Rand. Why was he so interested in leaving all of a sudden?

The cold air outside the lodge stunned Karen, although she felt flushed and warm. The street was deserted, the sidewalk bathed in shimmering moonlight. It reminded Karen of the night she and Rand had met. The stars were shining, but to gaze at them did funny things to her equilibrium.

Suddenly, Karen had the overpowering desire to dance.

"Rand," she whispered seductively, waltzing a few steps ahead of him, "may I have the pleasure of this dance?" She curtsied politely.

"Karen."

Was it impatience she heard in his voice? It must be the hiccupping; it was driving her crazy, too. "Then for heaven's sake, kiss me," she demanded. "That'll stop them."

"Stop what?"

Rand was definitely on a different wavelength, Karen mused, and giggled on another hiccup.

"The taxi's here," he told her, his hand gripping her upper arm firmly.

"But, Rand, I want to dance," she pleaded. Her lashes fluttered downward suggestively.

Rand ignored her and directed his attention to the driver. "I need to get some strong coffee into her."

The driver laughed as Karen hiccupped again. "Drive-through or restaurant?" he queried.

"Drive-through…definitely a drive-through."

Again, the driver laughed.

"But, Rand, I don't want any coffee." She forced herself to concentrate on him. His eyes were anxious, disturbed. That worried Karen. Was he angry? One arm cupped her shoulder protectively, as if she needed his strength to sit upright. The fingers on his other hand drummed a nervous tempo against the seat.

Her eyes narrowed. "You think I'm drunk," she said in an accusing, high-pitched voice that suggested absurdity.

"My dear Karen, another glass of champagne and I'd have had to carry you from the reception."

Karen giggled. "Honestly, Rand, I'm as sober as a"—she couldn't think of anyone sober—"a judge." She waved her finger wildly, as if to prove her point.

Rand snorted, but his mouth deepened into grooves as he suppressed a smile.

Karen's fingers crept to his face, caressing his jaw, outlining his mouth with the tips of her fingers. "Please kiss me," she whispered softly as her hands moved up and over his shoulders, meeting behind his neck, urging his mouth to hers.

At first, his kiss was slow and gentle, but Karen moaned, seeking deeper contact. She wasn't disappointed when his lips hardened and parted hers. Desire seared through her blood until Karen thought she would drown in the pleasure of it.

As he released her, she felt the cold air come between them and rested her head against his shoulder.

"Either your kisses are more potent than I remember," she said, smiling lazily, "or else I shouldn't be closing my eyes, because the whole world goes into a tailspin."

She could feel Rand's smile against her hair. "Then by all means protect Mother Earth and keep your eyes open."

Karen groaned when her alarm rang early the next morning. The shrill ring triggered a burst of pain in her head. When she sluggishly sat upright to turn off the offending noise, she thought her head would burst.

Slouching against the pillow, she groaned again, holding her head. Looking around her, she found her normally neat bedroom in a shambles; clothes littered the floor, and one shoe sat on the windowsill, while the other remained hidden from view. She could vaguely recall singing and dancing around the apartment as she undressed. Taking deep breaths, she calculated the consequences of staying in bed, but the call of responsibility soon moved her into action.

Once fortified with a cup of strong coffee and two aspirin, Karen showered and dressed. She lifted her eyebrows expressively when she located her second shoe in the bathroom sink.

Fifteen minutes before she was due to leave for work, Rand phoned.

"How are you feeling?" His tone was laced with concern.

"Don't ask." She tested her voice for the first time and found her tongue thick and her words husky. "I think I'll live if my head quits pounding." Memories of the night remained hazy; she could recall Rand saying something about coffee and a beautiful, sensuous kiss in the back of the taxi, but beyond that, the evening was veiled in her mind.

"I'm almost afraid to ask, but did I do anything out of the ordinary last night?"

She could hear his soft chuckle. "My dear, I've got enough information to blackmail you for life."

Her breath was forced from her lungs; things were worse than she imagined. "I was afraid of that."

"Just remind me never to argue with you again. I didn't know what lengths you were willing to go to to prove a point. From now on, if you insist most people don't really listen, I won't question the fact."

Karen laughed, wondering where she got the courage to pull anything so crazy. "I think everyone in the whole wedding party probably heard me but was too shocked to respond."

Rand did little to relieve her anxiety. "I think you've made your mark among my friends."

Karen's face remained tight and strained when the smile died. "I believe," she began awkwardly, "that I owe you an apology. I'm so sorry, Rand. I don't know what got into me."

"I'd say it was several glasses of excellent champagne," he interrupted smoothly.

Karen closed her eyes for a moment. "I feel terrible about the whole thing."

"Honey"—Rand's chuckle was warm and sincere—"I can't remember when I've enjoyed a wedding reception more."

Five

Thursday afternoon, the sky was thick with threatening gray clouds that promised rain. Karen rushed out one door, down half a block to the restaurant, and in another, where Judy was waiting.

Her sister waved as soon as Karen entered. "Hi." Judy smiled in greeting as Karen sat opposite her in the small booth. "I've got our order in; it should be here any minute."

Karen sighed appreciatively. "Thanks, Jude. It works out great when you can get here early and order for me. It's been a madhouse this morning. I didn't even think I'd get here at all for a while."

"It's a darn good thing you did." Judy laughed, her eyes sparkling. "You should have seen the look the waitress gave me when I ordered *two* chef salads."

Karen laughed, a natural release from the tension of a hectic morning. "What have you heard from Mike?" she asked just as the waitress brought their salads.

"Not much. He's miserable, counting the days till he can come home, but he loves his job and the challenge. Sometimes I wish he was like a normal husband with a nine-to-five job, but he isn't. It's something I learned to accept long ago."

Judy and Mike had been right for each other from the time they started dating in high school. Karen was almost envious that her sister had been so fortunate to have found her husband as a teenager. It was a fact Matthew had often used to convince Karen she was being overly choosy. But since Karen had been seeing Rand regularly, Matthew had all but ceased his demands.

"You're seeing quite a bit of Rand, aren't you?" Judy questioned unexpectedly. Her voice held a worried note, and she watched Karen closely.

"Not as much as I'd like." Karen was surprised by her sister's attitude. "Does it bother you that Rand is blind?"

Judy shook her head, quickly denying the implications. "Of course not."

"Then why the censure?"

"Karen"—Judy hesitated, looking uncertain and more than a little uncomfortable—"I know you like Rand, but I don't want to see you hurt. I think you should tread carefully with this relationship."

Karen studied her sister thoughtfully. *Liking Rand.* That was the understatement of the year. Judy and Karen had always been close, even as children. Almost five years separated them—a big difference when Judy was a sensitive teenager and Karen was a pesky younger sister. Even then, they had shared a special relationship. Yet, in all her years, Karen couldn't remember her sister acting in quite this manner.

"Things between Rand and me are going even better than I'd hoped," Karen told her sister, but Judy avoided eye contact, paying inordinate attention to her salad.

"Rand's just beginning to be comfortable with me; the defensiveness over his blindness is almost gone. More important, I sense he is accepting me into his life. It's more than I'd hoped to accomplish in such a short time. Although"—she smiled before continuing, as if she'd overcome an important hurdle in their relationship—"tonight is the first time we'll be alone together. His reader is sick, so I'm going to the school after work and read his students' papers to him. He's promised me dinner. More than a fair trade, I think."

Judy didn't mince words. "Do you love him?"

Karen didn't even hesitate. "More than I thought it was possible to love any man."

"Does he know it?" Judy still hadn't touched her salad.

Karen sighed heavily. "I'm sure he does." A hundred times, Karen had longed to speak freely of her feelings, but this was a sensitive area, and she knew she must be patient. Not that she doubted his feelings.

"If you love him, why don't you tell him?" An odd expression crossed Judy's face.

"I can't, Jude. Rand doesn't want to hear it. I know that's difficult for you to understand, but for now that's the way things have got to be."

Judy shifted uneasily, again giving the impression something was weighing heavily on her mind. "Are you sure of his feelings?"

Karen's soft mouth curved into a smile. "All right, sis, what is it?"

Judy looked all the more uncomfortable. "What's what?"

"Obviously, you've seen or heard something about Rand, and you're worrying yourself sick over it."

Judy sent her a sidelong glance, and her shoulders drooped forward in defeat. "Am I really so easy to read?"

Karen smiled with sudden humor. "My heavens, I've seen James and Carter less obvious."

Judy laughed, too, her smile more relaxed. "I was on campus the other day and saw Rand," she began, her fingers nervously twisting her napkin. "I knew who he was the minute I saw him. I mean, you've talked about him enough."

Karen knew Judy was taking a couple of classes at the university, and it didn't surprise her that she'd seen Rand.

"Only Rand wasn't alone." Her eyes met Karen's briefly. "There was a woman, a tall blonde, with him, and, Karen, I may be an old married lady, but I know a come-on when I see one. This woman was definitely on the make, and Rand was eating it up."

"That's Cora Dibner," Karen interjected on a long breath. "You don't need to tell me she's after Rand. The lady and I have met."

Judy sighed, visibly relieved. "I've been so worried. I don't think I've ever seen any woman that smooth. What gets me is that Rand seemed oblivious to what was happening."

Karen smiled ruefully. "As far as Cora is concerned, I think Rand is more aware than he lets on. I don't doubt that he can see through that layer of cool sophistication. Rand's no fool."

Judy studied her sister pensively. "For your sake, I hope you're right."

Karen went directly to Rand's office after work. She stopped only once at the ladies' room to check her appearance. Her lipstick had faded, and she freshened the honeysuckle-rose color and ran a quick comb through her hair. Impishly, she sprayed her favorite fragrance to the pulse points of her neck. Rand had commented once on the delicate white ginger scent she wore. He was sure to detect it again and smile at her womanly wiles.

"Karen?" Rand's welcome was both a question and statement.

She let herself into his office; the door between his office and his assistant's was open, anticipating her arrival.

"Yes, it's me." Her heart beat a little quicker each time she saw Rand; he was everything she'd ever wanted in a man, more than she dared dream she'd find. "I hope you're not one of those slave drivers who won't allow coffee breaks? I'm dying for a cup."

"Now, just a minute," Rand teased. "There's nothing in our contract about coffee breaks." His expression altered. "Hmm, you smell good."

Excitement churned inside her. "Good enough to kiss?"

"Definitely." His voice was both low and hoarse.

Karen floated into his open arms with the sense that this was where she belonged. The whole world could be at war, but as long as she was loved by Rand, there was nothing that could touch her. She wound her arms around his neck, marveling at the strength of his muscular shoulders. His mouth took possession of hers. It was a demanding kiss that parted her lips. Rand kissed her cheek, her ear, her eyelids, and when she groaned, he returned to her mouth. Again, Karen was trapped in a whirlpool—the warmth, the taste, the feel of him—until it didn't matter if she ever surfaced.

With her head resting against his chest, she could hear the erradic tempo of his heart and knew he was as affected by their kiss as she. His breathing was hoarse and uneven; his arm gently caressed her back as if he couldn't bear to let her go.

"I have the feeling that either we start work now or we'll spend the entire evening exactly like this." The reluctance in his voice thrilled Karen.

She agreed, knowing she'd have a difficult time speaking, almost regretting the need to pull herself away from the hazy fog of pleasure that blurred her mind.

Reluctantly, Rand withdrew his arms and sat on the corner of his desk, giving Karen his chair, the most comfortable in the office.

When Karen began reading, her voice was shaky and a bit awkward, but gradually she gained confidence, and her tone became steady and sure.

Rand's transformation from lover to professor was accomplished with an ease Karen envied. Could it be he wasn't as affected by their lovemaking as she? Quickly, she dismissed the thought. Rand had lived with rigid self-control all his life. He was as affected as she; it just didn't show.

After reading each paper, Karen wrote Rand's comments on top of the page. She found his grading system to be stringent and uncompromising, but she was impressed by his fairness and judgment. His comments to the students included some form of encouragement, but he didn't offer praise unless it was warranted.

At the end of the first stack of papers, Karen's throat felt dry and scratchy.

"You need a cup of coffee," Rand commented before

she began reading the next pile. "There's usually a pot of coffee in the kitchen."

Karen stood, stretching her tired muscles. "Do you want a cup while I'm at it?"

"I never drink and grade papers," he admonished her jokingly.

Karen laughed and suddenly couldn't resist kissing him. Rand's reaction was immediate, pulling her into his arms and deepening the contact. "Karen," he groaned in warning, "you're not making this any easier."

She straightened. "Sorry." Even now her voice sounded faintly raw from the lingering effects of his kiss.

"Karen"—he stopped her—"bring me a cup, after all. I'm going to need something to clear my head." His eyes were warm and loving. "You don't exactly encourage the sensible side of my nature. You know that, don't you?"

"Yes, sire," she answered saucily.

The next hour and a half were interrupted only by coffee breaks or when Karen had a question about something Rand needed to explain. They found they worked well together. Everything about them was right, Karen mused on a happy note.

"Didn't you say something about buying me dinner?" she asked quietly after marking Rand's comments on the last paper.

Rand walked across the office, flexing his shoulder muscles as if he were stiff. "I had Dorothy pack us a dinner. I hope you don't mind." His back was turned toward her.

"Dorothy?" Was there someone besides Cora she needed to contend with?

"Dorothy is Carl's wife." Rand paused, taking a deep breath before raking his hand through his thick hair. "The thing is, Karen, I don't like to eat in restaurants. Most blind people don't. It presents an unfamiliar environment."

Karen could have bit her tongue. How could she have been so thoughtless, so insensitive? She had made it necessary for Rand to admit something he considered a fault. It was a humbling experience that set him aside and made him appear different.

Karen was appalled at her own insensitivity. "You know, I thought I smelled something delicious when I came in this afternoon. But I couldn't very well accuse you of hiding prime rib in your desk drawer."

The tension faded from Rand's face. She'd done right by making light of his admission; apologizing would only have made the situation worse.

"Dorothy did pack roast beef. Between the ginger scent you're wearing and the aroma of beef, I've been like a man on the rack for the last two hours."

Karen drew a deep, troubled breath. "Well, which one of us would you like to devour first?"

Rand groaned and reached for her, pressing a hard kiss upon her lips. But before he allowed it to develop into something deeper, he straightened. "I think you'd better unpack the picnic basket before you find out. Carl put it in the coat closet against the wall."

Whoever Dorothy was, she certainly knew how to cook. The meal couldn't have been prepared or packed more efficiently. Karen spread the tablecloth on the thick carpet of Rand's office and unpacked their meal of French dip sandwiches made on crusty French bread. The beef, sliced thin, was piled on so high Karen doubted she would be able to fit the sandwich in her mouth. She poured steaming au jus into the bowls while Rand removed the cork from the bottle of wine.

"Fresh strawberries!" Karen exclaimed enthusiastically. "Where in heaven's name did she ever find strawberries this time of year?"

Rand chuckled, the sound of his laughter brightening the evening. "I never ask. The woman's a wonder."

As they ate, Karen's admiration for Dorothy grew. Everything was perfect, beautifully done.

"Ready for a strawberry?" Karen questioned, but when Rand reached for one, she restrained his hand and instead carried it to his mouth. Hesitantly, Rand accepted it, rubbing the juice from his chin as he bit into the tender pulp.

"Your turn," he insisted. Her lips trembled as his fingers touched her mouth, awakening within her a whole range of sensual sensations. When they kissed, the taste of fresh strawberries, mingled with the wine, was more potent than anything Karen had ever experienced.

His hands fell away from her shoulders as Rand took a deep, uneven breath. "I think we'd both benefit from some cold air."

Karen's breath wasn't any less jagged. "Yes," she said, finding her voice barely audible against the tightening in her throat. She was so intoxicated with her love for Rand that tears stung her eyes.

The night was cold and dark; the wind bit into Karen as they walked hand in hand across the campus. They needed the cold to put things into perspective, to remove them from the passion of the moment.

By mutual agreement, they chose the paved pathway leading to Commencement Bay. Lovers of all ages had used the path leading to the beautiful waters of Puget Sound. There was a freshness in the air, and Karen inhaled deeply, finding the faint odor of salt water pleasant. The wind whipped her hair across her face, but she ignored the cold, taking delight in the simple pleasure of walking along the beach with the man she loved. There was no need for words; it was their spirits that communicated. Rand needn't voice his love; his arm, pressing her possessively against his side, warding off the brunt of the wind, said it far more effectively than words.

Karen was too full of pleasure to speak. When Rand paused, stopping to gaze into the dark, cold night, the only sound was the pounding of the surf against the smooth beach. Somehow Karen found herself in his arms; their lips met in a fiery kiss that fused them together. Karen clung to him. He was her love, her life for all eternity. Nothing could ever make her happier than what she was at this moment.

"Oh, Karen," he groaned, his voice deep and pained.

"No." Her fingers hushed his lips. "Don't talk." She buried her face against his coat, feeling the roughness of his breath against her hair.

He walked Karen to the parking lot where she had left her car. Again, he kissed her, a featherlight kiss that teased and promised.

"I'll be out of town this weekend," he whispered into her hair. His finger gently circled the small of her back in a sensuous movement that melted her bones. "Meet me at the airport Sunday afternoon."

Karen seemed incapable of speech; his physical impact on her was complete.

"I'd like to show you my home." Gently, he released her from his embrace.

"I'd like that," she managed, extracting herself from his arms.

He opened the car door for her. "Drive carefully," he cautioned, and Karen watched him from the rear-view mirror as he stood in the lot until she was safely on her way.

Sunday afternoon, Karen chose a dark chestnut-colored wool skirt and a cream cashmere sweater with a single gold strand woven in a delicate pattern to wear to the airport. She debated between boots or her heels, finally deciding on the knee-high leather boots because it was raining. She was adding the final touches to her makeup when Matthew spoke.

"Ye seeing Rand again?" His eyes showed appreciation for Karen's natural good looks.

She turned sharply at the unexpected intrusion, her eyes angry. "Dad, you did it again. When will you learn to knock?" It was more a statement of indignation than a question.

"Lass"—Matthew gestured helplessly, showing impatience with himself—"I keep forgetting."

It was impossible to be angry with her father when she was in such high spirits. "Well, try, won't you?"

Karen knew he was just as likely to walk in unannounced the next time.

"Ye seeing Rand again?"

Karen knew he wouldn't be satisfied until she'd told him about their dinner date. "Yes, I'm meeting him at the airport. We're having dinner at his home near Graham."

"You love him, don't ye, lass?" The question was more of an announcement, and Karen couldn't deny the obvious. Besides, Matthew was a master in the art of inquisition and would have dragged the words from her one way or another.

"Yes, I do...very much." Self-consciously, she lowered her eyes.

Matthew flashed her a proud smile. "Randall Prescott will make me a fine son-in-law. You've chosen well."

"Dad," Karen said with indignation, "you're rushing things. There's been no talk of marriage."

"Aye, but there will be," he said confidently.

Karen laughed impishly. "If I have anything to say about it, there will be." It was impossible to imagine life without Rand now.

"Ye know, the course of true love between your mother and me wasn't smooth. I had my problems getting her to agree to marriage."

Karen was shocked. As far as she knew, her mother and father had been madly in love from the time they'd met.

Her eyes must have shown her surprise. "Your mother was the most beautiful girl I've ever seen. I took one look at her sweet face and knew I wanted her for my wife. But I was thirteen years older than Madeline, and her parents didn't take kindly to a thirty-one-year-old man courting their teenage daughter."

"Little wonder." Karen knew, of course, that thirteen years separated her parents, but she'd never thought of it in terms of eighteen and thirty-one. Nor had she been aware that her grandparents had voiced any objection to her father.

"Not only did Madeline's parents not trust me, but yer mother had more beaux than a movie star. For a while I became discouraged, but in time I was able to win her over."

"But, Dad, what did you do?"

Matthew followed Karen into the kitchen and bent close to whisper: "I've never told another living soul this, but I tricked your mother into marrying me. But not for a day did she regret it."

"You didn't," Karen said with a gasp.

"Aye, but I did."

Karen could hardly believe what she was hearing. "How did you trick Mom?"

His whole face broke into a wide, mischievous grin. "I whisked her away. By the time we arrived in Idaho, she'd agreed to be me wife."

Karen felt the sudden need to sit down. "You mean to tell me you kidnapped Mom?"

Matthew laughed boyishly. "It was hardly a kidnapping. I was just helping her make up her mind."

For a moment, Karen was dumbfounded. "Honestly, Dad, you astonish me."

"Aye, it was a brave thing, but your mother never regretted it. I knew she loved me."

Karen would have said more, but her doorbell rang. When she introduced Carl to her father, the two men shook hands respectfully. Karen slipped on her full-length leather coat, and the three left together. Matthew was invited to Evan and Milly Forsyth's for Sunday dinner and promised to give them Karen's love.

The drive to Sea-Tac Airport was accomplished in a companionable silence. Carl seemed to be a quiet, gentle man about the same age as Matthew. His loyalty to Rand was unquestionable. They parked with relative ease and waited in baggage claim.

Rand was the last passenger to arrive, and again the sight of this virile man sent her heartbeat racing. She experienced the urge to rush to him and hug him fiercely; instead, she walked forward almost hesitantly and whispered his name.

Smiling, Rand immediately held his arms open for her. Karen was there in a second, as if it were the most natural place in the world for her to be.

"Welcome home." Carl greeted him with a smile.

"Thanks, Carl. It's good to be home." He smiled at Karen, his look tender and warm. Slipping his arm around her waist, he added, "Very good indeed."

After a thirty-minute drive, Carl turned off the road and into a long driveway. Karen watched with growing anticipation for the first view of Rand's home. Having him invite her to his home held a special significance; Karen felt it was almost symbolic. The final defense was being lowered.

She tensed slightly as they drove down the winding driveway. The first view of the house left Karen awestruck. The house was magnificent, a long, sprawling, contemporary rambler. The large grounds were landscaped meticulously. Another smaller home stood in the distance and roused her interest.

Carl answered her unspoken curiosity. "The smaller house is for me and the missus." His voice was filled with pride.

Holding her hand, Rand led her into his home. He was confident and sure in the familiar surroundings; his movements were precise and made with ease. They stood in the elegantly tiled entryway that led to a sunken living room. The fireplace was lit, the flames reflecting a warm, welcoming glow. A solid-oak dining-room table was set in the formal dining room off the spacious kitchen. The candles flickering from the table's centerpiece cast dancing shadows across the bone china and crystal glassware.

"It's beautiful...everything's beautiful." Karen spoke with a sense of awe. Rand's personality was stamped in every piece of furniture, every room. He had allowed her into the inner sanctum of his life; this home was his pride. Shown a hundred different locales, Karen would have immediately known this house belonged to Rand.

Carl brought in the luggage with the instruction to call when Karen was ready to leave.

The door had no sooner closed behind him when Rand turned to her. Very gently, he took her face between his hands. "I've missed you." He bent forward and kissed her with a fierceness that spoke of longing and frustration. Karen responded with an urgency that matched his own. It had always been like this between them; that jolt of charged electricity that sparked the fire of awareness until every nerve sang with life.

He whispered her name, and then slowly released her. With her eyes still closed, Karen swayed toward him. Rand chuckled and kissed her again fleetingly before placing an arm around her shoulders and leading her to the dining room.

"Let's eat," he murmured, "while I'm still in control of my senses."

Karen would have willingly forgone the meal to have remained in his arms.

As before, Dorothy's cooking was superb. Karen

couldn't remember ever tasting chicken tetrazzini with such exquisite flavor.

After the meal, they decided to have their coffee in front of the fireplace in the living room. Karen cleared the table and brought in the coffee on a tray already prepared by the efficient Dorothy.

Enjoying the warmth of the fire, they talked for a long time. With her head resting against Rand's shoulder, his arm around her, Karen discovered they shared several interests. They enjoyed the same authors, and both played chess and were addicted to mellow music.

While Karen returned the coffee tray to the kitchen, Rand placed a CD featuring Rimsky-Korsakov's *Scheherazade* into his CD player. The melodious sounds filled the air as Karen returned.

"May I have the pleasure of this dance, kind sir?" She curtsied before him, her wool skirt brushing the cream pile carpeting. "As I recall, the last time I did this I was rudely rejected."

"The last time you wanted to dance, we were on a downtown sidewalk with half of Tacoma looking on," he remarked, his voice full of humor.

Karen giggled, lifting her arm in entreaty, her body already swaying to the music. "You have no sense of adventure," she chided him softly.

He gathered her in his arms, his body moving rhythmically with hers. "Every time I'm with you, it's an adventure." His hand arched her spine closer, pressing her body intimately against the hard length of his.

Karen closed her eyes and nestled against Rand, glorying in the dizzy emotions he could arouse within her.

They danced, although they barely moved, content

to be in each other's arms, lost in a world created only for them.

When the CD finished, they didn't move. The pressure of Rand's fingers at the base of her neck lifted her face upward to meet his descending mouth. Obediently, Karen's lips parted as she molded herself against him, responding with all her love to his deepening kiss. Her hands around his neck were winding a path through his hair, pulling him closer, igniting a slow-burning fire of passion between them until Karen ached.

The fierceness of his lovemaking awoke yearnings Karen had never experienced, and she moaned in surrender as Rand lowered her onto the couch. His hungry mouth claimed hers again and again while his hand slid intimately over her body, seeking the satin contours of her breasts. Caught in the powerful undertow of her love, Karen felt herself drowning in an ocean of sensations.

Suddenly, Rand raised his head, holding himself away from her. "No...no," he uttered harshly, his voice hoarse and barely distinct.

Suddenly bereft, Karen tried unsuccessfully to bring his mouth back to hers, struggling against him, holding him as if her life depended on his.

Angrily, his hand closed over her wrists, firmly pushing her away. He stood and strode across the room, his fingers raking his hair.

Bewildered, Karen sat upright. She was shocked by her wanton behavior, but equally disturbed by Rand's rejection. Her cheeks flamed red from embarrassment and the lingering effects of desire.

"Rand?" It was a muffled cry from her heart.

Rand sat down slowly beside her, gripping her shoulders, forcing her against him.

"Karen, oh, Karen…" His jagged breath was rough against her ear. "It would be the most natural thing in the world to carry you to my bed and love the very life from you. But there would be the reality to face in the morning. Heaven knows I want you. And right now you think you want me, too, but someday you'll thank me for this."

"Oh, Rand…" Her voice wobbled, and she clung to him as if being in his arms would prevent the new day rising. Let there be no tomorrow if she couldn't have him.

Gradually, the desire ebbed, leaving her confused.

Six

"Thank you, I had a wonderful evening," Karen lied with an ease that amazed her.

The elderly hostess gave her a sympathetic smile. "Do come again."

Karen smiled weakly in return; the lump in her throat had grown so thick she could barely swallow. She slipped into her coat and stepped outside, where Carl was waiting. Rand remained inside for several minutes. Why had he stayed? He couldn't possibly be enjoying this. Did he wish to humiliate her further?

Carl glanced at her quizzically. The strain about her mouth and the hurt in her eyes were impossible to hide; she looked away, not wanting anyone else to witness her pain.

Rand joined them.

The ride to Karen's apartment was completed in a wearisome silence that crowded the large vehicle.

Pride held Karen stiff. What had happened? Why was Rand doing this? Things had been strained between them ever since the night he'd invited her to his home. They had been together several times since, and on each occasion he'd grown less civil, less courteous. He was erecting the granite wall between them again, and Karen didn't know if she could stand it.

This evening's party had brought to a climax everything that was wrong between them. Perhaps it wouldn't have been such a disaster if Cora hadn't been there, but Rand had made every effort to make Karen uncomfortable. His attitude from the very beginning had been chilling, but once they'd arrived at the party, it was almost as if he'd forgotten her. He sat with Cora, rarely leaving her side, making excuses to touch her, attentive in a way he had never been with Karen.

Karen chatted with several people, attempting to ignore his behavior, but there could be no pretending when Cora flashed her a look of triumph. A look as loud and clear as if she'd shouted it across the room: Rand was hers, had always been hers, and would forever be hers.

"I suppose you're waiting for an apology?" Rand asked stiffly.

They sat as far apart from each other as possible. "Not unless you feel like making one."

His laugh was short and humorless. "I don't."

"Then it would be pointless, don't you think?"

He shrugged as if an apology were of little consequence either way.

When Carl stopped in front of her apartment building, Rand straightened. "Would you escort the lady to her door, Carl?" The command was issued as if he couldn't bear to even say her name.

Carl muttered something unintelligible under his breath. Karen didn't wait for him to open her car door, jerking it open with a violence that demonstrated the pain of this final humiliation. Had she come to mean so little to Rand that even the courtesy of taking her to her door was beyond him?

Her lips trembled, and she avoided Carl's probing gaze. "Don't bother, Carl," she spoke in a tight, shaky voice. "I'll let myself in."

"It's no problem, miss."

As he inserted the key into her lock, Karen looked back to the car. The streetlight illuminated the dejected, solitary figure inside. Rand had slouched forward, his hands covering his eyes, portraying the picture of a man weighted by an intolerable sadness.

Carl's eyes followed Karen's. "He's been under heavy pressure lately. I'm sure he didn't mean anything."

Tears welled in Karen's eyes; she blinked with the effort to hold them back. Gently, she placed her hand on the older man's arm.

"Thank you," she said softly.

"Well, you certainly look in better spirits than you did the other day." Judy took a slice of carrot from the tray; James and Carter quickly followed suit.

"Hey, you guys, cut it out. There won't be anything left for Rand." She slapped their hands playfully, her eyes laughing. "I feel a whole lot better." Her eyes met Judy's briefly, knowingly. "I don't know what's up with Rand, but you can darn well bet I'm going to find out."

Judy laughed at the spark in Karen's eye. "You know, I almost pity him."

"How do I look? Do you think I'm overdoing things a bit?" She was wearing the birthday dress Judy had made for her. Not only was it one of the loveliest things she owned, but it boosted her confidence, reminding her of the support and love of her family.

"You're lovely," Judy assured her quickly.

"Aunt Karen, can I light the candles?" James questioned enthusiastically.

"Not yet; I don't want to light them until right before Rand gets here."

Both boys gave a disappointed sigh. "All right, I'll tell you what." She playfully tousled the tops of their heads. "The next time you're over, I'll have a candlelight dinner just for you."

"Can I light the candles?" James asked again.

"Naturally."

"But I'd rather have hot dogs than the smelly stuff." Carter wrinkled his nose at the odor of marinating steak.

"I'll have you know that smelly stuff cost me a week's allotment for meat," Karen informed them indignantly. "But don't worry, if you want hot dogs, then we'll have hot dogs."

The boys gave their approval with a loud cheer.

"I think we'd better go. I don't want to be here when Rand arrives," Judy said after checking her wristwatch.

Karen was grateful. "Remember to keep Dad occupied and out of my hair. It would be just like him to drop by for a visit, and I don't want any interruptions."

Judy winked dramatically. "Gotcha."

Suddenly, Karen was unsure of herself. Was she doing the right thing by forcing the issue? "Are you sure everything is right? The wine goes with the meal? The candles aren't too much? I'm not overdressed?" she asked all in one giant breath.

Judy shook her head dismissively. "Settle down. Everything is perfect; you have nothing to worry about."

"You're sure?" Karen glanced around nervously.

"I'm sure. All right, boys, let's visit Grandpa." The boys ran ahead. Impulsively, Judy gave Karen a hug. "Good luck. Everything will work out beautifully; wait and see."

Karen wished she possessed the same confidence. Her fingers toyed with the gold locket Rand had given her as if she could draw solace and courage from its presence.

She was placing the finishing touches on the salad when the doorbell chimed. Karen hurriedly wiped her hands on the apron, then carelessly tossed it aside. Pausing for a moment, she closed her eyes to compose herself.

It had been only a few days since she'd last seen Rand, and yet her nerves raced at the physical impact of his presence.

"Hello." She greeted him with false cheerfulness and slid her hands up the lapels of his coat, anticipating his kiss. He hesitated before claiming her mouth. The kiss lacked tenderness or warmth, and Karen avoided another.

"I hope you like marinated steak," she said casually as she hung up his coat. His face looked tight and a little pale. "How about a glass of wine?"

Rand smiled faintly. "Do you have anything stronger?"

"Do you think you're going to need it?" she challenged.

He ignored the question and sat in the overstuffed chair Karen had purchased for its deep-cushioned comfort. But Rand didn't relax; his posture remained tense and straight. "I'll take the wine."

While Karen poured for both of them, her gaze rested briefly on Rand. His facial features, which suggested strength and pride, seemed more pronounced. She watched as he wearily rubbed the back of his neck.

When he accepted the wine, his eyes held a dark, unreadable light. As she sat opposite him, he withdrew a neatly wrapped package from his pocket.

"This is for you," he said tightly.

Karen took the package, her eyes widening with surprise. Was the gift a means of apologizing for his rude behavior these past weeks? Karen relaxed against the back of her seat, suddenly wanting to sing.

Her fingers fumbled as she removed the ribbon and paper. It was a jeweler's case; the name of an exclusive and expensive store was stamped in gold across the top. She hesitated for only a moment before opening the lid.

On a bed of red velvet lay a shimmering gold bracelet, one more beautiful than anything she'd ever hoped to own. She longed to go to him, touch him, thank him as only a lover could. Instead, she whispered softly, "I've never seen anything this beautiful. Thank you."

When she glanced at him, she was surprised to note his wineglass was empty and she'd yet to taste hers. She was reaching for her glass when Rand spoke.

"The bracelet is my way of saying goodbye." The words, savage and tender all at once, were spoken softly.

Karen was so shocked she nearly dropped her glass; part of the wine emptied into her lap.

"What did you say?" She was so stunned she hardly noticed the sudden wetness.

"I said," he began coldly, deliberately, "this is good-bye."

Karen searched his face, praying she'd find some evidence that would tell her he was joking. "You don't mean that."

He gave one of those abrupt, mirthless laughs she had come to hate. "I mean it. We're both adults, and I believe we can do this in an adult manner. I won't be coming here again, and I don't want you to make an effort to see me."

"Why?" The lone word was wrenched from her.

"Damn it, Karen, I'm tired of playing your romantic games. I think it's time you grew up." His body was stiff with determination, his face expressionless, a tight mask.

"I can't understand why you're doing this." Her eyes pleaded with him, implored him.

"Why did you *make* me do it like this? The things I've done to you in the last two weeks couldn't have driven the message home more forcefully. Why do you have to be so damn stubborn? Why did you keep coming back for more hurt, more humiliation?" Although his voice was forceful and steady, it contained an element of pain, as if he found it as difficult to say the words as it was for her to hear them. "I don't want you. Can I make it any plainer than that?" He was shouting at her, then paused and began again, more controlled. "I don't like myself when I'm around you."

Karen's throat muscles were so tight she didn't know if she could breathe much longer. "Please, Rand, don't do this to us." Where was her pride? She choked on a sob but swallowed it before it could escape and humiliate her further.

"*You* did this to us," he accused her harshly. "You and your trial relationship. Why in the hell couldn't you leave things alone? I didn't want you then, and I don't want you now. Do you understand?"

Hurt and anger flashed from the depth of her dark eyes. "I understand, all right. You're only half a man, a blind coward, and I've discovered I want a whole man. Would you just leave?" she screamed, but her heart was begging him to stay.

He stood abruptly. "I've heard enough."

"While you're at it, take the bracelet with you." She threw it at him, box and all; it hit his chest and bounced onto the floor, spilling onto the carpet.

"And this." She jerked the locket from her throat, snapping the delicate gold chain, and threw it at him with all her strength. Rand flinched as it hit him in the face.

"Now, will you get out of my life?"

She ran to her room; she'd be damned before she'd let him see her tears. She sat on her bed, her hands twisting nervously in her lap, noticing for the first time the stain of the spilled wine. The dress, the lovely dress Judy had spent so many hours sewing, would be ruined. In a panicked rush, she unzipped it, allowing it to fall to the floor. She needed to soak it, or the stain would never come out.

She turned blindly and crashed into the open closet door with a sickening thud. Pain stunned her for several seconds before she slumped to the floor, releasing a cry of anguish and pain. The tormented cry of a wounded animal.

"Karen, Karen…" Suddenly, Rand was there, rushing toward her. To her horror, he caught his foot on the edge of the carpet and stumbled into the room. Karen reached out to help him regain his balance, but her action sent him crashing to the floor. Rand grabbed her bare waist and twisted his body so he would absorb the full brunt of the fall. They lay on the floor, their arms and legs entwined, catching their breath.

Rand spoke first. "Are you all right?"

Her tears became sobbing hiccups. "No."

He shifted their position so he was above her. "Where's the pain?" The tender concern in his voice made her weep all the harder.

"My heart."

He groaned as his arms curved around her, gathering her against him while his lips unerringly located her eyes, kissing away each salty tear. He began at the corner of her face, kissing her forehead, her chin, her neck, her ears, before claiming her mouth in a kiss that was as fierce as it was devouring. Karen lifted her mouth to meet his, her trembling lips parting in anticipation.

They clung to each other, their hearts beating wildly as one. His lips followed a slow path down her neck and bare shoulder while his hand wandered over her back, over her hip, molding her soft, womanly body to the hardness of his. Their mouths met, slanting across each other with hungry impatience.

Karen's mind reeled, and she couldn't convince herself this was reality. A whispering sigh escaped her as Rand buried his face along the side of her neck, his mouth spreading hot kisses over her naked flesh. Karen caught her breath at the flood of pleasure, her fingers gripping his head, drawing him back to her lips. His open mouth sought hers in an urgent kiss that sent her world careening. His hands, sensuously caressing her hip, slipped upward, capturing the ripe fullness of her upturned breast, and she was swept along in a violent whirlpool of desire. Winding her arms around his back and pressing her full length to him, she answered his passion with her own.

Suddenly, Rand tensed, his muscles rigid with attention. Lifting his head, he listened attentively to the stillness, leaving her naked and bereft as he stood in anticipation.

"Rand?" Karen whispered, sitting upright.

"I thought I heard a noise." Wearily, he rubbed his hands over his face. He lowered himself onto the bed; leaning forward, he buried his face in his hands.

"I thought you'd gone." She covered herself with the housecoat from the end of the bed.

He smiled wryly. "I couldn't find my coat. What happened in here?"

She gestured weakly with her hand. "I was crying and didn't see where I was going."

He nodded, his face weary and pinched.

"Please, Rand," she pleaded, her voice wobbling dangerously, "don't do this to us."

He stiffened at the sound of her voice. "Don't…it's over."

"There will never be anyone who will love you as much as I do." Bitterness was etched in her pain-ridden eyes.

He stood abruptly, hurrying from her room. "I've got to get out of here. Damn it, Karen, my coat."

Tying the sash of her housecoat, she followed him into the living room and to the closet.

"Here." She handed it to him. "I'm going to let you go, and I'm not even going to say goodbye. We'll probably never meet again. You'll live your life, and I'll live mine. But I love you, Rand. I'll love you as long as I live, and someday, maybe not for a long time, you'll regret this."

The hand closed over the door handle was clenched so tight it became stark white. He didn't pause or acknowledge her words. Instead, he yanked open the door and left.

Karen jerked as the door slammed, crying as she had never cried, her breath coming in desperate gasps, the tears from her soul.

Hugging her arms protectively against her stomach, she sat in the chair Rand had vacated, curling into its softness like a hurt child seeking comfort from a parent. The gold locket and bracelet remained on the floor, and Karen stared at the glimmering gold for a long time before bending down to retrieve the pair. Clenching them to her breast, she rocked back and forth with an anguish too deep for tears.

She remained in the chair the entire night, her gaze watching the candles while they burned themselves out. First one, then the other, the last desperate flicker before extinction. The room went dark. Karen stared with sightless eyes into a moonlit, shadow-filled room, realizing the throbbing pain in her head would diminish, but not the pain in her heart.

The sun, gradually rising to announce a new day, spurred her into sluggish action. It took a careful application of makeup to camouflage the red swollen eyes as she dressed for work. "I'll make it through this day, and then I'll be all right," she told herself, knowing she was lying. It would be a very long time before she was all right again.

Until that day, Karen had had no idea how good she was at lying, how automatic certain responses became in one's life.

Late afternoon, she sat at her desk, examining the final details of a day's work, knowing she'd never find solace in her job, wondering if she'd ever find comfort.

Matthew's cheerful face was waiting for her outside her apartment. Karen avoided his eyes, praying he wouldn't mention Rand.

"Evening, lass."

"Hi, Dad. I'm kinda busy…" She didn't have the heart to tell him he couldn't come inside.

"'Tis fine. I'll only stay a minute." He followed her and sat at the kitchen table while she put on coffee to brew. When she gave him a sidelong glance, she found he was watching her with an odd expression.

"When will ye be seeing Rand again?"

Karen turned back to the countertop, closing her eyes for a moment at the searing pain. "I won't," she said flatly.

She could sense the shock that rocked him. "I'm sure I must not be hearing ye right," he said after a few minutes of stunned shock.

"Look, Dad"—her voice shook violently—"I don't feel much like discussing it right now."

"But ye love him," he cried indignantly.

"Of course I love him," she whispered through the pain.

"And he loves you?" This time, Matthew's voice was quiet and probing.

Karen couldn't keep her bottom lip from trembling. "Yes, he loves me…but love doesn't make everything right," she uttered in a hoarse whisper, blinking wildly to restrain the tears.

"But why?" her father asked in confusion. It was a question that had haunted Karen half the night.

"Because he's proud; he thinks he's only half a man and if I love him now, that love will eventually die when he loses his eyesight completely." She inhaled a shaky breath. "He wants me so much it's eating a hole in him; he had to push me away before it was too late." Karen grimaced with the memory that she had accused Rand of being half a man, lashing back where it would hurt him the most because he was hurting her so desperately.

Gently, a pair of hands settled on her shoulders and turned her around.

"Don't," she told him tautly, shrugging off his hands. "I'm a grown woman now. I'm not your little girl anymore."

Matthew ignored her, turning her into his arms, holding her close, his cheek resting gently against her head. "Even big girls require a father's comfort every now and then," he whispered.

Karen buried her head against his chest, the tension draining from her as she allowed the tears to come. "Oh, Dad, I love him so much."

"I know you do, lass," Matthew crooned. "Let it all out, darlin'. Let it all out."

A week passed. Matthew and Judy enfolded Karen in their love and support, trying to make sure she was busy, not letting her stay alone for any long length of time. Karen lost weight she could ill afford to lose, and her eyes developed dark shadows that cosmetics were unable to hide. When she wasn't working or with her family, she sat in the big overstuffed chair, looking pensive and lost.

Matthew seemed to feel talking about Rand would make things easier. Her father felt certain that once Rand had come to his senses, he would be back. Karen didn't bother to correct him.

Another week slipped by, and Karen knew she couldn't live like this much longer. Friday afternoon, she gave Tacoma Cable a two-week notice, drove home, and handed a similar notice to the apartment manager.

"Lass." Her father let himself into her apartment, his face hurt and confused. "What have ye done?"

Karen didn't pause. "I'm leaving Tacoma," she announced without emotion. Dark curls escaped the scarf she'd tied around her head. She was standing on the kitchen counter, cleaning out her top cupboards. Boxes littered both the kitchen and the living-room floor. "I should have done this two weeks ago." She dipped the cleaning rag in the bucket of hot, steaming water and wrung it out.

"But, lass, when Rand comes back…"

"Dad," she protested angrily, "when will you get it into your thick skull? Rand isn't going to come back. It's over between us."

Matthew grew visibly pale and sat down.

"Dad"—concern laced her voice, and she jumped down from the counter—"are you all right?"

He nodded weakly. "I'm fine." His eyes searched hers, holding a desperate appeal. "I don't want you doing something rash. You've been hurt, and seeking a geographical cure would be the worst possible thing for you. I told you before, things have a way of working out for the best. Just where are ye planning to go?"

Karen had expected an argument, and squared her shoulders defiantly. "Away... I don't know yet."

Matthew shook his head sadly. "I don't like this, lass."

Karen had known he wouldn't and that she hadn't heard the last of it. "I'm twenty-four years old, and I've barely left the state of Washington. I think it's time I learned to live a little, let my hair down, travel." Her enthusiasm was as phony as that of a used-car salesman. There was only one thing she wanted in life, and that was impossible. She couldn't chance meeting Rand. She couldn't stay. Not in the same city, not in the same state. Not in the same world.

Judy arrived an hour later; her eyes held an accusing, disbelieving look. "You've pulled some good ones in your life, little sister, but this takes the cake."

"Oh? What have I done now?"

"Do you realize you've got Dad worried sick?"

Karen flushed guiltily, dropping the pretense. "I know, but I've got to leave. I wish I could make you understand. Do you realize what it does to me every time I'm near the university, or see Uncle Evan, or even drive in downtown Tacoma? Someday it's going to happen. By fate or design, I don't know, but someday I'm going to run into Rand. I won't be able to take it." Her voice rose, and she took a moment to compose herself. "I'll fall into a thousand pieces. I know I will. If you and Dad think I'm running away, then all right, I'll admit it."

Judy sighed, her eyes filled with compassion. "I wish I had some magic formula that would take away the hurt, but I don't." She gave a weak gesture of helplessness. "I'm not convinced you're doing the wrong thing, like Dad is. But I do know we all love you. Let our love support you; let us be your strength." She paused for a minute and withdrew something from her purse. "Maybe if you read this, it'll help."

Karen accepted the letter, grown yellow with age.

"When Mom died," Judy continued, "Mike and I were stationed back East. Both boys were little, and I was stuck home alone most of the time. I had no family, no close friends, or anyone I could talk to about my feelings. I didn't know how to handle my grief. For weeks, I walked around in a haze of emotional pain."

Karen understood; her life had been a haze of pain since that last night with Rand.

"All I seemed capable of doing was crying. I know Mike was worried about me. He must have written Dad because I received this letter. It's the most beautiful thing Dad has ever given me."

Karen opened the letter and was greeted by Matthew's familiar scrawl. The date was exactly three months after her mother's death. It was a vivid memory. Madeline had suffered from a chronic kidney disorder, and when she contracted an infection, it didn't overly concern Karen or her father. She'd had several infections over the years. Karen had even felt her mother was getting better. Then one day she was in the hospital, insisting she should be home, and two days later she was dead.

Karen had loved and sorely missed her mother, too, but her concern had been for Matthew and the changes that had come over him after Madeline's death.

The letter showed the wear of many readings; the stain of Judy's tears marked the pages.

It read:

My darling Judy,

It hurts so terribly, doesn't it? But, my darling lass, we must learn to accept the pain. It is the price we must pay for having loved. I hold this ache of loneliness inside, and although I have loved and lost my beloved Madeline, I accept and gladly pay the cost. It is but a small price for the love we shared those many years. They have been good years, the best of my life. Sometimes I am overcome by my agony. I weep with you, my daughter. I pray God will surround you with His love.

Mike is worried about you. He loves you just as I loved my Madeline. Drink of his love; let it be your strength.

We must go on, just as life does. James and Carter need you just as Karen yet needs me. Accept the pain with joy…it was worth the cost.
Your loving father

Tears blurred Karen's eyes and spilled down her face. The end of her relationship with Rand was very much like her mother's death to Judy. She smiled through her tears, grateful for her sister's love. She, too, would pay the price for loving Rand, but now, because of a letter full of love and wisdom, she would pay the price with joy.

Judy may have accepted Karen's decision to leave, but Matthew made repeated efforts to dissuade her. Karen listened politely to his logic, sometimes doubting the wisdom of her actions, but never wavering from the decision.

Selling her furniture and packing her things filled

her last remaining days in Tacoma. It was the nights that continued to haunt her. She'd lie awake for hours in a reflective mood, wondering what she might have done differently to have won Rand. The sharp pain remained, and Karen pondered how long it would take for it to lessen. Sometimes, if she lay very still and closed her eyes, she could almost feel the warmth of his breath against her cheek. She'd shake herself, realizing she was doing the right thing by leaving. She couldn't bear the struggle to be free of him for much longer. All the memories were right here to torment her.

Only three days remained of Karen's two-week notice. Most of the things from her apartment had been sold. Only her bed and the large, overstuffed chair remained.

Because she couldn't sleep, she sat reading, finding it hard to concentrate and equally difficult to answer the doubts that bobbed to the surface of her mind. Karen realized, perhaps for the first time, how much she would miss her home, her city. If she were honest with herself, she'd admit that she didn't really want to leave Tacoma, but the alternative was just as unacceptable.

When the doorbell rang, it caught Karen by surprise. She glanced at her watch, curious who would be visiting so late.

"Who is it?" she questioned before unlocking the door.

"Rand," came the muffled reply.

Was it some cruel joke? Her fingers were trembling so badly she could barely open the door.

When he entered, Karen was as shocked by his appearance as his presence. He looked as if he hadn't shaved in days; the dark growth did little to disguise his haggard features. Gaunt lines of fatigue were etched about his eyes and mouth, as if he hadn't seen a bed in days. If he had slept, it was in the wrinkled mass of clothes he wore. His hair, normally so neat and well groomed, looked like he'd raked his fingers through it several times over.

"Rand?" His name was twisted from her in shock. She longed to touch him, to comfort him. He was in as much hell as she had been these past weeks.

His mouth twisted cynically. "All right, Karen, you win."

Seven

Karen walked into his arms, gently resting her head against his chest. His hold tightened until it was difficult for her to breathe. But it didn't matter, not as long as she was in his arms. Rand's face moved against her hair, as if he couldn't yet believe the feel of her. They stood entwined for a long time, not talking, hardly breathing, savoring the tender moment.

When Karen placed her arms around his neck, urging his mouth to hers, she felt his reluctance. The kiss began hard, as if he wanted to punish her; then, with a groan, his lips softened into a warm possession, and what followed was anything but punishment.

"Hold me, please, hold me." Tears blurred her vision, her voice betraying the anguish of the past month without him.

"I love you." His voice was thick with emotion as if he were confessing a guilt. "I could have withstood anything if I didn't love you so much."

"I know, I know," she whispered in soothing tones, remembering how hard he had tried to convince her otherwise. Tenderly, his hand brushed her tears aside. "I think I would have died if you hadn't come," Karen murmured. Already she had gone cold inside, withdrawing from her family and life.

Rand breathed heavily. "I'm here now." The words were clipped, almost angry.

His pride made him so defensive, Karen thought sadly. Knowing and loving Rand made her realize how much it had cost him to come to her.

"There's only one chair left in the apartment." She gave a tiny laugh and wiped the last happy tears from her face. "I'll have to sit on your lap."

The quizzical look on his face prompted her to add, "Everything else has been sold. I'm packed and ready to leave." Her arms automatically went around his neck as she positioned herself on his knees.

His hands tightened around her upper arms. "Were you so sure of me?" His look was weary, and there was a grimness in him.

"I wasn't sure of anything," she said, defending herself. Her eyes narrowed questioningly. Certainly he couldn't believe she had expected his return. In truth, she had never been more shocked in her life.

"I want the wedding to be small." The demand startled Karen. She hadn't expected him to mention marriage, not yet. Not that it mattered how many guests attended.

"Wedding?" Karen breathed in wonder as her heart soared with a new happiness. She began spreading kisses over his face, and fresh tears misted her eyes.

"Your father wouldn't accept anything less," Rand murmured caustically. "Nor would you."

Karen was too happy to question his decision.

* * *

They were married nine days later in Evan and Milly Forsyth's home. The preceding days were a whirlwind of activity as Judy, Karen, and her godmother rushed to have everything ready. Karen saw Rand only once, when they applied for their wedding license, and if he was curt and taciturn, she attributed it to nerves and the pressures of teaching. Because Rand had a speaking engagement in New York scheduled for the weekend of their wedding, it was decided that Karen would travel with him on a working honeymoon. Rand's mother lived in New York, and Karen was eager to meet her.

As Rand wished, the wedding was unpretentious, with only family and a few intimate friends attending. The Forsyth home was decorated with garlands and several bouquets of fresh flowers. Their sweet fragrance lingered in the air, their colors vivid. Karen felt she couldn't have asked for a more lovely wedding.

As Randall Franklin Prescott and Karen Madeline McAlister exchanged their vows, Rand's voice was firm and unfaltering. Karen's voice trembled slightly as she repeated hers. Her heart swelled with a burning love. Marrying Rand was the culmination of every romantic dream she'd ever had.

The wedding meal was served in the Forsyths' huge dining room. If Rand was somber and unusually quiet, no one noticed, for Karen was so obviously happy. Her spirits soared with an unrestrained freedom, yet she had just uttered vows that bound her for life.

It was late by the time they arrived at Rand's home. The stars were out in an ostentatious show, their brilliance lighting up the black velvet sky.

As Carl carried in her cases, Karen looped her arm

in Rand's, savoring the beauty of the evening. "This reminds me of the night we met." She smiled dreamily, placing her head against his upper arm. "Oh, Rand, I'm so happy… I love you so much." She longed to have him take her in his arms and whisk her over the threshold, but he paused, holding himself stiff and unyielding against her.

"My mother had a homemade sampler in the living room when I was a little girl. I've thought about it so often these past few days. I'd like to make one for our home."

Rand remained unresponsive, and Karen hugged herself to him. "Aren't you interested in what it said?" she asked with a gentle smile.

"I have the feeling you're going to tell me whether I want to hear it or not," he murmured.

Karen laughed. "It said, 'If you love something, set it free. If it doesn't return, it was never meant to be. But if it does, love it forever.'" She gave a long sigh. "I let you go that night. It nearly killed me to let you walk out of my life, but you've come back, and now I'll love you forever."

Rand jerked her arm from his. "That's just the point," he retorted angrily. "I didn't come back. You forced me into this farce."

"Forced you?" Karen asked in confusion. "I *didn't* show up on *your* doorstep. You were the one who came to me."

Rand gave a short, derisive laugh. "That I did, two hours before the deadline." He stormed into the house, leaving Karen standing alone and baffled. When she followed him, Rand had already poured himself a tall drink from a decanter of whiskey.

"I thought you said you rarely drink?" she asked accusingly.

He snickered. "I find I can't stand to be in your presence without something to dull my sense of decency."

"That's a rotten thing to say." What was happening to him? Why was he acting like this? Karen searched his face, hoping to find some clue of what was wrong. All she could read was contempt.

"That'll be all, Carl." Rand broke into her thoughts. "I'll call you when we're ready to leave for the airport."

Carl's eyes avoided Karen's, although she silently pleaded with him; for what, she didn't know.

As soon as the front door closed behind her husband's driver, Karen asked, "What...what did you mean when you said you came to me two hours before the deadline? What deadline?"

His face twisted malevolently. "Drop the charade, Karen. You're not going to fool me by playing dumb. I'd guessed you'd try something like this."

"Something like what? Rand, please, I don't know what you're talking about."

He emitted another sadistic laugh. "I walked into the whole thing like a lamb going to the slaughter. I have to admire you, Karen. You were more cunning than I thought possible."

"Rand?" she pleaded urgently. "I don't know what you're talking about."

"Sure you don't." He tipped his head back and drained the glass. "I needed that." Wiping his mouth with the back of his hand, he sat, leaning his head against the back of the couch. "Like a lamb to the slaughter," he repeated. "You must have been frantic when you saw your little ploy wouldn't work that night.

You hadn't counted on me handing you your walking papers so soon, did you? It was quick thinking on your part to pretend you'd hurt yourself. It got me into that bedroom." He ran his hand over his eyes. "I should have known something was up when you were practically naked."

"I'd spilled wine on my dress," she cried.

"Sure you did." His words were uttered in a harsh whisper.

Karen paced the living-room floor, her mind racing, her thoughts confused. Nothing made sense, least of all the things he was saying. "Rand," she whispered imploringly, "I'm going to ask you one last time. Please tell me what's going on."

He sat upright, flexing his shoulders as if he were going to ignore her. "What did you expect me to do? Welcome you with open arms? I don't take kindly to blackmail; I could hate you and your father for what you've done to me."

"Blackmail? Dad?" She glared at him, her face tightening with shock. Walking the full length of the floor, Karen poured herself a drink from the same decanter Rand had used, then choked and coughed after the first gulp. "Good grief, how do you drink this stuff?" Her eyes were watering, and she shook her head; her mouth felt as if she'd been sucking lemons. She moved back to Rand. "All right," she murmured tightly, "let's start at the beginning. I invited you to dinner—"

"Like a black widow to her web," Rand interrupted mockingly.

Karen clenched her hands together, fighting the urge to scream. "I invited you to dinner because…because I had to know what was happening with us."

"Ha!" Rand laughed sarcastically. "More likely to lure me to your bed so your father could find us."

"So my father could find us?" She echoed one of the short, bitter laughs he'd given her. "Really, Rand, if I'd gotten you into my bed, the last person I'd want to see is my father."

"So you say," he remarked flippantly.

Karen studied him closely again, feeling hurt and bewildered.

"I have to admit your duplicity worked well. I wasn't given much choice, was I? Since Evan Forsyth is your godfather, who do you think he'd believe?" His mouth twisted bitterly. "I haven't got ten years in at the university; you knew that. I'd stand a snowball's chance in hell of finding another decent position after Forsyth was through with me."

Even as understanding came, Karen refused to believe what she was hearing. Matthew had seen them together that night and was using what he'd witnessed against Rand, forcing him to marry her. She inhaled sharply. "The noise that night was Dad," she said incredulously, her voice tight with embarrassment.

"My contempt would be less if you'd admit your part in this."

"Damn it, Rand," she shouted, "I *am* telling you the truth." Suddenly, her knees became so weak she had to sit down. She sat tense and stiff in the chair opposite Rand as she pleaded with him. "Please listen to me." She spoke softly, enunciating each word. "I swear by everything I hold sacred that I had nothing to do with this."

Uncertainty flashed across his face, wrinkling his brow. "I could almost believe you…almost." His fingers twisted the wedding band, so recently placed on his finger, tying him to her. "But everything falls into place so neatly. You set up this trap for me…"

"I didn't, I swear," she cried.

"All right, you didn't, but why was it when I came to your room, thinking you were hurt, that I found you half-naked?"

"I already explained that," she pleaded. "I spilled wine on my dress. I had to take it off and soak it, or it would have been ruined. After I removed the dress, I bumped into the closet door."

"Your father just happened to walk in and witness that sordid little scene with us on the floor?"

Karen felt sick. "Dad… Dad has a terrible habit of walking into my apartment unannounced."

Rand's face turned sour. "Sure he does. You were so confident you had me trapped that you quit your job and packed your things."

"No! I'd decided to leave Tacoma…to move away." Karen could see it was useless; she couldn't argue or reason with him. Rand had already tried her and found her guilty. "Nothing I can say will make a difference, will it?"

"That's right," he jeered. "I have to admit you play the innocent well, but I've fallen for your deceit once. I won't be such easy prey next time."

A sick sensation churned her stomach; they could never build a marriage under the circumstances. "I realize you believe I was involved in this. I think I can even understand that." She spoke softly, her voice barely audible. "The evidence certainly points in that direction."

"What takes the cake is that you even had the marriage performed at the Forsyth home," he accused her again. "That was like rubbing salt in an open wound, my dear."

"That's the point, isn't it?" she asked, with pain-filled eyes. "I'm not your dear. You must hate me." Karen didn't know how she could sound so calm when she wanted to scream.

Rand's fingers tightened around the whiskey glass until Karen was sure the tumbler would be crushed into a thousand pieces. "I wish I could hate you," he whispered in a tone that reminded her of the night he'd returned and admitted his love almost as if it were a guilty secret.

"You once reminded me that we are two adults," she began shakily, gathering her resolve, "and that we should be able to handle things in an adult manner."

Rand nodded curtly.

"I can only apologize for my father's behavior. I don't know why he would do something so under-handed…"

"Karen…" Rand's voice rose threateningly.

Despondently, Karen realized Rand thought she was placing the blame entirely on Matthew's head.

"Please, let me finish," she asked, her voice stiff, polite. "I can only hope that someday you'll find it in your heart to forgive Dad…and to think kindly of me." She slipped the exquisite diamond from her long, slender finger and watched it slide off with a sadness she had never known. The ring had been on her finger for only a few hours, and Karen thought she'd rather have lost her finger than part with this symbol of their love. "I'm… I'm giving you the wedding ring back. I'll begin annulment proceedings first thing Monday morning."

Rand smiled stiffly as he accepted the diamond. "Maybe an annulment would be best."

"I'll have my things moved out before you return from New York," she said weakly, fighting back the first shock waves.

Rand's look became intent. "Where will you go?"

She turned away from him, tilting her head back and blinking wildly to keep the tears from spilling. "I… I don't know yet, but it won't matter. Once the annulment is final…" She left the rest unsaid, the words stuck in her throat.

Rand slouched forward, running his fingers through his hair. "You don't need to leave immediately. I'll be gone for the next three days. We both need time to think, to decide what we're going to do. By the time I return, I'll have the situation in perspective and a better grip on my emotions. I think you should do the same thing. We'll talk then. Is that agreeable?"

"All right," she murmured tightly. "I'll stay here for now and let my family assume I've left for New York with you. Maybe while you're gone, I'll come up with a solution to this mess."

"Until we decide, I'd like for you to keep the ring."

Miserably, Karen shook her head. "No… I don't think I should. Marriage is something very binding as far as I'm concerned. My parents were married for twenty-seven years, and if I place a wedding ring on my finger, I think my intention should be for a lifetime… not a three-day weekend."

Rand frowned slightly. "Whether we stay married or not, the ring is yours."

"I'd prefer it if you kept it for now." The ring would become very much like the bracelet he'd given her. Unless they stayed married, it could be only a painful reminder of what could have been.

Carl drove Rand to the airport an hour later. If he was surprised that Karen was staying behind, he didn't show it. Sadly, Karen stood in the open doorway as the car drove into the distance, watching until the lights faded and the car turned onto the main road. Rand's farewell had been cool, but the open hostility was gone. For that, at least, Karen could be grateful. Rand's face was drawn and tired as he'd stepped into the car, and Karen yearned to go to him and erase the finely strung tension between them. But she'd stayed where she was, watching him go.

Her suitcase remained in the master bedroom, a room indelibly marked by Rand's presence, and Karen avoided it as long as possible. Instead, she sat in the sunken living room, feeling lost and very much alone. Suddenly, she remembered this was her wedding night and could have wept with bitterness and disappointment.

Shortly after midnight, it began to rain, a steady torrent with mounting fury that pounded sheets of rain against the windows. Thunder rolled closer and closer; lightning flashed in jagged arcs across the sky. How quickly the storm had come; only a few hours before, Karen had been staring at clear skies and brilliant stars. The storm was like the day. It had begun with such promise; she had entered Rand's home as his wife, determined to do her best. Now, only a few hours later, her marriage was threatened, her life in turmoil.

When the phone rang, Karen was surprised. "Hello," she answered hesitantly. Surely Rand didn't receive many calls after midnight. More than likely it was a prank call.

"Miss Karen?"

The voice was familiar, and Karen recognized it immediately. "Yes, Carl, it's me."

He sounded awkward, as if he didn't often use the telephone. "I was phoning to see if you are all right… the storm and all."

"I'm fine, thank you. I'm not frightened by thunder and lightning. Did…did Rand get off okay?"

"I assume he and Miss Dibner were not delayed. I didn't stay to see the flight off."

Cora was with Rand. A sick feeling came over Karen's stomach. She had endured so much this day, the whole gauntlet of emotions from utter happiness to abject misery. Knowing Cora was traveling with Rand was almost more than she could bear.

"No, of course you wouldn't wait to see him off," Karen murmured, the lump in her throat building. "Thank you for your concern, Carl, but I'm fine."

"Let me know if you need anything," he offered soberly.

"I will." Her voice suddenly sounded frail and wobbly.

There was a pause on the other end of the line. "Good night, then."

"Good night." She replaced the receiver, looking around her helplessly. Rand and Cora. The picture of them traveling together when it was her and Rand's wedding night was almost more than she could bear. When the sobs came, she roughly jerked her hand across her face. If this was what love does, Karen decided, she wanted no part of it.

Stiffening her back, she turned out the living-room lights and walked determinedly into the master bedroom. Ignoring Rand's dominating presence, marked in every corner, she lifted her suitcase onto the king-size bed and took out her nightgown. It was a lovely full-length satin of pale blue that Judy had given her before the wedding. Karen took one look at it, stuffed it back inside the suitcase, and slammed the lid closed. Randall Prescott could fly across the country with another woman on their wedding night, but she…but she… The anger drained as quickly as it had flared.

Karen sat on the bed and lightly ran her fingers along the pattern of the multi-brown-colored bedspread. For an instant, she'd been ready to run, to surrender without so much as a confrontation. She couldn't stay, yet she couldn't leave. Releasing her breath slowly, Karen wandered from the room and found two other large-size bedrooms and a den that Rand obviously used as an office. She moved her suitcase into one of the other bedrooms; sleeping in the master bedroom was an agony she couldn't bear tonight.

Karen woke early the next morning, her heart heavy. She sat up, deciding to get away from the house for a while and sort through her thoughts. Evidence of the night's storm littered the yard; short branches of fir and pine from the trees that surrounded the property were scattered everywhere. Karen kicked them aside, her irritation so strong she failed to appreciate the freshness of the early-morning air. Heavy gray clouds continued to darken the sky, rain ready to pelt the earth at any time. Yet Karen noticed none of this.

"Just wait till I get my hands on you, Dad," she said

aloud, letting the branches receive the brunt of her
anger.

Did her father realize the impossible position he had
put her in? What could he possibly have been thinking?
Blackmailing Rand was an underhanded trick that went
against the very core of honesty she had always known
from her father. Karen wanted to shout at him every rotten name she knew. How could he have possibly done
anything so unscrupulous? Rand had every reason to
detest the backhanded methods Matthew had used to
get them married. And yet as much as she disagreed
with her father's schemes, she could understand why
he did it. Against the flint hardness of his will, against
his better judgment, Rand loved her. But that love was
doomed almost from the beginning. Without Matthew's
intervention, there would never have been a marriage.
Now it was up to Karen to see that they remained married. With a new resolve, she walked back to the house.

A movement out of the corner of her eyes caught
her attention, and she found Carl watching her from
the kitchen of his home. Impulsively, she gave him a
friendly wave and watched the smile grow on his face
before he returned her greeting.

"Miss Karen."

She turned to find Carl's long strides eliminating
the space between them. The calico kitten James and
Carter had given Rand was under his arm.

"Hello, Number Nine," she greeted the kitten softly.
She was more cat than kitten, and Karen was surprised
how much she had grown. "I wondered what had become of you."

"Mr. Rand asked the missus and me to keep the kitty
while he was away, but…"

"I'll take her," Karen offered, interrupting him to avoid explanations of why she was here and Rand in New York.

Carl handed her the cat. "With Mr. Rand gone so much of the time, the kitty seems to think of my place as home. The missus has tried to discourage her, but she stands outside the kitchen door and cries until we let her inside. My missus has a soft heart," he added.

Karen concealed a smile. No doubt Dorothy was a warmhearted soul, but it didn't take Karen long to realize Carl had a soft touch where animals were concerned. She'd found hay, food, and a salt block by the creek and knew he'd hauled it down the narrow path to feed the wild creatures in the woods.

"Now that I'm here, Number Nine will know her home," Karen said, her voice conveying the confidence of her newly formed resolve. "She's had her shots and everything?" Rand was sure to want her spayed as soon as possible.

"Oh, yes. First thing Mr. Rand had me do was take her to the vet."

"Thank you, Carl." The older man was fast becoming both ally and friend. Karen was grateful for both.

Without hesitation, Karen entered her new home, walking straight to the master bedroom. The cat followed her, jumped on the king-size bed, and curled into a little ball as if that were exactly where she belonged. *I'll do the same,* Karen decided.

One side of Rand's walk-in closet had been cleared for her things, and Karen spent the rest of the morning unpacking. She found herself singing, her confidence building. As she placed her things around the room, a sense of rightness replaced her insecurities. If her father could convince her mother to marry him, certainly she should be able to persuade Rand, who she knew loved her, that they should stay married. She'd face him with that quiet, unshakable McAlister resolve, she decided. Feeling as if a weight had been lifted from her, Karen slept in the master bedroom that night, finding courage in the fact that she was acting like a wife, waiting for her husband's return.

Rand's flight was due late Sunday afternoon. Karen waited impatiently as each minute passed with an incredible slowness. After pacing the floor innumerable times and checking the dinner she'd cooked, Karen decided she needed to vent some of her anxiety by walking.

She followed the same path she'd discovered the day before, a winding trail that led into tall trees alive with a natural beauty. When she returned, strolling leisurely into the clearing beside the house, she saw Carl's car had returned and was parked in front. Her footsteps hastened, her long strides filled with purpose.

"Hello, Carl," she called happily.

He gave her a frown that confused her and stepped into the entryway carrying Rand's suitcase. "I'll be heading home to *my missus,*" Carl quipped, his tone showing obvious displeasure.

He tipped his cap to Karen, his eyes avoiding hers. As Karen watched him go, her eyes clouded with confusion. Stopping to take a deep breath, she entered the house, but the welcoming smile died on her lips as soon as she moved through the door.

"Darling," Cora purred, her arms entwined around Rand's neck. "She must have left."

Eight

"But I haven't," Karen interrupted, fighting to keep her voice even and to hide her shock.

Gripping Cora's wrists, Rand forcefully removed her hands, which continued to cling to him. "Karen, I…" He sounded unsure and disconcerted.

"You must be exhausted from the flight, Cora," Karen interrupted again. If Rand wanted to give her an explanation, he could do it later, privately. "I'll have Carl drive you home." She returned Cora's cold glare with one of her own. Cora may have found encouragement in the fact that Rand had left her on their wedding night, but the woman had yet to discover the lengths Karen was willing to go to keep her husband.

Carl must have been waiting outside, because the minute his name was mentioned, he entered the house. "I'm ready to leave, Miss Dibner." He gave Karen a conspiratorial wink that did little to please Cora.

"Rand," she purred, giving the impression her feelings had been crushed by such a lack of welcome. But if she'd hoped for his support, she was again disappointed.

"As Karen says, you must be tired from the flight. I know I am."

"You will phone me?" Cora's attitude immediately changed from a feline on the prowl to the business-woman she was. Professionally, Cora was Rand's equal, her list of credentials as impressive as Rand's. The look she flashed Karen let her know she had yet to concede the battle.

"I'll contact you in the morning," Rand murmured without enthusiasm.

Her eyes filled with resentment; she gave Karen an almost imperceptible nod.

Karen returned with a slight dip of her head. "We'll meet again. Goodbye, Cora."

With a cool sophistication Karen envied, Cora gave her a meaningful sidelong glare on her way out the door. "You can count on it," she murmured for Karen's ears alone.

As soon as the door was closed, Rand crossed the living room and poured himself a stiff drink from the whiskey decanter. "I didn't mean for that to happen," he began, but his voice contained no apology, his pos-ture defensive.

"I'm sure you didn't," Karen murmured.

"Where were you?" he demanded. "I walked in the door expecting you to be here."

For the first time since his arrival, Karen began to relax. "I went for a walk in the woods out back. I wasn't exactly sure what time you planned on being here."

His face showed fatigue. "Did you discover the creek?" he questioned, then took a sip of his drink.

"Yes, I did." She was still standing in the same spot as when she'd come in.

"Carl has seen several deer drinking from it. I believe he's put some hay and a salt block out for them."

"I wondered about that," Karen said stiffly. Why did they have to talk to each other like polite strangers? Why couldn't they come to the matter that was uppermost in both their minds?

"Would you like something to eat?"

He shook his head dismissively. "I ate on the plane."

"Yes...of course you would." She glanced at the meal simmering in the kitchen, feeling chagrined. He was three hours ahead of the West Coast, and by his clock it was nearly eight. He would have eaten long ago.

Rand lifted his head and turned his face toward the kitchen. "You've cooked dinner?"

"I didn't go to any trouble; it's nothing special." She dismissed his concern and walked into the kitchen to turn off the oven. She had no appetite, and wouldn't until things were cleared between them.

He followed her, wrinkling his nose appreciatively. "What's this nothing special you're cooking?"

Placing a rebelling curl of soft brown hair around her ear, she turned her back to the stove. "Cornish game hens in orange sauce."

The beginnings of a smile threatened his stiff mouth. "If you consider this nothing, I'll look forward to your fancy meals."

She gave a small, nervous laugh. "Actually, I'm not a very good cook. I thought I'd ask Dorothy if she'd share some of her recipes."

"It was a very wifely thing to have dinner waiting for me."

Did she imagine an inquiry in his voice? If so, she wasn't likely to ignore it. "Yes, it was," she said as matter-of-factly as possible. "I... I am your wife, for the present, at least."

Rand scowled, and Karen's heart sank. She couldn't stand it for another minute. If he wasn't going to say something, she would. "I think the question remains of exactly how long I am to be your wife."

A muscle flexed in his jaw, and Karen could see the pride that narrowed his eyes. "Yes, that does seem to be the question. What have you decided?"

For a moment, Karen's stomach pitched unsteadily. Her hands twisted together, and she looked around, wondering why she had to have the most important discussion of her life in a kitchen with her back supported by an oven door because she was too nervous to stand upright.

"I've decided that my father played a dirty trick on the both of us. I know you believe I had a hand in this scheme, but I didn't."

Rand's mouth twisted.

"I know you don't believe me," she continued, her voice shaky. "Someday, I pray, you'll trust me enough to accept what I'm telling you as the truth. I do know"— she hesitated, her voice dipping slightly—"that I'm glad Dad did what he did. Admittedly, it was an underhanded trick, unworthy of my father, but you would never have married me otherwise, and Dad knew it."

"You knew that, too," he said tightly, accusingly.

"I only know you love me and that it hurt you just as much as it did me to walk away that night. I know that you'll never hold another woman in your arms without pretending it's me. I know that if you send me away, you'll always wonder about the life we could have had together."

"I never said I loved you." His upper lip curled into a defensive smile.

Karen's response was gentle. "You did the night you came back, the night of the deadline. But it doesn't matter if you spoke the words or not. I would have known, anyway. I've known for a long time. Do you imagine you could have hidden it from me the night we walked along Commencement Bay? Or any number of times since when you've held me in your arms?"

Ominously, Rand's jaw tightened. His fingers raked his hair in a savage motion. "All right, I love you, but it doesn't change things." The words were hardly an admission of tenderness, but more a biting accusation.

She met his fury calmly. "The only thing left to decide is the status of our relationship. Are we going to stay married, or are you going to allow that arrogant pride of yours to ruin both our lives?"

Karen could actually witness the inner turmoil etched so painfully on his profile. "No, we're married now. God knows it's not what I wanted for either of us, but the deed is done, and I haven't the strength to undo it."

"Okay," she whispered on a lengthy, drawn-out breath. Her love-filled eyes searched his face.

"All I know is I can't bear to face life without you now. I can't let you go again. It hurt too damn much the first time."

"I know," she said, assuring him of her own pain. Still, they remained apart at opposite ends of the kitchen. "Will you meet me halfway, Rand?"

His face relaxed, his look almost tender.

They walked into each other's arms, their grip tightening as if they never wanted to part again. When his mouth found hers, it was a gentle kiss that soon deepened. Karen's body flooded with warm excitement, and she moved against him sensuously, her arms locked around his neck.

No matter how deep their desire had run before, Karen had always tasted Rand's restraint. Now he returned his love and physical appetite in full. Their needs rose to a fever pitch; his kisses left her panting and breathless.

"I find I'm hungry," he whispered huskily against her ear. "I'm starving to death, but my want is not for food."

Karen gave a demure laugh, his words touching a spark of urgency within her. Tears of happiness glistened in her dark eyes as she spread happy kisses over his face. "Then let us wait no longer to dine."

Gathering her close, he kissed her brow and then her lips longingly, smiling down on her. "Yes, let us wait no longer to dine." He kissed her again, and her mouth parted in welcome. Again and again, their mouths met, each kiss more ardent, more rousing.

A soft sigh escaped Karen as she laid her head on his chest. His fingers brushed the soft curls from her neck, clearing the way for his lips.

Karen nestled against him, curving her womanly figure all the closer. "Will you carry me over the threshold?"

She could feel the smile against the satin smoothness of her neck. "It's raining outside."

"I meant the threshold of our bedroom," she whispered.

Rand groaned; their lips met again, rousing Karen until she gave a deep, heaving sigh of longing.

His hands caressed her back, sliding over her hips and buttocks, pressing her softness against his solid length. Bending slightly, he placed his arm behind her knees and lifted her from the floor. Her arms automatically went around his neck, and she rested her head on his shoulder. The tip of her tongue found the sensitive area behind his ear. When he gave a muted groan, she turned her attention to the thick column of his neck, spreading delicate kisses there until he shuddered.

A whisper of a sigh escaped her as Rand placed her with infinite care on their bed.

"Wait," she pleaded breathlessly.

"Wait?"

She thrilled to the impatience in his voice. "I'll be right back," she promised in a gentle whisper.

He released her reluctantly, his fingers never quite loosening their hold as she slipped from his embrace. The lovely silk gown her sister had given her was at the foot of the bed. Karen undressed, almost wishing Rand could watch her as she removed each item of clothing and placed it aside.

Wordlessly, she went to him and slipped her arms around his neck, urging his mouth to hers. They were locked in a frantic embrace, an all-consuming desire. Trembling, she buried her face in his shirt, her body shuddering with the effort to breathe. Their kisses were now wild and fierce; his hands loosened her gown and leisurely caressed her.

Unbuttoning his shirt, she placed her hands on his hard ribs, gliding them upward over the hair of his chest, her fingers caressing and stroking as his heart thundered beneath her palm.

"Karen, Karen," he rasped, his mouth seizing hers in a passionate kiss. Deftly, his fingers released the tie of her gown and slipped it away. Her soft breasts seemed to sear his chest, and he groaned before kissing her lips, then descended lower, spreading a molten path of desire that left Karen quivering with anticipation. She clung to him, eager to give herself to his passion. It was a tender, intimate moment, and Rand hoarsely whispered his love as he parted her thighs and gently entered her trembling body. Karen's eyes widened at the sudden influx of pleasure; she arched against him, murmuring her love, and surrendered to the swirling excitement.

Afterward, they lay together, Rand's arms protectively holding her as she rested her head against the cushion of his chest. Each was spent by the fierceness of their lovemaking.

When they spoke, it was whispered phrases of love, their emotions too strong to express with mere words what their bodies had said for them. Soon they slept in a deep, untroubled slumber.

Karen woke around ten, the room dark and still. A surge of love for the man sleeping beside her overcame her, and she nestled closer in the haven of his arms. Rand loved her as she loved him; together, they would build a good life. With a languid sigh, she rested her head in the crook of his arm. Playfully, her fingers ran through the hair on his chest. When he stirred, she asked him softly, "Are you awake?"

Karen could hear the amusement in his voice. "How do you expect me to sleep with your fingers driving me insane?"

Karen laughed, her arms tightening around him. "I'm hungry."

Rand turned so his body lay above hers, his mouth parting her lips with an urgency that almost startled Karen.

"Rand." She pressed her face against his throat. "I'm hungry for food."

He paused, although his hands enjoyed the freedom of her pliant, soft body. A low protesting moan followed her words as she slid out of his arms and climbed from the bed.

"Do you want something?" she asked while tying the sash of her robe.

Rand raised his brows and sat upright. "Yes, but I think it'll have to wait."

With a smile of contentment, Karen wandered into the kitchen and fixed herself a sandwich. Her stomach growled, reminding her she hadn't eaten since breakfast.

Rand was on the phone when she entered the bedroom. She sat on the bed, waiting for him to finish, her eyes studying the man she loved. There was a tenderness about him she hadn't seen before. The lines of fatigue were gone, and his eyes held a warm light.

"I've canceled my classes for tomorrow," he said, breaking into her thoughts. "It seems I have an urgent business matter that needs attending to at home." His eyes grew intense. "Come here, urgent matter."

A soft sigh slipped from her as she slid her arms around his neck. The thin piece of silk that was wrapped around her fell aimlessly to the floor.

"Karen," he groaned as his lips searched and found hers. She yielded to the urgency and clung to him, her smooth skin pressing against his muscular body. His touch was capable of drawing her strength as she responded to the intensity of his lovemaking. She was surprised by her abandonment as they came together again. They were caught in a whirlwind of spiraling sensations that hurled them upward to unscalable heights, then released them gently until they floated back to the reality of being in each other's arms.

They didn't speak; words would only diminish the wonder. Karen rested against him, and her cheek lay on his chest while he smoothed the tangles from her hair.

"I love you, Karen Prescott," he murmured softly; his voice contained a reverent note, as if he understood a love as deep as theirs could have been ordained only from above.

A loud ring roused Karen from the depths of sleep, but instead of reacting to the persistent peals, she incorporated them into her dream. Drawn naturally to the warmth beside her, she snuggled against Rand, folding her arms over his lean ribs. It was Rand's groggy "Hello" that brought her into reality.

Morning. Sunlight streamed into the window between a small crack in the drapery. With something akin to wonder, Karen marveled that she should be here with Rand, that they were man and wife, and that their love was secure and complete.

Unable to resist, she ran her fingers teasingly over his back. Rand shifted positions and sat upright. The telephone conversation continued, but it was distinctly a one-sided dialogue. All Rand murmured was "yes," "good," "fine," "okay."

It must be Cora, Karen mused, and stiffened when Rand issued an invitation for dinner that evening. The woman wouldn't accept defeat easily, and an uncomfortable chill ran through Karen.

When Rand replaced the receiver, Karen slid her arms around his middle. "Good morning, Mr. Prescott," she whispered tenderly.

Rand turned, looping his arms around her, his face buried in the softness of her hair. "Good morning, Mrs. Prescott."

Tipping her head back, she gently stroked his chin and guided his mouth to hers to kiss him with a lingering warmth.

The hall clock chimed, reminding them it was well into morning.

"It would be easy to spend the whole day making love to my wife, but we're expecting company for dinner."

"Yes, I heard. What time is she coming?" A heavy sigh slipped from Karen. She didn't want this wonderful day to be ruined by Cora.

"She?" Rand's brow twisted dubiously.

"Wasn't that Cora on the phone?"

His mouth compressed into a taut line. "No, that was your father. He's coming to make sure his little girl is a happy bride. Believe me, the invitation for dinner was issued grudgingly."

"Dad?" Karen's thoughts raced furiously. "You mean that was my father on the phone?" she asked again in disbelief.

"Matthew McAlister, the blackmailer himself, is entering the lion's den."

Karen's face grew serious as she studied Rand sitting on the end of the bed. The initial rush of pleasure at waking with Rand at her side quickly faded. She went to him, holding his head against her abdomen, stroking the hair from his face. "I want us to talk to Dad tonight." Her voice was sober. "Perhaps then you will believe me. Your trust is important to me."

Gently, he pushed her away as if her nearness disturbed his resolve. When he stood, his back was facing her. The silence hung heavy between them until Rand spoke, his voice somber, quiet. "No, there's no need to discuss our situation with your father. He would naturally deny you had any part in the marriage trap. Trying to make me believe your innocence is all part of the game. I'm not a fool, nor am I stupid. You're my wife now, but I think it would be better if we never mentioned how we came into this marriage. Doing so would only bring bitterness between us. Is that understood, Karen?" He turned around, his face proud and strong.

She searched but could find no words to answer him.

"But, Rand, please…"

"Karen"—his tone was stern—"you do yourself more harm than good by insisting you're innocent. Now, I said I don't want to talk about it."

"All right," she murmured tightly. "We won't speak of it again."

Rand didn't want to argue; Karen could see it in his face as it relaxed, his look almost gentle. "Now, how about fixing me breakfast? I'm starved."

Karen swallowed the tightness lodged in her throat. "Starved?" she returned, forcing herself to shrug off the hurt. "My dear husband, you've been feasting all night." She tried to sound gay and lighthearted, but the word *husband* nearly stuck in her throat.

As their relationship stood now, she was little more than a glorified mistress. She yearned to satisfy far more than his physical desires; she wanted to share his joys, his burdens, the everyday rituals of life that make a wife a wife. Rand wouldn't accept that from her yet. Not until she'd proven herself, had earned his faith and trust. There was little he would accept from her other than the delights her body could give him. For now, she must be content with that. Did her father have any conception of the hellish situation he had cast her into? she wondered wearily.

"I *have* been feasting all night." Rand's words broke into her thoughts. "But I fear having you once is like drinking salt water. I'll never be satisfied." His arms slid around her waist, his mouth seeking the gentle curve of her neck. "But for right now," he murmured thickly, "I was referring to something more basic, like bacon and eggs."

Karen snuggled against him, resting her head on his shoulder. If Rand's desire for her was only physical, she would accept that. In time, she would be able to tear down the bitter walls he'd erected against her. Eventually, under the determined onslaught of her love, he would be her husband, and she would be his trusted, cherished wife.

"Bacon and eggs?" She sighed, feigning disappointment. "And I was prepared to satisfy another hearty appetite…" She wasn't allowed to finish the sentence.

With a laugh, Rand lifted her from the carpet and placed her on the bed, his fingers eagerly searching for the opening of her gown. The unexpected action took her breath away. Before she could object, his mouth greedily claimed hers. When his head lifted from hers, Karen gave a weak protest. "Rand, I was only teasing."

"Don't act so outraged, my love. You did offer to satisfy my appetites," he murmured before planting another hungry kiss on her open mouth.

Karen responded fully to his passion, moving her body against him provocatively…

It was a long time before either of them entered the kitchen.

* * *

They spent a portion of the day arranging Karen's things around the house so Rand knew their whereabouts. He had a complicated system regarding the placement of his clothes and personal items. It showed Karen again the difficulties he encountered with partial eyesight and reminded her never to leave her things lying around. In his home, it was difficult to remember that he had limited vision. His knowledge of the house and everything in it was complete. The old saying "a place for everything and everything in its place" certainly applied to the system Rand employed.

Karen was arranging her small collection of ballerina figures on the living-room bookcase when Rand spoke. "Karen," he said with a faint huskiness.

Her cheeks were flushed with a warm glow of satisfaction as she turned around. "Yes?"

"We forgot something last night."

"Impossible." She laughed lightly and circled her arms around his middle, tipping her head back to study his face. His smile was warm and sensuous; his eyes glowed with a happiness she knew came from her love. It was a heady realization that the love they shared could change so much in each of them.

Because of Rand, Karen saw life with clear, more revealing eyes. She found herself ready to listen to others the way Rand listened. She was willing to look beyond pretense with business associates and acquaintances.

With Rand, there had been a definite softening. He was more relaxed and not as apt to erect the angry facade he had worn when they first met. Even his iron-clad will had shown signs of a willingness to compromise.

"We forgot your wedding ring." Rand withdrew it from his pocket. It lay in the palm of his hand. The solitaire diamond slid to his fingertips, and he manipulated it as if his hands were familiar with its feel.

Karen glanced at her naked left hand. She didn't need a wedding band to say she was his wife. Ring or no ring, she would always belong to him.

"Karen." His voice was low and earnest. "I want more than a weekend marriage. I want you for a lifetime." He took her hand, his fingers caressing hers until he singled out the ring finger. With a tenderness that was almost reverent, he slid the ring on.

"I'll love you all my life, Karen Prescott," he whispered, as if it was a vow.

Instinctively, Karen's arms slid over his shoulders as she brought his mouth to hers. As their lips met, Karen felt him shudder as he buried his face in the dark curls that fell over her shoulder.

Later, they sauntered hand in hand over the grounds, talking and teasing. Following the trail, they strolled to the creek and back.

"Would you mind if I went back to work?" she quizzed, watching Rand's face. It was a question that had troubled Karen. Her own feelings were mixed; her mother had never worked outside the home, but Karen was sure she'd quickly find herself growing bored without the challenge of a job. Being a housewife would mean a drastic change in her lifestyle, and she wasn't sure she wanted to make the adjustment.

Rand shrugged. "That's entirely up to you. In my opinion, you were foolish to quit. Did you think I would demand your presence day and night?"

Karen stiffened defensively. "I quit because I was

leaving Tacoma. I know you don't believe that, but it happens to be the truth."

His hand squeezed hers as if he wanted to punish her. "I thought we'd agreed to leave well enough alone? As for you returning to your job, I really don't care. My hours are long, and I'm often not home until late. You might do well to have some outside interests."

Karen bit back the hurt, wishing she'd never asked Rand's opinion.

The sun was setting, leaving a red glow on the horizon, when Matthew arrived, bringing flowers and a bottle of wine. Karen answered the door hesitantly, unsure how she'd greet her father; her feelings were mixed and ambivalent. She was grateful Rand was still in the shower.

"'Tis a sad day when a father is forced to beg an invitation to his own daughter's," he announced gruffly, handing her his gifts.

"'Tis a sadder day when said daughter's honeymoon is interrupted," Karen chided in return.

He hugged her close, and when he spoke again, there was an odd ring in his voice.

"I've missed you, lass." He studied her intently for a long, sober minute.

Two days before, Karen would have ranted at her father, called him an interfering old fool. His impudence had cast her into a sea of misunderstandings, creating an almost insurmountable lack of trust between husband and wife. Instead, she gently kissed his weathered cheek. "I've missed you too, Dad."

Matthew watched his daughter closely. "Are you happy, lass?" he asked with concern. His eyes held a troubled light, as if he were seeking far more than his words implied. Approval? Forgiveness? Praise? Condemnation?

Matthew's face looked wan and drawn, as if he'd been under a great deal of stress, as he well might have been, wondering about Rand and Karen. Seeing the question in his eyes, she couldn't berate him. "I'm happy, Dad."

"Rand?" His eyes wavered from hers.

"In time," she offered gently.

Matthew grinned as if relieved of a burdensome load. "Didn't I tell you things had a way of working out for the best?" he said, chuckling.

"I think you should repeat that for Rand's benefit," she teased lovingly.

"Did I hear my name mentioned?" Rand entered the kitchen, his hair still wet from the shower, his smile welcoming.

Karen gave a grateful sigh. She wasn't sure how Rand would react to her father. That morning, he'd made it clear he didn't wish to confront Matthew with the details of the marriage, but Karen feared he might harbor some resentment against her father.

"Welcome to our home, Matthew," Rand greeted, and the two men shook hands, an unspoken understanding between them.

Matthew relaxed and started checking under the lids of the pots bubbling on the stove top. "When's dinner?"

"Not until our other guest arrives," Karen said, trying to keep a straight face.

"Other guest?" Matthew quizzed.

Rand's brow wrinkled in question, but he didn't say anything.

"Yes, Dad. Rand invited the Widow Jackson."

Matthew's grin was wry until all three broke into hearty laughter.

While Karen placed the serving dishes on the table, she could hear Rand and her father laughing and joking together in the living room. She paused, watching them; her heart swelled with love for these two men. It was a relief beyond words that Rand showed no open hostility toward her father.

The lighthearted banter continued through dinner, and afterward, Rand challenged Matthew to a game of chess. Nothing could have pleased Karen's father more, and the board was soon set.

As before, Rand played the game entirely from memory. Karen moved the figures on his command, amazed how he could keep track of every move in his mind.

Matthew was an excellent player, and Rand a worthy opponent; the game dragged on, the skill of the two men evenly matched. Karen wasn't surprised when Rand won.

Matthew shook his head disbelievingly, moving the figures around the board, studying Rand's strategy.

Her eyes gleaming with pride, Karen turned and gave her husband a congratulatory hug.

"Well done, Prescott," Matthew said, but his eyes continued to study the board. "I accept defeat from you a second time, but want the chance to redeem myself."

With a lazy smile, Rand promised a rematch at a later date. Matthew left a short time later, and with a yawn, Karen closed and locked the front door behind him. Rand welcomed her into his arms with a smile.

"It's getting late," she whispered invitingly. Her fingers unbuttoned his shirt and teased his chest with light strokes before she wound her arms around his neck and drew his mouth down to hers.

Rand's lips moved hungrily over hers as he pressed her tightly against him until he shuddered with desire. "What is it about you?" he whispered thickly. "I'll never get enough of you, will I? Fifty years from now, I'll still be panting with desire for you." He led her purposefully toward their bedroom. Karen followed willingly but stopped at the doorway of one of the spare bedrooms, examining the room.

"This room will make a lovely nursery. What do you think, Rand?"

He stopped and became suddenly very still, his mouth drawn in a taut line. "I think there's something you'd better understand right now. There will be no children as a result of our marriage."

A shocked silence followed his announcement. Karen stared at him disbelievingly. "No children? But why?"

"For heaven's sake, Karen, think about it," he said bitterly. "I'm in no position to be any kind of father. Nor do I want children; they're an encumbrance I can live without."

"You're being unfair."

"Unfair?" He gave a short, derisive laugh. "You're a fine one to talk. If it had been up to me, I wouldn't have had a wife, either. If you want to talk about unfair, then we can talk about you and your father."

The cruel words struck her harder than any blow. "But, Rand…" she pleaded, then halted. A brooding scowl darkened his face, and Karen knew him well enough to recognize that arguing was useless.

"You got what you wanted, Karen. We're married,

but from here on, I make the decisions, and there will be no children. I don't ever want to discuss the subject again. The matter is closed." His tone was emphatic and hard as he strode away angrily, leaving her standing speechless in the hall.

An ache began to grow within her heart. She was married to Rand, a dream she believed would fulfill her every desire. But the deep womanly need to bear his child would be denied her. How easy it was to picture a dark-haired baby boy; Karen shook her head to cast the picture from her mind. Silently, she walked into their bedroom.

Rand was sitting at the end of their bed, bent forward, his face in his hands. He straightened when he heard her enter. "Karen, listen, it's bad enough having a wife I'll never see. I won't endure the same agony with a child." A hand moved wearily across his face. "Trust me in this. I know what you're feeling, but give us a chance. Together we'll build a good life; we don't need anything else."

Pictures of James and Carter flashed through her mind; she knew the love she felt for her two nephews was only a fraction of the emotion she would experience for her own child. She looked away; the searing, raw disappointment left an aching void in her heart. Gently, she went to him and traced the determined line of his jaw.

"Shall I take the precautions, or will you?" she asked in a tortured whisper.

Nine

"Karen?"

Faintly, she could hear Rand's call and carefully rolled from the bed. But when she attempted to straighten, her muscles knotted in protest.

"I'm coming," she called, stopping to rub the small of her back. When she limped down the hall from their bedroom, she could hear Carl's worried voice.

"All day she was out there. Wouldn't let me help; said I had enough to do without adding a garden to the list. Your missus is going to be real sore, mark my words. Real sore."

"Hi, honey. How was your day?" She greeted Rand cheerfully, belying the discomfort of her aching muscles. Her eyes narrowed as they fell on Carl. She could tell Rand of her foolishness herself; Carl didn't need to do it for her.

"I'm fine," Rand answered shortly. "What's this Carl is telling me about you working outside all day?"

"It wasn't all day," she denied, and winced from a shooting pain in her back. "It seems certain people are cursed with loose tongues around here. Isn't that right, Carl?"

The older man shuffled his feet, avoiding her eyes. "I'll be going home now." He turned to leave, but not before Karen saw the smile that crinkled the crow's-feet about his eyes.

Karen moved closer to Rand, wrapping her arms around his waist, then groaned softly. "Kiss me if you must, but please be gentle."

Rand scowled. "You crazy little fool. What were you doing, shoveling hard dirt?" He was both bemused and angry. He released her, and instantly Karen missed the warmth of his touch.

"I thought I'd plant a garden," she explained, flexing her overworked muscles, then flinching because even the slightest movement hurt. "My mother had a big garden every year. I don't think I ever realized how much work she put into it. The most I did was pull weeds. Believe me, I appreciate her efforts more fully now."

"If you wanted a garden, why didn't you say something?" he questioned, the irritation leaving his face. "I could have had someone come and rototill for you." He brought her back into the circle of his arms, his fingers gently rubbing the back of her neck.

His touch did insane things to her equilibrium, and she swayed against him. "I don't know," she responded huskily, her eyes closed, savoring the gentle caress of his hands. "I forgot, I guess." Clear thinking was almost impossible when Rand was holding her like this. His hands molded over her buttocks, lifting her pliant body against him. "Don't stop," she pleaded.

Rand's voice was low and husky as he murmured against her skin. "I have no intention of stopping."

Karen gave a sighing laugh. "I was referring to the massage. I could use a good rubdown."

With soft kisses, Rand closed her eyes. Again, the pressure of his arms increased as he lifted and carried her into the bedroom.

His fingers were soothing and gentle as he manipulated the sore muscles. Her flesh responded to the overwhelming comfort of his touch. She was encompassed in warmth; a fury of sensation assaulted her, and she yearned to roll over and bring his mouth to hers. Anything to satisfy this aching void he was creating within her. A small cry of pleasure slipped from her parted lips. But if Rand knew what he was doing to her, he ignored her plea until she released another soft moan.

His hand settled over her shoulder to gently turn her. Karen stared for a moment at the intensity that burned from his eyes. "You know what I want," he murmured thickly before lowering his mouth to hers.

A long time later, they rested, Karen's head nestled in the crook of Rand's arm. His fingers continued to explore her body by leisurely tracing an imaginary line around her breasts. The rounded flesh seemed to swell at his caress.

The meandering pattern followed down her abdomen. "I believe you're gaining weight."

"I know." She smiled, leisurely reveling in the power of his touch to arouse her. "It's Dorothy's recipes, but if you notice it, too, then it's time to go on a diet."

"Just as long as you only abstain from food," he whispered, claiming her mouth in a searing kiss that left her breathless.

Rand's breathing wasn't any more even, and when

he spoke, there was a hoarse quality to his voice. "I have some news."

"Good or bad?"

A smile lifted the corners of his full mouth. "I'll let you decide. I've been asked to participate in a lecture series across the country. The schedule isn't completed yet, but I imagine I'll be gone two, possibly three weeks."

The smile died on Karen's face, and she closed her eyes to block the loneliness a long separation would bring. Tears burned for release, and she brushed them away, angry with herself for being so emotional. "Will Cora be with you?" she questioned after a while.

"Of course Cora will be with me." His voice held a mocking note. "We are partners, you know."

"I thought we were partners, too? Remember me? I'm the wife you promised to love and cherish. I don't exactly relish twiddling my thumbs for several weeks while you go gallivanting across the country with another woman."

A scowl darkened Rand's face. "Karen, this isn't like you. Cora isn't another woman in the sense you're implying."

"Not from lack of trying, I bet," she snapped childishly, pulling herself from his arms and sitting upright.

"Karen?" Rand's voice held a puzzled note. His hands slipped over her shoulders to bring her back. "As for us being partners, if you recall…"

Abruptly, Karen twisted away. "Are you going to throw the fact you didn't want to marry me in my face every time we have an argument? You don't need to tell me your feelings on the matter. Believe me, actions speak louder than words."

"Karen, would you kindly listen to me?" he demanded, his mouth thinning angrily.

With her back facing him, she responded stiffly, "I'm listening."

"You could have fooled me," Rand murmured under his breath. Then he began again slowly. "Now, what I've been trying to say is this: Cora and I have been invited to participate in a lecture series. We have accepted the invitation. But there is no reason why you should stay here without me. I want you to accompany me on this trip."

"Oh." The anger drained from her all in one breath. "Oh," she said again, feeling chagrined and stupid. What was the matter with her? Why was she acting like such a shrew? "In that case, I'd like to do two things," she said softly, swallowing her pride. "First, I want to apologize for being so hotheaded, and second, I want you to know how very pleased I'd be to travel with you."

"Good," Rand said simply, holding her again.

Suddenly Karen came to the realization that Rand was trusting her now as he'd never done before.

Karen woke the next morning stiff and more than a little sore. When she started to get out of bed, she moaned as her stomach heaved unsteadily. Lying back against the pillow, she took deep breaths, afraid she would be sick.

"Rand," she murmured tightly, "I think I really must have done too much yesterday. I feel awful."

Tenderly, he brushed the hair from her face and kissed her forehead. "Stay in bed. I'll phone later and see how you're feeling."

"I'll be fine. Don't worry about me. Oh, if I'm not

here, don't worry. Judy and I are taking the boys to Point Defiance Zoo. I'd hate to disappoint them."

"They can make the trip without you," Rand said, tucking in his shirt. His brow was knit with concern.

"I won't go unless I feel better," she promised.

Rand's kiss was gentle as he tucked the blankets over her shoulders.

Karen watched him go, her heart full of love. After several weeks of married life, she was beginning to discover the joys and benefits of being Rand's wife. As he claimed, his hours were often long as he worked with Cora on a textbook they were compiling. Karen often waited up for him on the sofa, sometimes falling asleep. She'd been so tired lately. Rand woke her, rousing her by spreading tender kisses over her face. Drowsily, Karen would loop her arms around his neck and direct him to her moist lips. The evenings he was home, Karen would read aloud while they sat together, Rand's arms securely wrapped around her. Their taste in literature was surprisingly similar, and they explored everything from Kipling to Tolkien. In bed, she desired him as much as he desired her. Rand was the perfect lover, patient, tender, coaxing. They never spoke of the reasons for their marriage, but it was almost as if their love and need for each other had brought them together.

After a two-hour tour of the zoo and park, they were all hungry and tired. Dark clouds began rolling in to threaten the picnic that had been planned and packed so carefully.

"I wanna stay," Carter objected, ignoring the first drops of rain.

"We aren't going to let a little rain stop us, are we?" James echoed his dissatisfaction.

A few intermittent drops quickly became a fierce downpour, and the four ran to the parking lot without further discussion.

"I still want to have a picnic." Carter's voice dripped with disappointment as he climbed into the backseat of the car.

"Let's wait a few minutes; maybe it'll stop," Karen offered encouragingly. "If not, we'll have a special picnic at my house."

"All right!" both boys chimed.

"If we're going to wait here, I'll pour us some coffee." Judy opened the top of the thermos, and Karen's stomach pitched at the aroma.

She shook her head dismissively. "None for me, thanks. I don't know what it is, but coffee doesn't agree with my stomach lately."

Judy jerked her head up, and the liquid sloshed over the side of the cup and onto the seat. "Karen," she whispered in disbelief, eyeing her sister intently, "the first few months I was pregnant with James, I couldn't tolerate the taste or smell of coffee. I knew almost immediately when I was going to have Carter because the same thing happened. Even before the doctor confirmed my condition."

Karen gave a low laugh. "Well, I'm not pregnant. In fact, I'm sure I'm not," she said, more to assure herself than Judy. "Oh, heavens! Rand would be furious."

"What's pregnant?" Carter questioned, leaning over from the backseat.

"I'll explain later," Judy promised, studying Karen's worried expression.

A half hour later, the four were positioned under Karen's dining-room table, eating their lunch, when Rand entered through the front door.

"Karen, I'm home," he announced, shaking the rain off his umbrella.

Normally, Karen was there to greet Rand, but James and Carter were intent on playing a game of hide-and-seek.

"I'm here," squeaked James in an attempt to imitate Karen.

"James? Carter? Okay, boys, what tricks are you up to now? I suppose you've got your aunt tied up outside somewhere." He arched an amused brow toward the sound of their voices.

"Rand's certainly got my boys pegged," Judy whispered.

"We're under the table." Karen laughed as she watched his dark-trousered leg walk toward her.

"Under the what?"

"Come and join us; we're having a picnic," Judy explained, stifling her own laughter.

"It's times like these that make me wonder just exactly what kind of a family I married into." His face was smiling as he knelt down. "Just what will be required of me before I can talk to my wife?" he quizzed suspiciously.

"I'm here, Rand." Karen edged her way between bodies, sandwiches, and Number Nine to meet her husband. "Sit down and make yourself at home," she invited, and placed a welcoming kiss on his puzzled brow.

"May I remind you, I am home!" Humor glinted briefly in his expression. "I'm almost afraid to ask this, but just why are you eating your lunch under the table?"

"Because it's raining," the boys explained simultaneously.

"True," he reasoned, "but not inside the house."

"Well, it wouldn't be a picnic on top of the table, would it?" Karen asked him with an impatient sigh.

"There's logic in this someplace, but I swear it's beyond me." The humor in his smile held a wealth of love and warmth.

Karen regarded him curiously. "You're home awfully early. Is anything wrong?"

"Can't a husband come home early? May I remind you we've only been married a short while." His husky voice held a suggestive note, and Karen flushed.

"Finish your lunch, boys." Judy tipped her head back and winked knowingly at her sister. "It's time we left."

"There's no need to rush," Karen said, but she didn't insist they stay. Rand was rarely home early, and she selfishly wanted him to herself.

The picnic items were quickly packed while the boys protested. Judy ushered them out the door, and it suddenly became very quiet without the chatter of the two boys.

"Would you like some lunch? Are you hungry?" Rand stood beside her, and she turned, sliding her arms around his middle. Tilting her head back, she watched his expression alter.

"Starving." His mouth explored the side of her neck and sent shivers of delight shooting down her body.

"What would you like?" She melted against him, her heart thundering wildly.

"Don't ask silly questions," he whispered before claiming her mouth in a flaming kiss that left her weak and clinging. When he led her into their bedroom, Karen had no intention of protesting.

The nagging suspicion Karen was pregnant became a reality as the days passed. She'd refused to acknowledge the early signs, but there could be no denying the slight thickening of her waist or the added fullness of her breasts. Now it wasn't only coffee that upset her stomach; the smell of certain foods, especially bacon, would cause her to wretch. She found herself irritable, and it didn't seem to matter how much sleep she got, for she was constantly tired.

The first morning she lost her breakfast was the day Karen accepted the truth. Deathly pale and still nauseated, she staggered back to the bedroom and lay down.

With her arms cradling her stomach, she closed her eyes and let out a low moan of despair. "No, please, God, no." Rand would never believe she hadn't purposely gotten pregnant. The knowledge was sure to destroy the budding trust between them. She had worked so hard to gain his confidence in her integrity. How would she ever tell him? No possible explanation would make things right. And his reaction would defy comprehension.

Forcing herself to dress, she brushed her teeth, still feeling wretched and miserable. Her reflection in the bathroom mirror told her she looked as rotten as she felt.

Her sister had advised her to make an appointment with the doctor as soon as possible. But Karen had delayed, hoping against Las Vegas odds that she had some weird, unexplainable virus. *Some virus,* she mused. Her fingers trembled when she made the call. She wouldn't say anything to Rand until she was sure. His mother was coming for a visit, and she couldn't tell him before then.

Depression as heavy as Karen had ever experienced weighed on her. A baby. She found her hands resting on her abdomen while a myriad of emotions filled her all at once. A gentle smile touched her lips. A baby. This should be one of the most glorious days of her life, knowing that the love they shared had created this life growing within her.

Love. What a strange emotion, but not really an emotion at all; more an act of the will. Certainly it wasn't anything she could define. Did Rand really love her? Could she be totally secure in his love? He desired her physically. Was that love? He had accused and doubted her regarding their marriage. Was that love? As sure as the sun would rise on the morrow, he would doubt her again when he learned of this pregnancy. Was that love?

Hiding her symptoms from Rand became a worrisome game. The mornings she was especially ill, she would complain of being overly tired and stay in bed. Rand would lovingly accuse her of being lazy. Karen watched him dress, praying he'd hurry while she took deep breaths to delay the inevitable. The minute he was out the door, Karen would rush to the bathroom to empty her stomach.

Judy recommended eating soda crackers before rising in the morning to relieve the nausea. But when Rand complained of crumbs between the sheets and accused her of cheating on her diet, Karen laughed and promised not to eat in bed again.

A hundred times, she was grateful Rand couldn't see her. One look at her pale, bloodless cheeks and he would have guessed her condition immediately. That he hadn't put the facts together knotted Karen's stomach with guilt. His trust in her had become so complete that he didn't even suspect.

Karen was sure Carl knew. More than once she found his eyes following her, his look concerned and worried. She wasn't sure if he was anxious because she was obviously having such a bad time with the morning sickness or if he realized what this child would do to her and Rand's relationship. Either way, her eyes silently pleaded with him not to say anything. The look he returned assured her that he would not betray a confidence.

There was another problem Karen had yet to resolve. Number Nine was obviously pregnant.

"But Carl," Karen had protested, "I thought you said you'd taken her to the vet and everything had been taken care of."

"All her shots." Carl looked away nervously. "Number Nine was just a kitten then, and the vet wanted to wait a few weeks before having her spayed. I assumed you realized that. I'm sorry, Miss Karen."

She sighed in defeat. She couldn't be angry with Carl; it hadn't been his fault. If she hadn't been so wrapped up in her own problems, she would have known something was wrong when all the male cats started prowling around.

"Don't worry, Carl," she reassured him with a weak smile. "I'm sure Rand will understand."

"I'm sure he will, too," Carl told her, and Karen had the funny feeling he wasn't referring to the cat.

"But I don't understand how it could have happened." Karen's eyes pleaded with the doctor.

"It's not unusual for a pregnancy to occur even with the appropriate precautions, but judging from the look of things, I'd say you were already pregnant when you came for your first visit." Dr. Marshall offered Karen a reassuring smile. Since she was obviously so upset with her condition, he took the time to talk with her and answer her questions in a gentle, reassuring manner.

"Already pregnant?" Karen stared back in disbelief.

"I'm afraid so. I'd guess you were close to three months pregnant."

"Three months?" she whispered incredulously. Had she been so obtuse that she had not recognized even the most obvious signs? Dazed and unsure, Karen responded to the remainder of the appointment with little more than feeble nods.

Judy was waiting for her in the reception area. "Well?" She rose expectantly as Karen entered the larger room.

Karen stared at her sister with sightless eyes. "The doctor thinks I may be as much as three months along—"

"Karen." Although she shared her sister's anxiety, Judy didn't bother to disguise her pleasure. "Good grief, you won't be hiding this from Rand much longer. When do you plan on telling him?"

"I don't think it's a matter of when but how I'm going to tell him," Karen answered.

"But, Karen, the longer you delay, the more likely he is to guess."

"I know." Karen expelled her breath and looked to her sister helplessly. "I'll tell him soon."

After his mother's visit, Karen promised herself. Judy's look was skeptical.

Each day, Karen answered her sister's inquiring gaze with a negative shake of her head.

Rand had described his mother perfectly, and when she stepped off the plane, Karen spotted her instantly.

Eileen Prescott was tall and slender. Her blue business suit, smart and stylish, was a pleasant contrast to her hair, which was completely gray, cut fashionably short. There wasn't a striking resemblance between mother and son, but it wasn't difficult to tell the two were related.

"I see her," Karen said nervously.

"Relax, Karen. My mother's going to love you." His hand, resting on her shoulder, gave her an encouraging squeeze.

With swift, bold strides, Eileen Prescott walked directly to Rand. Karen stepped aside as mother embraced son.

She gave him a surly look. "Well, introduce me. I didn't fly two thousand miles to look at your dour face."

There was an affectionate smile in Rand's eyes as he held his arms open for Karen's return. "Mother, this is my wife, Karen."

Karen moved forward, still in awe of this overpowering woman. "Welcome to Tacoma, Mrs. Prescott." Her senses were clamoring under the woman's cold, unfriendly gaze.

Eileen ignored Karen's welcome. "Why, Rand, she's barely more than a teenager." It was the same gruff tone as before.

Karen eased herself closer to Rand, embarrassed and uncomfortable. The welcoming smile died on Rand's face, and he spoke sharply. "Woman enough, Mother."

Eileen ignored his tone and returned her attention to Karen. "I understand your father was an immigrant. The Prescotts can trace their family tree back to the sixteen hundreds. I expected Rand to marry within his own class," she stated stiffly, as if she doubted Karen's legitimacy.

The assertion stung. The McAlisters were of proud Scottish descent, and what they lacked in heritage was compensated for in pride. Karen bit back angry words, but Rand felt no such restraint and snapped angrily.

"Are you sure you wouldn't like to check out her teeth?"

There was dead silence. Eileen's severe expression altered to a twinkling smile, and she laughed, smiling at Karen with satisfaction. "Welcome to the family, Karen, such as it is." She stepped forward and gave her daughter-in-law a vivacious squeeze.

Astonished at the extreme change in mood, Karen was at a loss for words but managed a tremulous smile. "Thank you."

In the days that followed, Karen came to respect her unpretentious mother-in-law. Her manner was sometimes surly and forward, but it didn't take long for Karen to discover her warm and sincere heart.

Eileen discovered Karen's secret the first morning of her visit. As soon as Rand was out the door to school, Karen slumped in the chair, feeling wretched.

Eileen was waiting for her with a damp washcloth. "Are you going to be sick?" she asked abruptly.

Karen shook her head, closing her eyes to ward off the nausea. She was used to the gruff tone of her voice. Eileen spoke with a brusque affection that couldn't offend.

"I'm fine." Karen looked away.

Her mother-in-law's smile was tender and knowing. "Does Rand know?"

Miserably, she gave a negative shake. "Rand has made it very clear he doesn't want children. I don't know how I'm going to tell him."

"Doesn't seem to me he has much choice in the matter. He's going to be a father, like it or not." She made it sound so simple and matter-of-fact.

"I wish it were that easy."

"He can't place the blame entirely on you…it does take two. That son of mine can be such a fool sometimes. Leave him to me. I'll set him straight."

"No, don't. It's important that I be the one to tell him," Karen pleaded, and sat down as another wave of nausea threatened.

"Well, you'll have to tell him soon. I've been here less than a day and guessed almost immediately. Don't be a ninny about it. He's bound to be unhappy for a while, but he loves you." She paused and chuckled. "Rand surprised the heck out of me at the airport the way he stepped in to protect you. I didn't know he had it in him. First time he's raised his voice to me in twenty years." She laughed again, as if finding the whole situation amusing.

"He's my husband; it was only natural—" Karen began.

"Not so," Eileen interrupted quickly. "Rand and I have a special mother-son relationship. His father died when Rand was eleven. George was working in Alaska; we were desperately in need of extra money for Rand's medical expenses. We traveled from doctor to doctor, seeking the latest professional skill for his deteriorating eyesight, but no one could offer us hope. The public schools weren't equipped to teach the boy, and it meant sending him to expensive boarding schools for the blind. All this took money, so George accepted this high-risk, high-paying job in Alaska. He was there two years before being killed in a mining accident. The only frivolous thing he ever sent home was that locket you're wearing. It arrived after we received word George had been killed. I never could wear the thing; too many sad memories."

Karen fingered the locket that hung around her neck. It did hold special significance to Rand, perhaps because he assumed their love would end with the same bittersweet memories.

"Rand seemed to blame himself for George's death. Nothing I could say would lessen his guilt." Eileen continued speaking; even after all this time, reliving the memory proved painful. "In all the years since, Rand has been a model son. He's cared for my every need, given me every consideration. When he stood up to me the way he did at the airport, I knew he loved you. I needed to be assured of that. Things were mighty fishy when he arrived for his so-called honeymoon with that other woman. I've been wanting him to marry for years. He needs a wife, and selfishly, I wouldn't be opposed to a few grandchildren, but Rand would laugh and quickly change the subject. He mentioned you first thing off the plane, but I wondered what he was doing bringing me Cora when I wanted to meet you."

"Eileen?" Karen's fingers clenched tightly together in a nervous action.

"Speak up; I can't be expected to hear you if you insist on talking to the floor."

"Rand... Rand didn't exactly want to marry me."

Karen flushed as she related the events leading up to their wedding.

"Lordy me, your daddy's one sly devil." She laughed brusquely. "I can well imagine Rand's reaction to that," she said, laughing all the more.

Karen looked away.

"Don't look so put out. Rand wasn't totally opposed to this marriage, or nothing on God's good earth would have persuaded him to marry you. Being pressured was sure to ruffle a few of his proud feathers, but I know my son well enough to tell you he would have rotted in hell rather than marry someone he didn't want."

"But don't you see?" Karen murmured dismally. "He's sure to believe I tricked him with this pregnancy."

"No doubt he'll be as angry as a wounded bear, but given time, he'll come around. Now, don't be a quitter; give him time to sort through his feelings. If he said he was opposed to a family, it's not because he doesn't like children. Rand will make an excellent father. My only advice to you is to tell him soon. It's bound to go better for you if he hears it from your lips than if he discovers it on his own."

Acknowledging the wisdom of her mother-in-law, Karen had to agree.

Eileen returned to New York four days later, leaving with Karen's promise that she'd tell Rand about the baby soon.

Karen mentally prepared herself all the next day, determined to tell Rand about the baby right after dinner.

"It was nice having my mother for a visit, but quite frankly, I'm glad she's gone. I like having you to myself." Rand sat on the sofa, pulling Karen onto his lap; his fingers wasted no time unbuttoning her blouse.

Abruptly, Karen twisted away and stood. "Rand, no, don't touch me, please."

"Karen?" He sounded surprised by her sudden rejection.

She stood across the room from him, rigid with apprehension. Her hand rested protectively on the slight swelling of her stomach. "Rand," she told him boldly, her voice tight, "I'm going to have a baby."

Ten

The room crackled with a stunned silence; Rand expelled an uneven, disbelieving breath before his jaw tightened ominously. Despair flickered over his face, and he paused to run his fingers through his hair wearily. He was silent for so long, Karen didn't know how much more tension she could endure.

"Yell, scream, do what you need to do. But please, don't just sit there." She felt far more capable of dealing with his anger than the tormented ache in his eyes.

"All my life I've had to deal with people who feel that because I'm handicapped, I must also be mentally retarded. I expected more from you, Karen."

His words stabbed at her heart. She yearned to go to him, hold him, reassure him, anything but this intolerable, tortured look. He resembled a man defeated and friendless. He slouched forward, burying his face in his hands.

"I realize this is of little comfort to either of us at the moment, but I want you to know the doctor says I was already pregnant when I went to see him about birth control." Her voice faltered slightly.

Rand's head snapped up, his eyes blazing. The short, abrupt laugh was full of malice. "Get out."

Karen stared at him with disbelieving eyes.

"I said get out," he raged in white fury.

She choked back a sob, her voice raw as she spoke. "Just how far do you want me to go? Out of the room? Out of the house? Out of your life?"

Violently, Rand swung around, his hand slamming against the lamp, sending it crashing into the coffee table. The ceramic base shattered into a thousand pieces as his anger exploded.

Karen backed away from him fearfully as he stumbled from the living room. The picture windows vibrated as he slammed the front door.

Where would he go? Karen looked around her with the most helpless feeling in the world. A knot in her throat was so tight she could barely swallow. Her first inclination was to run after him, plead with him to understand. But it was useless, and she knew it. Miserably, she picked up the larger pieces of the broken lamp.

There was no use attempting to sleep; she couldn't until Rand was home. The car was gone; apparently, he had gotten Carl to drive him someplace. Possibly Cora's? She quickly cast the pain-inducing thought from her mind. A long time later, she heard the soft purr of the car engine as it died, and she sighed with relief. But Rand didn't come into the house. The time grew so long that Karen nervously stared out the window, hoping to see him. The yard—everywhere she could see—was deserted. Why did she have to love him so much? Why couldn't she just go to bed and let him work out the problem his own way? She'd been shocked, too, when she'd first realized she wasn't suffering from some obscure virus.

Was he walking in the woods? It was dark; he could hurt himself. Another half hour passed, each second interminable. Karen couldn't stand it anymore and carelessly threw a sweater over her shoulders.

"Rand?" she called, venturing down the path leading to the woods. "Please answer me."

The night was so clear and still. She stopped to listen, but everything was deadly quiet until Karen wanted to cry with frustration.

"Miss Karen," Carl spoke from behind her, and Karen swiveled around.

"Where's Rand?" Her eyes pleaded with him.

"I don't know." The older man's eyes avoided hers. "He had me take him to a bar, said he didn't want me to wait. But he was in a bad way; real angry, he was. I sat outside for a long time, wondering what to do. When I went back inside, Mr. Rand was gone."

Karen's hand squeezed Carl's arm. "I told Rand about the baby."

Carl's smile was wry. "I figured as much. Give him time; he'll come around. It won't be long before he'll be handing me a cigar as proud as any father; you wait and see."

Tears shimmered in Karen's eyes, tears of hope. "Thank you. I needed to hear that."

Carl patted her shoulder gently. "Do you want me to wait up with you? Neither of us is going to sleep until he's home."

"Dorothy?" Karen's gaze flickered back to Carl's house.

"Been asleep for hours." He chuckled softly.

With a slight nod, Karen accepted the man's kind offer. They walked to the house together.

Several hours later, the sound of a door closing and someone singing told them Rand was home. The words of the song were slurred and barely discernible.

"WHATCHA GONNA DO WITH A DRUNKEN BLIND MAN? WHATCHA GONNA DO WITH A DRUNKEN BLIND MAN? EARL-LIE IN THE MORNING."

Carl was immediately at Rand's side while Karen paid the taxi driver. The man gave her a sympathetic smile and drove into the night.

Rand's weight was giving Carl trouble as they weaved toward the bedroom. Karen hurried to help, slipping her arm around Rand's waist, accepting a portion of his weight as his arm fell haphazardly across her shoulders.

Rand staggered slightly, then paused as if suddenly realizing Karen was there.

"Karen, my sweet Karen." A haunted, tortured look came over his masculine features. His mouth twisted into a dark, foreboding glower. Angrily, he pushed her aside.

"Trick the blind man. Hurt the blind man. Fool the blind man," he shouted, madly waving his arms.

No one was more surprised than Karen when Carl unexpectedly lifted Rand, placing his bulk over his shoulder like a fireman. When Carl laid him on the bed, Rand was either asleep or dead drunk.

"He'll be all right until morning," Carl assured Karen as he stopped to remove Rand's shoes.

Numbly, Karen took a blanket from the hall closet, and laid it over his still body. A few minutes later, she

walked Carl to the door. When she returned to the bedroom, Rand was making sleeping noises, lost to the
world. Gently, she touched his face, the weight of unhappiness bearing hard upon her shoulders.

She slept in the spare bedroom, the room she thought
would make a lovely nursery. It seemed fitting somehow. When she woke, Rand had already left for school.
She looked at the unkempt bed and experienced a bittersweet agony. Trailing her fingers across the pillow
that had held his head, she was hoping to draw some
solace. Instead, she experienced an acute loneliness.

Rand wasn't home for dinner. Carl phoned to say
Rand was working late with Cora, but she guessed the
call had been made on his own initiative. It was after
midnight before she went to bed, lying awake until she
heard Rand enter. He undressed in the dark, pulled
back the covers on his side, and climbed into bed. Their
bodies were only a few inches apart, yet a whole world
lay between them. Karen was completely still, willing Rand to say something, anything. After a while,
she abandoned the hope and with an agonizing sigh
drifted into sleep.

First thing the next morning, she woke again, experiencing the now-familiar waves of nausea. Deep
breaths didn't help, and she rushed into the bathroom.
When she straightened, she found Rand's large frame
blocking the doorway.

"Are you all right?" he questioned tightly.

"I'm fine." Rand looked as drawn and pale as she
did.

"Does this happen often?" he asked again, gruffly.

Karen's voice sounded choked and small. "Sometimes two or three times a week."

His face twisted into a vicious smile, almost as if he was pleased she was experiencing some discomfort with this pregnancy. "Next time, close the bathroom door. The sound of you vomiting isn't a pleasant way to wake up."

"All right," Karen agreed, hoping to hide the hurt in her voice.

Leaving early and coming home later and later was a pattern Rand followed rigidly the next few days. Karen rarely saw him, and if she did, he didn't speak to her unless it was in gruff, impatient tones.

He was obviously overworking himself, skipping meals and not getting enough sleep. Karen's tortured gaze followed him.

Rand had told her to get out, but seemed unwilling to tell her how far he wanted her to go. The temptation was strong to pack her things, but Karen had never been a quitter, and this marriage was worth saving. If anything, her resolve to work things out grew stronger as the days passed.

Saturday morning, Karen woke with a queasy stomach but held her own until after breakfast; then she was sick again.

"Isn't there anything you can do about this?" Rand asked her impatiently after she reappeared in the kitchen.

"I'm usually okay if I can force down some soda crackers first thing. I try to keep some on the nightstand…" She paused at the look of disgust that came over Rand's face.

His upper lip curled into a snarl. "Those were the crumbs I felt in bed, weren't they?"

"Yes." She wouldn't lie to him even if it meant condemning herself.

Karen had never seen anyone's look turn as cold or hard.

"You're a deceitful bitch, Karen."

"Can't you understand?" she snapped. "I didn't plan this pregnancy."

"Just like you didn't plan our marriage?"

Karen dropped her eyes, her hands clenched tightly at her sides. It was no use trying to reason with Rand, nor would she again. If he loved her, truly loved her, then his faith in her integrity would eventually overcome his doubts. She couldn't force the issue.

Perhaps his irritation wouldn't have been so explosive if he hadn't gone to stroke the cat and discovered she was pregnant.

"Karen." His voice had vibrated through the house. When she didn't respond immediately, he shouted again.

She'd gone to the bedroom, taking her time. She wouldn't rush to him; she wasn't a servant who responded to threats and yelling. "What is it?" she asked calmly, ignoring his scowl.

"The cat." Anger furrowed his brow, and his mouth curved in a taut line. "Number Nine is pregnant, isn't she?" It wasn't a question, but an accusation, as if this, too, were something Karen had purposely done to thwart and undermine his authority.

"Yes," she responded simply, without explanation.

"Why wasn't I warned of the blessed event?" he demanded sarcastically.

She replied in mocking tones, "I would have been more than pleased to tell you, but I haven't seen you in nearly a week. And, shall we say, the timing was wrong."

Karen had never seen anyone angrier. His hands were knotted into tight fists; his dark eyes became as hard as steel, his jawline white and tense. "Get rid of the cat." The softly spoken words were more menacing than if he'd raged at her.

Karen gasped in disbelief; all attempts at impudence collapsed with his words. "You don't mean that."

His lip curled sardonically as he moved past her and into the den, his message clear.

Later, Karen went for a walk. Tears stung her eyes, and she tilted her head back to prevent their spilling. She followed the worn path leading into the woods and heard Carl's approach before she saw him. Hurriedly, she wiped the tears from her eyes and put on a bright smile.

"Good morning, Miss Karen." He greeted her with a broad grin.

"Been leaving little tidbits around for the animals again, I see." She responded in a teasing banter, belying the hurt that lay just below the surface of her smile.

He chuckled, and the sound of his amusement lifted her soul from the mire of self-pity. Likable, lovable, understanding Carl. Why did life have to be so complicated? Why couldn't she be more like this man, who wore a ready smile and looked as if he'd never known trouble or discouragement?

"Carl?"

"Yes'm."

"Rand found out about Number Nine."

The older man chuckled again. "I've been wondering about that bellow that came from your house this morning. Was he angry?"

Karen couldn't prevent a smiling response to his humor. Rand had sounded like a bull elk in his irritation. "He wasn't exactly pleased. I have to find another home for Number Nine."

The smile faded from Carl's weathered face. "I don't think he means that, Miss Karen. He seems to be saying a lot of things he doesn't mean lately." The dark eyes grew intense. "Me and the missus will take Number Nine. If Mr. Rand doesn't want her back, that's fine, 'cause we've been needing a mouser."

"But she's going to deliver the litter soon."

"Not to worry." Again, Karen was reassured with a grin. "We have several friends who need mousers."

Karen was afraid that if she spoke, her voice would crack and Carl would know how much his generosity had affected her.

Eyes dancing, he touched the tip of his cap and sauntered down the path.

"Carl?" she called after he'd gone several feet.

He spun around.

"Thank you." She couldn't hide the choke in her voice.

As she continued walking along the well-worn path, she could think, sort through her own feelings. For all the unhappiness she was experiencing, there was also a budding excitement beginning to blossom. A child was growing within her, a child created in love.

Rand and Karen were scheduled to leave for the lecture series next week. The thought of time alone together brought a surge of hope. Rand had purposely made separate flight plans so they wouldn't be traveling with Cora. He'd promised to make this trip the honeymoon they'd never had. Karen believed that only when they were separated from the pressures around them would Rand begin to accept the child. Six days; she could last another six days. The lecture series offered hope and promise.

When she returned to the house feeling refreshed and invigorated, she found Rand asleep on the davenport. The Braille book he'd been reading lay twisted on the carpet where it had fallen. As Karen picked up the book and placed it on the end table, an encompassing warmth filled her. In sleep, the gaunt lines of fatigue in Rand's face were relaxed. She brought him a pillow and blanket and impulsively brushed her lips softly over his cheek.

Baking chocolate-chip cookies gave her an excuse to stay in the kitchen and have a full view of her husband. It was obvious he was exhausted, and she guarded his sleep jealously.

The phone rang, jerking her attention to the kitchen wall. Karen raced across the floor to answer it before a second ring could sound.

"Hello," she greeted softly.

"Let me speak to Rand." It was the brisk business voice of his associate.

"He's sleeping, Cora," Karen said with a glance toward Rand to be sure the phone hadn't awakened him. "Unless it's important, I'd hate to disturb him."

A heavy sigh followed. "No, it can wait."

"I'll tell him you phoned."

"Do that," Cora said sharply, then added. "By the way, I'm sorry to hear you won't be traveling with us next week." Her tone suggested just the opposite. "Rand said you're much too ill with morning sickness to travel. I've had my flight plans rearranged so Rand and I can fly together. You'll tell him that for me, won't you?"

"Yes...yes, I will." Confused and hurt, Karen could only make a feeble response. "I'll tell him you phoned. Goodbye." She heard the click as the other end of the line was disconnected.

She stood there, the phone still in her hand, staring at Rand while tears brimmed in her eyes. Rand knew how much she'd been looking forward to traveling with him. How much she'd been counting on this trip. He hadn't even bothered to inform her of his change of plans. He was going to leave her behind, just walk out the door without her, without a word of explanation.

Replacing the receiver, Karen leaned her head back and closed her eyes. Instinctively, she wrapped her arms around her middle as a protective buffer to shield her unborn child. As if the baby could feel her hurt, her ache.

Perhaps she was being too optimistic regarding their marriage. Perhaps Rand would never accept her condition, never love or cherish their child. Perhaps he felt the necessity of being away from her to decide exactly what he wanted to do. Perhaps send her away. He had shouted for her to leave. Certainly the tension between them hadn't lessened.

Doubts, uncertainties, and questions pounded her from all sides, until her hands flew to her face as if to ward them off.

She needed to escape, too, but Rand had discounted any of her needs. He had been so angry with her because she'd hidden the pregnancy from him as long as she could. Yet he hadn't told her he'd changed their travel plans. Did that make him any less guilty? Rand had hoped to hurt her and had succeeded.

She waited until the cookies finished baking, then took a suitcase to the bedroom to pack her things. Where she'd go remained unclear—just away, she reasoned, to set order to her thoughts, decide what she wanted to do.

Carl was weeding the flower beds in the front of the house and glanced up when Karen quietly closed the front door. She jerked around when he spoke.

"Miss Karen, where are you going?" His eyes fell pointedly on the suitcase.

Karen looked away self-consciously, feeling like a cat burglar trapped in a bedroom. It was wrong to leave without saying a word. Everyone would worry, and she didn't want that.

"I'm not exactly sure where I'll go." Her eyes studied the tops of her shoes.

"Are you leaving Mr. Rand?"

"Oh, no," she denied instantly. "I just need to get away for a couple of days."

"Are you going to your family?"

"No." She couldn't put Judy and her dad in the middle of this. It would be unfair to all concerned; she hadn't even told her father she was pregnant yet. "I think I'll go down the Oregon coast. There was a little inn my parents loved, and they often vacationed there. It's someplace outside of Tillamook on the ocean. I think I'll head that way. Tell Rand where I am and not to worry. I'll be back in three days, four at the most. If you need to get ahold of me, Dad can tell you the name of the inn." She hesitated. "Take care of Rand for me, won't you, Carl?"

The older man gave her a toothy grin. "All right, Miss Karen, I will."

The drive down the rugged coastline was exhilarating, the scenery breathtakingly beautiful. Karen stopped at several scenic viewpoints to watch the waves explode against the huge, jagged rocks in majestic harmony. Several times she found herself wishing Rand was with her so she could describe the vivid colors and the brilliant beauty of the coast. Narrating a scene for him was one of the simple pleasures she enjoyed; it gave her a greater appreciation for the beauty of God's world. Rand had once told her after they'd made love that when he was holding her in his arms, it didn't matter that he couldn't see. For the first time in his life, he didn't hate being blind.

Now Karen wondered if he'd ever hold her again. The thought brought so much pain that she instantly rejected it.

The white shuttered inn her parents often visited was still there, but it was older and much smaller than Karen remembered. The family-owned enterprise had changed hands, but the new family was friendly and welcoming. Their teenage son carried Karen's lone suitcase upstairs, chatting the whole distance, offering advice about the best dinner spots, as it was nearing that time.

The room was small but adequate and had a panoramic view overlooking the ocean. Karen stood staring at it for a long time, watching the tide ebb away. The ocean mesmerized her; it was like watching sand sift through a bottle, wondering what would happen when all the sand was gone. The ocean was turbulent as the waves crashed along the beach, yet Karen found it soothing and relaxing after the long drive. She fell asleep without venturing from her room. She woke refreshed and hungry the next morning. In fact, she felt wonderful, better than any morning for three long months. A smile softened her mouth. Judy had claimed that if they were alike, the morning sickness would pass almost as quickly as it came—after about three months.

Karen was more like her sister than she realized. Anxious to enjoy the ocean air, Karen dressed in faded jeans, which fit snugly around her waist, and a pale purple short-sleeved sweatshirt.

"Good morning." She smiled at the boy who'd carried her suitcase the night before.

The returning smile was instantaneous. "Good morning."

"Want to recommend someplace for breakfast?"

It was the most enjoyable breakfast Karen had eaten in months. Without even a hint of morning upset, she took a long stroll along the undisturbed beach. It had rained during the night, hardening the sand, but as the sun appeared, drying the beach, it became impossible to walk in her tennis shoes. She paused long enough to remove them and flex her toes in the sand. She walked for so long that she lost sight of the inn. Her shoes were now used to store little treasures she discovered along the way, mostly small shells.

Pausing, she decided to rest before venturing back. The soft sand welcomed her weight, and she lay back, waving her arms to make a pattern of angel wings in the soft surface, then laughed at her childishness. How simple life would be if only she was a little girl again. Closing her eyes, she could almost hear her mother's worried voice telling her, "Karen, move back; the tide's coming in." But Karen had refused to leave her project, thinking her stubbornness would prevent the waters from sweeping away an afternoon's work.

"Matthew, do something. She'll be drenched," her mother had pleaded.

Helplessly, Karen had cried as her father had carried her onto the beach and she witnessed the sand castle washed away in minutes. Karen now felt much the same as she had then, the ache within her almost identical. That helpless feeling of holding on to something, then watching it disintegrate after having spent a part of herself in constructing it. Only this time it wasn't a simple sand castle; it was the love and marriage she had built with Rand.

Jerking herself upright, she brushed the sand from her pants. She'd come here to meditate, re-collect her thoughts; now she found them too painful and forced them from her mind.

For all her wanderings along the beach and the unaccustomed exercise, sleep remained elusive that night. After fighting herself and her thoughts, Karen rose and dressed, slipping outside into the moonlight. It had rained again that afternoon, but the skies were clear now, alive with glittering jewels that seemed to smile down on her. The wind was strong as it whipped her hair across her face. It felt good and right to be exactly where she was and who she was.

Karen found herself talking to the child, her hand placed over her stomach as if to communicate her thoughts. The baby had barely begun to form within her, yet the overwhelming love Karen felt for this tiny being was beyond description. Recognizing and accepting this overpowering emotion had a very calming effect on her.

Never again would she apologize to Rand for this pregnancy. This child had been created in love, her love for Rand, if not his love for her. That didn't matter anymore. Releasing a sigh from deep within, she strolled back to the room and fell into a deep, restful sleep.

The next morning fell into the pattern of the day before. Karen walked along the beach, her bare feet leaving imprints in the wet sand. Today, she would settle, if only in her own mind, the problems that existed between her and Rand.

A conversation she'd had with Judy at the zoo played again in her mind.

"I think I'd die if Rand and I had to be separated for a year. I love him so much it almost frightens me; Rand has become my whole life."

Judy had laughed. The wise, knowing, older- sister look had come over her. "It's amazing the things a woman can endure when it's necessary. I didn't think I'd ever survive without Mike, but I have, and I will."

Recalling their conversation, Karen realized that although she deeply loved her husband, she could make a life for herself and their child without him.

Symbolically, she built another sand castle, far from the water's edge. It was hard work, carrying buckets of wet sand onto the beach, but now the tide wouldn't steal it away. Perspiration wetted her brow when she finished; a dull ache throbbed in the small of her back. She waited until the tide came in, proud that her castle stood serene and secure. Tears misted her eyes; she was ready to face what awaited her in Tacoma.

The drive home was made with a sense of impatience. Karen left early the next morning and didn't stop for either breakfast or lunch. The instinct of a migrating bird seemed to be driving her home.

Home, she sighed, turning into the long driveway five hours later. She'd lived in the apartment for a number of months, and it had never produced in her the feelings this long rambler did.

Everything looked so peaceful, calm. Nothing had changed, yet everything looked different. She parked around back and glanced at her garden on the way past. After three days without hoeing, it was difficult to distinguish between plant and weed. The kitchen door was unlocked, and with dauntless courage she walked inside.

Karen stifled a gasp at the mess that lay before her. Dirty dishes, food, and utensils littered the table, countertop, and sink. It resembled the kitchen after James and Carter had prepared a meal.

Clothes and books were carelessly tossed about the living room; the drapes were closed, blocking out the afternoon sunlight.

Karen put her suitcase down and immediately opened the drapes, stooping to pick up several items along the way. The house smelled strange, as if no one had opened the windows and allowed fresh air to circulate in days.

"Damn it, Carl, I said leave me alone." The angry words were shouted and cutting.

Karen paused as a dejected figure moved down the hall. The sight of Rand shocked Karen, and she stared at him with disbelieving eyes. It looked as though he hadn't shaved since she'd gone. His clothes were wrinkled as if he'd been sleeping in them; his hair was a mass of tangles.

"It isn't Carl," she said quietly.

A flicker of pain touched his face as he stopped. "Karen?" he questioned as if he wasn't sure of the sound of her voice.

"What's happened?" The whole house possessed a sense of unreality; Rand would never live in such disorganization. "Have you been ill?" she questioned, gazing at him anxiously.

"Karen, Karen." He repeated her name incredulously, his voice raw and barely above a whisper. "Where the hell did you go?" he demanded, his back stiffening, ramrod straight.

A bewildered frown narrowed her brow as she went to him. "Where have I been?" she asked. "I told Carl where I was going. You were asleep when I left. I didn't want to wake you. Carl was supposed to tell you."

"He didn't." Rand's smile was contemptuous. "I suppose he thought letting me suffer was poetic justice." His hand ran wearily over his face and eyes. "It doesn't matter." Slowly, he turned, retreating to his den. Halfway down the hall, he paused, his back facing her. "Why did you go?" It was as if the question had been wrenched from him, had cost him more than she would ever know.

"Cora must have tried again to reach you. I apologize for not giving you the message."

"Damn it, Karen," Rand bit out savagely. "You disappear for three days and apologize for not giving me a telephone message? I don't give a damn hell about Cora right now. I want to know why you found it so sam-hell important to run out on me?" His hands were clenched so tightly the knuckles appeared white. He turned around, his face twisted, like a man pushed beyond his limit.

Karen watched him with a sad, almost pleading expression. His agony…hers. "Cora phoned to say she's had her flight reservations changed, so she'll be traveling with you since…since I won't be going with you, after all."

Her response angered Rand all the more. "Do you mean to tell me this whole disappearing act of yours was nothing more than a fit of jealousy?" he questioned between clenched teeth.

"Apparently so," she told him flippantly. "If it's jealousy to have the man I married take two honeymoon trips with another woman, then that's what I am. I won't question if it's reasonable or unreasonable; it's just the way I happen to feel."

Rand swore harshly under his breath.

"Well, what did you expect?" Karen asked. "More important, when did you plan on telling me I wouldn't be going? At the airport? We're supposed to leave in three days. Excuse me," she corrected herself with a bitter smile. "*You're* leaving in three days."

"You couldn't come," he shouted, his face red and angry. Then he paused, taking several deep breaths as if to calm himself. Gesturing with his hand, he added with a helpless, frustrated note, "You're sick every morning."

"If you'd bothered to ask, you'd have learned most of the morning sickness has gone." She looked away guiltily. It had only been the last couple of mornings that she'd felt like her old self. "It doesn't matter." She felt tired and defeated. Holding a conversation while ten feet of hall separated them seemed utterly useless. She returned to the living room, stopping to pick up clothes along the way. She deposited the pile on the sofa.

"Did you want to come?" Rand asked quietly.

"Of course I did. You could have asked me, Rand."

She heard his uneven sigh. "The lines of communication weren't exactly open last week, and as far as I'm concerned, you're angry over nothing." His voice was raised as he fought for control.

"That's what the baby and I are to you...nothing," she intoned sadly, and turned to witness the hard mask that slipped over his face.

"I don't want that baby," Rand shouted.

"You didn't want a wife, either," she reminded him.

Rand bit off another caustic reply and paced the floor, saying nothing.

"It's obvious I expect more from your love than you're capable of giving. Somewhere along the road, I got the twisted notion love implies trust and faith. You've accused and doubted me twice." She took a shaky breath, gathering her resolve. "You once told me to get out, but you didn't say how far you wanted me to go. I think that time has come."

Rand's expression remained impassive and stoic. If it hadn't been for the nerve that jerked in his jaw, she wouldn't have known the effect of her demand.

When the telephone rang, she ignored it. "Undoubtedly, it's for you," she uttered sarcastically. "Probably Cora wanting to confirm your plans."

Rand jerked himself around and strode toward his den. The phone went silent. Either Rand had answered it, or the caller had hung up; Karen didn't know.

She drew in a deep, calming breath and leaned her

head back to quell the emotion. She hadn't meant to say those things; her anger was hurting them both.

When Rand returned, his face was strangely troubled, the smoldering anger extinguished. "Karen, that was the hospital. Your father's had a massive heart attack. We must hurry."

Eleven

The blood drained from Karen's face, her hand flying to her mouth in shocked reaction. "Dear God, no," she gasped. "Rand, tell me he's all right, please."

"Carl's coming; we must hurry." Her husband's voice was tight with concern.

Later, Karen could hardly recall the tense drive to the hospital. She sat rigid with apprehension, her eyes closed. Matthew, her sweet, scheming, Scottish rogue of a father. Her lips moved in silent prayer, her spirit soothed by Rand's fingers tightly clenching hers, offering his support, his love.

Their shoes sounded loudly against the polished floors of the hospital as they hurried down the winding corridors.

Evan, Milly, and Judy were already there, sitting silent and frightened. It was as though they were in a stupor; no one reacted to Karen until Judy gave a feeble cry and stood.

"He's dying; surgery is his only chance."

Evan remained seated, his look despondent, his face

buried in his hands. When Karen entered the waiting area, he raised his hopeless, weary eyes to hers.

Milly, tears glistening in her eyes, could offer no encouragement.

"What happened?" Karen asked as if searching for some plausible reason for such a thing to happen to her father.

"I've known about his heart condition for a year now," Evan answered her, "but I had no idea it was this serious."

"Dad knew he needed the surgery but refused," Judy added, shaking her head as if she couldn't comprehend what was happening around her. "He was waiting to die," she mumbled incredulously.

"To die?" Karen echoed her disbelief. She looked quizzically to Evan for an explanation.

The events of the evening were exacting their toll. Evan stared back, his face white and drawn. "I didn't know. I swear to God I would have forced him to have the surgery if I'd known."

Karen still didn't understand; her gaze moved to Milly, helplessly searching for answers.

"Matthew learned his heart was bad, but decided he'd rather die and be with Madeline than prolong his life. He told us tonight before the aid car arrived that it was all right now that you and Rand were married. He needn't worry about you anymore."

Her father's strange behavior this past year suddenly became clear. All the dates he'd begun arranging for her, the pressure for her to marry and produce grand-children. His heart condition was the reason he'd co-erced Rand into marrying her. Matthew had known she loved Rand, and when things didn't look as though they were going to work out between them, he took matters into his own hands.

No wonder Matthew had looked so wan and pale at times. She knew that he missed her mother, but not to the extent that he would rather die than go on living. How stupid she'd been. It was as if the weight of the whole world had come crashing down on her. She had been closest to her father; she should have guessed what was happening, should have recognized the symptoms. Her father had been biding his time all along, hoping she would marry, forcing men upon her so she would be secure before his heart gave out.

"We were playing chess," Evan began, interrupting Karen's thoughts. "He just fell over. I thought he was dead."

"The doctor says that unless Dad has the surgery, he won't last the night. They're prepping him now. It doesn't look good, not good at all." Judy's voice cracked on a sob.

For the first time, Rand spoke: "It seems to me the lot of you have given Matthew up for dead. Matthew McAlister is a cursed old bulldog; once he's faced death, I doubt that he'll go without a gallant fight."

The doctor appeared, his face grim. Matthew was ready for surgery. Again, the older man explained the procedure, making it sound very routine, yet didn't minimize the risks involved. Karen and Judy could see their father for only a few minutes.

The sight of tubes and IVs brought reality to the seriousness of Matthew's condition. Slow tears wound their way down Karen's cheeks and chin as she stooped to kiss Matthew's brow tenderly. Judy remained at the foot of the hospital bed, her hand over her mouth to hold back her distress.

Matthew's eyes flickered open; he appeared drugged and woozy. Nurses were keeping a constant watch on his vital signs and hovered around the bed.

"Dad," Karen whispered, leaning close to his ear. "The granddaughter you've been wanting so long is due in five short months. She'd very much like to know her grandfather. Please live, Dad. Fight this."

Gently, the arms of a nurse comforted Karen, pulling her back from the bed. "We're ready to take him to surgery," she whispered soothingly. "Don't worry, honey. We'll take good care of your father."

Judy collapsed into tears, returning to Evan and Milly, while Karen stood alone in the hall until her father had been wheeled from sight.

When Karen entered the waiting area, she'd never felt so alone or so afraid. As if by instinct, Rand met her, wrapping her tightly against him, lending her his strength, his faith. Karen clung to her husband, desperately needing his support.

The night seemed endless, each second, each minute interminable. The small group huddled together, as if their presence would aid Matthew's battle for life. By dawn, the thin thread of hope remained taut and capable of snapping at any time. Yet Matthew clung to it obstinately.

Sometime during the long night, each one fell victim to despair and discouragement. Only Rand remained confident during the endless vigil. His gentle assurance lent strength, encouragement, and hope; all four leaned heavily on him.

When Dr. Phillips reappeared, clothed in a green

surgical gown, the family, watching his approach, remained paralyzed, afraid of what he would say, yet equally fearing the unknown.

Matthew had survived the surgery. He remained a critically ill man, and the next few days would hold the highest risk. Dr. Phillips advised them to go home and get some rest; there was nothing any of them could do to help Matthew's condition.

Rand, Milly, and Evan rose to leave, but Karen and Judy glanced at each other in unspoken agreement. They would stay, confident their love for Matthew was stronger than the power of death.

"Judy and I are staying," Karen told Rand.

"Karen," Rand coaxed softly, "come home. You won't be able to help your father any more here than you could at home. You need your rest. You'll only make yourself ill."

Stubbornly, Karen shook her head. "No," she whispered on a fervent note. "Judy and I are staying."

Rand didn't attempt to pressure her further. He left a few minutes later with the promise to return later that afternoon.

The hours merged together. Nothing mattered. There were no stars, no sun, no universe; nothing was of consequence while her father's life hung in a delicate balance.

The two sisters rarely spoke; the communication between them didn't require words.

The doctor had left word that Karen and Judy could visit Matthew for five minutes every hour, but only one at a time. When Karen went, she stroked his brow lovingly and murmured soothing phrases. Sometimes Matthew's eyes would drift open to gaze at her sightlessly, but his lashes lowered slowly, as if sleep had lured him back into her arms.

Seeing her father for only those few minutes wrenched at Karen's heart. He was so pitifully weak, so vulnerable. The picture of her physically strong, active father was far removed from the man who lay in the intensive care unit fighting for his life.

Rand returned and again attempted to persuade the women to go home and rest. Just as adamantly, Karen and Judy refused, fearing Matthew would wake, wanting them, believing with all their being they would instill in their father their own strength.

For a second time, Rand accepted their decision, remaining until late that night, having meals sent and ordering pillows and blankets when it became obvious neither of them would leave. Rand's quiet strength fueled Karen with desperately needed hope. She sat with his arms supporting her and relaxed for the first time in twenty-four hours. She was dimly aware of being lowered upon a soft cushion and covered with a blanket. A faint shadow stood above her, but the magnetic allure of sleep, sweet, blissful slumber, called, and she slipped into unconsciousness.

The next day followed the pattern of the first. Matthew's condition remained unchanged. Friends and relatives continued to visit, but there was no word, no hope to offer as Matthew clung to the delicate thread of life.

Rand was with them as much as possible, concerning himself with their basic needs of food and rest. He held Karen again until she fell asleep; she faintly recalled a caressing kiss on her cheek as she slipped into sleep on the third night of their vigil.

Early the next evening, the doctor appeared and for

the first time greeted Karen and Judy with an encouraging smile.

"Your father has made definite improvement today. He's awake and already giving the nurses a bad time." He seemed to find amusement in this and chuckled over some private joke. "Although the immediate danger has passed, Matthew must remain in the coronary care unit for several days, depending on his progress. From there he'll be transferred to the progressive care unit." Dr. Phillips took care to explain the details of Matthew's recovery and left with an optimistic smile a few minutes later.

After the unbearable wait, the news of Matthew's improvement was like a refreshing, life-giving rain after a summer drought. Karen and Judy hugged each other, the tension broken as happy tears blurred their eyes.

When Judy gave a small, strangled sound, Karen looked up, confused and unsure, to find her sister hurrying down the corridor. Walking toward them was Rand and her brother-in-law, Mike Turner.

Judy floated into her husband's arms and was enfolded in an embrace that spoke of worry, concern, and months of longing.

"How…when?" She didn't seem capable of forming a complete sentence.

Mike laughed. "Rand contacted the air force, and I was given emergency leave. I can see I'm going to appreciate my new brother-in-law." His smile was broad; then he sobered as if remembering the reason for his being there. "How's Matt now?"

"Better, much better," Judy supplied the information. "The doctor was just here. There's a long uphill road to recovery for Dad, but Dr. Phillips feels optimistic."

Rand rested his hand lightly across Karen's shoulder, and she slipped her arm around his waist. The simple contact brought a ray of hope to the problems they had yet to face regarding her pregnancy. When she glanced at Rand, she found him smiling smugly.

"What did I tell you? I knew that crusty old devil was going to make it." His expression altered. "It's time to come home. Evan and Milly are coming later. They'll phone if there's any change."

After three restless nights, catching what sleep they could on a lumpy davenport, both daughters were ready to agree.

The two couples left the hospital, and for the first time in three days Karen breathed in fresh air and looked toward the sun. Her eyes were lambent, her relief almost translucent.

Carl greeted her with anxious eyes but relaxed after she gave him a reassuring smile. "I don't need to ask how your father's doing, Miss Karen," he said. "The smile on your face answers all doubts."

"Dad's better, much better. Thank you for your concern."

The older man looked pleased. "The missus has dinner waiting. She'll be glad to hear your father is improving."

Everyone was being so wonderful. Karen felt a knot building in her throat, never having realized before how the loving support of friends could mean so much.

"Thank her for me," Karen murmured, holding back the tears.

Home held the comfort of familiarity, and Karen looked around her as if seeing it with new eyes. Flowers decorated the table; her collection of figurines on the mahogany bookcase stared back at her, providing solace that would have been difficult to describe with words.

The aroma of the meal warming in the oven couldn't deter Karen from the thought of a hot shower and washing her hair. As she entered the bedroom, she halted in midstep; the open suitcase on the bed caused her to stop and stare.

"Oh, Rand, the trip...the lecture series. I'd forgotten. You were supposed to leave today," she said, horrified. Everything was so confused in her mind; time had lost meaning as the days blended together. The trip, their argument, seemed so far removed, so distant. Not since the phone call from the hospital had Rand's leaving with Cora crossed her mind.

"I'm flying out early tomorrow morning. There's no question of you accompanying me," he said flatly, pulling his tie free and unfastening the top buttons of his shirt.

Was he referring to the pregnancy or her father? Karen was too weary to question him. "No, I suppose not," she mumbled, feeling dejected and sad. Rand was leaving with Cora, and all the things Karen had so desperately wanted to have clear between them remained to trouble her. All her efforts to normalize their relationship had been thwarted.

Rand was waiting for her in the living room, relaxing, his head leaning back against the chair, listening to the classical music they both enjoyed.

She sat opposite him, wishing he was on the davenport so she could be closer. "I want to thank you for all you did to help my family," she began, feeling awkward. "You were wonderful. None of us will ever forget it."

Rand frowned; his mouth twisted in a taut line as

if her words had displeased him. "I didn't do anything anyone else wouldn't have done," he told her flatly.

Karen looked around her; the welcome of her home had faded from the lack of warmth in her husband.

Rand was leaving in the morning. Nothing had been settled between them, and already the cold mask was slipping over her husband's face. A knot tightened the tender muscles of her stomach.

"If you don't mind, I… I think I'll skip dinner and go to bed," she added, hoping to hide the despair in her voice.

Rand shrugged noncommittally. "As you wish."

Karen returned to the bedroom, feeling depressed and weary.

The gentle caress of Rand's mouth woke her the next morning. The alarm had rung, sounding as if it'd come from a far-off distance, but that had seemed so long ago. Karen welcomed the warm touch as he rolled her over, his mouth seeking hers. Automatically, her lips parted, savoring his ardent kiss. Her silken arms wound around his neck as his hand slipped under her nightgown, capturing the rounded fullness of her breast.

Karen gave a muted groan; Rand hadn't touched her like this since she'd told him about the baby. She was starving for his love and responded with all the hunger of weeks without him.

"I've got to go or miss the flight," he murmured low in her ear as his other hand stroked her exposed thigh.

"Can't you stay a bit longer?" she questioned, drugged with desire. Unfastening his suit coat, her arms circled the broad expanse of his back, stroking, caressing, drawing him to her.

Rand's mouth parted hers hungrily, and she clung to him, arching her back.

He groaned hoarsely. "I'll catch another flight."

Matthew was awake for Karen's visit later that morning. He was pale and so weak that his smile was no more than a slight quiver at the corners of his mouth. He struggled to speak, frustrated until he managed one word.

"Bairn?"

Karen flashed him a proud smile, her eyes sparkling with happiness as she nodded. "A granddaughter, we're hoping. Who told you?" He was unlikely to have remembered her frantic whisper that night.

Matthew rolled his head, indicating the nurse near his bed.

Mrs. Thomas looked away guiltily. "I hope you don't mind my telling him, dear. He needed a bit of good news."

Karen assured her it didn't matter; she'd liked Mrs. Thomas immediately. The kind eyes and reassuring manner had done much to relieve Judy and Karen during the bleakest hours.

"I hope this dirty old man isn't giving you problems," the nurse said with a wink as she connected another IV bottle to the stand above Matthew's head.

For an instant, angry fire sparked in her father's eyes, and Karen smiled at the sight, strangely comforted by this small display of anger.

Rand phoned that evening to assure Karen he'd caught his flight and had arrived in Chicago safely. He sounded relaxed and less tense than she could remember since finding out about the baby. It was a little thing that showed her Rand was beginning to come to terms with her pregnancy. Their conversation lasted only a few minutes, but when Karen replaced the phone, she closed her eyes, confident for the first time things would work out between them.

Matthew was much more alert the next two days as his strength gradually returned. Karen's visits remained short, and on several occasions she enjoyed the banter between her father and Mrs. Thomas. Their quick wits were well matched, and Matthew appeared to find solace from the tedious days in the good-humored teasing.

His first words to Karen the next morning were a plea for food. "Karen, lass, I'm starving to death. Will you see what you can do to get me off this sugar water and onto some real food?"

Even before Karen could assure him she would, Mrs. Thomas moved to his bedside.

"Feisty this morning, aren't you?" she said, hands on her hips, her flashing blue eyes glaring at Matthew.

He lowered his brows disapprovingly. "How can a man be anything else when he's near fainting from hunger? If you were any kind of a nurse, you'd see about getting me some food."

"Listen here, you meager-witted, croaking toad. If you had any brains in that buffooned head of yours, you'd know none of the patients in the intensive care unit are allowed solid food. Be patient for once."

"Meager-witted toad, is it? Well, you're nothing more than a domineering battle-axe."

"Dad!" Karen's gaze bounced from one to the other. Mrs. Thomas's eyes were sparkling with delight; she loved this teasing raillery. Her father's mouth quivered with the effort to suppress a smile.

"Go tend your patients, nurse, but let it be known ye sorely task my temper."

"Thirty years of nursing and I've yet to meet a more ill-mannered, ill-tempered man." She continued to make busywork around Matthew's bed and, meeting Karen's eye, gave a girlish wink.

Karen's gaze followed the older woman as she moved around in the large, open area. Catherine Thomas's hair was completely white, and Karen guessed her age to be close to Matthew's. The woman's deep-blue eyes seemed to dance with mischief, and her smile was ready and warm. It was easy to picture this woman with her father; somehow it seemed right.

Rand telephoned from Kansas City the next evening and laughed as she related the scene between Matthew and Mrs. Thomas.

"It sounds to me like a little romance is brewing between those two."

"I was thinking the same thing myself," Karen confessed. "I've often wondered how I'd feel if Dad showed interest in another woman. I loved my mother so much, and Dad loving someone else is almost painful. But I like Catherine Thomas immensely. I wouldn't feel bad at all if they got to know each other better." The picture of the couple together brought a charmed smile to Karen's face. "What a pair they'd be. Mrs. Thomas is barely five feet tall, and Dad's well over six feet."

"Karen, I don't want you interfering with those two."

"Randall Prescott, I wouldn't!" She was surprised he would even make such a suggestion. Her back stiffened with resentment.

"Of all the couples in the world, you and I know what it's like to have someone intrude."

You and I, he'd said. Did Rand finally accept her innocence in the contrived marriage? So much had been said the night of her father's open-heart surgery to help her understand his strange behavior; Karen had wondered if Rand had understood the implications. Matthew was aware that Rand and Karen were in love, but he also knew his time was limited with a bad heart. Forcing the marriage had been a desperate act by a desperate man.

"Yes, I guess *we* do," she said evenly.

"How are you feeling?"

In the past, Karen had always responded with a flat "fine." Now that Rand possibly accepted that she hadn't tricked him the first time, maybe he would be willing to accept the truth about her pregnancy. Perhaps it was time to begin talking about the baby.

"I'm doing much better now that the morning sickness has passed."

"Good." The one word came out abrupt and clipped. They hadn't spoken about the pregnancy since the night of Matthew's heart attack. Rand's response didn't encourage her to continue, but she ignored the unspoken warning. "I've had to buy some new clothes," she added, forcing herself to sound bright and cheerful. "You'd hardly believe how rounded I've become since you left."

"I'm pleased you're feeling better." He didn't attempt to disguise his displeasure or the chill in his voice. "I'll phone tomorrow night. Goodbye."

"Goodbye." The line had already been disconnected; the buzz continued to drone for several moments before Karen replaced the receiver.

When Rand phoned again, they talked briefly, but he

didn't inquire about her health. It was as though he were purposely avoiding the slightest reference to the baby.

Most of the discomforts of the early months of the pregnancy had passed, but her emotions remained sensitive and fragile. For several nights afterward, Karen had a difficult time sleeping, continuing to mull the problem in her mind.

It was a day for rejoicing when Matthew was transferred to the progressive care unit. His condition had improved so rapidly that even Dr. Phillips was surprised.

Catherine Thomas followed the small party down the corridor to the new ward, beaming a proud smile. Her delight at his improvement was apparent as she joked and laughed along the way.

Catherine stopped at the nurses' station and said, loud enough for Matthew to hear, "Keep your eyes on this ole buzzard, girls. He can be more trouble than a nursery full of newborn babies."

"Ha," Matthew emitted harshly, but his eyes followed Catherine without even a hint of anger.

Karen and Judy exchanged meaningful glances.

"How long before I get any decent food?" Matthew asked eagerly.

"Patience, my dear man, patience." Catherine grinned sheepishly at the girls on her way out the door.

"Dad"—Judy glanced out the window as if finding the street below an intriguing sight—"is there a Mr. Thomas?"

"Of course there's a Mr. Thomas," he boomed, his voice angry. "There must be a thousand Mr. Thomases in the world, but if ye're referring to Catherine, she's a widow."

Color rose in Judy's cheeks, but she managed a weak "Oh."

When Catherine reentered the room, Matthew's eyes widened appreciatively. His gaze fastened on the large serving of chocolate pudding. "Grand, pudding is one of my favorite—"

He didn't get to finish his thought. "But, Matt, this isn't pudding." She gave Judy and Karen a wicked smile. "This is strained liver."

A disgusted sound came from Matthew. "It seems I'm beset by a cruel woman who delights in punishing a sick man." But his laughter joined theirs.

Rand had been away for almost two weeks, and Karen was miserable. She wasn't sleeping well; so much had been left unsaid between them. Karen discovered the pleasure she enjoyed in simple things diminishing because he wasn't there to share them with her. She worked in the garden, listened to mellow music, and eagerly awaited his daily phone calls. These were mostly a disappointment. Their conversations remained stilted and formal because neither would speak openly of what was uppermost in their minds.

With Rand gone, the baby was becoming more and more the focal point of Karen's world. The forming child moved often now; the first light fluttering, as delicate as a butterfly testing its wings, had confused Karen. She wasn't sure if it was something she ate or the baby. Gradually, the movements grew stronger, more pronounced, and Karen didn't doubt the source.

Rand phoned early one morning, early for Karen, midmorning for him in Cleveland. She was still in bed, her hands pressing against her abdomen, feeling the baby's movement.

"I know you don't want to hear this," she told him, her voice high with enthusiasm, "but I'm lying here feeling the baby kick. I mean a good solid kick."

"You're right. I don't want to hear it," he said dryly.

The balloon of happiness burst, leaving Karen speechless and unbelievably hurt. "Whether you face the fact or not"—her low voice wavered—"I'm going to have a child, your child. I did not create this child on my own. The baby is part you, part me. This should be one of the happiest times in our marriage, yet I'm afraid even to mention the baby. What am I supposed to do, Rand? What do you want from me?"

He sighed heavily. "I've told you repeatedly I don't want that baby," he said bitterly. "You seem to be living under the misconception that given time, my feelings will change. They won't. I'll have nothing to do with that baby. You've chosen to become pregnant against my wishes; as far as I'm concerned, the baby is yours, not mine. Don't expect me to touch it, hold it, or in any way have anything to do with it."

The baby was an *it* to Rand, a nonentity, unworthy of importance.

"Maybe you don't want me, either," she whispered through the agony.

"Maybe I don't," he returned.

His rejection knotted her stomach into a tight ball of pain. "That doesn't leave much to be said, does it?"

A long pause followed. "No, I guess it doesn't."

Fifteen minutes after the phone call, Karen remained in bed, the enormity of their conversation crushing against her heart like a huge boulder.

In effect, Rand was saying it was him or the baby. How could she possibly choose between the two? The image of a child the father refused to touch or acknowledge ripped at her soul. Loving them both so much would tear her in two. Rand was asking the impossible.

If this was the way he wanted things, forcing her to decide, then the decision would be an easy one. They had no marriage. Rand was selfish, hurtful, and totally unreasonable; he had been almost from the beginning of their marriage. They had made a mistake by not getting an annulment.

Karen jerked the suitcase from the closet and set it on the bed, throwing her clothes from the drawers into it without thought or organization. Her vision was blurred with unshed tears, her lips pressed tightly closed to restrain the sobs.

How naive she'd been to believe their love would conquer all their differences. Rand didn't need her; he'd just told her he didn't want her, either. Maybe it was time to prove she was perfectly capable of making a life without him.

She'd leave him this time, really leave him, not another three-day jaunt down the Oregon coast. A small, hurt laugh came from deep inside; three days without her and Rand had fallen apart. How did he expect to live without her, and for that matter, how would she ever make it without him?

She paused, sitting on the end of the bed, her tortured gaze moving around the room and sensing all the love represented there.

How could they ever settle anything when separated by hundreds of miles? Their telephone conversations frustrated them more than settled anything. They needed to sit across from each other and talk out their problems. Other than never being able to see the baby, Karen had no idea why Rand objected so violently to the child. There could be no more running, no more telephone conversations, when it was too easy simply to hang up the phone rather than talk things out. She needed to know his feelings, his thoughts; she needed to explain hers.

Tilting her head back, she closed her eyes as waves of depression rippled over her. Rand wasn't due home for another ten days. He was in Cleveland; she was in Tacoma. It couldn't wait; they'd delayed discussing it for too long. She'd simply have to go to him…the sooner the better.

The flight touched down at nine o'clock Cleveland time. Karen was tired and hungry. The conviction she was doing the right thing was reinforced by every mile of the journey. As the hours passed, Karen recalled Rand's mother telling her she need only be patient. Rand would make a good father; would accept the child. Carl had told her that Rand would be handing out cigars, proud as any father. Karen need only believe this herself, trust in his love.

By the time she'd collected her luggage, gotten a taxi, and arrived at Rand's hotel, it was after ten. The clerk gave her Rand's room number and kindly offered to keep her suitcase, since she hadn't been able to locate him. Rand didn't respond to either the telephone call or the knock when they tried his room. Discouraged, Karen went into the restaurant for something to eat while she waited.

Where would he be this late? Cora hadn't answered her telephone, either. Were they together? With so many other things on her mind, Karen didn't want to think about Cora.

Seated in the dimly lit restaurant, Karen read over the menu. She hadn't eaten in hours, but nothing sounded appetizing. Where was Rand? She almost asked the question aloud.

As she laid the menu aside, the sound of a laugh, Cora's laugh, caught her attention from across the room. The lighting was low. At first, Karen was sure it wasn't them; it couldn't be. A bubble of hysteria rose in her throat. Rand and Cora were sitting together across the room, their heads close together like lovers sharing intimate secrets.

Numbly, she stood. Her heart hammered irrationally as she approached their table.

"Hello, Rand, Cora," she said in a complete monotone. A sick feeling rose in her throat as she saw Cora's hand holding Rand's.

"I'd advise you to remove your hand from my husband's, Cora. Otherwise, I'll have to create a scene in this very nice restaurant."

Twelve

"Please excuse us, Cora." Rand offered the other woman an apologetic smile and stood.

"You don't need to make apologies for me, Randall Prescott." Karen's gaze narrowed menacingly on Cora and was surprised by the lack of challenge. Was she so confident of her hold over Rand that she needn't show the least concern? Karen was studying the other woman so intently she didn't hear the parting words Cora issued Rand.

Rand held Karen's upper arm. "Thanks, we're going to need it."

Neither of them said a word until they entered the elevator.

"Let go of my arm," Karen demanded coldly.

Rand's mouth twisted, his look hard and resolute. "Like hell!" But his hold relaxed.

Karen didn't struggle; it would have been useless, anyway.

Once inside his room, Rand leaned against the closed door. "Just what kind of game are you playing?" he questioned, his voice hoarse.

Karen was trembling fiercely. She didn't trust her voice.

"Karen," he demanded again.

Turning her back to him, her arms cradled her chest to ward off the cold, the ache, the hurt. Tears coursed a haphazard route down her face, the strength of her will unable to abate their fall. Every breath became a sob, wrenched from her heart.

He clasped her shoulder to turn her toward him. "Karen, please don't cry," he pleaded.

Closing her eyes, she averted her face, burying her chin into her shoulder, her body shaking with uncontrollable sobs.

Rand brought her head against him, supplying the loving support she needed so desperately.

"I can't stand it when you cry," he said.

She gave a short, almost hysterical laugh. Almost from the time they'd met, all she'd done was cry. The power Rand had to hurt her was so sharp it was incomprehensible.

"Don't, please." Gently, his lips moved against her hair. His hands, which had been holding her, now began a caressing provocation over her shoulders, back, and hips.

His mouth sought the gentle curve of her neck. Just as powerful as his ability to hurt was his power to comfort, to love. His mouth found hers, claiming the trembling softness with a gentleness that caused her knees to quiver. His lips hardened in possession, and Karen could taste the salt from her tears on his mouth.

"No," she mumbled imploringly, breaking the contact and burying her face in his chest.

"Karen."

She could hear the rawness in his voice and knew he was as affected by their kissing as she. His chin moved against her hair as if he couldn't bear to release her from his arms.

"We need to talk." She was surprised by the strength in her voice.

"I know." His hold relaxed slightly, but she remained in the protective circle of his arms. "I've tried to contact you all day. Even Carl wouldn't answer. I've been sick with worry. I thought you'd left me for sure this time."

Lifting her face, she watched his reaction. "Would you care if I'd left you, really left you?"

Almost angrily, he broke the embrace and strode to the other side of the room, clenching his hands at his sides as he paced the floor. "Yes, I'd care." He ground out each word as if it were a weakness he was confessing. "I need you." He turned around, and his face shone with the intensity of his feelings.

"What about the baby?" she asked, her voice shaking violently.

Karen thought she glimpsed pain in his eyes. "I never wanted the child."

Her shoulders hunched forward in defeat until the baby kicked, almost as if the child were saying she must fight for her father's love. Approaching Rand, she took her husband's hand and placed it against the budding roundness of her abdomen. Rand resisted at first until he felt the activity. A sense of wonder came over his face, and for a second, Karen was sure she witnessed a flicker of pride move across it.

"That's the baby?" he asked incredulously. "He's so strong."

Karen smiled. Rand had referred to the baby as *he,* not as *it*.

"The doctor says I'm carrying the baby high; that's why I'm showing as much as I am."

Karen was sure he hadn't even heard her as his hand moved over her stomach in a gentle caress, his eyes proud but tortured.

"How can I be any kind of father?" The raw pain in his voice shocked Karen. "I'll never see this child. More than that, I'll never be the kind of father a child needs."

"Rand"—her voice shook with her own pain— "that's not true."

He emitted a dry, bitter laugh. "You know what's going to happen, don't you? It's inevitable. One day that child is going to be embarrassed to have me as his father. I'll never be able to do the things other fathers do." His voice trembled with emotion as he strode across the carpet like a man pushed to the limit. "I don't want that baby, Karen, but I'm trying. At least give me credit for that."

She watched him with a sense of unreality. "Rand?" She had once stood in his office reading over his accomplishments, with the realization that there wasn't anything this man couldn't do. He'd overcome obstacles and prejudices she could only imagine, but the thought of this new life they'd created frightened him beyond all else. "You're afraid, aren't you?"

He didn't bother to deny her accusation. "I'm scared to death," he bit out savagely, his face white and drawn.

"Rand…"

"No, let me finish. It's always been important to me to be completely independent. I've struggled for that. Now, within the space of a few short months, I find myself responsible not only for myself but first a wife and now a child."

"I entered your life with the subtlety of a racing locomotive, didn't I?" she asked with a tender smile.

His returning one appeared involuntary. "Now the baby is doing the same thing to the both of us."

Karen's smile relaxed, and she watched Rand with questioning eyes. "You believe me now, don't you? I didn't purposely get pregnant."

Rand's mouth thinned. "Yes, I realized that almost immediately, but I was confused and hurt. I lashed out in anger. I wanted you to suffer, and yet every time I purposely hurt you, I suffered, too. I created my own hell. Then you were gone for those three days, and I nearly went insane. I couldn't imagine what my life would be like without you now. Your love has affected every facet of my existence. I almost ruined what we have, didn't I?"

"No." Her voice wavered slightly, a lump of happiness choking off her words. "I could never leave you."

"Then, this morning, when I phoned and you started talking about the baby, I went cold inside. My stomach knotted into a ball of pain, and I knew I'd lost. I was going to love the baby. Perhaps I was even subconsciously happy you were pregnant. I got scared. All I could think of was all the things a father should do... things I'll never be able to do."

"But, Rand"—her hand gripped his arm—"don't you realize what you have to offer is far more valuable than shooting baskets or tossing a baseball? Why is it you feel that being a good father is synonymous with being a jock?" She sighed, her voice husky with emotion. "Just being the person you are is more important than any physical feat you could ever accomplish."

"But, Karen…"

"No, let me finish." She stopped to kiss his throat softly but found the temptation too strong; fearing it would lead to other things, she broke the contact. "I fell in love with you almost from the time we met. It didn't take me long to see past the angry facade you wore. I was sick with disappointment when I didn't hear from you after the Christmas party. I knew then that I'd never meet anyone who would be more of a man than you. When we started seeing each other on a regular basis, it was like every dream I'd ever hoped to fulfill." She gave a small, nervous laugh. "Every woman has a picture of what she'd like in the perfect man. Some see him as tall, dark, and handsome. You're all of those, but I've known lots of men who fit that description. It was your sensitivity, your intelligence, your strength, both physical and emotional, that attracted me. When you decided to break off our relationship, it was like dying. I knew that although someday I would probably love and marry another, I'd never love anyone as much as I loved you. It was a dreadful thing Dad did to us. Such trickery goes against everything I've ever known from my father. I understand why he did it now. But even before I knew his reasoning, I was glad he'd forced your hand."

Gathering her close in the haven of his arms, he gently parted her moist lips in a kiss that kindled a fire of warmth and need that quickly spread through her body. But Rand also showed restraint, as if what they must say to each other was more important than the desire between them.

"As much as I resented your father's interference in my life, I realize he acted in the only way he could. I would never have married you otherwise, for the same reasons I didn't want the baby. I left New York alone after the wedding with a harrowing ache eating at me. Your wedding ring was in my pocket, and every time I touched it, the ring felt like it had seared my skin. I kept remembering how you said you wanted a marriage that would last a lifetime and you weren't interested in a three-day weekend. You'd been so shocked, so genuinely surprised, when I told you about being forced into the marriage. It was like being pulled apart. I was caught in the middle of a tug-of-war between my intellect, my will, and my desire for you." He paused for a moment as if the memory continued to haunt him. "I wanted to hate you, make you suffer for all the agony I was enduring. At the same time, I desperately wanted to believe you. I yearned to hold my wife in my arms and love you as any husband. But most of all, I realized it didn't matter what you'd done or how deceitful you'd been. I couldn't deny myself any longer. I desired you as I've never wanted anything in my life. Do you remember when I replaced the wedding ring on your finger?"

Karen smiled softly. "I'm not likely to forget."

"Your wedding ring burned my pocket the whole trip. I couldn't keep myself from fingering it, as if touching it would ease the ache of not having you with me. I couldn't return to Tacoma fast enough to place it where it belonged. And then you weren't there."

"But I was," she reminded him mockingly. "When I hurried into the house, Cora had her arms wrapped around you."

"I could have choked her for that, but I'll explain

the situation with Cora in a minute." Gently, his hand caressed her cheek. "I hurried back to put the ring on your finger. Suddenly, you were there, and I realized, ring or no ring, you were my wife."

"About Cora?" Karen questioned.

"Yes, Cora." Rand expelled his breath in a long, drawn-out sigh. "At one time, she may have harbored some hope of the two of us getting together. But she realized such expectations are useless. I'm very much in love with my beautiful wife."

Karen held herself stiff. "That wasn't exactly the impression I got tonight when I saw you in the restaurant."

Rand's returning grin was wry. "I've behaved like a madman most of the day. I tried repeatedly to get ahold of you and couldn't. I was positive I'd really done it this time. I'd lost you, driven you away. I booked a flight home for tomorrow morning. It was the soonest I could get out. Cora was, I guess you'd say, comforting me, assuring me that things would work out between you and me."

The unyielding stiffness ebbed from Karen. "From now on, if you need any comfort, come to me."

"Don't worry, honey. Cora knows where she stands."

Rand wasn't explaining the complete situation to her. A lot had been left unsaid, perhaps for the better. This was her husband; she trusted his judgment.

"And the baby?"

"My attitudes aren't going to change overnight. I'd rather you weren't pregnant. The thought of this child terrifies me more than anything I've ever faced. I'm trying to accept the fact we're going to have a family, but I'll need time."

Karen swallowed tightly. "I can't ask for anything

more than that. The baby and I need you. We're willing to do whatever it takes, to wait as long as you need. Your daughter and I will simply have to learn to be patient."

Rand's arms tightened their grip around her, and he buried his face in her hair. "A daughter?" He looked surprised. "From the time you first told me you were pregnant, I've assumed the baby would be a boy."

"My dad has wanted a little granddaughter for years, and I've promised him a girl. Would you be unhappy with a daughter?" Karen questioned in afterthought.

"In truth, I'd rather you weren't pregnant at all. But as long as you and the baby are healthy, it doesn't matter what you have."

His words of indifference still had the power to hurt, but she disguised their effect. "Good, because I'm hoping for a girl." Unable to resist him much longer, she gave Rand a kiss.

Rand's laughter held a musical note. "I swear you're still more McAlister than Prescott."

With a warm smile, Karen cupped his face and drew him down invitingly to her waiting lips. "I'm feeling very much like a Prescott right now."

Rand sucked in his breath and groaned before his mouth hungrily claimed hers.

Her response was automatic as she wrapped her arms around his waist and pressed her face to his shirt. Rand smoothed her hair; then his hands ran through it, tangling it between his fingers, and his mouth descended to the slim column of her throat. Nestled in the comfort of his arms, Karen yawned. Their emotional talk that morning, the hurried flight to Cleveland, the time difference between Cleveland and Tacoma, were all

demanding their due, and before she could prevent another, she yawned again.

Rand sighed and gave a soft chuckle. "Come to bed,
my love. You're exhausted."

"I am." Karen was too tired to argue.

They undressed, and a few minutes later, she was
again securely settled in her husband's arms. A pang of
hunger reminded her she'd hardly eaten all day.

"Rand," she whispered, "I'm starving—" She wasn't
allowed to finish. Rand's mouth claimed hers again as
his hands began a gentle exploration of her breasts.

"Me, too," he whispered huskily before claiming her
mouth in a rousing, twisting kiss that left Karen weak
with longing. This wasn't exactly what she had in mind,
but she didn't bother to correct him.

When Karen and Rand returned to Tacoma almost
two weeks later, Karen was amazed at the rate of Matthew's recovery. Although she'd spoken to him daily,
she was unprepared for the healthy flush in his cheeks
or the smile in his eyes. Karen was convinced Catherine
was responsible for the renewed vitality.

"Karen, lass." Matthew flashed her a happy smile
as they sauntered into the hospital room. "Rand, welcome. How was the trip?"

"Good," he responded simply, but the hand holding
Karen's tightened. The trip had been the honeymoon
they'd never had. It was a time of reassurances, settling
doubts and misunderstandings, and days of wondering
at the strength of their love for each other.

They rarely spoke of the baby. One morning, Karen
had awakened to the feel of Rand's fingers traveling
lightly over her abdomen in a gentle caress. They had

both felt the baby's kick. Quickly, Rand jerked his hand away as though unprepared to touch this child or begin the simplest form of communication. Rand had told her he needed time; she must learn to be patient. Rushing things would do more harm than good.

"Dad, you look wonderful." Karen hugged him, her eyes aglow with a warm light. "Catherine," she greeted, and impulsively gave the older woman a hug. It was the first time Karen had seen the other woman out of a nurse's uniform and she was pleasantly surprised by her attractiveness.

"I should be going," Catherine offered, reaching for her purse. "Your family's here to visit now."

"I'd like you to stay." The unspoken message in his eyes was clear.

A smile widened Catherine's mouth, and she conceded.

"How are you feeling, lass?" Matthew's grin widened as his gaze rested on Karen's rounding stomach.

"Fine, Dad." She looked away self-consciously, praying he wouldn't go on about the baby in front of Rand. She wanted to warn him, plead with him to drop the subject, for she could already sense Rand's withdrawal.

"I guess I should have warned you, Rand. The McAlister women are a fertile group. I no more than hung my pants over the bed with Madeline and we had two girls before I knew what had happened. And as I recall, Judy had no trouble getting caught with James and Carter, either."

Karen stiffened, her smile frozen on taut lips.

"I could have done with a warning," Rand replied stiffly, but if Matthew noticed anything was wrong, he didn't show it, laughing off Rand's remark.

Karen continued her daily visits to the hospital, but as the days passed, Matthew's attitude became withdrawn. He was often melancholy, although he attempted a cheerful facade.

Several days later, Karen asked, "Where's Catherine? I haven't seen her in a while."

"She's busy, lass," he explained stiffly, "too busy for an old man."

"I know you asked me to stay out of this," Karen told Rand that night, "but I know something is wrong. Dad's miserable, and other than a few brief visits, I don't think Catherine's been to see him at all."

Rand's expression tightened. "Karen, your father is old enough to handle his own affairs. What's between him and Catherine is none of our business."

She gave him a determined glance. "I'm going to visit Catherine."

"Karen," Rand said with a note of warning.

"I'm only going to say hello," she assured him, her eyes glinting with mischief.

Forced to wait for several minutes, Karen sat in the waiting room that had been a prison of anxiety the first days following Matthew's surgery.

"Karen!" Catherine joined her; a smile of welcome didn't reach her eyes. "Your father's not worse, is he?" There was no disguising the note of anxiety in her voice.

"No, Dad's doing fine. How have you been? We've missed you. We *all* have." She hoped the inflection in her voice conveyed the message.

Catherine glanced nervously at her hands. "I've been busy."

"That's what Dad said."

Catherine avoided eye contact, her face slightly drawn.

"All right," Karen demanded, "what is it with you and Dad?"

"There's nothing between your father and me," Catherine responded tightly, and stood.

"Catherine!" Karen murmured in frustration.

With an exasperated sigh, she turned around. "You're more stubborn than your father. I don't know what's wrong, but every time I've been to see him lately, I get the impression he'd rather I didn't come anymore. I think it's obvious that he's recovering and doesn't want me around. I'm nothing but a bossy old woman. I do wish him the best."

Karen watched Catherine return to her ward. What was wrong with her father? Why would he behave in such a way?

"I don't understand it, Rand," she told him later that evening. "Why would Dad act like that toward Catherine?"

Rand arched an exaggerated brow. "Karen, I want your promise you won't interfere in this. What goes on between Matthew and Catherine is none of your business."

"But, Rand—"

"No buts," he insisted. "Your father's behavior isn't so difficult to understand. He's going through a period of readjustment. He may love Catherine, but he wants to be sure he can offer her a healthy man. Let him work this out himself."

As the days progressed, Matthew showed renewed strength; his discharge date was set for the end of the week. When Rand and Karen visited the next night, they found Matthew out of bed, sitting in a chair waiting for them.

"Rand, Karen, I need to be talking to ye."

His tone was so serious, Karen wondered if the doctors had found a complication to his heart condition.

"Sit down," Matthew ordered.

Karen complied, her hand reaching for Rand's. She'd never seen her father act so nervously.

"Lass, I've already spoken to Judy and received her blessing; now I'm seeking yours. If ye have no objection, I plan on asking Catherine Thomas to be my wife. I love her," he told them simply, directly.

Karen could have cried with relief. "Dad, of course. I love her, too."

"Congratulations, Matthew," Rand added.

It wasn't until they were alone that Rand chided Karen affectionately. "Now, didn't I tell you things have a way of working out themselves without your meddling?"

Karen gave a happy laugh. "I knew you couldn't resist that, but I didn't know you were the kind of husband who would stoop to saying 'I told you so.'"

Rand's mouth twisted humorously. "Sure I am."

Matthew and Catherine were married at the end of October and left almost immediately afterward for a two-week honeymoon in Scotland and England.

Rand and Karen drove to the airport with them, excitedly waving them off. Rand was unusually quiet as Karen drove home.

Later, as Karen sat on top of their bed, brushing her hair before changing into her pajamas, Rand asked, "Now that all the rush has passed, how do you feel?"

She paused, her hands resting lightly on her stomach. "Tired." As the pregnancy had progressed, Karen had lost the ability to move gracefully. The baby's first gentle movements now resembled the activity of a soccer team.

"I don't want you driving the car any longer," Rand declared casually.

Her look was puzzled. "Why ever not?"

He walked away from her, hanging his clothes in the closet, as if reluctant to let her know his reasons. "Because."

A faint smile quivered at the corner of her mouth. "All right, if you insist." Rand was worried about her, about the baby, but was unwilling to admit as much.

"I do." His words were abrupt. "Either Carl will take you where you need to go, or if he can't, perhaps your sister"—he hesitated—"and, Karen, please wear your safety belt."

"I promise," she said gently.

Another month passed, the longest month of her life. Rand didn't mention the baby or her pregnancy. He touched her, held her in his arms, loved her with a tenderness that was beyond description, but he never spoke of the child. A hundred times, Karen wanted to cry out that her time was drawing near, that he'd have to hurry. She couldn't bear it if the baby was born and Rand refused to have anything to do with their baby or couldn't love him or her. Somehow Karen felt the infant would know, would sense Rand's reluctance, and the thought of that rejection brought a harrowing ache within her heart.

With only a couple of months remaining, Karen didn't think she could grow much larger. Even getting up from a sitting position proved to be a difficult task.

Judy reminded her that large babies ran in the family and that James and Carter both weighed more than eight pounds at birth. But even she looked upon Karen with worried eyes.

Following her regular visit to the doctor in December, Karen sat in her living room with brooding thoughtfulness. As she stared into the distance, a lump began to form in her throat.

"Do you think Rand will be angry?" Judy sat opposite Karen; her eyes sparkled in excitement.

"Of course he's going to be angry. I suppose I shouldn't be so shocked, but how was I to know anything was unusual? I've never had a baby before."

Judy chuckled softly. "To be truthful, I suspected something. I could understand it when you looked down and couldn't see your shoes, but when you lost sight of the floor, I knew something was up."

Karen's voice wobbled uncontrollably. "How can you joke? Rand will be here in a few minutes. He didn't want one baby. How am I supposed to tell him it's a multiple birth?"

"You've really done it this time, little sister." Judy chuckled. "If I wasn't so delighted, I'd sympathize with you. But I think twins are wonderful."

The beginnings of a small smile formed. "I think I could be happy about it, too, if only I could be sure of Rand's reaction."

After Judy left, Karen entered the bedroom that had been transformed into a nursery. Running the tips of her fingers over the pink-and-blue-plaid wallpaper, she glanced around the room with mixed emotions. Rand had given her a free hand to do as she wished, never asking what she had done, not listening when she told him. She had tried to discuss names for the baby with him. Rand had cut her off, telling her she could choose any name she wanted. Little by little, she could see a softening in him, but it was so infinitesimal. How would he react to the news she was having twins?

The doctor had been so reassuring, so kind. When he had first suggested the ultrasound, Karen had been surprised. The results confirmed his suspicions, and Karen didn't know if she should laugh or burst into tears. She chose the latter. Of course, the doctor had no way of knowing Rand's attitude regarding the pregnancy.

"Karen." The front door opened, and Rand called for her, his voice eager.

"I'm in here." She walked out to meet him.

"How did things go with the doctor today?"

She stiffened slightly. "Fine."

Rand kissed her softly, his lips teasing hers, but his hold tightened as the possession of his mouth hardened.

"My childbirth classes begin next week. I can't wait any longer if I'm going to take them at all." Her eyes studied his face. "Will you come with me?"

His face darkened, and a scowl narrowed his eyes. "No, I'm not ready, Karen."

A lump of painful hoarseness tightened her throat. "That's okay. I understand." She broke from his embrace and moved into the kitchen. "I… I better start dinner."

Rand nodded, and Karen saw the flicker of sadness that passed over him.

Karen couldn't sleep that night. There didn't seem to be a comfortable position, and turning over was a difficult task. She lay on her back, staring at the ceiling in the moonlight, wondering how she could even broach the subject of a multiple birth when Rand couldn't accept or love even one child.

"Are you awake?" Rand whispered.

"I'm sorry. Am I keeping you up?"

"No." He rolled over, cradling her head on his shoulder. "I can't sleep, either." His fingers gently caressed the length of her arm. "I love you, Karen."

"I know," she whispered, the lump in her throat constricting.

"Honey, I'm trying as hard as I can. I know you're upset about me not attending those birth classes with you, but I can't force this. It's got to come naturally."

Rand believed the reason she had been so quiet and withdrawn that night was because of his reluctance regarding the classes. She hadn't the courage to tell him otherwise. Perhaps when he was more comfortable with her pregnancy, was closer to accepting the baby, then she'd tell him.

"Did you tell him?" Judy asked the next day.

Abjectly, Karen shook her head. "I couldn't."

"Honestly, Karen, when are you planning to tell the poor guy? On the delivery table?"

"If I have to. What do you suggest?" she questioned sharply. "He's trying to come to terms with his feelings for one child. I can't suddenly announce there's more."

"He's been so good to you."

"I know, Rand's been wonderful. But it's all me, not the baby."

"I don't understand."

Karen inhaled deeply. "He follows me around like a lost puppy. The other night, I found him standing outside the shower listening in case I fell. He calls two or

three times a day and canceled his speaking engage-
ments close to my due date. He's even hired Dorothy
to do the housework for me. I'm barely allowed to lift
a finger around my own home."

Judy chuckled, dimples forming in her pink cheeks.
"It's a good thing. I don't imagine you're able to do
much."

She laughed. "It takes me an hour to get dressed.
I've only got a few weeks left before the baby comes.
And as far as I can see, Rand's no closer to accepting
this child than he was in the beginning."

"Chin up, kid. Things will work out," Judy spoke
reassuringly.

The first glimmer of hope came a week after the
break of the new year. Rand arrived home with a large
box under his arm.

"Hi, honey. I'm home."

"I'm in the kitchen," she called, drying her hands on
a terry-cloth towel. Her back had been aching most of
the day. Finally, in an effort to take her mind from the
dull pain, she'd baked Rand's favorite cookies.

"What are you doing?"

"Dishes," she replied weakly. The ache seemed to be
moving slowly from her back to her stomach.

He paused behind her, slipping his arms around her
swollen stomach, caressing her roundness. "Leave them
for Dorothy. I've got something for you—a present."

"For me?" She brightened, noticing the large box on
the table for the first time.

"Go ahead; open it."

Lifting the lid, Karen stifled a cry, tears shimmering
in her eyes. "Oh, Rand," she murmured tightly. "Oh,
Rand." Inside the box, wrapped in tissue, lay a giant

teddy bear. He had said the present was for her, but he had gotten it for the baby.

His hug was warm and gentle. "Hey, why the tears? If I'd known you were going to cry, I wouldn't have gotten it."

"I'm just so surprised," she said, sniffling, before he brought his mouth down to hers.

Sitting through dinner was an uncomfortable task. The pain in her back and abdomen seemed to grow more intense as the night progressed.

"Karen, are you feeling okay?" Rand asked as they got ready for bed.

Rubbing her hands over her stomach, she hesitated. "I don't know… I feel funny."

"Funny?" He straightened. "How do you mean 'funny'?"

"I've had a backache all day, and now it seems to be traveling around to my stomach. I think it might be a good idea if we started timing these pains."

The blood drained from his face. "Pain? You said you felt funny. You didn't say anything about pain."

Her hand traveled down his tense jaw. "Relax, Rand. I'm sure it must be false labor. It's almost three weeks too early."

"I'll call the doctor."

"Don't do that. It's much too soon even if this is the real thing."

An hour later, there could be no denying the pain that constricted her abdomen.

"I'm sorry, Rand, but I think we should call the doctor. This pain is too intense to be anything but real."

"Dear God." For a moment, Rand remained frozen,

as if in his own silent terror. "You're sure?" he questioned.

Again, Karen was seized with another contraction, taking deep heaving breaths before she could respond. "Yes," she groaned softly, "the baby's coming."

"Carl." The name was wrenched from Rand as panic seemed to fill him. "I have to phone Carl…then the doctor."

"Honey, settle down. I'm all right; everything is fine." For the first time, Karen saw that Rand was troubled, unsure. "Rand…if you'd prefer it, I could go to the hospital alone."

"No." He nearly shouted the word. "I'd go insane sitting at home worrying about you. I want to be there when…the…our baby is born."

A minute later, Carl was knocking on the door, his face tight and anxious. "Miss Karen, are you okay?"

"It's too early," Rand repeated, as if hoping against hope she was teasing.

"It is too early," she agreed with a soft smile, "but I'm afraid no one bothered to tell the baby that."

"Oh, God."

The drive to the hospital was a bad dream. Rand kept telling her it was weeks too soon—she must be mistaken—and then shouting at Carl to hurry.

Karen was met at the hospital door by one of the nursing staff, who took her into the obstetrics ward. It was more than an hour later before she saw Rand.

He looked pale, drawn, his hair a mess, as if he'd jerked his hands through it several times.

"Karen." He caught her fingers, holding them tightly to his mouth.

She bit into her bottom lip to keep from groaning as

she was wrenched by another pain. "Rand." Her hand smoothed his hair away from his face. "Listen, there's something I must tell you."

"No, you listen. I love you… I've done so little to deserve your love. The thought of my life without you is unbearable."

Tears blurred her eyes, and she drew a ragged breath. "Oh, Rand, I love you, too." Again, her stomach hardened and contracted. Against her will, she whimpered softly as the pain ebbed.

"Nurse," Rand cried, "my wife is in pain. Do something."

"Rand, you must listen to me…it's about the baby."

The white-capped nurse rushed into the room. "Mr. Prescott, there's nothing we can do now to ease your wife's discomfort. The doctor's on his way." The woman sounded so calm and sane against the frantic cries of her husband.

Karen smiled tenderly at this man she loved. "Rand"— she placed his hand on her stomach—"please listen, because I want to be the one to tell you." She paused as the grinding agony ripped through her once again.

"Tell me what?" he asked as she relaxed.

"Rand." She kept her eyes shut, afraid to look into his eyes, then couldn't help herself. "We're having twins."

"Twins," he bellowed, then repeated it incredulously. "Twins?" He shook his head as if stunned. "I should have known to expect something like this."

"Are you angry?"

"No," he denied instantly.

Again, Karen was gripped by the tormenting pain. Rand kissed her hand several times. "My love," he whispered as if the pain was his own, "let us work together to bring these new lives into the world. Show me what I can do to help you."

Her eyes shining with an infinite tenderness, Karen smiled softly.

Several hours later, after the delivery, Rand joined Karen in her hospital room. She was exhausted but radiant, content and happy as her husband sat beside her and kissed her.

"How are they?" she questioned softly.

A look came over him, unreadable at first, myriad emotions. There was pride, satisfaction, and a wealth of love. "They're perfect, Karen. The nurses let me hold Jody and then Jenny. It was incredible to touch and feel our daughters. For the first time, I realize that you and I are bound together by far more than vows. The whole while you were in labor, I was experiencing this terrible guilt because I hadn't wanted a family. Then suddenly they were there, and I knew I would love these little girls beyond reason, as I love their mother."

Karen held his hand against her breast. "I love you."

"My wife, my lover, the mother of my children. You hold my life and everything important in the palm of your hand." Tenderly, he took her hand, lifted it to his lips, and very gently kissed her palm.

* * * * *

PROMISE ME FOREVER

One

Joy Nielsen brushed a dark strand of curly hair away from her face and straightened her shoulders. She stood in front of the closed door, strengthening her resolve. She'd been told what to expect. Absently her hand smoothed the pants of the uniform she wore as a physical therapist. This was a new case, and she couldn't help feeling apprehensive after listening to Dr. Phelps.

Determined, she forced a smile and opened the door. Quickly her brown eyes scanned the interior. Although the sun was shining, the drapes were closed and the room was filled with dark shadows. A solitary figure in a wheelchair stared silently into the distance.

With purpose-filled strides, Joy walked into the room.

"Good morning, Mr. Whittaker. I'm your physical therapist, Miss Nielsen. I believe Dr. Phelps mentioned I was coming."

Silence.

Undeterred, Joy pulled open the drapes and paused momentarily to take in the beauty of the California coast. Huge waves crashed against the beach. The sky was the bluest of blue and not a cloud was in sight. Joy sighed with appreciation.

"Close the drapes." The harshly whispered words were barely audible.

Joy ignored him. No one had mentioned her patient was so young, mid-thirties at most. His hair was dark and needed to be trimmed, his eyes were like that of a caged lion—fierce, and at the same time hopeless and angry. It wasn't difficult to see that this man had once been vital and proud. But he was close to being broken. That was the reason she'd been hired.

"It's a beautiful morning. I was up at dawn and saw the sunrise."

"I said close the drapes." There was no doubting the command a second time. He squinted against the light.

"I'll be bringing in breakfast in just a few minutes, if you'd like to get ready."

His mouth thinned. His two large hands rotated the chair to her side.

"Would you like to eat on the deck?" she asked.

Ignoring her, he leaned forward, grabbed the drapes' pulley, and tugged them closed.

Expelling a frustrated sigh, Joy turned to him, hands on her hips. No, she wouldn't let this man get the better of her. It would be best for them both if he recognized early on that she wasn't like the others.

The room was again dim, with only a minimum of soft light. Dragging a chair to the double glass doors, she unhooked the pulley, opened the drapes, and tossed the cord so that it caught on the valance.

"If you prefer to have the drapes closed, then do it yourself."

His eyes seemed to spit fire at her, but he said nothing. Although his face was covered with at least a day-old beard, Joy could see the nerve twitch in his jaw.

"I'll be back in five minutes with your breakfast," she told him. She closed the door on her way out and paused to inhale a deep breath. Dr. Phelps hadn't understated the situation; Sloan Whittaker could easily be her most difficult case.

The white-haired woman Joy had been introduced to earlier that morning glanced up expectantly when Joy entered the large, modern kitchen.

"How'd it go?" Clara Barnes asked.

"Fine," Joy assured the older woman.

As Clara chuckled, a network of wrinkles broke out across her weathered face. "I've been working for Mr. Whittaker too many years to accept that. Odds are you won't last the week." The cheery tone carried a note of challenge.

"I'll last," Joy said as she poured a glass of juice and set it on the tray.

A brow flicked upward approvingly. "I said to Mr. Whittaker's mother the minute I saw you that you'd be the one to help Mr. Whittaker be his ol' self again."

"He has to help himself. There's only so much you or me or anyone can do," Joy explained, and lifted the breakfast tray from the kitchen counter. She didn't mean to sound rude or discouraging, but it was best to set the other woman straight. She wasn't a miracle worker.

"Mr. Whittaker's mother will be here this afternoon. I know she'll want to talk to you."

"Let me know when she arrives." The swinging kitchen door opened with a push of her shoulder.

Sloan had wheeled across his room. He glanced up when she entered. His look was hard and unwelcoming. "I'm not hungry."

"No, I don't imagine you work up much of an appetite sitting in the chair, do you?"

His eyes narrowed menacingly.

"Well, if you're not hungry, I am." Joy walked onto the verandah and set the tray on the table. She made a small production of lifting the silver-domed food warmer. A thick slice of ham, two fried eggs, and hashbrowns filled the plate. An order of toast was wrapped in a white linen cloth and set to the side. Joy deliberately slid the knife across the ham and lifted the first bite to her mouth. "Delicious," she murmured with closed eyes.

Twice she felt his gaze on her, but she said nothing. When she had finished, she stood and walked to the far side of the long deck. The view was fantastic. Sloan Whittaker must be more than bitter to block this beauty from his life. But then, she knew what it was to be immune to the lovelier things of life.

"I'll take the tray back to the kitchen and send Paul in to help you bathe."

He ignored the comment. "You didn't drink the orange juice." He reached up and lifted it from the tray. There was a suppressed violence about the way he handled the glass—as if he wanted to hurl it at her. "The hired help eat in the kitchen. Remember that."

She shouldn't have smiled. Joy realized that too late. Without warning he emptied the contents of the glass on her uniform. An involuntary gasp escaped as the cold liquid ran down her front. Calmly she set the tray aside. Their eyes clashed and held as she struggled to maintain control of her temper. "I'm sure that was an accident, Mr. Whittaker."

"And I assure you it wasn't." His hard gaze held hers.

"That's unfortunate," Joy returned, and without a backward glance she emptied the remains of her luke-warm coffee in his lap. Not waiting for his reaction, she took the tray. "I'll send Paul in," she announced crisply, and left.

Her hands were trembling when she came into the kitchen. Sloan Whittaker's arrogant pride was definitely going to be a challenge. But he'd learn soon enough. The display of temper pleased her. He hadn't lost the will to fight. That was good; in fact it was very good.

Clara looked up from the sink, her eyes widening as she noted the juice stain.

Joy laid the tray on the counter and smiled wryly. "I had a small accident," she explained.

"Sure you did," Clara muttered with a dry laugh, and lifted the empty plate from the tray. "Well, I'll be. Mr. Whittaker ate his breakfast," she cried in open astonishment. "First time in six months that he's cleaned his plate. You are a miracle, girl. What did you do?"

Joy couldn't put a damper on the woman's enthusiasm. "I'm afraid that's a professional secret, but I promise to let you in on it before I leave."

Smacking her lips, Clara beamed a brilliant smile. "I always said that once Mr. Whittaker started eating again he would walk. He won't ever be strong unless he eats."

"I couldn't agree with you more," Joy replied with a soft sigh. "But after such a large breakfast you should keep his lunch light. Nothing more than broth, but do me a favor and cook his favorite meal tonight."

"I will, miss, that I will."

Pleased with herself, Joy walked down the hall to her room. She understood Sloan's frustration. His story was a familiar one. His car had skidded on a rain-slick road and smashed into a tree. The bare facts had been related by Dr. Phelps. Only when Joy pried further did she learn he had lain in the twisted wreck for hours in an agony beyond description before anyone found him. The initial surgery had saved his life, but in his weakened condition the operation to relieve the pressure on his spinal column had to be delayed. Months passed before he was strong enough to endure the next difficult surgery. Now there were no guarantees. Dr. Phelps told her there was feeling in Sloan Whittaker's legs, but the pain remained intense, and Sloan had decided to accept the wheelchair rather than endure the agony of learning to walk again.

Joy didn't need to be a psychologist to know that a man who resigned himself to a wheelchair had far more reason than pain. Something had happened to make him lose the will to use his legs. She'd know what it was before finishing this assignment.

After six months, the bitterness had built a thick wall around him. It wouldn't be easy to crack that granite fortress, but Joy was determined. She wanted to be the one to help him.

Entering her bedroom, she paused again to take in the expensive decor. The room was decorated in a powder-blue color scheme: the wallpaper contained tiny bluebells, the azure carpet was lush and full. The flowered bedspread matched the walls and drapes. Joy had seen pictures in magazines of rooms like this, but she'd never imagined she would be sleeping in one.

Money could buy a lot of things, and in Sloan's case it had bought him the privilege of choosing life in a de-luxe-model wheelchair.

Opening her closet, she took out and changed into a fresh uniform. She rinsed out the juice stain in the private bath off the bedroom. Once she'd turned off the water, she could hear the angry words coming from the room next to hers. Apparently Sloan wasn't in any better mood.

Paul had seemed the perfect type to deal with Sloan. He was an easygoing, laid-back sort of person who recognized a good thing when he saw one. His job entailed helping Sloan bathe and dress each morning, stimulating his leg muscles with massage, and lifting weights. Paul Weston was a body man, and he had been given free use of the equipment in the room off the kitchen— equipment Sloan had once used.

Now that she was here, she'd see to it that Paul's duties were increased. She was going to need his help. One of the first things she planned to do was get Sloan Whittaker into his swimming pool whether he wanted to go or not. And for a time she was going to need Paul to get him there.

She had finished reading over the medical reports kept by the previous therapists when Clara came to tell her Mrs. Whittaker had arrived.

Glancing at her watch, Joy raised a speculative brow. "She's early."

"Mrs. Whittaker's anxious to meet you," Clara explained unnecessarily.

The older woman, seated on a long white sofa, was the picture of grace and charm. She was delicate and fine-boned, her hair silver and stylish. She glanced up when Joy entered the room. Joy watched as the smile died on her lips.

"Miss Nielsen, I can't tell you how pleased I am to meet you," she said with a frown.

"Is something the matter?"

"It's just that I expected someone older," she admitted.

Joy's back remained straight as she sat across from the older woman. "I'm twenty-eight," she said in a deliberate, casual tone.

"But Dr. Phelps explained that…" She let the rejoinder fade into silence.

Joy's eyes held the older woman's. "I can assure you that I'm perfectly qualified for the job."

"Oh, my dear, I didn't mean to imply otherwise. It's just that there is so much resting on you. I'm at my wit's end with that son of mine. I've all but given up hope."

"To do so would be premature."

"Have you met Sloan?" Her eyes were anxious.

"This morning."

"And?" she inquired gently.

"And he's bitter, resentful, in pain, mad as a wet hen at the world and everyone in it."

"His last therapist stayed only one day."

"I may not look like much, Mrs. Whittaker," Joy strived to assure the woman, "but I can guarantee it's going to take far more than a few angry words for me to pack my bags."

The woman looked relieved. "I can't tell you how pleased my husband and I are that you agreed to take this assignment. Dr. Phelps has nothing but good things to say about you, and quite honestly I don't know how much longer my husband can continue managing the company."

"Pardon?"

Margaret Whittaker lifted the china teacup to her lips and took a sip before continuing. "I'm sorry, dear. I assumed Dr. Phelps told you."

"No, I'm afraid he didn't."

Margaret Whittaker sighed, drawing Joy's rich, brown eyes to the carefully disguised age lines that fanned out from the older woman's eyes and mouth. "My husband came out of retirement after Sloan's accident. I'm afraid the pressure is more than Myron can cope with. We'll be forced to sell the business unless Sloan can assume some of the responsibilities soon."

Joy frowned thoughtfully. "I'd like to talk to your husband when it's convenient. I can't make any promises, Mrs. Whittaker, but I would think involving your son in the business again would be in his own best interest."

"Yes, but…" She looked disconcerted, and Joy noted that her hands shook as she replaced the cup to the saucer. "Sloan's convinced he will never walk again. He's given up."

"Mrs. Whittaker, I think you should realize that a man like your son never gives up. Although he wouldn't let you see it, he's fighting. No matter what he says or does."

The silver-haired woman paused, her hands folded primly on her lap. "You're very wise for your years." She regarded Joy thoughtfully. "I apologize for doubting. I can see that you're exactly what Sloan needs."

"I hope I am," she murmured softly, "for your sake and for Sloan's too."

The soft hum of the wheelchair sounded behind them. Sloan's look was hooded as he moved into the room.

"I wasn't aware you'd arrived, Mother." A sarcastic inflection laced his words.

"I was introducing myself to Miss Nielsen. I hope you appreciate how fortunate we are to get her."

"Oh, yes." His light, mirthless laugh was filled with disdain. "About as lucky as I was the night of the accident."

"Sloan." Margaret Whittaker breathed his name in protest. But his dark head had already turned away, effectively cutting off any further discussion. "You'll have to forgive him." Anger trembled from the sharp edge of his mother's voice.

Joy glanced up, surprised. She would have thought Margaret Whittaker was the type of woman who would never lose her poise. The small display of temper showed Joy how desperate the situation had become for Sloan's mother.

"Don't worry, Mrs. Whittaker. I understand."

An hour later Joy wandered into the kitchen. Clara was busy fixing lunch. "Mr. Whittaker's tray's ready. He has all his meals in his room these days."

"I'll take it to him," Joy volunteered. She wouldn't avoid another confrontation.

She knocked once before swinging open the door. "Good afternoon. I imagine you're anxious for this."

"Then you imagined wrong."

"Listen, Sloan, we can do this easy or we can do this hard. The decision is yours."

"Nothing in my life's come easy," he returned sharply.

Joy's laugh was filled with challenge. "You're sitting in this showroom house with people fighting to wait on you, and you want my sympathy? You're looking at the wrong woman."

He tipped his head to one side and glared at her. "Get out—or I'll throw you out."

"If you want me to leave, you'll have to do it physically. That's pretty tough for a cripple."

His nostrils flared. "Don't be so confident."

"Oh, I'm sure." She tossed the words at him flippantly. "I run two miles every morning, and in addition to being in great physical condition, I could flatten you with one swift punch. Look at you," she returned smoothly. "You've been sitting in the wheelchair for six months. Your muscles are weak and limp. I doubt that you could lift your own weight. But if you want to try, don't let the fact I'm a woman stop you."

A muscle jumped along the side of his jaw. With a violent shove, he propelled the wheelchair onto the verandah. For now, Joy recognized, he was running; he didn't know what else to do. But the time was fast approaching when he'd have nowhere to go.

Before she left, Joy set up the meal tray. A satisfied smile spread to her eyes as she regarded the meager contents. She'd bet hard cash Sloan Whittaker was going to eat his lunch.

When she returned she noted that she'd been right. He'd devoured every bit and would probably look forward to dinner.

"I'm taking you outside now," she told him in a silky, smooth voice.

"No, you aren't."

She didn't argue. Instead she stuck her head out the door and called Paul.

Almost immediately the muscle-bound young man stepped into the room.

"I'd like you to take Mr. Whittaker to the beach."

"No," Sloan shouted.

"Do as I say, Paul," Joy encouraged.

"You so much as touch my chair and you're fired." The way he spoke proved that the threat wasn't an idle one.

"She told me you'd say that."

"Don't do it." The thin line of Sloan's mouth was forbidding.

Uncertain, Paul glanced to Joy for assurance. They'd had a long talk and had reached an understanding where Sloan Whittaker was concerned.

"You can't fire either one of us. You realize that, don't you?" she explained in a bored voice.

"Like hell."

"As I understand the situation, it's your family who hired us, and therefore we work for them. Not you."

Joy could have kissed Paul as he effortlessly pushed Sloan out the bedroom door. Only at rare times had she seen such barely restrained rage. Sloan's face was twisted with it as Paul directed the chair out the back door and onto the sheets of plywood they had laid on the sand to help manipulate his chair.

The day was gorgeous, and a gentle breeze ruffled the soft brown curls about her face.

"Is that all?" Paul looked to her and she nodded, indicating he could leave.

Slipping off her shoes, Joy sat on the soft beach and

burrowed her feet in the warm sand. Lifting her face to the soothing rays of the sun, she closed her eyes, oblivious to the angry man beside her.

After several minutes of contented peace, she lowered her gaze and turned to Sloan. He sat erect and angry, like a prisoner of war. He *was* a prisoner, she mused.

"Tomorrow we'll start with the therapy."

"What therapy?"

She ignored the censure in his voice. "Your first session will be in the morning with me. I'd thought we'd start in the pool. Later in the afternoon Paul will be helping you tone up the muscles in your arms."

His hands grabbed hold of the arms of his chair in a death grip. "What has my mother told you?" He breathed the question.

Joy let the sand drain out of her closed fist, watching it bounce against the beach. "Plenty."

"I refuse to fall into your schemes."

"We'll see about that." She rose lithely and rolled up the pant legs to her knees. The ocean was several hundred yards away, and she ran down to the water's edge. Her big toe popped the tiny bubbles the surf produced. The sun felt soothing and warm, and she basked in the beauty of the afternoon. When she glanced back she saw that Sloan had somehow managed to turn his chair around and with a determined effort had begun to wheel the chair toward the house.

For now she'd let him escape. His pride demanded as much.

Joy didn't see him again until later that evening. She wasn't surprised when Clara proudly exclaimed that Mr. Whittaker had eaten his dinner.

The sky was pink with the setting sun when she un-packed her flute and stood on the verandah. The music flowed from her unbound and free. There'd been a time Joy had to decide between a musical career and the medical profession. Once the decision had been made she had no regrets. She was a good therapist, and she knew it. Cases like these were her best—and for a rea-son. Absently she stopped playing and rubbed her thigh.

"Don't quit."

The words surprised her, and she turned around. Sloan had rolled his chair onto the verandah and was only a few feet from her. Foolishly, Joy hadn't realized their adjacent rooms shared the deck.

Wordlessly she lifted the flute to her lips and played her favorite pieces. Lively jigs followed by the sweet soulful sounds of the classics.

"Where did you ever learn to play like that?" he asked in a whisper.

It was the first time she had heard him speak with-out being angry. "I started as a child. My father was a musician."

His strong profile was illuminated by the darkening sky. Her eyes fell from the powerful face to the chair, and her heart wanted to cry for him. Arrogant, noble, proud—and trapped.

No. Swiftly she jerked her gaze free. The last thing she wanted was to become emotionally attached to a patient. For now Sloan Whittaker needed her, but that would soon change, and he would be free from the chains that bound him. As he became independent to live and love again, he wouldn't want or need her.

Joy had never fooled herself—she wasn't a beauty. Dark hair and equally dark eyes were probably her best features. Her mouth was too small to be sensuous, her nose a little short, her cheekbones too high. The Sloan Whittakers of this world wouldn't be interested in a hundred-pound misfit.

"Good night, Mr. Whittaker," she spoke softly.

"Miss Nielsen." He remained on the deck while Joy turned sharply and entered her room, closing the sliding-glass door after her. Her heart was pounding wildly, and she placed a calming hand over it. What was the matter with her? It would be utter foolishness to become attracted to this man. Two, maybe three months at the most, and she would be leaving.

Joy woke with the alarm early the following morning. The sun hadn't broken the horizon as she pulled open the drapes and stared into the distance. Quickly she dressed in sweatpants and an old gray sweatshirt. She hadn't run on sand before, and wondered about wearing tennis shoes.

The house was quiet and still as she slipped out the kitchen door. A chill ran goose bumps up her arms, and she jiggled them loosely at her sides as she performed the perfunctory warm-up exercises.

An angry gust of wind nearly toppled her along the beach as the surf pounded the shore. Heedless to the blustery force, Joy picked up her heels and ran. The first quarter-mile was always the hardest. Her lungs heaved with the effort. Sand sank in her shoes, making it almost impossible to maintain her usual pace. Soon she discovered it was much easier if she ran close to the water, where the sand was wet.

When she figured she'd gone a mile or more, she turned and headed back. The house was in sight when she spotted a seagull walking along the shore dragging its wing. Slowing her pace, she watched as the poor creature pitifully attempted to fly. After several tries the large bird keeled over, exhausted. Realizing the pain it must be enduring, she stopped running hoping she could find some way to help. When she took a tentative step toward it, the gull struggled to sit upright and flee.

Speaking in soothing tones, she fell to her knees in the sand. "Long John Seagull, what are you doing here?"

The bird hobbled a few steps and fell over.

"It looks like you need a friend," she said softly. "Stay here. I'll be right back." With urgent strides, Joy raced toward the house.

Breathlessly, she stumbled into the kitchen.

"Dear heavens, are you all right?" Clara stood with her back to the sink.

Out of wind, all Joy could do was nod.

"You scared me clean out of my skin."

"Sorry." Joy managed. Not wishing to wake Sloan, she moved quietly down the hall to her room. Only yesterday she'd unpacked several emergency medical supplies. She gathered what she thought she'd need in a large shopping bag, found some tough garden gloves, and hurried out of the room.

"You headed for a fire?" Clara asked as Joy scurried through the kitchen a second time.

"No. I found an injured seagull. I'll be back as soon as I can."

"But, Miss…" Clara called after her.

With the wind beating against her face, Joy returned to her newfound feathered friend.

A half hour later her back ached and her fingers felt swollen and numb with the continued effort of trying to help the bird while not being cut by his powerful beak. As far as she could tell, the wing hadn't been broken, only injured. After carefully applying some antibiotic cream and binding it to his body with a strip of gauze, Joy felt confident the gull would heal.

Long John didn't look pleased when she picked him up and carefully placed him in the sack. A movement out of the corner of her eye captured her attention. She straightened and placed a hand above her eyes to shield them from the glaring sun. She saw that Sloan was on the verandah, watching her. Even from this distance she could see that he was displeased.

"His bark is worse than his bite," Joy informed the bird, who stuck his head out of the sack and looked around. "Don't worry. I know a safe place for you."

Her hair was wet from the shower when Joy came out of her room and closed the door.

"What were you doing this morning?" The question came at her like an arrogant challenge.

"Running," she replied, and rotated to face Sloan.

He glared at her. "I saw you working on something."

"I found an injured seagull. His wing," she added. "Are you ready for breakfast?"

Sloan's gaze hardened and shifted to her eyes. "You like to play the role of the rescuer, don't you? Birds, animals, people. Well, get this straight, little Miss Miracle Worker. I don't need you, and furthermore I don't want you. So get out of my life and stay out."

"My, my, we're in a fine mood this morning," Joy said cheerfully. "How do you want your coffee? Lukewarm and in your lap, or perhaps over your head?"

In return she saw a hint of a smile. "Would it be too much to ask for it in a cup?"

"That depends entirely upon you," she said softly. "Don't go away. I'll be right back."

A few minutes later she brought in his breakfast tray. "You'll be pleased to know I ate in the kitchen," she said, a mocking reminder of his earlier statement.

Again a near-smile came over him.

"I thought that would please you," she said.

On Joy's instructions Clara had prepared a much lighter meal this morning. A warm croissant was served with butter and homemade strawberry jam. She poured his coffee and set the pot to the side.

"I'll be back in a few minutes with Paul."

"I don't need him this morning," Sloan said stiffly.

"Are you already in your suit?"

"My suit?"

"We're going swimming, remember?"

Sloan laughed coldly. "Not likely."

"It'll probably hurt, so prepare yourself."

"Miss Nielsen," he muttered grimly, "there's no way in God's green earth that you're going to get me in that pool, so kindly accept that and save us both a lot of trouble."

"We'll see," she returned lightly.

The grooves around his mouth deepened with defiance. "Has anyone ever told you that you're a stubborn bi—"

"I do find such language unnecessary." She effectively cut him off by pivoting and walking away.

An hour later, dressed in her one-piece turquoise swimsuit, Joy dived into the deep end of the pool. Her slim body sliced through the water. She surfaced and did a couple of laps, enjoying the feel of the cool water against her skin.

When she paused she found Paul standing outside the pool, looking ill at ease and uncertain.

"Whittaker isn't pleased about this."

"I don't imagine he is. If necessary, bring him down here naked. He's coming in this pool one way or another."

"You're sure?"

"Very," she repeated confidently. "Throw him in, if necessary."

"If that's what you want."

Waiting in the shallow end of the pool, Joy could hear Sloan long before seeing him. An angry torrent of abusive words were followed by the sight of a red-faced Paul.

"Thank you, Paul." She smiled at Paul and then glared at Sloan. "The time has come to separate the men from the boys."

Two

A slow smile spread across Joy's face. "Come on in. The water's fine."

"I could hate you for this," Sloan growled.

"I've been hated by better men than you," Joy informed him cheerfully. She didn't doubt Sloan; her job was to channel some of his angry intensity into the exercises. Clara had told her how much Sloan had loved the pool, swimming laps early every morning. He would again if she had anything to do with it. "Put him in the water, Paul."

She turned and dived into the blue depths, feeling slightly guilty that Paul was left to deal with the abusive end of Sloan's temper. By turning away she offered him the privacy to climb into the water without her seeing Paul lift him. His pride had taken enough of a beating lately, and she didn't want to make this any more difficult than it already was.

When she surfaced at the far end of the pool, Joy noticed Paul was standing back from the pool's edge, his look unsure.

"That'll be all." Treading water, she raised one hand and waved, indicating she wanted him to leave.

Sloan was sitting on the steps that led from the shallow end, his look foreboding. "Let's get this over with so I can get out of here."

"All right," she agreed, swimming toward him. Her arms cut through the water as she stroked. Because of the distance separating them she couldn't hear the savagely muttered words, which was probably just as well.

He held himself rigid, and one hand gripped the side of the pool.

"I've always loved to swim," she announced, and playfully dipped her head back into the cool, aquablue water.

Sloan's dark gaze followed her actions.

"When I was a child, my father was the one who taught me," she said. "I loved those days. We could never afford a pool like this, but summer evenings when Dad got off work, my brother, mother, father, and I went swimming in the pool at the park."

Sloan looked bored.

"It seems ironic to me that my father would drown," she continued. Her unflinching gaze met Sloan's. "For a year afterward I couldn't go near a pool. In some obscure way I think I wanted to punish the water for taking my father."

Sloan exhaled a short, angry breath.

Joy's mouth formed a humorless smile. It'd been a mistake to speak of her beloved father. She couldn't understand why she had—especially with Sloan Whittaker.

"For now all I want you to do is familiarize yourself with the pool. Tomorrow I'm going to start you on a series of exercises. I won't try to kid you. These movements are going to hurt, but they're supposed to."

"Do you want me to leap for joy with some pie in the sky dream you have of my walking again?" he said and his eyes snapped fire.

"No, but I'll tell you this. Progress will be slow enough; if you fight me, it'll only take longer."

"In other words, a lot of pain and only a little progress."

"That, Mr. Whittaker, is up to you."

"If it was up to me, you'd get the hell out of my life."

She couldn't hold back her amusement and a smile twitched at the edges of her mouth. "I'll be happy to leave, but when I go that wheelchair will be in the attic."

His fist slammed against the water, spraying it along the pool's tiled edge. "Spare me from optimistic women."

"Starting tomorrow, Paul will be taking you to the whirlpool before our session here. There are several reasons for that, none of which would interest you, I'm sure."

His impassive expression didn't alter.

"You can go for now. I'll see you at lunchtime."

"Don't hurry."

The sun's golden rays bathed his pale features. Joy realized that only a year ago Sloan Whittaker would have been bronze and sun-browned. Once he had been a compellingly handsome man, but pain had chiseled blunted, abrupt lines in his face. His dark eyes seemed to mirror the agony of the past months. Mournful and intense. Joy had seen it before, but never had it affected her like this. In some degree she gave a part of herself to each of her patients. Her greatest fear was that Sloan Whittaker would take her heart. That she couldn't allow.

"I won't hurry," she answered at last. "I'm not any more anxious to see you than you are me."

"At least we understand one another."

Joy called for Paul and swam laps as the young man helped Sloan out of the water. She again offered him privacy to salvage his pride.

Later when she brought in his lunch he regarded her skeptically. When she delivered the tray to the kitchen, Joy was pleased to note that he had again eaten a decent meal.

That night, after the sun set, she picked up her flute and stood on the balcony to play. A gentle breeze stirred her hair and felt like a whispered caress against her smooth skin. The sounds of the Beatles' classic "Yesterday" filled the silence. She loved the song.

Joy paused when she finished, noting that Sloan had rolled onto the balcony and was staring into the still night.

"You can't bring back the past," he said. The words were filled with regret.

"No," she agreed softly, "you can't. Today, this minute. Now, is all that matters."

Again she played the songs she loved best. Michael Bublé and Josh Groban, mellow sounds that produced a tranquil mood within her.

She sighed as she lowered the musical instrument. The day had been full, and she was exhausted. "Is there anything I can get you before I go inside?" she asked softly, not wanting words to destroy the mood.

At first it didn't appear that he'd heard her. He rotated the wheelchair so that he faced her. "How about new legs, Miss Miracle Worker?"

"I'm fresh out of those," she replied evenly. "I'm afraid you'll have to make do with the ones you've got."

Joy heard him exhale and knew her comment hadn't pleased him. After a moment, she turned away. "Good night, Mr. Whittaker."

He didn't reply, and Joy guessed that he wasn't wishing her anything good.

The next week was miserable, an unceasing confrontation of wills. Sloan fought her every step of the way. Several times it was all she could do not to retaliate out of her own frustration.

She hadn't minced words when she told him the exercises were going to cause him pain, although he never indicated that she was hurting him. He worked with her because he had no choice, and although he didn't resist her as she manipulated his legs, he didn't aid her, either. Some mornings after their session Joy noticed how ashen his face was as he struggled to disguise the pain. The lines of strain were deeply etched about his mouth. He rarely spoke to her, seeming to prefer sullen silence to open confrontation. Apparently he'd learned early that the biting, sarcastic comments rolled off her as easily as the pool water, that she could give as well as she took. In some ways a mutual respect was beginning to blossom, but it didn't lessen the intense dislike he felt for her or the frustration she experienced knowing she wasn't reaching him or gaining his trust. Although getting him in the pool and exercising his legs was good, she'd failed in the most important area.

Sloan came onto the balcony at night as if waiting

for her music. Rarely did he comment, silently wheeling back into his room when she'd finished.

On Saturday Joy rose and dressed at the usual time. Her heart felt weighted, and she wasn't sure why. The crisp morning air felt cool as she slipped out the back door. First she checked Long John, the seagull she'd found and was nursing. He didn't like the confines of the fenced portion of the yard, but like Sloan he was trapped and unable to flee. The bird squawked and hobbled to the side of the yard when she opened the gate. Several times he had lashed out at her hand, once drawing blood. He didn't trust her, again like Sloan.

For six days she had worked with them both and had failed to earn more than a grudging respect. At least the bird wanted his freedom. But Sloan had no will to walk or reenter the mainstream of life. What would make a man content to sit in a chair? Perhaps this was all another battle of their wills, in which he was determined to prove he didn't need her.

Long John squawked, and Joy focused her attention on the bird. "Good morning, fellow," she whispered. "Are you glad to see me?"

The gull stared at her blankly.

"Don't worry, I'm not any more popular with the master, either." She yearned to reach out and comfort her winged friend. She wanted his trust, as she wanted Sloan's, at least enough so that the bird would allow her close enough to touch him. But he wasn't confident enough yet. Moving slowly, she placed a bowl of cut-up fish and high-protein gruel on the ground and filled his bowl with fresh water. On her knees, she held herself motionless for several moments, hoping he would be hungry enough to overcome his natural reserve. It didn't take her long to realize that the bird wouldn't eat as long as she remained in the yard.

Releasing the latch, Joy let herself out of the gate and locked it. For a time she stayed and watched, but Long John defiantly remained where he was. The pungent scent of the ocean greeted her as she walked along the shore. A gentle mist wet her face and hair, and she ran a hand along both sides of her cheeks. Tonight she would go out, do something special. She needed a few hours of escape. An evening away would help her perspective.

As she turned and headed back for the house, a solitary figure on the balcony caught her attention. She hesitated, hands thrust deep into jeans pockets. It seemed Sloan Whittaker was watching her. Maybe he was hoping she'd leave and never return.

The morning followed its usual routine. Joy brought him his breakfast.

"Good morning," she greeted with a smile. "You were up bright and early this morning."

His response was muffled and gruff.

"Long John seemed to be in an identical mood when I brought him his meal."

"Long John what?"

"The seagull," she explained as she set the tray on the desk.

"Good grief, don't tell me you've still got that poor creature."

"He's improving, which is more than I can say…" She let the rest of what she was going to say fade when Clara appeared in the doorway.

"Mr. Whittaker's here to see you."

"Bring him in, Clara," Sloan instructed briskly.

The older woman shifted from one foot to the other. "Mr. Whittaker said he wanted to talk to Miss Nielsen."

Sloan's gaze swiveled to Joy for a long, considering look. "What could my father possibly have to say to Miss Nielsen?" he demanded.

"I'll take notes, if you'd like," Joy volunteered.

"Don't bother."

Joy felt his gaze burning into her shoulder blades as she stepped out of the room.

Even Clara seemed puzzled that the senior Whittaker sought out Joy. The question was in the older woman's eyes as Joy took a left turn into the living room.

"Miss Nielsen." Myron Whittaker stood and extended his hand. He was tall and as large as Margaret Whittaker was petite. His shoulders were as broad as a wrestler's, his hair white and receding from a wide forehead. Joy's hand met his and was clasped firmly.

"My wife mentioned that you would like to speak to me."

"As a matter of fact, yes. I'm glad you've come." She sat in the large modern chair across from the distinguished-looking man. It wasn't hard to tell where Sloan got his compelling features. Father and son were a lot alike.

"It's only fair to tell you how pleased my wife and I are that you've agreed to take on Sloan's case."

"I think I'm the lucky one. I've never had the pleasure of working in such elegant surroundings."

"Yes, well…" The older man cleared his throat. "We want you to know we appreciate what you've done."

"I haven't done anything yet," Joy admitted wryly. "But part of your son's recovery will depend on you."

"Anything." He rubbed a hand across his face, his eyes tired.

"Part of Sloan's therapy will be mental as well as physical. He's got to be brought back into life, given responsibilities." She hesitated and leaned forward slightly so that her elbows rested on her knees. "Your wife mentioned that you've assumed Sloan's job in the company since the accident. In some ways this is good, but the time has come for you to return those duties to your son."

"How do you mean?"

"Decision-making, paperwork. These are things that can be done from the house. At least come to Sloan when a decision needs to be made. Part of the problem with your son is that he feels useless. Prove to him he's needed."

"He is," Myron returned forcefully.

"Don't overpower him," she suggested. "Start with updates and reports that will keep him in tune with what's happening. Then gradually lead into the other matters. I don't know that much about your business, but I'm sure you'll know how to approach this." Dr. Phelps had told her that the Whittakers owned a ski equipment company. Joy had never skied, but from Sloan's home and lifestyle it was easy to see the business had been a profitable one.

Myron Whittaker looked down, but not before his dark eyes conveyed the toll of the last months. "I'm not sure of anything anymore."

"Your son's going to be fine, Mr. Whittaker." She leaned forward and gave the elder Whittaker's clenched fist a reassuring pat. "He's strong-willed and determined."

Tears glistened in the proud man's gaze. He closed his eyes and gripped her hand with his own.

"My, my, isn't this a touching scene." Sloan wheeled into the room. "My physical therapist? Honestly, Father, I think you're lowering your standards unnecessarily."

Myron Whittaker sprang to his feet, his face twisted with rage. "You will apologize for that remark."

Joy's gaze swiveled from father to son. Sloan's hands gripped the wheels of his chair until his knuckles were white. His mouth was slanted and scornful.

"Wheelchair or no wheelchair, I won't have a son of mine make that kind of suggestion."

"Mr. Whittaker, please." Joy could feel the hot color explode in her face. "This isn't necessary."

"It most certainly is," he barked.

How often Joy had heard that same tone of voice. Father and son shared more than looks.

Sloan's hard gaze hadn't relented. "I regret the implication," he managed between clenched teeth.

"If you'll excuse me." Joy hurriedly left the room. Her heart felt as if she'd completed a marathon as she let herself into her quarters. Her hands shook as she slipped into the swimsuit. The decision this morning to get out, go to a movie, anything, had been a good one. Sloan Whittaker was getting to her. Keeping a cool head with this man was essential to success.

When she slipped out of her room and into the hall, she could hear the angry exchange between Sloan and his father. Joy wanted to shout at them both. Arguing would solve nothing. She bit into her bottom lip tightly and moved outside.

Paul was lounging in a chair by the pool when she came out. "Morning," he said. "How's it going?"

Joy rolled her eyes expressively, and Paul laughed. "He's really something, isn't he?"

"You can say that." Her relationship with the other staff members had relaxed considerably. Almost everyone called her Joy. Since she and Paul worked directly with Sloan she felt a certain camaraderie with him, although they rarely had time to talk for more than a few minutes at a time. "How are the afternoon sessions coming?"

Paul shrugged. "Better, I guess. At least he's stopped yelling."

"In other words, he submits, and that's about it."

Paul nodded.

"The good news is that when he yells we know he's involved." Absently, Joy slipped off her sandal and dipped her foot in the water. "This lackadaisical attitude concerns me."

"He's all but given up."

"I refuse to accept that," Joy murmured. "A man like Sloan Whittaker isn't a quitter. I think he's afraid to show he cares simply because he cares so much." Joy felt Paul's gaze and glanced up.

"I think you're right."

Joy was glad Paul agreed. "I'm betting on it."

Clara ambled toward them, wiping her hands on the ever present apron. "Mr. Whittaker told me to say he's ready for you now."

"I'll be right there." Paul sat up and stretched his arms high above his blond head. "See you in a few minutes."

"I'll be ready." Joy waited until he was out of view before dropping the terry-cloth cover and stepping into the water. It gently lapped against her waist. Lowering her lashes, she lay back, paddling her hands at her side to keep afloat. Even with her ears in the water she heard the approach of Sloan's chair. But she remained with her back to him until she was certain Sloan was in the water.

As she straightened, their eyes met and clashed across the distance of the pool. Her attention was diverted by Paul, who waved.

"See you later, Joy."

"Joy?" Sloan spit out the word distastefully. "Your name is Joy?"

She wouldn't rise to the barbed comment.

"Talk about irony." His laugh lacked warmth. "A torturer named Joy. It's almost hysterical."

Little he could say or do would intimidate her. She'd done verbal battle with him far too often to fall prey to another needless confrontation.

"Are you ready?"

"No." He held himself stiffly against the side of the pool. One elbow was elevated onto the tile rim, supporting his weight.

Undeterred, Joy swam to his side. Viciously he lunged for her, his fingers gripping hold of her upper arm.

She attempted to shrug free, but his grasp was surprisingly strong.

"I hope it hurts," he said cruelly.

"Let go."

"What do you know of pain?" he sneered. "How can you possibly know what it is to lie in a hospital and pray to God you'll die just so the agony stops?"

With her jaw clenched, Joy tried to pry his fingers loose. Already she could imagine a bruise forming.

Sloan tightened his grip. "What could you know of pitying looks and lost dreams?"

She struggled, and demanded a second time, "Let me go."

"Does it hurt? Good, it's supposed to." His eyes darkened with emotion. "Be objective about it. Isn't that what you said to me? Your turn, Miss Miracle Worker."

Boldly she met his gaze, and to her horror tears welled, blurring her vision. His hand relaxed, setting her free. As she pulled away she heard him utter a frustrated groan. Twisting her upper torso, she dived under the surface. The water felt cool against the flushed skin of her face. When she thought her lungs would burst, she surfaced and found herself at the far end of the pool. An angry bruise had turned her skin black-and-blue. Her arm throbbed.

"Paul," Sloan shouted. The muscle-bound man appeared almost immediately. "Get me out of here," he muttered thickly.

Paul glanced at Joy, who nodded and turned her back to the pair. Sloan had asked her what did she know about pain? It was funny enough to make her want to laugh.

Purposely she avoided Sloan at lunchtime. Clara took his meal in to him and returned with a worried frown. "Didn't so much as touch it. His favorite soup, mind you."

Alone at the kitchen table, Joy released a broken sigh.

"And you're no better," Clara accused. "You've done nothing more than rearrange the food on your plate. What's going on around here?"

"I guess it's an off day. Everyone's entitled to those now and then."

"Off day?" Clara clucked. "The air around here feels like an electrical storm passed through. And Mr. Whittaker and his son fighting? I don't know when that's happened." She wiped a hand across her brow, and her face narrowed. "And you look like you've lost your best friend."

Joy gave the older woman a weak smile. "You're right," she said with determination. "I need a change of pace. Don't fix dinner for me tonight. I'm going out."

"I'd say it's about time." Clara nodded approvingly. "Pretty young thing like you should be out having fun every night."

Joy laughed. Young she couldn't deny, but pretty was something else again.

She wouldn't be able to avoid Sloan forever, but she gladly relinquished her duties that afternoon. Without explanation, Paul seemed to know she needed the break. When she took part of the day off to go shopping, no one questioned her. At the time she was hired, the Whittakers had told her to set her own hours.

Although Joy browsed around several shops, she didn't buy anything. It felt good to get away, if only for a few hours. She checked the newspaper and drank coffee in a small café. A movie she wanted to see was playing, and Joy decided to take one in later.

Clara was busy in the kitchen peeling apples when Joy returned.

"Did you enjoy yourself?"

"It was nice," Joy admitted, and handed the woman one long-stemmed rose. "This is for you."

"Joy." She took the flower and sniffed it appreciatively. "What are you doing buying me flowers?"

"Well, actually, I didn't buy it," Joy admitted grudgingly. "I picked it from the bush outside."

Clara laughed and gave her a spontaneous hug. "I knew the minute I saw you what a dear girl you are."

Joy sat on the countertop, dangling her feet over the edge and talking to Clara for several minutes. She had the impression Clara wouldn't allow many the privilege of invading her home territory so freely. She stayed in the kitchen until dinner was almost ready.

Luxuriating in a bubble bath, she hoped to wash away some of the unpleasantness of the day. A smile came to her. Could one ever wash away hurts and pains? Dear heavens, she was becoming philosophical.

The sky was painted a bold shade of pink, and Joy paused to admire the vibrant color as she slipped a full-length silk robe on and tied the sash.

How could the night be so beautiful when the day had been so ugly? Joy mused. Without thought, she wandered onto the balcony. The palms of her hands rested against the painted rail.

"Lovely, isn't it?"

Joy froze.

"Sometimes when I sit here and stare into the sunset, I can almost forget." The whispered words were spoken so softly that Joy had to strain to hear.

The sound of Sloan's chair told her he was coming toward her. She didn't move.

A finger traced the pattern of the ugly bruise on her arm. "Did I do that?"

"Yes," she answered without turning.

"Dear sweet heaven," he muttered, his voice suddenly thick. "You must hate me."

"No," she replied softly, and turned her face to him. "I don't."

Again he ran his index finger along the bruise. His touch was gentle, almost a caress, as if he wanted to blot out the pain he had caused.

"I'm going out for a while tonight," she announced.

He dropped his hand. "A date?"

"No." She shook her head. "Just a movie. I'm going alone."

His hands rolled the chair back a couple of feet, then swiveled it around, presenting her a view of his back. "Have a good time, Joy."

A frown creased her brow. She found it hard to understand this man. "Thank you."

He hesitated a second before wheeling into his room.

Joy watched him go. Sloan regretted the incident that morning with his father and later with her in the pool. He was a man driven to the limits of his endurance. Mentally, Joy pictured him standing at a crossroads. He would either choose life or a living death. Unconsciously she brushed the hair off her forehead as a smile came to her. Interestingly, she had viewed him standing, and not in a wheelchair. Why such a nonsensical thing should lighten her spirits she didn't know.

Joy was whistling on her way out the front door. She hadn't been hungry and had skipped dinner. All of a sudden she felt ravenous. There wasn't time to stop and get something before the movie, so she decided to wait until after.

The show was a light comedy that made her laugh, and heaven knew she needed a reason to smile.

On the way down the coast highway, Joy pulled off at a fast-food restaurant. She hadn't paid much attention to the kind of food until she stepped out of the car. Fish. The tantalizing aroma of deep-fried fish and crisp French fries filled the air.

Joy read over the menu and absently wondered if Sloan knew about this place. He would have, of course, since it was only a few miles from the house. But how long had it been since he'd tasted something like this?

"Can I help you?" An eager-faced youth leaned halfway out the order window.

"Yes." Joy's eyes didn't leave the menu that was painted in bold-faced letters over the grill. "I'd like a double order of fish-and-chips. And a Pepsi."

"Will that be all?"

"No, make that two orders," she added impulsively.

"To go?"

"Pardon?" Joy's puzzled gaze found the girl's.

"Do you want to eat here or take out?" she asked in an impatient breath.

"Take out."

Even as she paid for the meal, Joy wondered what had possessed her to do anything so foolish. No use lying to herself—she'd bought the second fish order for Sloan.

The lights to his room weren't visible from the front of the house. Joy carried the grease-stained white sack into her bedroom and immediately went out onto the balcony.

His drapes were open, but the room was dark. He often sat alone with the lights off. Sometimes she thought he preferred it like that. He could hide in the shadows, but not in the light.

Tentatively she knocked on the sliding-glass door and opened it just a crack.

Silence.

"Are you awake?" She whispered the question, not wishing to disturb him if he happened to be asleep. Her eyes adjusted to the dim interior and searched the room. He sat in the corner, his chin propped up by his fist.

"How was the movie?"

"Great."

His chuckle was filled with quiet humor. "Why are we whispering?"

"I don't know." She slid open the door. "I didn't have dinner, so I stopped off at a fish-and-chips place up the road."

"Not Mobey Jake's?"

"I didn't notice the name, but it had a neon whale flashing off and on."

"That's the one. The food's terrific."

"I brought you an order back too."

An uncomfortable pause followed her announcement. "Isn't that fraternizing with the enemy?"

"Could be," she agreed with a secret smile. "But my mother once told me I'd catch a lot more flies with honey than vinegar. But then, my mother never met you."

Three

A contented feeling moved through Joy as she sat up in bed and stretched. Linking her fingers high above her head, she arched her back and released a long, drawn-out yawn.

She couldn't remember an evening she enjoyed more than the one spent with Sloan. He had chuckled when she relayed the movie plot and the antics of the characters. It was the first time Joy had heard the sound of his laughter. The feeling it had produced was warm and pleasant. She had seen him grit his teeth and muffle groans as she manipulated his legs, but never his amusement. How much more she preferred dark eyes that crinkled with laugh lines to ones that struggled to disguise pain.

She dressed in jeans and a loose-fitting T-shirt. Some of the fish fillets had been left over, and she wanted to see if Long John would eat out of her hand. Great strides seemed to have been made with Sloan, and she was eager to see if the injured gull was willing to accept her as his friend.

"Good morning, L.J.," she greeted as she let herself into the yard. The gate latched behind her as she stepped to the food bowl and bent down extending her hand. "See what I've got here? Fish," she answered her own question in reassuring tones. "And I happen to know gulls are particularly fond of fish. I'm not so sure about fried fish, but I think you ought to give it a try."

With an ambling gait that reminded her of Clara Barnes, the bird took a step in her direction.

"Obviously you've got keen eyesight," Joy encouraged her feathered friend.

When the bird was only a few inches away, she edged closer, wanting him to take the fish from her. Almost immediately Joy realized her mistake. The razor-sharp beak sliced into the back of her hand instead of the food. Blood gushed from the open cut. Inhaling a sharp breath, Joy dropped the fish and jerked upright. In a protective movement she held her hand to her body and hurried out the gate. Blood seemed to be everywhere. The gull had apparently cut a vein. The pain was sharp as she quickly stepped back into the house. Clara wasn't in the kitchen. Joy was grateful she didn't have to make unnecessary explanations. From the flow of blood, it looked as if she might need a suture or two.

Intent on escaping unseen into her bedroom, Joy nearly stumbled over Sloan, who was wheeling down the wide hallway.

"Joy, why the rush?"

"I'm sorry," she mumbled, pressing her hand to her shirt. "I didn't mean to startle you."

"You're hurt."

Sloan's pallor became sickly. He swallowed and narrowed his gaze on her hand.

"I'm fine."

"You need a doctor."

"What I need is to see how deep this is."

Stepping into her room, she moved directly to the bathroom sink and held her cut hand under a slow faucet. In the background she could hear Sloan yelling for Clara. Within moments the red-faced cook came rushing into the room.

"I got cut. It's no major catastrophe. Darn, it looks like it may need to be sewn up." Angry at herself for her own stupidity, Joy felt like stamping her foot. Didn't she know better than to rush something as delicate as trust? As an injured bird, she would have probably reacted the same way.

"I'll get Paul to drive you to urgent care." With agitated, worried movements, Clara rushed out of the room.

The fuss everyone was making didn't lessen Joy's feelings of self-reproach. A small towel was wrapped around her fist and held protectively against her stomach. Joy grabbed her purse off the dresser, fumbled with the clasp, and took out her car keys.

Sloan was gone, but she could hear him speaking to someone on the phone. His voice was angry and urgent. Footsteps could be heard rushing up the stairs.

"What happened?" Paul directed the question to Joy.

"I got cut. It's my own stupid fault. But it looks like I'm going to need a few stitches. A vein's been sliced."

A pale Sloan rolled his chair from his room. "Dr. Phelps is on his way."

"Dr. Phelps," Joy repeated, aghast. "You didn't call him, did you?" The whole situation was quickly becoming ridiculous. "You don't ask a noted surgeon to make a house call for a few stitches," she shouted sharply.

"Paul," Sloan shouted, no less calm, "get her into my room."

With a supportive hand under her elbow, Paul led her into Sloan's quarters.

"This is ridiculous," she hissed under her breath.

Sloan wheeled in after her. "Sit her in my chair."

"I might get blood on it," she protested.

"For once, just once," Sloan ground out between clenched teeth, "will you do as I ask?"

Pinching her mouth tightly shut, Joy plopped down on the expensive leather recliner. Paul hovered over her and Sloan rolled his chair back and forth across the room.

"For heaven's sake, you two look like you expect me to keel over dead any minute." Her wit didn't please Sloan, who tossed her a fiery glare. "Look at you." She directed her words to Sloan. "You're absolutely pale. Do you mean to tell me that after everything you've gone through you can't stand the sight of blood?"

"Shut up, Nielsen." The authority in his voice brooked no resistance.

"Well, for heaven's sake, would you stop doing that. You're making me nervous."

"Doing what?"

"That." She pointed her finger at his chair. "You've got to be the only man in the world who paces in a wheelchair."

Paul chuckled, and she tipped her head back and rolled her eyes expressively. "How could you have phoned Dr. Phelps?" she asked, and groaned with embarrassment.

"You've lost a lot of blood." His voice pounded like thunder around the room.

"I'm fine," she nearly shouted, and bounded to her feet, stalking to the far side of the room. Her angry glare met Sloan's as they stared at one another, the distance of the room separating them.

"How'd it happen?" Paul inserted, apparently in an attempt to cool tempers.

"It was my own stupid fault." She watched as Sloan's hands tightened around the arms of his chair in a strangling hold. "I tried to get L.J. to eat out of my hand…"

"L.J.?" Sloan interrupted.

"The seagull I found."

"She named him Long John," Paul explained with a trace of humor. "Rather appropriate, I thought."

"I didn't ask what you thought." Sloan's mouth twisted sarcastically. "I want that bird destroyed."

"No." Joy's voice trembled with rage. "You can't kill something because it was protecting itself. I told you, the whole thing was my fault."

"I don't want the seagull around," Sloan shouted.

"Then I'll find someplace else."

The air between them was as cold as an arctic blast.

Paul moved to the center of the room. "Interestingly enough, I happened to read the other day that there aren't such things as seagulls. Kittiwakes, black-backed gulls, and herring gulls, but technically there are no seagulls."

Speechless, Joy stared blankly at her muscular friend until she recognized that he was placing himself between her and Sloan, granting them each the space to cool their tempers.

Clara could be heard fussing in the hall. "This way, Dr. Phelps."

Everyone's attention was centered on the door as the tall, dark-haired doctor entered the room.

"Dr. Phelps," Joy began, "I'm so embarrassed."

"Anyone that lets a stupid bird slash their hand in two deserves to be," Sloan inserted dryly.

Joy darted him a warning glance.

"Now that I'm here, I might as well have a look." Professional and calm, Dr. Phelps set his bag on the desk and hung his light coat over the back of the chair.

"And since you're here, you might as well check Mr. Whittaker," Joy suggested. "I'm sure he's due for an enema or something."

The good doctor chuckled as he removed the towel from her hand. A fresh supply of blood oozed from the laceration as he pried it gently with his fingers. "Nothing a couple of stitches won't cure," he murmured.

"I have most of the supplies you'll need in my room," she told him, and stood, leading the way.

The necessary equipment was laid out across the small tabletop as Dr. Phelps injected the topical anesthetic. Nonplussed, Joy watched him work. Having seen this so many times in the past, it amazed her how unaffected she could remain when it was her own hand.

The dull ache continued after he bandaged the hand in white gauze.

"How's it going with Sloan?" he asked as he worked. They'd only talked briefly one time since she'd taken over the assignment.

"I'm not sure," she answered honestly. "I'm beginning to think some progress is being made, but it's too soon to tell."

"I don't know of anyone else who could reach him."

His compassionate gray eyes searched hers. "Have you told him yet?"

"No, but he'll see soon enough."

The dark head bobbed in agreement. "If you have any problems, don't hesitate to call me."

"I won't."

"And listen, it might not be a bad idea to keep this hand out of the water for a few days."

She laughed softly. "Sloan will love that."

"Speaking of the man, I'll check him, since I'm here." He discarded the items he'd used and closed his bag. "I'll give you a call later in the week."

"Thank you, Doctor."

"I'm glad to finally be in your debt. You're the one who continues to save me." The good-natured smile left him as he noted her hand. "Go ahead and remove those sutures yourself in a week or so. Use your own judgment."

Dr. Phelps left a few moments later and Joy lay back against her pillow, intent on resting her eyes for a bit. Before she was aware of it, it was afternoon and she'd been asleep for hours.

A blanket had been laid over her, and she recognized it as one from Sloan's room. How had he gotten in? The door to his quarters had been widened to accommodate the wheelchair, but hers hadn't. A gentle breeze ruffled the closed drapes, and she realized the sliding-glass door had been left open.

What a puzzling man Sloan Whittaker was. Rubbing the sleep from her eyes, Joy sat up and swung her short legs off the mattress. Already, half the day had been wasted.

Someone knocked softly on her bedroom door.

"Come in," Joy called.

Clara opened the door and came in carrying a large tray. "I thought you might like something to eat."

"But you didn't need to bring it to me," Joy protested. "I'm not incapacitated, you know."

"Mr. Whittaker insisted that you take the rest of the day off. You rest and I'll bring in your meals."

"But, Clara, that's ridiculous."

"Mr. Whittaker was real worried about you. I can't remember a time he acted like this."

Leaning against the pillows the cook had fluffed up against the headboard, Joy laughed. "For all his bark, our Mr. Whittaker is a marshmallow. Did you see how pale he got when he saw the blood on my shirt? For a minute I was afraid he was going to pass out."

Clara's look was thoughtful. "Mr. Whittaker doesn't like the sight of blood. At least not since the accident."

The humor drained out of Joy's eyes. She was being callous. Of course seeing all that blood had bothered him, especially since he'd lain helplessly in a pool of his own.

The lack of sensitivity robbed Joy of her appetite. She made a token attempt to eat so as not to arouse Clara's suspicions and tucked a few items inside a napkin to give L.J.

After changing into a clean blouse for the third time that day, Joy carried the half-empty tray into the kitchen. "Thanks, Clara. Lunch was delicious."

"Since you're up, I think Mr. Whittaker would like to talk to you. He's in his room."

"Sure," she agreed, and swallowed tightly.

With the blanket clenched to her breast, Joy tapped

lightly on Sloan's door and waited for his answer before entering.

They eyed one another warily. "You wanted to see me?"

"Not particularly," Sloan snapped.

Shrugging off his gruff welcome, she laid the blanket at the foot of the bed. "I'll see you later. By the way…" She hesitated, her back to him. "Thank you for putting the blanket over me."

"I didn't."

Joy frowned curiously. He was lying, and she didn't know why. Later, as she walked along the windswept shore, Joy guessed that he didn't want her to know he was concerned.

Paul saw her and waved as she climbed atop a sand dune. Joy raised her good hand and returned the gesture. It was another gorgeous April afternoon. How quickly she was coming to love this beach, this house, this… Her mind refused to form "man." So much of herself was tied up with this case: her skill, her ego, the almost desperate desire to help lift him from the mire of self-pity. The dangers were clear, but as long as she was aware and protected herself, she would be safe.

With long-legged strides, Paul raced to her, feet kicking up sand as he ran.

"How do you feel?" she queried.

"Great."

"Feel up to another confrontation with the master?" she asked in a teasing voice.

"Naw, it's much more fun watching you two argue. But since you're a bit under the weather, what would you like?"

"You've still got that plywood around, haven't you?
Let's get him down here on the beach."

"He isn't going to like it," Paul warned.

"Heavens, so what's new? Sloan Whittaker doesn't
like anything."

Together they laid down the thick boards of wood.
Paul insisted on wheeling Sloan down, and Joy didn't
argue. She didn't feel like arguing with Sloan, not today.
Her hand throbbed; foolishly she'd refused anything
for pain when Dr. Phelps asked. Sitting and soaking
up the sun sounded far more appealing than a verbal
battle with Sloan.

"I suppose this was your idea, Nielsen," Sloan
ground out as Paul pushed the chair down the wooden
planks.

She pretended the wind had blown the words away
by cupping a hand over her ear.

"You heard me."

"Could be."

Paul glanced from one to the other and chuckled.
"He's all yours. Let me know when you need me."

"Thanks, Paul." She watched as her friend headed
back to the house.

"You enjoy doing this, don't you?"

"Doing what?"

"This kind of garbage!" He hurled the words at her
savagely, as if venting his anger would lessen his confusion. "You seem to have the mistaken impression that
once thrust into the beauty of nature I'll forget all my
troubles and thank God for the gift of life."

"No." She sat in the sand beside him, her bare toes
burrowing under the granules. "I thought a little sun
might add color to your face."

"You're lying."

"If you say so," she agreed pleasantly, tilting her face upward and coveting the golden rays. "You know, Whittaker, if you didn't work so hard at disliking this, you could come to enjoy it."

"Never."

"Want me to bury your feet in the sand?"

"No," he hissed.

"Then be quiet. You're destroying my peace."

"Good. I haven't had a peaceful moment from the day you arrived."

She ignored him, pretending not to hear his movements.

"Nielsen."

Opening her eyes, she quirked her head inquiringly. Sloan dumped his sweater over her head. "That's what I think of your loony ideas."

"For a cripple, you're mighty brave."

"And you're a sad excuse for a woman. Don't you wear anything but pants? What's the matter, are you afraid to let a man see your legs?"

"Legs," she cried dramatically. "You want legs, I'll give you legs." Rolling to her feet, she pulled up her pants to her knees and pranced around like a restless filly. The sight of Paul escorting a tall blonde halted Joy in midstride. Stopping completely, her hands fell lifelessly to her side and she took a huge breath. "It looks like you've got company."

"Company?" Sloan barked. "I don't want to see anyone. Send them away."

"It's too late for that." Joy studied the other woman. She would have killed for a figure like this blonde's.

Tall. Willowy. Every brick stacked in the right place. And a face that would stop traffic.

As the two drew closer, the woman's pace increased. "Oh, my darling, Sloan. No one told me. Oh, Sloan." She fell to her knees and buried her perfectly shaped head in his lap. The delicate shoulders shook with sobs.

Sloan's hand lifted, hesitated, then finally patted the blonde's back.

Joy took a step in retreat, not wishing to be a witness to this scene. Sloan's eyes found Joy's and cast her an unmistakable look of appeal.

"I'll leave you two alone."

"No," Sloan barked, silently demanding that she stay.

"Maybe you'd enjoy some iced tea? I'll be back in a jiffy."

"Nielsen?" Sloan's low voice threatened.

"I'll be right back." Wickedly she fluttered her long lashes at him.

Paul carried a lounge chair for her while Joy managed the tray with two tall glasses of fresh iced tea each with a slice of lemon attached to the side.

Apparently the blonde had composed herself. Dabbing her eyes with a waded tissue, she stood at Sloan's side, her blue eyes filled with compassion and sweetness.

"I'm afraid Chantelle can't stay," Sloan announced, and his gaze narrowed menacingly on Joy. "Paul, would you kindly escort her to her car?"

In true gentlemanly fashion, Paul placed his arm around the blonde's shoulders and whispered comforting words to her as he walked her toward the house.

"Nielsen, you do that to me again and I'll—"

"Do what?" she inquired innocently.

His hand sliced the air dramatically. "Couldn't you have done something? I thought you were my self- appointed rescuer. Well, rescue me! The minute I really need you—off you fly with the excuse of getting iced tea."

"What in the Sam Hill did you expect me to do?"

"I don't know. That's your job, isn't it?"

"No," she snapped back, then started to laugh.

"What's so funny?" he demanded.

"You! Think about it. It's a sad commentary on your life when you want me to rescue you from the arms of a beautiful woman."

A poor facsimile of a smile came and went. "Couldn't you see she was throwing herself all over me, oozing pity?"

"Women like to cry," she explained patiently, and sat down in the sand cross-legged. She took a tall glass and handed him the other. "It gives us a reason to appear feminine."

"And Chantelle knows how good she looks with tears clinging to her lashes. Her big, blue eyes staring into mine."

"You sound like you've made lots of women cry."

"Hundreds," he returned sarcastically.

"I wouldn't doubt it." Joy laughed lightly.

"What about you?"

"I don't know of any women who've cried over me," she teased, the wind blowing her soft brown curls across her high cheekbones.

"You know what I mean."

Staring in her tea, she shrugged lightly. "Only one."

"Who?"

Joy swallowed around the tight lump that formed in her throat. "My father."

They were silent after that.

"Tell me about your family," Sloan said after a long time.

"My father was a senior high music teacher and band director, my mother was a stay-at-home mom. There's only my brother. He's two years older, lives in Santa Barbara, has a wife and two children."

"Is he as gutsy as you?"

"Doug? Yes, only in a different way. He's a policeman."

"You said your father drowned." The words were issued softly. His voice inflection made it a question.

Arms wrapped around her knees, she stared out at the waves gently lapping the shore. "He died in Mexico, three summers ago. Mom and Dad flew down to celebrate their anniversary. Two little boys, about eight and ten, tourists from Texas, got trapped in the undertow." She paused, reliving the horror of that summer again. "Dad managed to save one. He died with his arms around the ten-year-old. My mother looked on from the beach helpless." Even blandly stating the facts brought tears to her eyes, and she touched her forehead to her knee, not wishing him to witness her distress. Once her breathing had returned to normal, she lifted her head. "My father was a wonderful man."

"I already knew that," Sloan murmured, and, reaching out a hand, lightly stroked her hair. His touch was gentle. Joy hadn't expected his comfort and expelled a whispering sigh at the warm sensation that cascaded over her from the touch of his hand to her head.

"What about you?" she asked to purposely change the subject.

"There's only me. I think my parents wanted a larger family, but mother had a difficult pregnancy and the doctors advised her not to get pregnant a second time."

"Were you always…"

"Rich?" he finished for her.

"That's not the word I would have used, but yes."

"The company's been in the family for three generations. This summer house is a new acquisition."

"This is your summer home?" Her gaze flew over her shoulder to the magnificent structure behind her. The idea that it was a summer home shocked her. This was the sort of place anyone would dream about living in all year long.

"Usually I live in a condo in Palm Springs, but I have apartments in Switzerland and New York. Had," he corrected on a bitter note.

Her mouth dropped open and she widened her eyes and swallowed. "Oh."

"For heaven's sake, don't go all goo-goo-eyed on me."

Joy forced her mouth closed.

"Actually, this house belongs to my parents. Does that make you feel any less intimidated?"

"Yes." She gestured weakly with her hand. "Sure."

"Does that shocked look mean I'm going to get a little respect?"

"No." She shook her head emphatically. "It means I'm asking for a raise. I hope you realize I'm still paying off a government loan for my college education."

He chuckled then. The rich, clear sounds were carried with the wind. Joy tossed her head back and smiled at him. This moment was one she would treasure when it came time for her to go; Joy was sure of it. The sun. The sand. The sea. And the sound of Sloan's full laugh.

Jumping to her feet, she took off toward the sea.

"Hey, where are you going?" He called after her, his brow creased in thick lines.

"To look for seashells." Swinging her hands high at her side, she walked backward, taunting him. "Want to come?"

"Yes!" he shouted, surprising her. "Bring one of those pieces of wood forward. Once the chair gets on wet sand, you can push me."

"Push you?" Her laugh was musical. "Wheel yourself, bub."

His dark eyes sparkled. "All right, lazy. I'll do the heavy work."

Joy did as he suggested, dragging the wood around until they managed to manipulate the chair close to the shore.

"Come on, I'll race you."

Sloan quirked his mouth to one side. "Trying to take advantage of a cripple, are you?"

"I was going to even the odds," she added with an offended look.

"Sure you were."

"No, honest." She crossed her heart with her index finger and burst into peals of laughter at the look on his face. "Okay, okay, I'll run backwards."

"And hop on one foot?"

"No. That's too much."

"All right. On your mark, get ready, go," Sloan shouted.

Joy paused, hands on her hips, looking on helplessly. His arms worked furiously as he rotated the large wheels.

"Hey, I wasn't ready," she shouted at him.

"Tough." The wind brought the lone word back to her. She watched as the muscles of his upper arms flexed with the effort.

Serious now, Joy turned around and began to jog backward. Within a minute she was even with him. "Let's negotiate," she protested, gasping for breath.

"Do you concede?"

"Anything."

Sloan stopped and swiveled the chair around so that he faced her.

Soft laughter rose within her, and until she regained her breath Joy leaned forward and rested her good hand on her knee. "You cheated," she chided him. "I wasn't ready."

"You looked ready to me."

Her back was to the ocean, and she heard Sloan's shout of warning just as the wave crashed against her legs, hitting the back of her thighs.

Sloan dissolved into fits of laughter at the shocked look that came over her.

"You did that on purpose," she gasped in outrage.

"I didn't, I swear it."

Flinging her hand forward, she managed to catch enough water to spatter him with a few drops. Not to be deterred, she waited until the next big wave came in and scooped as much water as her cupped hand would hold. Giggling and breathless, she ran toward him, stumbled, and fell forward.

In split-second response, Sloan reached out to catch her, breaking the impact of the fall. But to her horror,

Joy pulled him out of the wheelchair and took him with her to the ground.

He lay partially on top of her. "Joy." His voice was urgent. "Are you all right?"

"Disgraced, but otherwise unruffled. And you?" Her back was pressed against the rough sand.

He didn't answer her. Their eyes met, and a flood of warmth swept through her. The laughter was gone from his gaze, and she stared back wordlessly, almost afraid to breathe. Joy knew she should break away, do something, anything, to stop what was happening. But the hunger in his look held her motionless. She didn't blink.

Slowly he lowered his head, blocking out the sunlight. Their breaths mingled as his lips hovered a hair's space above her own. No longer could she see his face. Her heart was crying out to him, begging him to stop and at the same time pleading with him to continue and kiss her. It was no use fighting her clamoring sensations, and she closed her eyes.

Very gently, as if in slow motion, Sloan fit his mouth over hers. At first his lips barely skimmed the surface, as if he didn't want this but couldn't help himself.

But when Joy slid her hands around his neck, his mouth crushed hers, forcing her lips to part. Fiercely he wrapped his arms around her, half lifting her from the sand.

Abruptly he released her and rolled to the side so that they lay next to one another on their backs. Joy felt the cold air and kept her eyes closed. She shouldn't have let this happen. It could possibly undermine everything she had struggled to build in this relationship.

"You asked for that," he said bitterly. "You've been

asking for it all day. Are you satisfied now? How does it feel to be kissed by a cripple? Or is this one of the extra services you provide for all your patients?"

Four

"Mr. Whittaker's breakfast is ready," Clara announced as she set the tray on the kitchen counter. The older woman studied Joy. "You want me to take it in to him?"

For a moment the offer was tempting. But Joy couldn't. Sloan would know why, and he must never guess the effect his kiss had had on her. How stupid she'd been to have let it happen. Now she must pay for her foolishness.

"Air's been a mite thick between you two," Clara mumbled as she set a pan in the sink and filled it with tap water.

"What do you mean?" Joy glanced up guiltily.

"I don't suppose you'd think ol' Clara would notice. But things got real quiet after you and Mr. Whittaker were on the beach yesterday. Mr. Whittaker didn't eat dinner, and neither did you. Then later you didn't play that clarinet the way you have most nights."

"Flute," Joy corrected. "You're right. I didn't play. My...my hand was hurting."

Unconcerned, Clara hummed a soft tune. "You want me to take him breakfast?"

"No," she said with a forced smile. "I'll do it."

Balancing the tray on her knee, Joy knocked loudly on Sloan's door twice. Purposely she'd avoided him the remainder of the day, hoping that if she put some distance between them after what had happened on the beach they could both look at it with perspective. But the nagging questions persisted. How could anything that felt so good, so right, be a mistake?

"Come in," Sloan growled.

Forcing a smile, Joy opened the door. "I can see you're in your usual good mood this morning."

"What's so good about it?" Sloan demanded, and pivoted his chair around so that he faced her. "It's just like any other morning for a cripple."

"You're not a cripple." Her eyes focused away from him as she placed the tray on the desk.

His laugh was short and derisive. "But isn't that what you're so fond of calling me?"

Joy inhaled a calming breath. "I call you one to get a rise out of you. You're a smart man; I'd have thought you had that figured out by now."

"Not many men I know roll around in one of these things," he challenged, and his hand patted the large wheel of his chair.

"It's true that you and that chair are constant companions." Joy wasn't going to argue with him. "But in your mind you're running free."

"How do you know what's in my mind?" he protested, his eyes darkening.

"It's not so difficult," she returned thoughtfully, her back to him.

"Oh?" Again his voice was thick with challenge.

"What is this? An interrogation?" Joy whirled around and leaned against the desk, her hands behind her. "Remember, it's Monday morning. You'll have to make allowances for me on Mondays. It takes my heart ten minutes to start beating once I crawl out of bed."

"You ran this morning."

Joy turned around and lifted the silver warming dome off the breakfast plate and set it aside. "How'd you know that?"

"I watched you."

"Oh." It was crazy, the effect the information had on her. Joy's hands felt clammy and her face warm. She didn't want him invading her thought life this way. When the time came for her to leave, it would only make matters more difficult. And when she left, Joy vowed, she would walk away from Sloan Whittaker intact. Whole. She wouldn't leave this man her heart.

"What's that?" Sloan's words cut into her musings.

"What's what?"

"That." He pointed to the breakfast tray.

"Oatmeal, toast, and juice." She looked at him with a blank stare.

"I hate oatmeal."

"Rolled oats are good for you," she countered with a smile.

"Yes, but have you ever asked yourself what they rolled them with?"

"No," she admitted with a small laugh, "I can't say that I have. Do you want me to have Clara cook you something else?"

He looked up at her, his eyes wide and disbelieving. "Nielsen, you're mellowing."

Joy's nerves suddenly felt threadbare. The need to escape was overpowering. "Maybe I am," she agreed. "But don't count on it," she murmured, and made her exit from the room.

Her hands were trembling as she leaned against the wall in the hallway. She needed its support. With a determined lift of her chin, she straightened and returned to the kitchen. This wasn't like her, but there seemed to be a lot of things she didn't understand about herself anymore.

"Problems?" Clara questioned, her large brown eyes watching Joy with concern.

"None. Why?"

Clara's look was disconcerting. The older woman was too observant not to notice the high color of Joy's flushed cheeks.

"You need to talk to ol' Clara?"

"No, I'm fine," Joy dismissed the offer. "But thanks anyway."

"Anytime."

The sounds of Clara humming followed Joy down the hallway to her room. The door clicked, and she walked across the room to stand in front of the mirror. She forced herself to do an assessment of herself. Twenty-eight, never been married. Not unattractive, but certainly not beautiful. She wasn't another Chantelle, the blonde who looked gorgeous with damp lashes. Joy's hair was cut short and curly. With so many hours in the pool every day, it was the most practical style.

Turning sideways, she placed her hands on the underside of her breasts and lifted them. They were probably her best feature. If it weren't for those, most people would think she was a young boy. That was the problem with being so short. Petite, her mother claimed. Joy called it just plain stubby.

Within seconds Joy had determined she was headed for a lot of heartache if she allowed this awareness for Sloan to continue. In all the years she'd been working, this was the first time she had faced these feelings. A patient was a patient, and she had never allowed herself to forget the code of ethics.

The session with Sloan in the pool didn't go well. Both of them were on edge. The ability to work with one another, although grudgingly, was gone.

Sloan struggled to disguise his pain, and with every wince Joy had to force herself to continue. She didn't need to be reminded that it hurt. She knew.

"Are you going to do the exercises today or not?" Sloan questioned in a vicious tone, angry and impatient.

"What do you think I'm doing?" she shot back. Unconsciously Joy realized that she hadn't been working him as hard, because his pain was affecting her.

When the next series of manipulations had been completed, Sloan was left in little doubt that she was doing her job.

Later that afternoon, Joy entered the fenced yard to see L.J. The bird hobbled to her, and Joy bent down to talk to her creature friend.

"Hello."

L.J. squawked loudly, and Joy laughed.

"So you can talk. I was beginning to wonder." She held out her bandaged hand. "Did you see what you did?"

The seagull tilted its head at an inquiring angle.

"Well, don't worry. I know it was an accident. But it was a good lesson for us both." She crumbled up bits of fish and some other leftovers in his dish, then stepped back. Almost immediately L.J. began to eat. Joy stayed with him until he'd finished.

That evening she watched television with Paul, but a half hour later she couldn't have told anyone what she'd seen.

When she returned to her room, Joy couldn't decide if she should play her flute or not. But music was a basic part of her life, and she didn't know if she could go without it two nights running. Playing had always calmed her spirit and soothed her.

Her options were few. If she stayed in her room, she would be depriving Sloan of the pleasure he received when she played. It seemed almost petty to put her desire for solitude above what little enjoyment he received from life.

Dusk had cast a purple shadow across the horizon when Joy stepped onto the verandah. She paused to inhale the fresh scent of the sea and closed her eyes. The winds were whispering and gentle when she raised the musical instrument to her lips.

As always, the music flowed naturally. But tonight it was dark and deep, unlike the mellow tunes she normally enjoyed.

"You practicing for someone's funeral?" Sloan asked in a bitter tone.

Joy paused and lowered her flute. She'd been so caught up in the music she hadn't noticed he'd come outside. He stayed several feet away, his profile illuminated by the setting sun.

She shook her head. "No."

"Could have fooled me."

Ignoring him, she played again, forcing out a lively, popular tune. Before realizing what had happened, she slipped into the intense mournful music a second time. When she recognized what she'd done, she stopped mid-measure.

"Will you play at mine?" Sloan asked, his voice a mere whisper.

"Play at your what?" She didn't look at him, her gaze focusing on the tumbling waves that broke against the beach.

"My funeral."

"That's a morbid thought. You're not going to die," she said seriously, her own voice a soft murmur. "I won't let you."

His light laugh couldn't hide the pain.

"Do you want something?" She didn't need to explain what. When it came to painkilling drugs, Sloan was sensible. He never took anything unless the pain became unbearable. The fear of becoming addicted to the medication was always present, and he seemed well aware of the dangers.

He expelled a harsh breath before answering. "What I need is for you to kiss me better." His voice was low and seductive.

Joy didn't breathe; the oxygen was trapped in her lungs. Her hand tightly clenched the railing as she closed her eyes. The battle to alleviate the pain from his eyes with a gentle brush of her mouth over his was almost overpowering. The knowledge that one kiss would never be enough was the only thing that stopped her.

"Want me to call Chantelle?" A fingernail broke

against the freshly painted surface of the railing on the verandah. Still she didn't move.

"No." The word was released in an angry rush.

With her back to Sloan, she heard him return to his room.

Joy breathed again.

The following morning Joy walked into the modern-style living room. "Good morning, Mr. Whittaker."

Myron Whittaker placed the coffee cup in the saucer and stood. "Morning."

"You asked to see me?"

"Yes, I did. Sit down, please." He motioned with his hand to the chair opposite him.

Joy sat on the edge of the leather cushion and primly folded her hands in her lap. The Whittakers were wonderful people who loved their son and were willing to do whatever was necessary to help him return to a normal life again. "How's Sloan?" his father began.

"There's been some improvement. I imagine within a few weeks he'll be able to start work on the mats and the parallel bars. From there it will only be a matter of time before he can advance to the walker and then the cane."

The older man lowered his gaze. "Yes, the cane."

Joy didn't need to be told what Sloan's father was thinking. "From what I can tell, your son will always have a limp. The cane will be necessary."

Myron Whittaker glanced up, and Joy had the funny sensation that although he was looking at her, he wasn't seeing her. "That's not it," he admitted absently, and shook his head. "I was remembering…thinking…" He let the rest of the sentence ebb away. "We used to play tennis, Sloan and me. Twice a week."

Joy could see no use in dwelling on things past. "It's unlikely that your son will play a decent game of tennis again."

He lifted the coffee cup to his mouth, and Joy noted that it shook slightly.

"I've done as you suggested and brought some work from the office. Heaven knows I'm not able to keep up with it all."

"I think bringing Sloan back into the mainstream of the business can only help," Joy murmured.

"I was hoping to go over a few of the things with you."

"With me?" Her gaze shot to him. "Surely you don't expect me to discuss the business with your son?"

"To be honest, I was hoping you would bring up the subject with him. Sloan and I had a parting of ways on my last visit. At this point I feel it would be better if we didn't see one another for a while."

"You can't mean that."

Myron Whittaker stood and paced across the marble floor. He had his back to her.

"Sloan and I have always been close. Don't misunderstand me. I love my son."

"I'm sure you do."

"It hurts me to see him in that chair. There are so many things I wanted in life for Sloan, and now everything seems impossible." He dropped his foot and turned around. "The last time I saw Sloan we said some bitter, hard things to one another. I don't know if it would be a good idea for me to see him now. We both need time."

"But that's something you don't have," Joy countered, and released a slow breath. "Sloan regrets what happened just as much as you. Clear the air between you, make amends. Then bring up the business aspect of your visit. If you'd like, I could tell him you're here."

The agreeing nod wasn't eager. "If you think I should."

"I do."

Sloan was in his quarters, his head resting against the back of the chair, eyes closed.

When Joy tapped lightly on the open door, he straightened and opened his dark eyes, which narrowed on her.

"Your father's here to see you."

At first Sloan said nothing. "Tell him I'm busy."

"That would be a lie."

"When did you get so righteous?" Sloan tossed the question at her flippantly.

Joy made a show of glancing at her wristwatch. "About five minutes ago."

Sloan ignored the humor. "I don't want to see him."

"He's your father," she reminded him.

"Do you want me to wave a banner?"

Maybe Joy wouldn't have reacted so strongly if her own father was alive. "That comment was unworthy of you, Sloan."

"Listen, Miss Miracle Worker. This is between my father and me. I'd advise you to keep out of it."

"No."

The barely controlled anger showed in the tight set of his mouth. His eyes were afire. "Stay out of this; it's none of your business. You seem to think you've got me wrapped around your finger. You're wrong. I refuse to allow you to dictate to me my personal affairs. Is that understood?" His voice gained volume with each word until the room seemed to shake with the sound. "Get out, Joy," he warned in a dangerous tone. "Get out, before I say something I'll regret."

She took a step in retreat, then stood her ground.

Sloan advanced his chair across the room until he was directly in front of her.

"He's your father," she murmured. "Don't do this to him. Don't do this to yourself."

"Stay out of it, Nielsen," Sloan ground out between clenched teeth.

In the past Joy had found ways around Sloan's pride. Now, facing his steel-hard resolve, she felt defenseless. There was nothing she could say or do.

Sloan's father stood when she entered the living room.

"I can tell by your face what he said. Don't bother to explain."

"I'm sorry, Mr. Whittaker," she added in a weak voice. "I feel terrible."

"Don't." He looked away as though assessing his visit and then reached for his coat.

"I shouldn't have forced the issue."

He snapped the briefcase closed, his back to her. "Give me a call when you think…" Again he let the rest of the sentence trail away.

"I will." Joy walked with him to the front door. "I'm sure everything will work out fine."

Gravely he shook his head. Not for the first time, Joy noted the tired, hurt look in his eyes.

She stood on the front steps until his car rounded the bend in the road. Without questioning the wisdom of her actions, she marched through the house and into Sloan's room.

"That was a despicable thing to do."

"I told you to stay out of it," he stormed back.

"I won't."

Sloan escaped onto the verandah.

"You can't do this to your own father. He loves you. Seeing you like this is tearing him apart."

"You're right, it is," Sloan shouted, appearing in the doorway that led outside. "Don't you think I can see the pity in his eyes? He's no different from anyone else. I don't want his sympathy. I can't stand to see him stare at me that way."

Some of the intense anger drained out of her. "I'd give anything to have my father look any way at me," she whispered.

"Don't confuse the issue with sentimentality."

"Oh, Sloan," she moaned, and exhaled a wistful sigh. "Can't you see what you're doing? You're driving everyone who loves you out of your life."

"That's my choice," he returned bitterly. "I can see and do as I please."

"But you can't play tennis with your father."

The color fled from his face as his eyes hardened into cutting diamond chips. Fierce anger shot out from him. "You're right about that, Miss Miracle Worker. I'm not going to play tennis with my father. But then, I'll never play much of anything physical again, will I? So what's the difference?"

The urge to fall to her knees and hold him was so strong that it was all Joy could do to turn and walk away.

To say Joy was miserable was a gross understatement. Paul attempted to lighten her mood by taking her out to dinner.

"I blew it." They sat at an umbrella table at Mobey Jake's. The neon whale flashed directly above them.

"Don't be so hard on yourself, kid."

Joy nearly choked on a French fry. "Kid?" she repeated. "How old do you think I am?"

The muscular shoulders lifted with a heavy shrug. "Twenty, maybe."

"Thanks." Joy laughed.

Paul laid his fish on a napkin and looked up thoughtfully. "You should laugh more often."

One corner of Joy's mouth lifted in a bittersweet smile. "There's not much excuse to laugh in this business. I wish my patients could understand that it hurts me as much as them."

"One patient, you mean," Paul inserted.

Joy looked out over the coastline instead of directly at Paul. "One patient," she agreed.

"Are you falling for this guy?" A frown marred his forehead.

Paul was nothing if not blunt. Joy felt the heavy thud of her heart. It beat so loud and strong that it seemed someone was pounding on her with a hammer. She reacted that way when someone spoke candidly.

"I hope not," she replied truthfully. "I've enough problems handling Sloan Whittaker without involving my emotions."

"If you need a shoulder to lean on, let me know."

"Thanks, Paul." Joy meant that sincerely. She'd never worked with nicer people than Paul and Clara.

It was dark by the time they returned to the house. Since Clara had the day off, Joy had cooked Sloan's dinner, and she was grateful when Paul had delivered it to him.

The porch light was on, but the house was dark. As Joy let herself into her room she noticed there were no lights on in Sloan's. Apparently he'd opted for an early night.

Not wishing to wake him, Joy carried her flute down to the beach. She stopped long enough to check L.J. and give him the leftover fish. The bird seemed to want out, and when Joy held open the gate, L.J. hobbled after her.

The two found a log not far from the house. Joy sat, buried her bare feet in the sand, and began to play. For a while L.J. stayed close to her side, but it didn't take much time for him to stray. As long as she could see him, Joy let him wander. The difficulty came when it was time to return to the house. L.J. enjoyed his taste of freedom and wasn't willing to go back to the small fenced area. Joy had to round him up like a sheepdog herding a stray lamb.

Laughing and breathless, she let herself into the house.

"What were you doing out there?"

Sloan.

"What are you doing up?" Joy had never known Sloan to come into the kitchen.

"I asked you first." The room remained dark.

Joy's eyes soon adjusted to the room's interior. Only a few feet separated her and Sloan.

"I… I was on the beach."

"That much I knew."

"Why are you here?" Her hand gripped the knob behind her.

"I heard you playing."

"I'm sorry if I woke you," she interrupted. "I didn't mean to."

Sloan wiped a hand over his brow. "I couldn't sleep. Did you and Paul have a good time?"

"Yes. We went to Mobey Jake's."

"Bring me anything this time?"

"No, sorry. I didn't."

He dismissed her apology with a wan smile. "What took you so long coming inside? I was worried."

Sloan concerned about her? After this afternoon he had all the more reason to want her out of his life. In her eagerness to mend the rift between father and son, she had only done harm. Sloan was right; it wasn't any of her affair.

"Joy?" He seemed to be waiting for her answer.

"I was bringing L.J. home."

"You and that bird." His mirthless laugh was filled with irony. "I was ready to call out the National Guard."

"I'm sorry—for everything," she muttered.

Her apology produced a stunned silence.

"Did I hear you right? Joy Nielsen, gutsy Miracle Worker, actually admitting to a fault? Are you feeling well? Do you need a doctor?"

"I'm fine," she said with a shaky laugh. "Sloan, I feel terrible about today. You were right. I should never have stuck my nose where it doesn't belong."

The amusement drained from his eyes. He extended a hand to her, palm open.

Scooting out a kitchen chair, Joy sat so that their gazes were level. With appreciation for his accepting her apology, she placed her hand in his.

"Friends?" he questioned.

Joy nodded. "I prefer it to being enemies."

His hand closed tightly over hers, his thumb sensuously rotating against the inside of her wrist. "I do too." His eyes holding hers, he lifted her fingers to his mouth.

Joy tugged, and immediately Sloan released her hand. The potential for danger was powerful and strong. If she let Sloan kiss her fingers, it wouldn't be enough; she'd want to taste his mouth over hers. She couldn't risk weeks of hard work for something as fleeting as physical attraction.

Awkwardly she stood and backed away. "Good night, Sloan. Sleep well."

Somehow Joy managed to keep from running into her room. By the time she closed the bedroom door, she was trembling. Covering her face with both hands, she paced the carpet, her heart pounding like a trapped fledgling. Either she came to her senses or resigned from this case. The matter was simple. She was a professional therapist, sensible and proficient. She knew better than to nurture this powerful physical attraction. In the end she would leave the cripple, not Sloan. But just as she recognized she must rein in her feelings, she knew she couldn't bear to leave him now.

The next morning, Joy was in the pool doing laps when Paul brought Sloan to the water's edge. Once placed on the side of the pool, Sloan could lower himself into the blue depths.

Treading water at the deep end, Joy waved. "I'll be right there."

"Don't hurry on my account," he shouted back.

A smile flashed from her eyes, and with even strokes Joy swam toward him.

"You look bright and cheerful this morning." Sloan

had been up, dressed, and eating breakfast by the time
Joy returned from her run. Normally he delayed starting the day as long as possible. Joy remembered the
first few days after she'd arrived the struggle she had
had just to keep his drapes open. Sometimes she forgot
how far they'd come. But seeing him now, she was reminded how much farther they yet had to travel.

Clara hurried onto the patio. "Sorry to bother you,
but Mr. Whittaker Senior is here."

A hardness stole over Sloan's face. "Who does he
want to see this time?" The question was barely civil.

Joy bit into her lip to restrain an angry response.

Clara wiped her hands on her apron, obviously flustered. "Mr. Whittaker says he wants to talk to you." She
directed her answer to Sloan.

"Tell him I'm busy."

"We can do this later," Joy inserted eagerly. "I'll
come back…"

"No." His angry shout shut her off.

"Sloan, please," she whispered.

"Do as I say, Clara." He directed his attention to the
housekeeper, his dismissal final.

With a quick bob of her head, Clara turned and hurried toward the house.

His narrowed gaze swung to Joy. "Was this brilliant idea yours?"

Joy returned his stare speechlessly. Was Sloan implying that she had sent for his father?

"Is it?" he shouted.

"Of course not. What are you suggesting?"

"I saw the two of you together," he hissed. "I'm not
stupid. You two have something up your sleeves. Let it

be known right now. I don't want any part of it. Is that understood?" The last words were shouted.

"Something up our sleeves?" Joy echoed incredulously. "Your father is half killing himself to maintain the business. *Your* company, I might add. He's dying in stages. In case you'd forgotten, your father's retired." Joy paused to draw in a breath. "Are you so self-absorbed that you haven't stopped to think what his life has been like since your accident? Not only is he worried sick about you, but he's taken over your position in the company—with all the stress and worries. But you, Mr. High and Mighty, you're so caught up in self-pity, all you see is yourself."

Sloan's face became sickeningly pale. "You don't know what you're talking about."

"Are you accusing me of lying now, too?"

"What can you expect me to think? My parents told me Harrison was in charge of the company."

"Have you looked at your father lately, Sloan, really looked? Can't you see what's happening to him?"

Sloan went completely still, like a lion alert before the attack. "If what you say is true, it's Dad's own fault. He should have given everything over to Harrison the way he said he was."

"Are you really so uncaring?" His lack of concern shocked her.

His blistering hot gaze swept over her contemptuously. "What do you know of any of this?" he shouted. "Safe and warm in your secure little world, it must be easy to sit in judgment of something you'll never comprehend." A muscle worked convulsively along the line of his jaw.

The desire to tell him was overpowering. "What do

I know?" She repeated his question with a half laugh. "Maybe it's time you found out exactly what I do." She swam to the steps that led out of the pool. "You asked me once about pain. Believe me when I tell you I'm well acquainted with it." She stood and placed one foot on the painted step. "You told me once you'd lain in a hospital bed wanting to die. I did more than want. I begged."

She turned to him then, the hideous scars that marked her thighs in full view. When she glanced at him she was prepared for the shocked look, even the repulsion he couldn't hide. She'd viewed it before when others saw her scars.

"Paul," she yelled, and hurriedly donned her terry-cloth wrap. "Mr. Whittaker wants out of the water." Unable to bear another minute in Sloan's presence, Joy turned and ran into the house.

Five

"Joy," Sloan called after her, but Joy only increased her pace.

Paul met her halfway to the house. He stuck out a hand and stopped her. "You okay?" His finger brushed a tear from her cheek.

"Fine," she lied. "I'm fine."

Clara gave her a funny look as Joy came through the kitchen, but she didn't stop to explain.

Once in the privacy of her room, Joy slumped into a chair and covered her eyes with one hand. She'd only been sixteen at the time of the accident. A school cheerleader. But she would never be again. The scars were cleverly disguised with the proper clothing, so that no one need ever know. But their ugliness affected her more mentally than physically. She ran, she swam, she played tennis, could, in fact, do almost as much as before the accident. She had her father to thank for that, but even he couldn't force the look of shock and revulsion from people's eyes when they saw her misshapen thighs for the first time.

Joy changed back into her uniform and held a cool

washcloth over her eyes, hoping the cold water would take away the redness. Tears were the last thing she wanted Sloan to see. He held enough aces in his hand as it was.

Clara was stirring something at the stove when Joy entered the kitchen. "Mr. Whittaker's been saying lots of things he doesn't mean lately," she commented, her back to Joy.

"Mr. Whittaker didn't say anything to upset me, so don't blame him for something he didn't do. He's confused enough without all of us turning on him." It would be unfair to have the others think Sloan had caused her to cry.

"I still think Mr. Whittaker had better take a good, long look at himself."

Joy pretended not to hear. "Do you mind if I take some of these leftovers to L.J.?"

"Isn't that bird well yet?"

"No. It'll be a long time before his wing heals completely."

"Go ahead, then."

"Thanks, Clara." She took out bits and pieces of meat and fish she knew the gull would eat.

Joy spent a good portion of a half hour with L.J. He allowed her to touch him freely now—a small victory, but one that encouraged her.

When she came back into the kitchen, Sloan's lunch tray was ready.

"Take it in to him while it's hot."

Joy hesitated. She'd rather not see Sloan. He was sure to ask her questions she'd prefer not to answer.

"Go on," Clara ordered.

The door was open, and Sloan appeared to watch her

anxiously. Joy was sure a niggling uncertainty showed in her eyes.

"Set the tray outside today," Sloan ordered. "I feel like looking at the ocean."

Still and silent, Joy did as he asked. He joined her at the round, enameled table on the verandah. He examined his lunch, lifting the warming dome and unrolling his silverware from the linen napkin. "Did Clara forget the pepper?"

Briefly Joy's eyes scanned the tray. She was sure she'd seen it earlier. "Would you like me to bring it to you?"

"Please."

With obvious reluctance, Joy returned to the kitchen.

Sloan's eyes followed her as she came onto the deck. "Will you have your lunch with me?"

She focused her gaze on the view of the sky and the sea. A light breeze ruffled the silky, soft curls. Absently she smoothed the hair from her face.

"Joy?" he prompted.

She blinked, forcing herself to look at him. "Not today."

"Tonight then?"

Joy felt drained. "Why?"

"I think we should talk."

"About what?"

Sloan expelled an impatient sigh. "There's no need to be obtuse."

She turned around to face him then, hands clenched so tight that her long nails cut into her palms. "Like everyone else who's seen my disfigurement, you're dying of curiosity. What happened? How long ago? Whose fault was it? I'm not a morbid sideshow."

"I wasn't thinking that," he said tautly.

"Don't lie to me. You're no different. Did you think you could hide the revulsion? Don't you realize I've seen abhorrence often enough to recognize it?" she accused in a choked voice.

"That's not true."

"Oh, for heaven's sake, spare me." Joy shook her head, not wanting to argue. She retrieved the pepper shaker and pointedly placed it on the table and left.

As she walked away, Joy could almost feel the dagger penetrate her back. Sloan was angry. She had watched as he struggled to control his temper. For the first time in her memory, he'd succeeded.

Joy waited until Paul came for Sloan after lunch before she returned his tray to the kitchen. He'd hardly touched his lunch. But then, neither had she.

Adjusting a wide-brimmed straw hat on her head, she took a well constructed straw basket and headed for the beach. On several occasions she'd wanted to go beach-walking to look for seashells, but had yet to bring back more than one or two. The need to explore, to escape, to get away, was stronger today than ever.

When she stopped to check L.J. she noted he was quickly finding his protective home a prison and she decided to bring him with her. Readily the bird hobbled behind her when she opened the fence gate.

Her first find was an unbroken sand dollar, and she bent over to retrieve it from the wet shore. As she did, L.J. came to her side. He pecked away at grass, eating bugs and things she decided she'd prefer not to know. The two of them were content and happy. Two against the wind, two against the sea. Two cripples against the world.

The day was perfect as only a California spring-time could be, and when Joy turned back to return to the house, she noticed the figure in a wheelchair coming toward her.

She paused, her feelings undecided. One half of her was demanding that she run the other way. Avoid him as much as possible, cast his curiosity and pity away. But the other half of her yearned for the comfort and understanding that could only come from another facing like circumstances.

There was irony here. None of her other patients had ever known. But she had never worked with anyone like Sloan Whittaker. His effect upon her was far more powerful than anyone else's, which made him dangerous in ways she still hadn't fully comprehended.

With L.J. hobbling behind her, Joy slowly sauntered toward Sloan.

"How'd you get out here?" she questioned when they met. Her eyes refused to meet his.

"You're a smart girl. Figure it out."

Hoping to display a lack of concern, she lightly shrugged her shoulders.

"Is it so dark and horrible that you can't tell me?" The question was issued so softly that for a moment Joy wasn't sure he'd spoken.

"It happened a long time ago. Some things are best forgotten."

"What you mean is the painful memories."

"I'm not going to argue, if that's what you want."

"It's not."

She stood stiffly at his side.

"Show me what you found?" he requested gently.

Joy didn't know how to deal with him when he was

kind or tender. She felt far more comfortable dealing with his pride and anger.

When she didn't immediately respond, Sloan took the basket out of her hand and fingered the assortment of shells and rocks she'd collected. He lifted his eyes and his frowning gaze studied her. "You didn't want me to know, did you?"

"No," she quipped.

"You would never have told me if it hadn't been for my fight with my father."

Joy's eyes met his. Was that pain she heard in his voice? "Probably not."

"Why?"

"Why?" She angrily threw the word back at him. "You like perfection, especially in your women. I saw Chantelle. The china-doll face, with the figure a woman like me would die for. She's perfect right down to the mascara on the tips of her lashes and the uniformly shaped fingernails."

Her words seemed to anger him. "You're not like Chantelle."

"That's just what I said," she concurred.

"Not in the ways that matter."

Her voice quivered as she struggled not to reveal the hurt his words inflicted. "I can't tell you how many times kindhearted people with good intentions told me that it didn't matter if I was scarred because it was what was on the inside that counted. I don't need to hear it from you."

"Now you're twisting my words."

She shook her head and pinched her lips together.

"You are the most incredibly beautiful woman I know."

Joy released a short, disgusted sound and stormed away. His rolling laughter stopped her. "What's so funny?" she demanded, swiveling around, hands on her hips, feet spread in a defensive stance.

"You are!" he shouted, the wind carrying his words. "Don't you remember how you said it was a sad commentary on my life if I needed you to rescue me from beautiful women?"

"I remember." She didn't lessen the distance separating them.

"I tell you how beautiful you are and immediately you act like I've given you the biggest insult of your life."

"I am not beautiful," she shouted back.

"Then why do I have to struggle not to kiss you? Why do I lie awake at night and wish you were in bed with me?" The violence in his voice stunned her.

Joy flinched at his words. "You don't know what you're saying."

"You're right. Not only am I a cripple, but I'm weak in the head."

"You won't get an argument out of me about that." A gust of wind nearly lifted the hat from her head. Joy caught it just before it flew off. Long John squawked, diverting her attention, and when Joy looked at Sloan he had his back to her and was slowly progressing along the beach.

Unwilling to join him, but equally unwilling to leave him on his own, Joy sat and waited. She lay back in the sand and rested her eyes. Could it be possible that Sloan was attracted to her? The thought was heady enough to cause her heart to beat wildly. Sloan Whittaker was more tempting than any man she had ever known. But she would never fit into his world. Sloan was best left in the hands of women like Chantelle. The two of them belonged together. She was a physical therapist that would pass in and out of his life in short order. A year from now he'd have trouble remembering her name. Joy couldn't afford to lose sight of that.

She must have drifted into sleep. The next thing Joy knew Sloan let out an angry curse, and she sat up, surprised.

"You can call off your attack bird."

"Long John," she yelled. Sloan was sucking the side of his index finger.

"What happened?"

"Nothing."

"And you always suck your finger?"

"I do when it's bleeding."

"Let me see."

"No."

"My, my, aren't we brave," she murmured, coolly aloof.

"If you saw this cut you'd think so in earnest."

"Sloan, please. Did L.J. hurt you?"

"Only my pride. It seems your feathered creature doesn't make friends easily."

Joy gave a frustrated sound and fell to her knees at his side. "For heaven's sake, quit acting like a child and let me have a look at it."

His hand cupped the side of her face, raising her eyes to meet his. A heavy sensual awareness rippled through her, and it was all Joy could do not to place her hand over his and close her eyes. She was tampering with fire, and she knew it.

"It…it doesn't look bad."

"I told you it was only a scratch."

"I wouldn't want…"

"What wouldn't you want?" His voice was low and seductive as his hand cupped the other side of her face. "I can't help this," he whispered huskily. "Hate me later." His mouth gently kissed her chin, her eyes, the end of her nose, and caressed her cheek before softly parting her lips.

She should have stopped him. It wasn't him she'd hate later, but herself. Her arms slid around his neck; her fingers stroked the hair that grew thick there.

Sloan's mouth sought hers, and she moved her face against his until finally, when their lips met, Joy was beyond coherent thought.

The kiss was hard and demanding and showed an expertise she had only rarely experienced. The tip of his tongue outlined her lips. Joy thought she would die from the pure pleasure as his mouth crashed down over hers.

His hand slid down her nape, his thumb moving in a slow rhythmic circle against her sensitized skin. He pushed the neckline of her dress off one smooth shoulder, his mouth blazing a trail of soft kisses that led to the scented hollow between her breasts. When Joy emitted a small protesting sound, Sloan tightened his hold and raised his mouth to the nape of her neck.

"Don't say it," he ground out in a fierce whisper. "I know what you're thinking."

"You couldn't possibly know."

"For once in your life, don't think. Feel." His mouth was on hers. The kisses became longer, more languorous, as he pressed their upper bodies as close together as possible.

"No…no…" She dragged her mouth from his. Stiffening, she pulled away. At first Sloan didn't want to let her go; Joy could sense as much as he tightened his grip. But after the first sign of struggle he released her.

Joy slumped on the sand beside him.

"Don't say it." The command was whispered harshly.

"I won't," she returned unsteadily. "I... I think we should get back to the house."

"Not yet." His voice was softer. "Sit with me for a while."

Joy's first reaction was to refuse. Together, alone like this, was dangerous for both of them.

She brought her knees up and circled them with her arms. For a long time they sat in silence. When she felt Sloan's gaze on her she turned to face him. Their eyes met. Hers, she was sure, were soft, lambent, the effect of his kisses evident; his tired, strained.

Joy looked away. "I was only sixteen." Her voice was barely above a weak whisper. "I was a cheerleader on the way home from a Friday night game when the school bus was hit by a train. I... I don't remember much of the accident. Only the sound of screams and realizing they belonged to my friends...and to me. My father told me I was trapped inside. Everyone told me how lucky I was to be alive." She gave a sad laugh. "For a long time I didn't think so. At least if I was dead the pain would go away."

"I thought the same thing," Sloan added in a gruff whisper. His hand rested on her shoulder as if some contact with her, even the light touch of his hand against her bare skin, was necessary.

"The doctors assured my family I'd never walk again. The damage was too extensive, multiple. My father wouldn't accept that. He insisted on a therapist."

She paused and bit into her bottom lip. "It hurt so much I thought I'd die."

"And I had the audacity to ask what you could possibly know about pain." His voice was filled with regret.

"You didn't know. My mother couldn't stand to see me suffer like that. I know it wasn't any easier on Dad, but he was there every session encouraging me, loving me, helping in any way he could. I'd be in a wheelchair today if it wasn't for my father."

"You told me once the only man you'd ever made cry was your father."

Joy nodded. "With the therapist's help, Dad learned the manipulations and assumed some of the exercises. I wanted to give up so many times. But Dad wouldn't let me. He prodded, pried, bribed, and when the pain was the worst he cried with me. But not once in the next two years would he let me quit."

"It took two years for you to walk again?"

"Two of the longest years of my life."

"I can imagine."

"If it weren't for the scars I don't think anyone would guess."

"No. Have you ever considered plastic surgery?"

Joy stiffened defensively. "My medical bills were staggering. My family gave me back my life. The disfigurement can be hidden. No, the thought has never entered my mind."

"I've offended you and I didn't mean to. I'd like to do that for you, Joy. My gift to you for everything you've done for me."

"I haven't done anything."

"How can you say that?"

"Easy. Want me to do it again?"

"Joy." He ground out her name in frustration. "Why is it every time I try with you it backfires? I think you're wonderful just the way you are. The scars don't bother me. Keep them, if you like."

"I like." She stood and brushed the sand from her dress. "Paul and Clara will be worried. We should head back. Do you want me to push you?"

"No."

Joy had gone several feet, but Sloan didn't follow. When she glanced back expectantly, she saw that he hadn't moved, his gaze resting on the rough ocean. "You coming?" she called.

He turned toward her and nodded, but it was several long moments before he did so.

By midnight the house was as quiet as a funeral parlor. Joy remained in her room reading, or at least made the pretense of involving herself with a bestselling mystery plot.

The light tap against the sliding-glass door that led to the verandah startled her. She threw back the covers and quickly donned her housecoat.

"I couldn't sleep either." Sloan sat outside the door. "Don't lie and tell me you weren't awake."

"I was up," Joy conceded.

"Why didn't you play tonight?"

Since their meeting on the beach, Joy had avoided Sloan as much as possible without arousing suspicions. "I didn't feel up to it."

"Don't kid yourself. You weren't up to facing me."

"All right," she stormed. "I didn't want to see you. But it didn't do me much good, did it?"

"I can be as stubborn as you. Come out here and sit awhile."

Joy doubted that. "It's late." She searched for an excuse.

"That's never stopped you before. I bet you didn't know I could see you out here with your flimsy silk nightgown pressed against you in the wind."

Joy decided the best thing to do was refuse to be drawn into his game. "I'm hungry," she said on a falsely cheerful note. "I think I'll fix myself a sandwich. Do you want one?"

"You know what I want," he whispered as he carried her hand to his lips.

"No!" She pulled her fingers free as if his touch were red hot. She didn't know what he wanted. Didn't want to guess, because whatever it was, her heart was willing. "I'm going to the kitchen."

"Then I'm coming too."

Her heart seemed to plunge into her stomach. Was there no escape? "It's your house," she returned with remarkable calm.

His laugh was short and mirthless. "At least we can agree on something."

Joy sliced a banana into thin pieces and laid them across a thick layer of peanut butter on bread. "Want half?"

Sloan's look was skeptical. "Peanut butter and banana?"

"It's good. Honest." She handed him half and poured them each a glass of milk.

Sloan joined her at the table. "I've been thinking all night of ways to thank you. But I never did have a way with words."

"Thank me?" She regarded him quizzically.

"I know what it cost for you to tell me about your accident. Even now, just talking about mine produces a cold sweat."

The bite of sandwich nearly stuck in her throat. She swallowed around it and reached for the milk. As she stood, the chair scraped against the floor. "I think I'll go see to L.J. before going back to my room."

"Running, Joy?" he taunted softly.

She was glad her back was to him so that he couldn't see the flame of color that heated her face. "You're being ridiculous."

"I'll see you in the morning."

"Good night, Sloan."

The pause was only momentary before he whispered his own farewell. "Night, Joy."

Clara was busy in the kitchen when Joy returned from her run early the next morning. "Yum, that smells good. What is it?" Joy peeked under the lid of something cooking on the stove.

"Food. Now scat."

With a laugh, Joy took an apple off the table centerpiece and took a bite out of it. After a long run, she felt exhilarated.

"Here." Clara stopped her. "Take Mr. Whittaker his tray, will you?"

"Already?" Sloan wasn't normally up at this time of day.

"He's up. He called me soon after you left."

Clenching the apple with her teeth, Joy carried the tray down the long hallway. Her knock went unanswered. Resting the breakfast on one knee, she turned the knob and walked unheralded into Sloan's quarters.

Two steps into the room she stopped cold. Sloan and his father were busy going over some papers. Both father and son were so intent, neither was aware she was there.

Six

The apple fell out of her mouth, bounced, and rolled across the floor.

Myron Whittaker glanced up from the paperwork spread on the top of the large oak desk. "Good morning, Miss Nielsen. Could you set that tray outside? I'm hoping Clara sent an extra cup. I could use coffee this morning."

Sloan's expression was brooding. "Joy's my physical therapist, not a servant."

"I... I don't mind," she stuttered. "Really." She placed the breakfast tray on the verandah and came back through Sloan's room.

"Joy." Sloan stopped her. "Good morning."

His smile was devastating, her answering one weak but happy. "Good morning." A flowing warmth seeped into her limbs as she exited from the room.

"Does she normally dress like that?" Sloan's father's words followed her into the hallway. With a half laugh, she bit into the corner of her bottom lip. She was wearing baggy gray sweatpants and an old T-shirt.

Mindful of her appearance, she returned with the

extra coffee cup and picked up the apple that had rolled halfway under Sloan's bed. "I'll be out of your way in a minute."

"No problem," Sloan assured her. She left in a rush, but not before she caught the look of concern in Myron Whittaker's eye as he glanced from Joy to his son.

Joy didn't need to be told what he was thinking. Sloan's father was worried. He didn't want Sloan to fall in love with her—and with good reason. Joy wasn't stupid. Myron's picture of Sloan's future wife was someone like Chantelle—as well it should be. Joy would never fit into the Whittakers' world; Sloan's wealth and lifestyle were as foreign to her as propositional calculus had been in her college days.

Later, the spray from the shower relaxed her muscles and soothed her body, but the look in Myron Whittaker's eyes continued to disturb her. He was right—she couldn't argue with him. Now she had to do her part to protect her heart and Sloan's.

Father and son worked until almost noon. Joy was sitting on a stool chatting with Clara when Myron walked into the kitchen. He looked relaxed, pleased, his eyes smiling.

"I owe you more than words can express," he said sincerely to Joy. "You've given me back my son. I'm going to see that you receive a generous bonus."

"Please, Mr. Whittaker, that's not necessary." The harsh lines of strain about his eyes and mouth had relaxed. That was all the appreciation Joy wanted to see.

"Nonsense." He dismissed her plea with a wave of his hand.

It was easy to see that arguing would do her no good. Myron Whittaker could be as stubborn as his son.

As soon as he left, Joy returned to Sloan's quarters to take back the breakfast tray and see if he was ready for their session in the pool.

"This was your idea, wasn't it?" he stormed as she walked into the room.

The anger in his voice stopped her. "Yes." She wouldn't deny it.

"Well, all I can say is thank God. You wouldn't believe some of the things that have been going on. How my father could make some of these decisions is beyond me."

A tiny smile broke out across her mouth. Joy battled to suppress it.

"What's so funny?" He didn't sound pleased.

"Nothing. Do you think you're going to have time to squeeze in the therapy today?"

Sloan set the papers he was working on aside. "I'll make the time."

Joy's mouth fell open.

"Don't look so shocked. You want to see me out of this thing, don't you?" He patted the rubber on the wheel of his chair.

"I'll get Paul and meet you in the pool."

"See you." He paused and glanced at his wristwatch. "Fifteen minutes?" He made it a question.

"Fine."

Joy was doing laps when Paul delivered him to the pool. Sloan sat on the edge watching her.

"Don't you ever get tired?" he called after a while.

Joy stopped and treaded water. "You should have said something. I didn't know you were there."

"You look like a sea nymph. That turquoise suit in the blue water leaves little to the imagination." His look was absent, his words thoughtful. "The scars were the reason you were always in the water ahead of me. It's also why you choose to wear pants."

Joy ignored his observations. She didn't want to talk about herself. "Are you going to come in the water or not?"

Sloan's smile was filled with warm amusement. "What will you give me if I do?"

"I think it's more of a question of what I'll do to you if you don't." The sound of his laughter rang in her ears as she swam toward him. She stood in the shallow end. "You're in a good mood today."

"Yes, I am," he agreed. "I can't tell you how good it feels to be needed again. Just looking over some of the things my father brought showed me how much things had slacked off since I've been away." He lowered himself into the water. "You knew that, didn't you?"

"Everyone needs to know they're wanted."

"Even you?" The words were whispered on a husky breath.

"Even me," she returned crisply. "Now let's get to work."

"Always business. Don't you ever let loose and have some fun?"

"Of course I do. In fact, I'm going out tonight." The statement came off the top of her head. But the idea was a good one. She needed to check her apartment in Oxnard, a small town a few miles up the coast highway, and it wouldn't hurt to call a friend and make a night of it.

Sloan's mouth twisted, drawing in his facial features. The look in his eye chilled her. "Anyone I know?"

"I'm sure you don't. It isn't like we run in the same circle, is it?"

"No, I guess we don't," he admitted, and stared at her.

Sloan was strangely quiet, almost brooding, for the remainder of their session. Even when she took him in his lunch, he did little more than give her a polite nod of acknowledgment.

That evening Joy's own feelings were mixed. She was sorry she'd said anything to Sloan about going out, and forced herself to dress in her best suit: black pants and a soft cream blouse with matching jacket. A strand of pearls graced her neck. While freshening her makeup, Joy tried to convince herself she was doing the right thing. The physical attraction between her and Sloan was growing more powerful every day. Of the two, she was the one who had to keep a level head, because she was the one who stood to lose the most. On the way out of the house, Joy stopped in the kitchen and told Clara where she could be reached in an emergency.

"I think it's time you took a day off, if you don't mind my saying so," Clara murmured as she dried the pots and pans from dinner.

"I don't mind," Joy agreed and impulsively hugged the older woman.

"Must say you look beautiful."

"Thanks, Clara."

"Don't suppose Mr. Whittaker's taken a look at you yet?"

"I haven't seen him since dinner." Quickly Joy changed the subject. "You know where you can reach me." Joy realized the housekeeper was much too observant not to have noticed what was happening between Joy and Sloan.

"Got it right here." She patted her apron pocket. "Let your hair down, girl."

"Honestly, it's only three inches as it is," Joy said with a small laugh as she opened the swinging door that led out of the kitchen.

She was in the marble-floored entryway when Sloan spoke.

"Don't you ever wear dresses?"

Joy stopped and turned. He was in the living room, almost as if he'd been sitting there waiting for her. His hard expression was a shock. Sloan hadn't looked like that since the first days after her arrival.

"Sometimes," she answered softly. "Usually full-length ones so I can be assured no one is going to be shocked if they happen to catch a glimpse of my scars."

"That's considerate of you," he muttered.

"It's not consideration. It's protection for my ego. These days women wear pants most anywhere, so it isn't any faux pas if I do."

His eyes held hers. "You look nice."

"Thank you."

"Have you decided where you're going yet?"

"Dan and I are going to dinner."

"Dan?"

"An old friend."

"How old?"

Joy inhaled a deep breath. "You're being ridiculous, you know that, don't you?"

"I suppose I am. Go on, go. Have a good time." He jerked the wheelchair around so his back was to her.

"Oh, boy, here it comes." Joy flew into the room and stood in front of him.

"Here what comes?" he barked.

"That 'poor little boy' act. You want me to feel guilty. You've even gone to great lengths so I'll experience this terrible guilt."

"Now you're the one being ridiculous," he declared, but his eyes refused to meet hers.

"Poor crippled Sloan has to sit home while his physical therapist Joy paints the town." She raised her eyes heavenward in a mocking gesture. "I suppose you're planning to wait up for me, too?"

Sloan's nostrils flared as his eyes narrowed. "Get out of here."

"That's what I'm trying to do," she returned flippantly, and swung the strap of her purse over her shoulder in a defiant action.

She was halfway out the door when she heard him draw in a quick breath and utter something violent. Joy decided she would prefer not to know what he'd said.

The small apartment in the heart of town looked exactly as she'd left it. Joy walked around, inspecting each room. She'd only been back once since moving into Sloan's. The rooms were compact and unappealing after the luxury she was accustomed to living in these past weeks. In some ways Joy doubted that her simple life would ever be the same again. Certainly her heart wouldn't. If she had a whit of common sense she'd pack her things and leave him now before their feelings for one another developed further.

A quick knock on the door was followed by a blond head. "I thought I'd find you here."

"Hi, Danielle." The one thing about tonight that Joy regretted was letting Sloan assume she was seeing a man. It seemed childish now, but vital at the moment.

They ate at a Chinese restaurant and drank several cups of tea while chatting over old times. When Danielle suggested a movie, Joy readily agreed. After a quick phone call to Clara, she sat through a nondescript movie. No matter how hard she forced herself to watch the screen, her thoughts continually drifted back to Sloan.

Danielle and Joy parted after the show, and Joy drove back to her apartment. Her watch said it was only ten. Much too early for her to head back to the beach house. If she was going to feel like a criminal because she took a night off, then he could sit and wait.

The television on, Joy slouched across a lumpy couch and laid her head against the back cushion and closed her eyes. When she opened them again it was well past two o'clock. Oh, heavens, she hadn't meant to stay away this long. If Sloan had waited for her he'd be in a fine mood by now.

When she pulled into her parking spot in front of the house, she took in several calming breaths. Mentally she prepared herself—for what she wasn't sure.

The porch light was on, and another in the long hallway that led to her room. She turned off the outside light and tiptoed into the entryway. "You look like a thief in the night." A deep voice flew out from the living room.

Startled, she let out a gasp. Her hand flew to her breast. "What are you doing there?" she demanded defensively.

"In case you've forgotten, I live here."

"I didn't mean that to sound the way it did," she apologized. "You frightened me."

He moved closer to her. "Did you have a good time?"

"Wonderful," she lied.

"How was Dan?"

"Good." She took in a deep breath. "Is this an interrogation?"

"No, just curiosity."

"I didn't mean to stay out so late." She could have kicked herself the minute the words slipped past her mouth.

"Time flies when you're having fun, or so they say."

"Yes, well, I think I'll get to bed."

"Did Dan kiss you good-night?" The question came abruptly, issued with impatience.

"I don't think that's any of your business." Her hand tightened around the strap of her purse.

"You don't look like you've been kissed."

"Sloan, please." She released the words on a sigh.

"At least when I kiss you, there's no doubt. Your eyes grow warm and gentle, your face is flushed, and you have a look about you that begs for more."

Joy looked away, but not before she saw the way Sloan's fingers bit into the arm of his chair.

"Does Dan make you feel the way I do?" he continued, his voice raspy and deep. "Does your heart beat faster when he holds you? Or is it just the thrill of having a man, a real man, one you don't have to look down to?"

"Stop it," she cried, her voice strained and weak. "You don't know what you're saying." The temptation was to cry out that he was more man than she'd ever known, all the man she'd ever need. Were he never to take another step, she couldn't love him any more than she already did.

Joy inhaled a sharp breath, her eyes rounded at the startling realization. For days she'd been struggling with herself, refusing to accept the truth. Now, in her anger, she acknowledged her true feelings. It was too late; she was already in love with him.

"Joy?" Sloan paused and took her hand. "Are you all right? You look like you're sick."

"I'm fine," she mumbled, and pulled her hand free from his. "I just need to lie down." She felt like she was staggering as she rushed down the hall to her room. Of course, she wasn't, but it seemed her whole world had crumpled in on top of her and the weight was more than she could possibly manage.

"Joy, wait," Sloan called out after her, but she ignored him and firmly shut the bedroom door.

Even after she'd changed clothes and crawled between the fresh sheets, Joy couldn't sleep. Unreasonably, she was angry with Sloan. Irritated, because he knew as well as she did what was happening between them and had done nothing to stop it. Her feelings, emotions, and heart were only playthings to him, a small diversion until he was walking again. She could almost hate him. Almost.

She lay there for what seemed like hours, unable to sleep because every time she closed her eyes pictures of Sloan would flash into her mind. Not content with dominating every waking minute, he was determined to haunt her sleep as well. The room felt hot and stuffy. Throwing back the covers, Joy opened the sliding-glass door just a crack. A faint moaning sound stopped her. She had to strain to hear. Sloan.

Was he in pain? Thoughtless of her bare feet, she slipped outside. Sloan's glass door was also cracked. The sound of his moans was more distinguishable now, in addition to a faint thrashing noise. Joy peeked inside his room.

Sloan was asleep and in the throes of some horrible dream. His head tossed from side to side, his blankets a twisted mess around his legs.

"Sloan." She hurried to his bedside and placed a restraining hand on both shoulders. "Wake up. You're having a dream." Lightly she shook him. "Sloan, it's a dream."

He jerked himself upright, leaning the brunt of his weight on one elbow. For a second he looked at her blankly, then released a small cry of relief. "Joy, good heavens." His eyes were filled with some unspeakable torment. Forcefully he pulled her into his arms, his breathing hoarse and uneven. "Oh, Joy." His open hands caressed her back, shooting a tingling fire down her spine. "I thought I'd lost you," he continued. "You were in the school bus screaming for me to help you, and I couldn't get out of the chair."

"I'm fine, I'm right here," she assured him, her hands brushing the hair from his face. Her heart cried out to him.

"I couldn't bear to lose you now." He twisted his upper body, bring her onto the bed beside him. Positioned so that he was above her now, his anguished eyes stared into hers. "Don't stop me. I need you so much," he murmured before his mouth rocked over hers.

She gave in to him unselfishly, parting her lips with all the eagerness of her newly discovered love. Her hands roved his back, reveling in the muscular feel of skin under her fingers. He was warm, vital, and for this moment, this night, hers.

His mouth left hers and pressed against the gentle slope of her bare shoulder.

"You've been drinking," she whispered.

"Yes." He continued to kiss her neck, his tongue making moist forays against the sensitive skin. "It was the only thing that kept me sane tonight while waiting for you."

"Oh, Sloan. You didn't drink after taking any medication, did you?"

"Don't 'Oh, Sloan' me. I know what I'm doing. For once stop being my therapist and be my lover?" His mouth blotted any objection she might have voiced.

Joy was reeling with the potency of his kisses. His exploring hands cupped the soft undersides of her breasts.

"You shouldn't," she protested weakly.

"Do you want me to stop?" he whispered against her ear, his warm breath caressing her lobe.

"No," she admitted, her arms entwined around his neck, "don't stop."

Desire, raw and fierce, ran through her blood, spreading a path of fiery awareness that left no part of her untouched. Her senses were in turmoil. No longer did she question right from wrong. No longer did it matter.

Sloan's kisses grew more deep, more passionate; their effect drugged her into submission and demanded a response. Trapped in the warm, rushing tide of her love, Joy responded freely, wholly. His lips began a downward path from the sensitive cord of her neck. Her long fingernails dug into the rippling muscles of his back as she arched, wanting to give more, needing to receive more.

"Joy," he moaned, and bruised her mouth with a scorching possession. "Do you realize how long it's been since I touched a woman like this?"

The whole world came to a sudden, abrupt halt. A woman. Any woman would have done. She was convenient, here, now. A passing fancy until he was ready for the Chantelles of this world.

Dragging her mouth from his, she pushed him away. "No more," she whispered, and struggled to sit upright.

Sloan went still. "Are you hurt? What is it? What did I say?"

The question was almost ludicrous. She was dying, and he wanted to know if he had caused her pain.

"Joy?" He raised himself up and brushed the hair from the side of her face. "What's wrong?" His tender concern was nearly her undoing.

"Let me go," she cried, her voice pitifully weak. She shut her eyes, and waited for him to let her go.

"Not until you tell me what's wrong." His voice was thick with frustration. "Are you crying?" A finger brushed the wetness across her cheek. "Joy, please. Tell me what I did."

"It has been a long time since you've touched a woman," she whispered achingly at last. "So long that you'd hold any willing woman."

"That's not true. I can't think of anyone else when you're in my arms. It's you I want," he muttered thickly. "Only you."

"That will change," she said confidently, "and soon."

He groaned her name.

"Please let me go," she pleaded, her voice quivering uncontrollably.

With a frustrated exclamation, Sloan rolled off her and stared at the ceiling as she raced out of his room as if the devil himself were in pursuit.

For two weeks they treated one another like polite strangers. To avoid the curious stares of Clara and Paul, Joy took long daily walks along the beach. No longer did she play her flute on the verandah at night. L.J. was her companion and friend, often hopping along behind her on a walk.

On the first night of the third week, Joy delivered Sloan's dinner tray. He sat, his gaze centered on the ocean. Joy left it on the table outside.

"Can we talk?" he asked without looking at her.

Joy bit into the soft fleshy part of her inner cheek. "What do you want to talk about?"

"Us."

"No," she answered emphatically.

"All right, we won't talk about us. We'll simply talk."

Joy moved to the railing, watching the rumbling sea. The scent of the ocean filled the early evening. A gentle breeze brought in a salty spray. She turned and propped her elbow against the railing. "I don't know if we have anything to say to one another."

"That's a negative thought. I've never known you to be pessimistic."

"Oh, I can be," she admitted with a sad smile.

"Yes, I noticed."

"If you don't eat, your dinner will get cold." Her mouth felt suddenly dry, yet her hands were moist to the point of being clammy. She should have packed her bags and walked out the morning after she'd given in to his kisses. But she couldn't, not before it was time. When he was walking, at least on crutches, then she'd go.

His gaze fell on the tray she'd brought with her. "Leave it. I'm not hungry."

"Have you been busy?" She knew he met daily with his father now, and she had seen his light long into the night.

"Very."

"That's good."

He came closer to her side. "In some ways it's helped me..." He let the rest trail away.

"Helped you how?"

His smile was wry. "You said the subject was taboo."

"Oh," she said, and swallowed tightly.

Paul shouted from the far side of the yard and waved. Joy gave a guilty start. She'd told him she would join him for dinner at Mobey Jake's. They went there often now.

"I've got to go."

Sloan's mouth thinned with impatience. "I understand."

Quickly she moved into her own quarters and grabbed a light sweater.

"Joy." Sloan had followed her and slid open her glass door. "Will you play tonight? I've missed that." His smile was slightly off center, and her bones felt like liquid. "Almost as much as I've missed having you as my friend."

"I've missed it too," she murmured, refusing to look into his eyes.

"Hurry back, my Joy."

The words were issued so softly Joy was sure she'd misunderstood him.

Paul brought her a double order of fish-and-chips and joined her at the umbrella-covered table in the sun. The large order was far bigger than Joy could manage, but she automatically bought the double fish so there would be enough for L.J.

"You and the boss getting on better?" Paul questioned. Their camaraderie and mutual respect had grown over the weeks. They were a team, pressing toward one goal—Sloan. He would walk one day, and the credit would be due them all.

"I guess so." She wiped the corner of her mouth with the napkin and lifted one shoulder in a lopsided shrug.

"Sometimes I wonder how you two can work with one another, the ice is so thick."

"You have a good imagination," Joy denied uneasily.

Paul lifted one thick brow expressively. "If you say so."

Joy dunked a French fry in a small container of ketchup. "I do."

Later, she brought her flute onto the verandah. She hadn't played three notes when Sloan joined her. She lowered her instrument and offered him a smile.

"Are you taking requests?"

"Sure, what would you like to hear?"

"'Yesterday,'" he replied without hesitation.

Joy remembered the first time she'd played the song. Sloan had angrily proclaimed that yesterdays were gone forever, that they couldn't be brought back. Bitterness had coated his words. Now his voice was filled with hope.

The sweet melodic sounds of the Beatles' classic

filled the night. When she was finished, there was a poignant pause.

"Why did you request that song?" she asked in a whisper, not wanting conversation to ruin the mood.

"Because I wanted to share with you some of my yesterdays."

"How do you mean?"

"Follow me," he answered cryptically, and turned sharply, leading the way through his quarters. Once he was in the hallway he paused in front of the door that was opposite her room. "Haven't you ever wondered what was in here?"

"No," she answered honestly. "I assumed it was probably your parents' room."

"Go on, open it."

Joy turned the knob and stepped inside. Because his chair wouldn't fit through the narrow doorway, Sloan remained in the hall.

The interior was dark, and she felt against the side of the wall for the light switch. Once she located it, she flipped it on. Immediately light sprayed across a room filled with awards, trophies, and sports equipment. Plaques lined one entire wall. On closer inspection, Joy saw that each one had been received by Sloan. There didn't seem to be anything he hadn't tried and mastered. Baseball, volleyball, skiing, bowling, and hockey.

Confused, she turned around, her smooth brow marred in thick creases. "All these are yours?" she asked incredibly. "It's unbelievable."

"I was quite the jock."

She picked up and inspected one of the smaller baseball trophies. "You were just a boy." She lifted her gaze to his.

"My father is credited with mounting most of these things. The albums on the desk—" he pointed to a large flat-topped desk on the far side of the room "—are filled with newspaper clippings from the time I could hold a tennis racket."

"My goodness, it's enough to take my breath away."

"I was good."

"I don't doubt it."

"I'll never be as good again."

Joy didn't mince words. "No, you won't. Does that bother you terribly?"

The look in his eyes seemed to peel away every defense barrier she'd carefully constructed these past two weeks.

"It did, but you changed that."

"Me?" The one word echoed across the room.

"I accepted the wheelchair as my fate—until you came. It wasn't a conscious decision, but one I can see as clearly now as if I'd signed the contract in blood. I was a winner with remarkable talent and skill, if I was to believe everything that had been written about me. I had the world by the tail; I lived the good life. And then it all came tumbling down on top of me. After the accident I decided that if I had to be half a man the rest of my life, then I'd be no man at all."

Joy understood what he was saying. She came and knelt by his side.

"It wasn't the pain that bound me to the chair, but the fear." He took her hand and squeezed it tight. "I'm going to walk again, Joy Nielsen, because you had the foresight to understand what was happening to me on

the inside. And just as you had your father, I have you."
Very gently he lifted her hand to his mouth and kissed
it.

Her heart plummeted to her stomach. Gratitude was
what Sloan felt. Overwhelming gratitude, nothing more.

Seven

"You're sure about this?" Sloan regarded her skeptically.

Joy sat on the thick blue mat on the weight-room floor, her legs crossed Indian fashion. "Trust me."

"You said that when you asked me to roll around like a man whose clothes had caught on fire."

"Now I want you to crawl just like a baby."

"How much longer before I can work on the parallel bars?" He eyed the set she'd brought in.

"Not long, I promise. If you want, I'll test you for strength again today."

"No." He shook his head, and Joy could all but taste his disappointment.

"Don't push yourself so hard. You're doing remarkably well."

"But the progress is so slow."

"It isn't," she replied emphatically. "Look how long you sat in that chair—months. You can't expect to be out running again in a matter of a few weeks."

"Tell me what's next."

Joy must have repeated the procedure to him fifteen times, but she didn't hesitate when he asked again.

"Lying to crawling, crawling to kneeling, kneeling to standing."

"From there to the parallel bars, the walker, and lastly the cane," he finished for her.

"There's a light at the end of the tunnel."

"I'm just beginning to see it."

"Good." She smiled brightly. "I knew you would."

"Should I pretend I'm a dog and bark?" he asked as he moved into the crawling position.

"Go ahead." Joy laughed. "It'll give Clara a good laugh."

Sloan gave an Academy Award performance that left both Joy and Paul laughing.

"Mr. Jewett's here. I haven't seen Dale in nearly nine months."

The laughter drained out of Sloan's face and his eyes turned icy cold. "Send him away. I don't want to see him. Is that understood, Clara?"

"But Mr. Jewett's been your friend since you were a boy."

"It doesn't matter. I don't want to see anyone."

Joy tossed a glance to the obviously flustered Clara, then back to Sloan. Angrily Sloan reached out from the mat and grabbed the side of his wheelchair. With a violent shove he sent it crashing against the wall. The chair tilted onto its side and fell over.

"What's wrong?" she asked quietly, and knelt at his side. "Who is the guy?"

"A friend."

"You have a funny way of showing it."

"When I want your advice, I'll ask for it," he growled.

"That wasn't advice," Joy returned. "I was simply stating an opinion."

"Then keep those to yourself."

"Fine." She stood and wiped the grit from her hands. Walking across the room, she up-righted the wheelchair and brought it to his side. "I want you to make the transfer yourself today."

"I can't."

"Don't give me that, Whittaker."

"What is this? Put the cripple in his place time?"

"Figuratively speaking, I think that's it."

"Kindly leave before I say something I'll regret later."

Joy's mouth formed into a humorless smile. "Gladly." Arms flying at her side, she stormed into the kitchen, plopped down on a chair, crossed her legs, and took three deep breaths.

"What's with that man lately? Mr. Jewett and Mr. Whittaker have been friends for a whole lot of years. Friends shouldn't treat one another like that. It's not right, it's just not right. But no one pays a mind to ol' Clara. No one," she emphasized.

"What's the matter with me lately?" Joy answered Clara with a question of her own. "I used to give as good as I took."

Clara apparently chose to ignore Joy. "I said to Mr. Jewett that Mr. Whittaker wasn't feeling like himself today. That's what I said because I know later Mr. Whittaker is going to want to see his friends again. No need to offend him. I did the right thing, didn't I?" Clara's look was eager.

"You did fine."

Clara clucked, and a look of relief relaxed the wrinkled face.

"Are you sure there isn't any reason Sloan wouldn't want to see his friend?"

"Mr. Whittaker sent all his friends away after the accident. He didn't want to see anyone. Mr. Jewett came around for a long time, but Mr. Whittaker wouldn't see him. Same as now. It's not right to treat friends like that."

"What's not right?" Sloan entered the kitchen and boldly glared at the cook.

"To send friends away," Joy answered for Clara.

Briefly, renewed anger flashed from his eyes. "You two are beginning to sound like henpecking wives."

"Mr. Jewett's been your friend for as long as I can remember..."

With a burst of energy, Sloan wheeled himself out of the room, apparently not wishing to become involved in an argument.

Joy didn't see him again that afternoon. After his time with Paul, he met with his father and spent the remainder of the day in his room on his computer.

Joy sat on the beach with L.J. until dinner, wondering if she should press this thing with Sloan. She understood what he was doing all too well. She'd done it herself. Friends, especially ones who were whole and well, were a reminder of things that would never be again. Even Danielle, her best friend since high school, the one person who knew her so well, couldn't help or understand the adjustment Joy was making.

In some ways Danielle had hurt more than she helped. She came to visit, eager to share tidbits of news and gossip from school. Joy hadn't wanted to know or

hear any of it. School, boys, teachers were so far removed from her life then that it only served to widen
the gap between them.

Sloan met Joy that night on the verandah. She was
sitting watching the sunset, a fiery ball of orange lowering into the ocean.

Sloan pulled up beside her. "Beautiful, isn't it?"

Smiling, Joy nodded. "I don't think I'll ever get tired
of looking at it. The whole world seems so peaceful and
serene. It's hard to remember the tragedies reported on
the evening news when everything's so calm here."

"I often feel that way too."

She felt at ease with Sloan, relaxed, so unlike their
first days of constant confrontation. Those times
seemed in the distant past now. She turned to smile at
him and noted the signs of stress about his mouth. His
dark eyes looked tired.

"You're strung out from working all day," she whispered. "You should go to bed."

Teasing warmth kindled in his gaze as he smiled
slightly. "Now that, my dear Joy, sounded suspiciously
like an invitation."

The gibe was a gentle one, and Joy couldn't take of-
fense. "No. When I issue an invite to my bed there won't
be need for any speculation." Joy had hoped to sound
breezy and sophisticated, but it came out all wrong. She
could feel Sloan's puzzled gaze run over her.

"You're blushing, which leads me to believe you
haven't had a lot of experience with men." His short
laugh was soft, almost caressing.

Joy straightened. "I don't like the sudden turn of this

conversation," she said stiffly. "Let's go back to what a beautiful sunset it is."

"Your cheeks are nearly as bright as the sky."

"Would you stop?" she demanded.

"No," he chided, and linked his hands behind his head, obviously enjoying himself. "Why?"

"Why what?"

"You're innocent…clearly you…"

"Honestly, Sloan, you're embarrassing me," she said, cutting him off. "Don't, please." She hung her head and pretended to be studying her fingernails. The sound of his moving drew her gaze. Sloan had turned his chair around and parked himself beside her so that only a few inches separated them. A finger under her chin turned her face to him.

"For most of my life I've stayed away from women like you." Joy swallowed uncomfortably. His eyes were tender, infinitely gentle.

"That was until I met you," he went on. "I'm pleased you are who and what you are. I wouldn't change a single thing about you." His hand slid behind her neck, urging her mouth to his.

Confused and unsure, Joy stiffened; she knew what would happen if she let him kiss her. It would be lighting a match to gasoline. The feelings Sloan produced in her weren't a small spark, but a raging forest fire. She wanted him so much, but at the same time was all too aware of where it would lead.

He dropped his hand at her resistance. The puzzled look in his eyes deepened into pain. "Is it always no to every man?"

She looked away and nodded, because speaking was almost impossible.

"Is it the scars?"

"No."

"Then why?"

One shoulder was lifted in a halfhearted shrug, urgently hoping he'd change the conversation. "I'm not exactly a sex goddess."

"There's never been anyone I've wanted more."

Bounding to her feet, Joy stalked to the far side of the deck. "Stop. Please. I find this whole conversation inappropriate."

"If I promise not to mention it again, will you come back and sit with me?"

Joy didn't find the teasing light in his eyes encouraging. "Promise?"

"Scout's honor." Solemnly he raised his index and middle fingers.

Joy returned to the cushioned wrought-iron chair and relaxed.

"But then, I was never a Boy Scout," he inserted.

"Sloan!"

"I promise, I promise."

Joy sat and brought up her knees, resting her chin on top of one. "Tell me about Jewett." Joy could sense him drawing away from her. Not physically, but mentally.

"He's a buddy," Sloan returned in a tone that discouraged further discussion.

"A good friend?"

Irritably, he expelled his breath before answering. "At one time."

"Not now?"

"I know what you're doing, Joy," he breathed impatiently. "And I don't like it."

A gentle breeze ruffled the soft curls about her face,

and Joy laughed lightly. "I love turning the tables on you."

"I don't want to talk about Dale or any of the others."

"Why not?"

"Because—" he hesitated "—because I'm not the same person I was before the accident."

"Dale knows that. He doesn't need a psychology degree to realize you've changed," she explained in a patient voice. "You couldn't help but change."

"The only friend I need is you."

"But I couldn't possibly hope to meet all your needs."

He cocked his head, and a teasing smile flirted at the side of his mouth. "You could try."

Joy ignored the glint in his eyes. "I did the same thing to my friends. Looking back, it's easy to see that my ego was involved, because I didn't want anyone to see me like that. Nor did I want to hear who was going with whom and what couple had broken up. My life had gone beyond all that, and it seemed trivial and petty. They'd come with pitiful looks and talk as if I'd had brain damage."

"Exactly," Sloan agreed.

"But I didn't consider the fact that they needed me. I was their friend, and they loved me. It hurt them to see me the way I was, and desperately my friends wanted to do something, anything to help. For a long time I wouldn't let anyone near me. Then one day Dani—"

"Dani?" Sloan questioned.

"Danielle, for real," Joy supplied.

"Not the old friend Dan you had dinner with not so long ago?"

"One and the same," she supplied with a puzzled look.

Sloan went completely still, and she watched as the

muscles worked along the side of his jaw. "You little devil. You did that on purpose."

Too late, Joy realized exactly what she had revealed.

"You purposely let me assume that you were going out with a man."

"Yes...well," Joy floundered.

"I sat here half the night going crazy thinking about you in the arms of this Dan. You should suffer for what you put me through." He wheeled around so suddenly, Joy was caught completely off guard.

Somehow she managed to escape his grip as she scurried out of the chair. Laughing, she ran down the deck, Sloan in hot pursuit. When she'd gone as far as possible, she turned, the wood railing pressing against her back. Joy stretched out a pleading hand. "Sloan." She couldn't keep the laughter out of her voice.

"Yes, my trapped little rat?"

"Would it do any good to apologize?"

"Not when I've got you where I want you." Slowly he advanced toward her, one inch at a time.

"Sloan," she pleaded a second time. Frantically she looked around for an escape.

"Mr. Whittaker, where are you?" Clara's high-pitched voice could be heard coming down the hall. There was a slight hesitation as the older woman stepped onto the verandah. "Oh, Mr. Whittaker, I was hoping I'd find you here."

"Yes, Clara, what is it?" Sloan's voice was thick with impatience.

"If you'll excuse me." Joy sauntered out of her corner and wickedly fluttered her long lashes. "It seems to have gotten a bit chilly out here all of a sudden. I think I'll take a drive into town."

"Are you going to meet Dan again?" Sloan taunted.

"Not tonight," she said with an exaggerated sigh. "But I think I'll give Mark a call."

His eyes narrowed for an instant before a smile broke out across his powerful face. For now she would escape, his eyes were telling her, but the time was fast approaching when he would extract his due.

"Are you ready?" Joy's voice was soft with encouragement.

Sloan nodded. Joy didn't know how he could be so calm. Her stomach felt like it had twisted to double knots. Even her mouth felt dry, her throat scratchy.

The parallel bars loomed before him. Sloan positioned the wheelchair so that he could reach up and pull himself upright.

Joy watched him with a ballooning sense of pride. Once he was upright, he beamed her an off-center smile.

"Well?" he probed. "How am I doing?"

Joy shook her head, because she was afraid the lump that filled her throat would make her words sound irregular and he would know how happy this new triumph made her. This was only the beginning.

"I don't think I realized how tall you are," she said at last.

Sloan continued to work his way across the bar, each movement cautious and measured. His face was furrowed with concentration.

"And I don't think I've ever realized what an elf you are."

"I am not," she denied.

His laugh was rich and deep. He stopped when he

came to the end of the long bars and awkwardly turned around.

Joy watched him with her heart in her throat. She need not have worried; he was doing wonderfully well.

"Joy," he called to her, and she was immediately at his side.

"Yes?"

"Stand here." He indicated a place beside the bars. When she did as he asked, he manipulated himself around so that they stood facing one another. She came to just an inch or two under his chin. "An elf," he affirmed, "but a perfect one. Look how well we fit together." A hand grazed her cheek and cupped her neck. "I've been waiting weeks to kiss you like this. Don't deny me now."

Joy could refuse him nothing. Had he asked for any part of her she would have given it to him gladly with all the love pent up inside.

When his lips touched hers, she released a small, weak cry of happiness. The kiss was sweet and gentle and left her craving for more. Somehow Sloan managed to keep his balance as he cradled her head against his chest and pressed his face into her hair.

"Thank you, Joy," he murmured, and again she was reminded that his emotions were confused, interwoven with a deep sense of gratitude.

"Has something happened to Sloan?" Margaret Whittaker rushed into the living room. Her face was pale and tight. Myron Whittaker followed close on his wife's heels.

"Not at all," Joy hurried to assure them. This whole

production was Sloan's idea, and she was reluctantly playing her role. "Please sit down."

Myron eyed his wife and shrugged his shoulders. "You say Sloan's fine?"

"Yes." For a moment she was sure her smile gave her away. "Perhaps you'd like some coffee while you're waiting?"

"Please," Myron answered for them both, and stopped to run a hand across his forehead.

Joy excused herself and rounded the corner, pretending she was going into the kitchen.

"You should be shot for this," she told Sloan in a heated whisper. "They're both worried sick."

He was standing. The U-shaped walker accepted his weight as his hands gripped the metal bar. Joy continued to marvel at how tall he was. Tall and vital. But even the wheelchair had been unable to diminish the aura of powerful virility that was so much a part of him.

A happy smile skittered across his face.

"What's so funny?" she demanded.

"You. I still can't believe I let such a pip-squeak boss me around. I must have been weak in the head."

"Not weak," she countered brightly, "but exceptionally smart."

He bent his head and kissed her lightly on the cheek. "Don't tell me to break a leg."

She smiled, one that came deep from within her heart. "All right, I won't."

With a slow gait, every step deliberate and practiced, Sloan moved out of his hiding position in the hall. Joy stayed where she was, the sound of his steps, the drag of the walker against the floor, magnified in the enclosed area. She didn't need to be told the cries from

Sloan's parents were ones of surprise and happiness. In her own way she was inexorably happy. The time was fast approaching when she must leave. Sloan wouldn't need her anymore.

"Clara, Clara." Myron Whittaker's voice boomed through the house.

Joy stepped aside as Clara bustled out of the kitchen.

"Bring out a bottle of my best champagne. There's cause to celebrate again."

"Joy," Sloan called to her.

Purposely she had stayed out of view. This was a time for family; she didn't want to intrude.

"Joy," he repeated, and she stepped around the entrance to the hallway and into the living room.

"Where did you go?" he questioned, his eyes watching her, his look vaguely troubled. "I thought you were right behind me."

Margaret was dabbing the corner of her eye with a scented handkerchief, and when she saw Joy she hurried across the room and hugged her tightly. "My dear Miss Nielsen, Myron and I owe you so much."

"Dad's bringing out the family's best." Sloan's eyes were bright with excitement.

"Do stay, dear," Margaret insisted. "After all, it's you we all must thank."

"Nonsense." Embarrassment heightened the natural color in her cheeks.

Sloan wrapped an arm around Joy's shoulders. "Mother, we owe this little pint-sized woman more than words can express."

A look of undisguised concern flickered briefly over Margaret Whittaker's eyes. Joy saw it but was certain Sloan was unaware of his mother's look.

Myron Whittaker returned with champagne and several glasses. A great production was made out of opening the bottle. Laughter filled the room as the bubbling brew foamed onto the marble floor.

Joy accepted the glass and stood stiffly apart from the cozy family scene by the fireplace hearth. Her smile was strained, but when Sloan's father offered a toast her response was genuine. She smiled warmly at Sloan, afraid her heart was in her eyes. Then purposefully she looked down into the sparkling liquid before taking a sip.

"This is fantastic," Sloan said, and reached for the half-empty bottle.

"French, of course," Myron Whittaker bragged. "Some of the world's finest."

"Honestly, dear, you sound like an advertisement."

Watching the small family interact naturally with one another produced an ache Joy knew she would endure for years hereafter. She would never fit into the Whittakers' social circle, with their wealth and position. It wasn't difficult to tell that Sloan's parents were concerned with their son's obvious attraction to her. And with good cause, Joy acknowledged.

"We must have a party." Margaret Whittaker's words broke into Joy's troubled musings. "Invite all your old friends."

Joy could almost visualize all the wheels turning in his mother's head.

"Here, of course," she continued. "It'll be easier for you that way. We'll invite the Jordans and the Baxters and the Reagans and the Considines."

"Mother." Sloan's sharp tone caused Margaret Whittaker to pause.

"Yes, dear?"

"There will be no party."

"Of course there will. You've been out of circulation for months. People are beginning to ask questions."

"Let them. There will be no party," he repeated forcefully.

"But, Sloan." His mother's eyes were soft and pleading. Joy didn't know how anyone could refuse the woman, and sincerely doubted that it happened often.

"I'm tired. Joy," Sloan called for her, and held out his arm. "Help me back to my room."

Joy set her nearly full champagne glass down on an end table and strode across the suddenly silent area.

"Don't say it," Sloan murmured as they reached his room and he lowered his weight in the wheelchair.

"Say what?" Joy asked, pretending not to know.

"For most of my life I've fallen into Mother's schemes, but not anymore. I have nothing in common with the Baxters, or any of those people."

Joy straightened, standing in the doorway, one hand braced against the wooden frame. "Don't look at me. That's your decision."

"Then why do I feel guilty?" He slammed his fist against the rubber wheel.

"Parents have the knack of doing that to us sometimes."

Sloan whipped a hand across his face. "I mean what I say, and Mother knows that. It'll be interesting to see what lengths she'll be willing to go to get her own way. I love my mother, but I'm not a fool."

It didn't take even twenty-four hours for Joy to learn exactly what Margaret Whittaker had in mind. Mid-morning, Clara handed Joy a phone message that asked

Joy to meet Margaret Whittaker in the best restaurant in Oxnard for lunch. Joy dreaded the confrontation.

"You look nice," Sloan commented as she brought in his lunch tray. "Where are you headed?"

"I have an appointment in town."

"Oh?" He arched one thick brow curiously. When Joy didn't elaborate, he continued. "Anyone I know?"

"Honestly, who said I was meeting anyone? It could be with the dentist." Over the years Joy had gained a certain amount of poise. She didn't want to mislead Sloan; nor did she wish to cause ill will between mother and son.

"What time will you be back?" he questioned.

"You're beginning to sound like my guardian," she accused teasingly with an underlying tone of seriousness.

Sloan reached out and took her hand, squeezing it lovingly. Even his lightest touch was enough to cause chaos with her emotions. A tingling awareness spread up her arm. "That's the last way I want you to think of me." He smiled at her, his voice deep and calm while his eyes shone into hers.

Joy nodded and backed away. The need to escape was growing to the point of desperation. If she couldn't disguise her feelings for him, then everything would be lost and she would have to leave.

Margaret Whittaker was already seated when Joy arrived.

"My dear, how nice of you to come."

"How thoughtful of you to invite me," Joy murmured, hating small talk and knowing she would be

forced to endure at least an hour of it until Sloan's
mother came to the point of the meeting.

The waitress arrived, filled Joy's water glass, and
handed her a menu. Joy ordered almost without looking.
She doubted that she'd be able to choke down anything
more than a salad. Already she could feel the sensitive
muscles of her stomach tighten.

"Such lovely weather this time of year, don't you
agree?" Sloan's mother murmured the question.

"Yes." Joy nodded. Her right hand surrounded the
water glass, collecting the condensation. "May is my
favorite month."

"You've done remarkably well with Sloan."

"Thank you."

"Believe me when I say I know how difficult he
can be."

"He was in the beginning, but gradually he came to
accept me as his physical therapist."

"How much longer will it be before Sloan's completely independent?"

"A few weeks, not much more than that." She swallowed a sip of ice water. It slid down her throat, easing
the building tightness.

"One of the reasons I invited you here today is to
ask about Sloan's social readjustment. I'm sure you've
dealt with situations like this before."

Joy hadn't, but didn't say so. "I believe that, given
time, Sloan will readjust automatically."

"I had hoped he would agree to letting me throw a
party in his honor. He knows how much I love parties,
and everyone has been so concerned. It seems like such
a good way to help my son. Don't you agree?"

"I really couldn't say, Mrs. Whittaker." Uncomfortable, Joy lowered her gaze. So this was the reason Margaret Whittaker had invited her to lunch.

"Has he mentioned the party to you?"

"Not since yesterday."

"What did he say then?" the older woman probed.

"Mrs. Whittaker, please," Joy said, and breathed in softly. "I don't think it's my place to relay your son's feelings."

"But I had so hoped." She gave Joy a softly pleading glance, not unlike the one Joy had witnessed so recently.

The waitress arrived with their salads. Joy smiled her appreciation and reached for her fork. She didn't need to take a bite to know the meal would taste like overcooked mush.

"I think that if you talked to Sloan..." Margaret Whittaker continued, her gaze centered on the meal. "What I mean to say is that I've noticed the way my son looks at you."

Joy's heart leaped into her throat. "What do you mean?"

"It's only natural that Sloan would feel a certain amount of gratitude toward you. He respects and likes you. If you were to ask him about the party, I'm sure he would agree. Won't you, dear?" she quizzed softly. "For Sloan's sake?"

Eight

Joy laid the fork beside her untouched salad. "I sincerely doubt that my asking will have any effect on Sloan's decision."

"But you will try?" Margaret Whittaker entreated.

"Yes," Joy agreed, nodding reluctantly, when what she wanted was to keep Sloan to herself for the rest of her life.

As Joy returned to the beach house, she knew what she had to do. Sloan's mother had made the position clear. Joy's responsibilities went far beyond the physical therapy Sloan required. He was almost to the point of walking on his own now. Her last duty would be to bring him back into the mainstream of life.

Hands clenching the steering wheel, Joy drove to the shoulder of the highway and stopped completely. The scenery was spectacular. Huge waves pounded the rocky shoreline. Large gulls swooped low in a sky that was cloudless. Heaving a sigh, Joy lowered her face until her brow pressed against her coiled hands. What Margaret Whittaker was really asking was that Joy relinquish her love. Of course, she had been subtle, but genuinely concerned that Sloan fit back into the life-style he had known before the accident. One that excluded Joy.

Sloan was in the hallway when Joy rounded the corner, eager to escape to her room unseen. She stopped abruptly when she saw him.

Large-knuckled hands gripped the walker. Slowly Joy raised her eyes to meet his.

"How was your appointment?"

"Fine."

A smiling knowledge lurked behind his dark eyes. "You don't look pleased about it. What's the matter, did the dentist find a cavity?"

"I wasn't at the dentist."

His mouth curved in a smile, the look deliberately casual. "I suppose my mother's been at it again."

Joy attempted to disguise her surprise. "How'd you know where I was?"

"I didn't. But I happen to know my mother. I didn't think she'd let this party thing drop so easily." He shifted his weight, and Joy recognized that he was getting tired.

"Go back to your room and I'll bring us coffee."

Sloan agreed, and Joy returned a few minutes later with two cups of hot coffee and freshly baked cookies from Clara.

When Sloan saw the tray he lifted one dark brow. "You expect this is going to take a while?" The look he gave her was both amused and curious.

"It could," Joy responded noncommittally.

Her hand shook a little as she handed a cup to Sloan.

"You are nervous." The sharp gaze followed her movements.

"Not really," she said, attempting to smooth over her telltale tremble. With her cup resting on her knee, Joy sat across from Sloan, who was at his desk.

"All right, let's have it. What's Mother said to you?"

"Nothing so terrible."

"I can imagine."

"Don't," Joy said quickly in defense of the older woman. "You've spent a hellish nine months; I don't think you realize how hard this has been on your parents."

His mouth narrowed slightly. "I admit things haven't been easy for any of us."

"Now that you're walking again, your mother needs the assurance that things are going to be the way they once were."

Sloan rubbed his hands together, the movement marked with frustration. "I'm not the man I was nine months ago."

"You are and you aren't," Joy murmured, staring into the steaming black liquid.

Sloan's frown was curious.

"In some ways you can't change," Joy continued. "Certainly not who or what you are. But you're bound to see things differently. Life is suddenly precious, and what was once important means little to nothing." She sat awkwardly on the edge of the straight-backed chair. "I don't know if any of this makes sense."

"It makes perfect sense. That's exactly how I feel."

"The struggles, the pain, have made you…"

"Us," he interrupted, immediately linking them together.

"Us," she altered, and swallowed. The tightness in her throat was mounting until it felt as if someone's hands were around her neck in a stranglehold. "I know how it was with me. My whole world revolved around my family. I felt secure with them. I didn't want to face the world. People can be cruel, and I wasn't sure I could handle it if someone saw my scars." Her voice contained the rawness of remembered pain, but she continued steady and even. "Now that time has come for you too."

"Or so my mother says," Sloan murmured dryly.

"And I agree."

"Has it come down to taking sides?"

"I hoped it wouldn't," Joy whispered.

"Apparently, Mother's conned you into believing this party idea of hers will bring me back into the social circle?" His tone was cynical.

"Your mother hasn't conned me into anything. She's concerned and wants what's best for you."

"And has appointed herself as my guardian to issue me back into a life I want to leave dead and buried."

Joy's responding smile was crooked despite her best effort.

"You find this situation comical?"

"No." She shook her head while her finger absently made a circular motion around the top of the cup. "You remind me so much of myself. The thing is, Sloan, as much as you'd like to remain a hermit in this beautiful retreat, there's a whole world waiting for you."

He emitted a harsh, bitter sound that Joy chose to ignore.

"My point is that I believe your mother may not be so far off base with this party idea. For weeks now, I've battled again the fortress you built against the outside world. The time has come to face these doubts straight on."

He was silent, intense, and to all appearances hadn't heard a word she'd said. "You're asking me to let my mother go ahead with the plans for this party."

"Yes." Her voice was faintly husky.

Sloan closed his eyes and uttered a low, frustrated groan. "By heaven she's done it again." He slammed his hand against the top of the desk, shooting pens and papers in every which direction.

Joy gasped, and her hand flew to her breast.

His mouth pinched tight, Sloan's head bobbed in cynical acknowledgment. "She knew the only person in the world I'd do this for was you."

"It's got to be for you, Sloan." If they didn't end the conversation soon, Joy was convinced she'd break into tears.

Margaret Whittaker couldn't possibly understand what she had asked of Joy. Not only must she relinquish her love, but she must give Sloan back to a life he claimed he didn't want.

"All right." Sloan ran a hand along the side of his head, smoothing the dark hair. "I'll call Mother and tell her I'll agree to this stupid party idea of hers."

"Thank you." Joy stood before a sob escaped and humiliated her. "I'm sure you won't regret it."

"I already do." Sloan's muttered words followed her out of the room.

The party plans were set for the following weekend. Clara couldn't hope to manage everything, and extra help was brought in. Margaret Whittaker became a permanent fixture, bustling in and out, a flurry of activity following her wherever she went. The house, staff, everyone was thrown into an unbelievable tizzy.

As much as possible, Joy stayed out of the way. Tuesday she phoned Danielle to see if there was a possibility of their getting together that Saturday night, but Danielle had already made plans. Not wishing to involve herself, Joy decided to spend the night at her apartment and return the following Sunday morning.

Sloan joined her on the verandah the night before the planned gala event. He stopped his walker beside her and waited until she'd finished playing the musical score on the flute.

"Do you see what you've done?" he teased, referring to the party.

"Does your mother do everything like this?"

"Everything," Sloan confirmed with a chuckle. "But I admit this one tops the cake. I think Dad nearly had a stroke when Mother handed over the caterer's bill."

"I hope you don't mind if I slip out early tomorrow afternoon—" She wasn't allowed to finish.

"Slip out!" he repeated angrily.

"Yes, I thought I'd spend the night at my apartment. You don't need—" Again she was interrupted.

"Don't need!" he shouted unreasonably. "Listen here. It's because of you that I agreed to this whole fiasco. I have no intention of letting you get out of it."

"But I can't be here."

"What the blazes do you mean by that?"

Not for weeks had Joy seen Sloan so angry. "I... I don't belong there."

"The only reason I agreed to this craziness my mother schemed up was because you'd be with me."

"But, Sloan, these are your friends. I won't know anyone."

"You'll know me."

A feeling of desolation stole over her. "But I don't have anything to wear to something like this."

"Take tomorrow off and buy yourself a dress," he shot back.

"It doesn't matter what I say. You have an answer." Her chin jutted out defiantly.

"You're right. And you'd better decide soon. Otherwise this whole affair is about to be canceled."

Nervously Joy trailed her fingers along the railing. "But I don't want to go. I'll stick out like a sore thumb."

Sloan's sharp laughter filled the night. "And you think I won't? There's no way I'll endure tomorrow without you. Now, do you agree, or will I be forced to start a war within my own family?"

Her mouth thinned with anger and regret. "I don't like this, Sloan Whittaker. I don't like it one bit."

L.J. offered some comfort early the next morning when Joy walked along the sandy beach and plopped down on a log. With short strokes, Joy smoothed the gull's feathers down the back of his head.

"It isn't working like I'd planned," she complained. "Not at all."

L.J. cocked his head undisturbed. A few other seagulls flew overhead and landed down the beach. L.J.'s interest piqued as he squawked loudly. The returning sounds seemed to excite him, and he scurried toward his friends, his feet leaving wet indentations in the sand.

Joy's heart plummeted to her feet as she watched the

bird she had come to love hurry away. Would she lose him? L.J. was tame now, at least for her. She couldn't help wonder if he'd fit back into the life he'd once known. She was almost glad when he turned around and hobbled back to her side. The gauze that held his wing against his body was what restrained him. Joy knew she shouldn't be glad, but she was.

The remainder of the morning and all afternoon was spent shopping. Joy gave up counting the number of dresses she tried on. By afternoon she was weak with worry. It didn't matter what she wore; nothing could change what she was: somewhat plain, short, and scarred.

The dress she finally chose was a deceptively simple design with elegant lines. The wide white belt contained a rose pin. By the time she made her decision, Joy had given up caring. The sales clerk told her it was lovely. Joy was convinced the sales clerk was prompted by the thought of a big sale.

The hairdresser styled her short hair in bouncy curls that made her look like the comic strip character Betty Boop. Joy washed it out when she got home.

Sloan was nowhere in sight, and Joy stayed in her room, preferring not to interfere with everything that was going on around the house.

The knock on her bedroom door surprised her. She stood, running a light hand over the black skirt before answering.

Sloan, dressed in a dark suit and tie, stood supported by crutches outside her door. The sight of this virile, handsome man was enough to steal her breath. His smile was devilishly enticing and slashed deep grooves around his mouth. His dancing dark eyes were directed at her and slowly took in every inch of her appearance. Apparently, what he saw pleased him, as an immense look of satisfaction showed in his eyes.

"Will I do?" The words stuck in her throat and sounded almost scratchy.

His answering nod was absent. "I see you every day, but this is the first time I've ever seen you all dressed up."

"I feel like a fish out of water."

"And you look like a princess. My Joy, you are a beautiful woman." He said it as if it surprised him.

She felt the color seep up her neck. "And you, Sloan Whittaker, bear a striking resemblance to Prince Charming."

"So it's been said," he teased. "Shall we?" He proffered his elbow. Joy rested her hand lightly against the crook of his arm and inhaled a deep breath, readying herself for the ordeal.

"I'll be the envy of every man here," he whispered reassuringly, and paused in the hallway just out of view from the living room. "Relax. You're as stiff as starched underwear."

Under any other circumstances Joy would have laughed, but she felt like a coiled spring, her nerves in chaos.

"Joy." Her name was issued on a soft reassuring note. The gentle brush of his lips on her cheek sent a warm glow over her. "Now smile."

She painted one on her lips and prayed it would effectively disguise her nervousness.

People had already begun to arrive. Joy didn't know a soul, not even the help who sauntered in and around the guests with trays of drinks and hors d'oeuvres.

Just before they entered the room, Sloan paused and inhaled a deep, calming breath. Filled with her own misgivings over this evening, Joy had forgotten what an ordeal this must be for Sloan. She glanced at him, a protective spark burning in her eyes.

Sloan's mother was at their side the minute they entered the room. Dressed in a lovely silver creation, she looked years younger. Diamonds graced her neck and hung from her ears. The scent of gardenias followed her.

"Ladies and gentlemen," Margaret Whittaker announced solemnly, "the guest of honor, my son Sloan."

Sloan tossed his mother a look of severe displeasure, but graciously smiled at the small audience.

A flurry of introductions followed, for Joy's benefit. After five minutes she gave up trying to remember names and faces.

A path was cleared for Sloan as he purposefully made his way into the room. He chose a far corner chair and set the crutches at his side.

"Joy," he whispered tightly. "Get me something to drink. I'm going to need it."

Joy felt exactly the opposite. More than at any time she could remember, she needed her wits about her. But getting something nonalcoholic in this crowd might be impossible.

A waiter was readily available. Joy lifted a long-stemmed wineglass from the silver tray. "Would it be possible to have a Coke or something?"

"Right away, madam."

Joy relaxed. Maybe this wouldn't be as bad as she'd assumed. Sloan took the wineglass out of her hand and placed an arm around her waist.

"Sit here." He indicated the padded arm of the chair.

When she did as he requested, Sloan kept his hand where it was. Joy knew she should object. The reason for this gathering was to bring Sloan back into contact with his friends—and that included women.

Joy spotted Chantelle a few minutes later. Blonde. Beautiful. Perfect. Everything Joy would never be. Chantelle laid a thin cobwebbed lace shawl over Clara's arm and smiled beguilingly into a tall man's eyes. Obviously her date. Joy relaxed.

"What was that for?" Sloan asked, his hand tightening possessively around her.

"What?"

"That sigh," he returned.

"Chantelle's here."

"Joy, whatever you do, don't leave me."

"Sloan?" She couldn't understand him.

"Don't 'Sloan' me. I want you here as protection."

"I'm your physical therapist, not your armed guard," she whispered back. Silently she gritted her teeth.

"Joy," he said again entreatingly. "If someone makes one condescending remark or patronizes me, I won't be responsible for my actions. I need you as a buffer."

"A pillow would have done as well. Why drag me into this? Haven't you any consideration for someone other than yourself?"

"Hello, Sloan." It was the man who had come in with Chantelle. He stood directly in front of them.

"Dale." The greeting was sadly lacking in warmth. "Forgive me for not standing up," Sloan mocked.

"That I can overlook. It's the constant brush-off you've been giving me these past months I'm having a hard time forgiving."

"I'd think after the first few times you would have gotten the message."

Dale directed his attention to Joy. "Since Sloan is delinquent in introducing us, I'll do it myself. I'm Dale Jewett, Sloan's friend, although that at the moment is questionable."

"How do you do," Joy responded primly. So this was the man Sloan had repeatedly sent away.

"I think there's something you should understand right now." Sloan's voice was coated in ice. "My tennis days are over, skiing no longer appeals to me, and my golf game is shot."

Dale laughed and loudly slapped his knee. "You mean that's what's been bugging you all these months? Do you think I care if you can do any of that?"

Joy slid off the seat. Sloan had released his hold, and didn't seem to notice that she'd moved. "If you'll excuse me a minute."

Sloan didn't answer. Joy stepped aside and watched as Dale pulled up the ottoman and sat down. Within seconds the two men were engrossed in conversation.

The waiter delivered her Coke, and Joy stood in the background. Someone she vaguely remembered being introduced to engaged her in a conversation, but Joy was only half listening, making monosyllabic responses when required. Apparently the woman was a distant cousin of the Whittakers and had heard all kinds of good things about Joy from another cousin.

Dale was joined by Chantelle, who proudly held out her left hand. A solitaire diamond sparkled from her ring finger. Joy felt like jumping up and down and applauding. She watched as the two men enthusiastically shook hands.

Sloan turned and started to say something, unaware she had left. His eyes briefly scanned the crowd until they found her. They narrowed slightly, indicating he wanted her.

"Excuse me, please," Joy told the friendly cousin. The Coke glass in her hand, she sauntered back to Sloan's side.

"You rang, master?" she teased.

His arm came around her waist. "The funny-girl is Joy."

"We've met," both Chantelle and Dale said at the same time, and laughed. The two were so obviously in love that Joy instantly shared in their happiness.

"From what I understand, you're the one responsible for this minor miracle."

"No, the credit goes to Sloan. The only praise I can accept is being tenacious enough to stick it out with him."

"This little lady pinched, poked, prodded, and punished me."

"All in the line of duty," Joy joked.

"Sometimes above-and-beyond duties call," Sloan inserted dramatically.

Another couple joined them. Again Joy was introduced, his hand at her waist keeping her possessively at his side. When he handed her his empty glass, Joy stood to go refill it for him.

Dale had broken through the brick wall that Sloan had erected, and now the sounds of his laughter could be heard above the rest. The crowd around him had grown so large that Joy didn't bother to push her way through.

"Didn't I tell you what a good idea this party was?"

Margaret Whittaker brushed past, cheerful and happy. "Myron and I couldn't be more pleased with everything you've done."

She held the fragile stem of Sloan's drink with both hands. "Thank you," she murmured humbly.

"We'd like to give you a generous bonus." Her husband had mentioned the same thing once before. Joy didn't want or need a bonus. It was enough that she had accomplished what she set out to do.

"Really, Mrs. Whittaker, that won't be necessary."

"Of course it's necessary. Now don't argue."

Joy was quickly learning that the Whittakers were accustomed to having things their own way. It wouldn't do her any good to argue.

Myron joined his wife, his hand cupping her shoulder. "Good evening, Miss Nielsen."

"Hello," she returned. "It's a lovely party."

"Are you enjoying yourself?"

"Very much." The lie was only a white one.

"Juliette's here." The words were directed to his wife.

Margaret was instantly alert. "Do you think inviting her was wise?" A curious note of concern entered her voice. "Juliette and Sloan were quite serious before the accident," the older woman explained.

"Oh." Joy struggled to sound as natural as possible.

"I'm so hoping they get back together again."

Joy tensed.

"They were perfect for one another."

"What happened?" Joy wanted a reason to hate the mysterious Juliette. Had the woman walked out on him after the accident?

"All Sloan's doing, I fear. He didn't want anyone around. I'm afraid he hurt her terribly."

"Don't worry, dear," Myron Whittaker commented. "I'm sure now that Sloan's walking they'll patch things up."

"What has been your experience in cases like this?" Margaret asked. Both parents looked to Joy.

She forced a reassuring smile. "I really couldn't say."

A middle-aged woman came up and whispered something in Myron's ear. He nodded.

"Miss Nielsen, would you mind checking with Clara in the kitchen. It seems we've run out of hors d'oeuvres."

"Of course not."

Her nerves felt raw as she sauntered into the kitchen. Clara was busy working with the caterers, placing large shrimp onto a silver platter.

"How's it going in here?" Joy asked.

Clara looked up, startled. "My goodness, what are you doing in here?"

"Mr. Whittaker sent me to see how the goodies are holding out."

"What he really wants to know is if the little pink fellows have made their debut yet." She held up a shrimp.

"I guess you could say that." She smiled.

"Tell him to hold his horses, for heaven's sake. There's only so much we can do all at one time."

"All right, I'll tell him. But if you don't mind, I'll use more delicate terms."

Clara's look was perplexed, her brow knit in deep creases. "Now scat before something spills on that pretty dress."

Sloan's wineglass was still in her hand as she returned to the party. The Whittakers were out of sight, and Joy suspected Myron had purposely sent her away in order to bring Juliette to Sloan's attention. It was probably best. Joy didn't want to meet someone that was perfect for him.

"There you are." Chantelle stepped to her side. "Sloan sent me to find you."

Joy took in a breath to make her voice sound calm. "I imagine he's ready for his drink. I got waylaid."

"His drink?" Chantelle returned hesitantly. "No, Dale got him a refill earlier. Sloan wants you."

What lovely words, Joy mused as she followed the blonde through the crowd.

Several people were standing in front of Sloan, some leaning against the furniture, drinks in hand, a friendly crowd that responded with laughing eagerness to his witticisms. The attention didn't bother him, but unnerved her.

Their eyes met and Joy stopped midstep. She didn't want to be thrust into the middle of this, and silently she relayed as much. Her hands balled into fists as she stood outside the circle of friends. She didn't belong here, and he knew it.

Someone whispered Juliette's name, and Joy's attention was diverted to another blonde who moved gracefully across the room toward Sloan.

A hush fell over the crowd.

"Hello, Sloan," the other woman's musical voice greeted him.

Joy couldn't listen, couldn't watch. Abruptly she turned away and for a timeless second was frozen into immobility as the sound of Sloan's warm welcome reached her.

Somehow she made it back to her room, which felt stifling and hot. The sliding-glass door made a grating noise as she opened it and stepped onto the verandah. Arms hugging her waist, Joy raised her face to the heavens. From the moment she arrived, Joy had known this would happen. There was no one to blame but herself. She was the foolish one to have given her heart to Sloan Whittaker.

Tonight had magnified their differences. From the instant she'd stepped into the party it'd been apparent she didn't belong. Sloan's world was light-years away from anything she'd ever known. He was accustomed to wealth, influential people, and a certain amount of power.

Her job was almost complete, and she couldn't be anything but happy with how things had worked out. Her heart, however, was weeping for the man who had cried out for her in his sleep. "I thought I'd find you here," Sloan spoke from behind.

"You should be with your guests," she mumbled, not turning.

"Why didn't you come back?"

She could hear the sound of his crutches as he moved closer to her side.

Tension crackled in the space separating them.

"I couldn't." Her weak voice was barely audible.

"That's not an answer."

"All right, I don't belong in there. Is that what you want me to say? Because it's true." Her lower lip quivered slightly.

"Don't give me that garbage." His words exploded into the still night. A hand on her shoulder turned her around.

Joy hung her head. "How's Juliette?"

"Fine. We didn't talk long. I was too eager to find you." A hand stroked the curve of her neck and down her shoulder. The other found its way to the back of her neck. A fiery warmth rushed down her spine. "How long is it going to take you to learn that the two of us belong together? We're a team."

The pressure of his hands brought her up onto her tiptoes.

"Don't," she pleaded, and her voice trembled. "Sloan, I can't bear it. Please don't."

His hand closed more firmly around her neck, bringing her against the solid wall of his chest. "Don't you know yet how much I love you?" His voice was incredibly gentle, caressing her upturned face.

Agony was tearing at her heart. "You can't love me."

"But I do." His mouth moved against her hair in a rough action. The heat of his body burned through the flimsy material of her dress. His heartbeat hammered erratically against her palm.

For a moment she managed to elude his searching kiss, but when his mouth found hers, all protest died. She wound her arms around his neck and gave herself completely to his probing kiss. Everything went spinning, a magical merry-go-round that ascended to dizzying heights. Feeling boneless, she molded her body to his. Sloan had once said that they fit perfectly together. For the first time, she was able to test how accurate his statement was.

"Come on, my Joy," he whispered against her nape. "As much as I want to stay here and hold you the rest of our lives, we have to go back." He chuckled softly. "At this point, it would be best to avoid Mother's wrath."

Nine

Joy sat on a burned-out log along the beach. Her flute lay across her lap and L.J. hobbled about her feet. The early-morning air contained a crisp chill, but Joy was only vaguely aware of her surroundings.

"I should be the happiest woman in the world," she told the attentive seagull. "Sloan said he loved me last night." She raised the flute to her lips and played a few mournful notes. "Talk to me, L.J. Tell me why I feel so miserable."

The bird looked back at her blankly.

"Come on," Joy moaned regretfully. "This isn't doing any good. Let's go back."

She stood and continued to play as she walked along the sand-covered shore, L.J. trailing behind. Once she glanced back, and a smile lit up her face. She felt like a pied piper.

When the house came into view, she noted that Sloan was standing on the verandah, looking out. She paused and waved. He returned the gesture, but even from this distance she could see that something was bothering him.

He was still outside when she put L.J. back into the fenced yard and returned to her room. She carelessly laid the flute across the mattress and joined Sloan on the deck.

"What's wrong?"

He glared at her for a moment, his look thoughtful. "I didn't know you still had the bird."

"He's just like a pet now."

"The two of you made quite a pair walking on the beach like that." Somehow he didn't sound like it was a pleasant sight.

"Something's troubling you. What is it, Sloan?" She placed her hand on his forearm, and he covered it with his own.

"You say the bird is tame. For everyone?"

"No, only me. But I was the one who treated him and I'm the one who feeds him."

"Hasn't he ever given any indication he wants to be free?"

"No…" She stopped, remembering his reaction the other day when some gulls were near.

"I notice his wing is still bandaged. I'd think by now it would be healed."

Joy straightened her back and took a step in retreat. "What you're suggesting is that the time has come to set the bird free." She struggled to take the protest out of her words.

"I know how you feel about him."

"You couldn't possibly know. I found him; I was the one who took care of him. He eats right out of my hand now. He's tame, I tell you. He doesn't want his freedom; he's content to stay here." Her voice became thinner with every word as she argued.

"You're right," Sloan reasoned. "The bird is yours; you're the one who worked with him. I'm just asking that you think about it."

Joy tried to smile, but the effort resulted in a mere trembling of her mouth. She squared her shoulders. "I think you're right. L.J. deserves a better life than this." Abruptly she turned around, intent on doing it while the strength of her conviction remained strong.

"Where are you going?"

"To set L.J. free."

"It doesn't have to be done now."

"Yes, it does." Unreasonably, she felt like shouting at him.

Her mouth was set in a firm line as she marched down to the back portion of the yard and opened the gate. She didn't need to say a word for the gull to come rushing out. Like a tiny robot, he followed her down to the beach.

Tears blurred her eyes as she knelt at his side and unwrapped the gauze bandage from his wing. Carefully she extended it, checking for any further damage. There wasn't anything that she could see.

"We've become good friends over the last few weeks, haven't we, Long John?"

He tested his new freedom, then quirked his small head at an inquiring angle when he experienced the first unruffling of his broad wingspan.

Joy bit into the corner of her bottom lip at the happy squawk he gave.

"The time has come for you to go back to your other friends." Her voice was incredibly weak.

The bird continued to stare back at her.

"Go on," she urged. "Fly away. Scat."

He didn't budge.

"Sloan's right," she spoke in a whisper. "He told me it was time to set you free." Joy choked on a sob. "But it wasn't you he was talking about. Sloan's ready too. Long John," she groaned. "This is hard enough without your making it any more painful." She rose and brushed the sand from her pants. "You're free. Go." She waved her arms, indicating that he should fly away.

Still he didn't move.

Joy began to run, and to her horror the bird followed behind as he'd done so many times in the past.

"No." She shouted and continued waving her hands in an effort to frighten him away.

He looked at her as if he were laughing.

She picked up a pebble and tossed it at him. It bounced a few inches away.

He let out an angry squawk.

"Go," she shouted with all her strength. Just when it didn't look as if anything she did would make any difference, another gull swooped onto the beach.

"Your friends are here," she told him in a gentle voice that probably confused him all the more. "Go to them. It's where you belong."

He glanced from her to the sky. Testing his wing a second time, he rose and hovered in the air above her. He seemed reluctant to go.

Standing completely still, Joy placed a hand over her mouth and raised the other in a final salute to the bird she had come to love. Burning tears streamed down her cheeks.

Her heart breaking, she stayed on the shore until he was out of sight. She turned, and the beach house loomed before her.

Almost from the beginning she had found similarities between Sloan and L.J. They were two of a kind. In the beginning each had been arrogant and proud. She had been the one to tame them, and she must be the one to set them free. The decision was long overdue. Sloan didn't need her anymore. Within a matter of days he'd be able to go from the walker to the cane. Why had she waited? It only made the parting more painful.

Her lower lip trembling, Joy returned to the house. Mercifully Clara wasn't in the kitchen, and Joy hurried down the hall to her room. The suitcases were under the bed, and she knelt down to pull them out.

The first thing she packed was her flute in the small black carrying case that resembled a doctor's bag. Without rhyme or order she began tossing her things inside the open bags.

When the largest one was filled, she dragged it off the bed and out of the house. Somehow she managed to get it into the back of her car. Sloan was in the hallway outside her bedroom when she returned. Without a word, she scooted past him.

"What are you doing?"

"Packing."

He laughed. "You're kidding."

"No," she said forcefully, "I'm not."

"You can't mean it." He sounded shocked.

"Isn't it obvious?" she returned flatly. "Look in my room. My bags are out; my clothes are on the bed. To put it plain and simple, I'm leaving."

"But why? I don't understand."

Holding her expression tight, Joy released an impatient sigh. "What's there to understand? My job is finished. You're up and around. That's what I came here for. Now it's time to move on." She strived to sound as unemotional as possible.

She saw his hands tighten around the metal bar that supported him. "It's that damn bird, isn't it?"

"Of course not."

"I knew the minute you left that something was wrong. Let's talk about it, at least. Don't just walk out."

"Mr. Whittaker." Clara ambled down the hall. "I haven't seen Joy this morning."

"She's here," he replied, obviously irritated by the interruption.

"But she didn't bring you breakfast."

"She claims she's leaving," Sloan announced.

"No." Clara emphatically shook her head to deny the truth. "Joy wouldn't leave without saying something. That's not like her."

Joy came through the doorway carrying as much as possible under both arms. Only one suitcase remained. "I was coming back to say goodbye to you and Paul."

"But not me?" His look cut her to the quick.

She didn't answer.

"Joy." Frustration coated his voice as he stepped aside to allow her to pass. "Why are you doing this?"

"Because I have to, don't you see?"

"No, I don't," he returned angrily.

Joy hurried out of the house and threw her things into the car. She paused long enough to take in several deep, calming breaths.

Clara was standing in the front doorway, her face tight with concern. "What's happened?"

"Nothing." Joy attempted to brush away the house-keeper's doubts. "The time has come for me to leave, that's all. You knew from the beginning I would eventually go."

"But not like this, so sudden and all."

"Sometimes it's better that way. Clara, you've been a dear. I'll never forget you." Briefly she hugged the warm, generous woman. "Where's Paul?"

"He's gone into town," Clara replied, her look preoccupied.

"Then give him my best. I can't wait."

"Why can't you?" Clara demanded in uncharacteristic sharpness.

Joy didn't answer; instead she stepped back into the house and headed straight to her room. Sloan was inside waiting for her. He slammed the door shut after she entered.

Hands clenched, Joy whirled on him. "Why'd you do that?"

"I'll lock you in here until hell freezes over if you don't tell me what's going on."

"What's there to explain? The time has come for me to take on another case, that's all."

"But I need you."

"Nonsense. Everything I do, Paul can do," she explained tersely.

"That's not it, and you know it."

Her chin jutted out in challenge. "I know nothing of the sort." Her hand closed around the suitcase as she lifted it off the bed.

"Doesn't last night mean anything to you?"

Joy's greatest fear was that he would bring up his love. Silently she prayed God would give her strength. "Of course it does. But those feelings of gratitude are common—" She wasn't allowed to finish.

"It isn't gratitude." He was all but shouting now. "What does it take to reach you?"

With the suitcase in her hand, she rolled it across the floor.

"Don't walk out on me, Joy...we both know that in time you'll regret it."

A sad smile briefly touched her mouth; she would come to regret this day? Slowly, she turned to face him. "Goodbye, Sloan. May God grant you a rich and full life." At the moment her own felt empty and desolate. Tears clouded her eyes as she turned around, her back to him, one hand on the door.

"Don't leave me. Not like this." A wealth of emotion filled Sloan's plea.

The temptation to turn around and run into his arms was so strong that Joy felt as if she were fighting an invisible force that was pulling her apart.

"Goodbye," she repeated, her voice trembling and weak.

Something exploded behind her. Joy swung around just in time to see Sloan hurl a vase against the opposite wall. It shattered into a hundred pieces.

"Go ahead, then, go," he shouted, knocking the bedside lamp aside. "You're right. I don't need you. Get out of my life and stay out." Defiance glared from his dark eyes.

All color drained out of her face as she stood frozen and immobile.

"What are you waiting for? Do I have to kick you out the door?" He took the walker and slammed it against the dresser. "Like you said I don't need you."

Joy understood all too well. Swallowing, she walked

out of the room. Her legs felt as if they could buckle under her, but somehow she managed.

Clara stood in the entryway, wringing her hands. "Sure gonna miss you around here. It won't seem the same with you gone."

"Thank you, Clara." Tears ran freely down her face. "Take care of him for me." Her voice was breaking, and she paused to take in a breath, then tilted her head toward Sloan's room so Clara would know what she meant.

"I will, but it's you he needs."

"He'll be fine."

"But will you?"

The confirming nod was weak. "I think so."

Without looking back, Joy walked out of the house, climbed in her car, started the engine, and pulled away.

"I won't do any more private cases," Joy emphasized as she spoke into the telephone receiver. She knew that Dr. Phelps was upset with her, but Joy had learned her lesson. Never again.

"You're sure? The money is good," Dr. Phelps persisted.

"The money is always good."

"You did a fabulous job with Whittaker."

"Thank you." Joy bit her lip to keep from asking how he was. Three weeks had seemed more like three years.

"I understand you're working at the Sports Clinic now."

"Yes, I started a couple of weeks ago."

"How do you like it?"

Joy couldn't very well admit it was boring, unchallenging, and that every day away from Sloan she was dying a little more. "It's regular hours, no hassles and…"

"Crummy pay," Dr. Phelps finished for her.

"And that," she agreed with a weak laugh.

"I can't talk you into this case?"

"No, I'm afraid not."

"Should I try again?"

"You can try, but I doubt if I'll change my mind." She knew Dr. Phelps was disappointed in her. "I'm sorry," she murmured, and replaced the receiver.

Her hand rested on top of the phone. No less than twenty times after she'd left Sloan, she'd been tempted to call and see how things were going. The only thing that had stopped her was the fear that Sloan would answer. Some nights she had lain awake and allowed her mind to play back the memories. They'd shared some happy times, good times. Her favorite had been when they'd sat on the beach, Sloan at her side, his hands fingering her hair.

So many times they'd sat on the verandah late at night and discussed a myriad of subjects. Amazingly, their tastes and opinions were often similar.

Joy hadn't expected to miss his companionship so much, nor his friendship. Sloan had been her friend, a very good friend.

A long sigh escaped her as she tucked her feet under her in the big overstuffed chair. Joy rested her head against the back cushion and closed her eyes. Three weeks, and she'd yet to sleep an entire night through. She felt exhausted and frustrated with herself.

The decision had been the right one. Both times. L.J. was free to join his own kind and live the life he was meant to. Just as Sloan was now. She would no more fit in Sloan's world than she would in L.J.'s. For a time they would miss her. It would be a natural reaction. But later those feelings would change. Soon, if not already, Sloan would realize she'd been right. What he felt was gratitude, not love. Her only desire was that in the future he would think kindly of her.

Days took on a regular pattern. She rose early and continued with her running, sometimes going as far as five miles.

Her work offered few challenges. Patients were shuffled in and out of the treatment room every thirty minutes, sometimes longer, depending on the nature of the damage. The clinic specialized in treating sports injuries. Usually little more than ice packs, electric muscle stimulation, and a workout schedule with weights. But there was little personal satisfaction.

Usually Joy didn't eat until late in the evening. Her appetite was nearly nonexistent. Clara's good cooking had spoiled her, and when it came to fixing herself something to eat it was easier to open a can or toss something in the microwave.

Friday night, after a long week, Joy left the front door of the apartment open while she sat drinking from a glass of iced tea, her leg draped over the side of her chair. Her attention flittered over the glossy pages of a woman's magazine.

When the doorbell buzzed, Joy assumed it was Danielle, who sometimes stopped in unexpectedly. Unlooping her legs, she set the tea aside and sauntered to the door.

The welcome died on her lips. Was she hallucinating? Dreaming? Sloan, standing erect without the aid of crutches or walker, stood before her.

Dressed in tan slacks and a blue knit shirt, he looked compelling and handsome. The vigorous masculine features broke into a ready smile.

"Hello, my Joy." The lazy, warm voice assured her that her mind wasn't playing cruel tricks.

"Sloan." His name slipped from her lips as the magazine fell to the floor. She stooped to retrieve it, conscious of her rolled-up cotton pants and bare feet.

"Aren't you going to invite me in?"

"Of course," she muttered, her voice trembling as her fingers fumbled with the lock on the screen door. "You're using the cane." The observation wasn't one of her most brilliant. But she knew how hard he must have worked in the three weeks since she'd last seen him to be using the cane.

"Yes, but only for a few days." The limp was barely noticeable as he walked into the room.

"You're doing great." It was so good to see him that she had to restrain herself from throwing her arms around him. Her heart was singing a rhapsody.

"Thanks."

Her hands were clenched self-consciously in front of her. "Would you like something to drink? I made some fresh iced tea earlier. From scratch, the way Clara does."

"That sounds fine."

Joy felt like skipping into the kitchen. Her mind whirled at the virile sight of him. He looked magnificent. Oh heavens, why hadn't she washed her hair tonight? She was a mess.

"Make yourself comfortable," she said, and motioned toward the chair she'd vacated. "I'll only be a minute."

Joy had opened the refrigerator door and taken out

the pitcher of tea before she noticed that Sloan had followed her.

"Aren't you going to admit it's good to see me?" His gaze shimmered over her.

"It is," she said, and beamed him a bright smile. "It really is. You look great."

"So do you."

The tea made a swishing sound at the bottom of the glass as she poured it over the ice cubes. Her hand shook as she added a lemon slice to the side of the tall glass. When she held it out for him, Sloan's hand cupped hers.

"I've missed you, my Joy."

"And I've missed you." She forced a light gaiety into her voice.

Sloan set the tea on the counter without releasing her hand. His eyes held her prisoner as he tugged gently on her arm, bringing her closer to his side.

"I want you to come back."

"Oh, Sloan," she murmured miserably, and dropped her gaze. "You don't need me; I can't come back."

"I love you, Joy. I've loved you from the time you held up your head and walked out of the pool, letting me see your scars. Proud, regal, and so beautiful I nearly drowned just watching you."

"Don't, Sloan, please." She injected a plea into his name.

"I can't change the way I feel. I love you."

Backed against the kitchen counter, she was grateful for the support it gave her. "Listen to me, please."

"No," he said, and sighed heavily. "I listened to you the last time. Now it's my turn."

"All right." Her hesitation was pronounced. She

didn't want this, but there was little choice. Nothing he could say would change her mind.

"I know what you're thinking."

"I'm sure you don't—"

"It isn't gratitude," he interrupted her, his voice heavy with building frustration. "We're a team; we have been almost from the day you arrived. We were even injured in the same kind of accident. I could have fallen off a cliff skiing or broken my back a hundred different ways. But I didn't. We like the same things, share the same ideals. I am thankful for what you did, I can't deny that, but it's so much more."

"I'm a therapist." She placed her palm across her breast in an identifying action. "I've worked on tons of cases like yours. Patients always fall in love with their therapists. It's common knowledge that it happens all the time."

"In other words, I'm one of the scores who have fallen for you."

She avoided the question. "What you feel isn't a true emotion, but one prompted by appreciation for what I've done."

Sloan took in a deep, angry breath. "In this case I think you outdid yourself," he returned flatly.

"Your parents' bonus check was very generous." Her heart was crying with the agony she was causing them both.

His handsome face twisted with something she couldn't read.

"You're wrong," he argued. "I know what I feel. I'm not a young boy suffering from my first case of puppy love." His voice was low and rough with frustration, almost angry.

"The thing is, we've been through a lot together. We've worked hard; I've seen you at your best and your worst. You've shared a part of yourself with me that probably few others have ever seen. It's only natural that you would come to think you love me. Believe me when I say sincerely that I've never been more honored."

"Don't say that. I want to share my life with you. I want you to be the mother of my children and stand by my side in the years ahead. When I wake up at night, I want to feel your softness at my side. Tell me you want this too."

"Sloan." Tears blurred her eyes as she lifted her gaze. She loved him desperately and at the same time hated him for what he was forcing her to do. Perhaps now he wanted these things. But later that would change. His gratefulness would diminish and he'd realize what a terrible mistake he'd made.

"Say it, Joy. Tell me you want me." His hands, warm and possessive, cupped her shoulders.

"You're being unfair." Her throat felt raw, and it throbbed.

"I'm being more than fair. All I ask is a simple straightforward answer. I love you; I want to marry you. Yes or no?"

She stood, unable to formulate the word, not when every part of her was crying out for her to go to him. A huge lump had a stranglehold on her voice.

"Joy?" he prompted. "Just say yes." His voice was a caressing whisper. His fingers pressed lightly into her shoulder as if that would encourage her.

Tightly she closed her eyes, unable to bear looking

at him. A tear squeezed through her lashes and ran down her cheek.

With infinite tenderness, Sloan kissed the moisture away.

"No." Somehow the word managed to slip out.

Joy felt his shock.

"I see." He dropped his hands from her shoulders. She blinked through a curtain of tears. "I'm sorry; so sorry." She felt raw and vulnerable.

"Not to worry." The grim voice was cutting. "I appreciate the honesty." He turned abruptly and moved out of the kitchen.

Dazed, hurt, dying, Joy watched him leave as the tears slid down her face. He didn't hesitate.

Ten

Mutely Joy walked to the screen door to catch one last glimpse of Sloan as he strolled out of her life. His limp was more pronounced now, his shoulders hunched. Joy bit viciously into her bottom lip, and the taste of blood filled her mouth. Never had anything been more difficult; never had anything been more right.

Someday the hurt would go away and she would be stronger for it. At least that was what Joy told herself repeatedly in the long, dark days that followed. She had no energy. Listlessly she lay around the house. Food held no appeal, and she began skipping meals. Her weight began to drop. She wouldn't allow herself the luxury of tears. The decision had been made; she had done the right thing. It would be useless to cry over it now.

Five days after Sloan's visit there was no doubt that summer had arrived in Southern California. Heat and humidity filled the tiny apartment, and Joy turned on a fan in hopes the small appliance would stir the heavy heat.

The thin cotton blouse stuck to her skin, and she unfastened the second button. Perspiration rolled down the hollow between her breasts.

Impatiently she walked into the kitchen and took a soft drink out of the refrigerator. Empty calories for an empty life, she mused as she ripped the pull tab from the aluminum can.

Her cell rang, and she felt like plugging her ears. There wasn't anyone she wanted to talk to. Not her mother. Not her brother. Not even Danielle. No one. The whole attitude was so unlike her that Joy knew it was important to shed this dark apathy as quickly as possible.

"Hello." Her voice held little welcome.

"Hi, Joy. This is Paul. How you doing?"

"Paul," she spoke into the mouthpiece, surprise raising her tone. "I'm fine. How are you?"

"Great. Listen, I know this is sudden and all, but how about dinner? We could meet at Mobey Jake's."

"I... I don't know." She hesitated. Why torture herself? Paul was sure to mention Sloan.

"Have you eaten?" he asked.

"No. It's too hot to eat."

"Come on," Paul encouraged. "It's the least you can do, since I didn't get so much as a goodbye when you left. That still rankles." He was playful and teasing.

Joy laughed, and the sound surprised her. It'd been weeks since she'd found anything amusing. "All right," she agreed, "but give me an hour."

"Do you want me to pick you up, or can you meet me?"

"I'll meet you."

Mobey Jake's held fond memories. The flashing neon whale, round tables with faded umbrellas, and some of the best fried fish on the California coast. The first barrier she had hurdled in her relationship with Sloan had been the night she had brought him an order of fish from Mobey Jake's. Even L.J. had liked this fish the best. And who could blame him?

Joy was sitting at a table that overlooked the seashore far below when Paul arrived. He came from the direction of the beach home, which answered Joy's first uncertainty. Paul was still with Sloan. She had to wonder if Sloan sent him to talk to her. As soon as the question formed, she knew the answer. Sloan did his own talking.

Paul parked the older-model convertible and waved. Joy returned the gesture. He looked fit, tan, and muscular.

Tucking the car keys in his jean pocket, he smiled as he strolled toward her. "You look good." The hesitation was slight enough for her to notice.

"I don't, either."

"Lost weight?"

"A few pounds." Her fingers curled around the tall foam cup. "I'm ready to order." She changed the subject abruptly, not wanting to be the topic of their conversation.

She waited while Paul stood in line at the window and placed the order for their meal. He returned a few minutes later with their standard. Joy looked at the large double order of fish, knowing there wasn't an L.J. to eat the leftovers. The memory of her little friend tightened her stomach.

"I don't suppose you've seen L.J.?" She looked up at Paul.

"That darn bird of yours? No, I haven't."

"I wonder what ever became of him."

Paul shrugged his shoulders and slipped a large piece of fish into his mouth. Avoiding her gaze, he looked out over the scenery. "Don't you wonder about anyone else?"

Deliberately obtuse, Joy returned, "Of course I do. How's Clara?"

"Ready to quit."

"Clara? I don't believe it. She's been with the Whittakers for years."

"Neither one of us can take much more of what's been going on lately."

Joy nearly choked on a French fry. "Oh?"

"Aren't you interested?"

"I don't know." Joy managed to sound offhand and unconcerned, when she was terrified Paul would even mention Sloan's name.

"I understand where you're coming from," he began, "and whatever's between you and Sloan is none of my business, but something's got to be done."

"What do you mean?"

Paul took a swig of beer and with deliberate casualness placed it back on the table. "I shouldn't trouble you with this. After all, you were the smart one to get out when you did."

"Paul!" For the first time, Joy wanted to shake the younger man. "Obviously there's something you want me to know. Now either get it over with or shut up."

"It's Whittaker." Paul sounded uncertain now.

"Well, for heaven's sake, who else would be causing you any problems?" Joy was quickly losing her patience.

Paul avoided her gaze, fingering the fish. "He's in a bad way."

"How do you mean? Did he fall and hurt himself? Why didn't anyone let me know? Paul, does he need me?" All her concerns rushed out in one giant breath.

"He needs you all right, but not because of any fall."

"What do you mean?"

"I wish I knew. Listen, I don't know what happened last week, but Whittaker hasn't been the same since he came back from seeing you."

Joy hadn't been the same either. "How's that?"

"For nearly three weeks he practically killed himself—and me," Paul added sheepishly, "so that he could walk with the cane. His goal was to come to you. He never said as much, mind you, but it was understood. I don't know what you said, or what *he* said, for that matter, but Sloan's been locked up in his room ever since."

"I don't believe it."

"It's true. Ask Clara. He shouts and throws things at anyone who comes near him. If you think he was an angry beast when you first came, you should see him now. I think he's drinking, too."

"Oh, no." Joy's shoulders sagged. "Oh, Paul, no."

Joy hardly slept that night. Everything Paul told her seemed to press against her as she tossed and turned fitfully.

Before the sun came up the next morning, she was dressed in the same outfit she wore while working with Sloan. The ride down the highway was accomplished in short order, and she pulled into the long driveway that led to the beach house. Pausing, she looked appre-

hensively at the closed drapes and prayed that she was
doing the right thing.

Clara answered her timid knock and gave a cry of
welcome when she saw it was Joy.

"I'm so glad you've come." She hugged Joy briefly
and hurried on to explain. "I just didn't know what to
do for Mr. Whittaker anymore. He doesn't want to see
no one. He hardly eats and keeps himself locked up in
that room. Not even his father, but he'll see you, Joy.
It's you Mr. Whittaker needs."

Joy's returning hug lacked confidence. "If he thinks
I went through months of work so he can lock himself
away and sulk, then I'll tell him differently."

"That-a girl." Clara patted her across her back. "I'll
be in the kitchen cooking breakfast. Mr. Whittaker will
eat now that you're here."

"You do that."

"I'll fix my best blueberry waffles. I'll cook some
up for you too."

Food was the last thing that occupied her thoughts,
but Joy gave the old woman an encouraging nod.

Hands knotted at her side, Joy squared her shoulders
and marched down the hall to Sloan's room. Boldly she
knocked long and hard against his door.

"I said leave me alone."

Pushing in the door, Joy was immediately assaulted
with the stale and unpleasant odor of beer. Wrinkling
her nose, she proceeded into the room. Dirty clothes
littered the floor, the bed was unmade, and the sheets
hung off the edges.

In the dim interior, Joy didn't see Sloan at first.
When he spoke, her attention was drawn across the
room to the far corner. He sat in the wheelchair, the

cane lying on the floor at his side. Two or more days' growth of beard darkened his face. His normally neatly styled hair was tangled and unruly. Paul hadn't been exaggerating when he said Sloan was in a bad way.

"What do you want?" The anger was unable to disguise his shock.

Joy didn't answer him; instead she walked across the room and pulled open the drapes. Brilliant sunlight chased away the shadows and filled the room with its golden rays.

"Get out of here, Joy."

"No." Hands on hips, she whirled around. "What's the matter with you?"

He didn't bother to answer. Instead he stood, limped across the room, and closed the drapes. "Wasn't it you who said if I wanted to keep the drapes closed I'd have to do it myself? I just have. Now get out."

"Oh no you don't," she flared, and jerked the drapes open a second time. Not an inch separated them.

Sloan squinted with the light. "Who the hell let you in here anyway? They'll pay with their job when I find out."

"What's that doing sitting in here?" She pointed to the wheelchair. "When I left, it was because you would never need that thing again." Now she was angry, just as angry as Sloan.

"Is that what it takes to bring you back in my life? A wheelchair?"

"No," she cried. "But I didn't spend long, hard weeks working with you so that you could sit in the dark."

"I thought I told you to get out of here. This is my life, and I'll live it as I please," he shouted back harshly.

"Not when I've invested my time in it you won't."

"I need a beer." A hand against the side of his head, he looked around the room, carelessly throwing clothes and anything that impeded the search.

"Alcohol is the last thing you need."

"Go home, little girl. I don't want you."

"Sloan, for heaven's sake, look at what you're doing to yourself. This is ridiculous."

"No more crazy than your coming here. I don't need your devotion or your pity."

"Pity?" She nearly choked on the word. "I can't believe you'd even suggest anything like that."

"You've made your feelings crystal clear," he told her roughly. "If it isn't sympathy, what is it?"

Joy pressed her lips together.

"Why are you here?" he demanded a second time.

"I... I don't know why," she lied, and stalked across the room, arms hugging her waist. He shouted at her again, and she grimaced, not even hearing the words. "All right," she cried, "you want to know why? I'll tell you. I didn't go through the agony of giving you back to the Chantelles of the world so you could waste your life."

"Have you gone crazy?"

"Yes, I'm nuts, and another week like the last one and I'll be carted off to a mental hospital." She knew she was being irrational, but she had lost the power to reason. She didn't know what she'd planned to say when she walked into his room. But nothing was going right, and everything looked so hopeless.

"Joy." An incredulous note entered his voice. "Do you love me?"

Joy opened her mouth to deny herself again, but the words wouldn't come.

"Do you?"

"Yes," she snapped.

"You idiot. You crazy idiot," he muttered, and pulled her into his arms, his hold strong and sure. He expelled a rush of air and relaxed against her.

Somehow Joy had never heard anything more beautiful.

"Why did you send me away?" His breath stirred the hair at the crown of her head.

She slid her arms around his neck, reveling in the feel of his body close to hers. "I couldn't let you waste yourself on me because you're grateful."

His arms tightened around her. "Grateful." He spat the word out. "I've come to almost hate that word. What does it take to convince you that what I feel is love?"

"Thirty years?" she breathed, and laid her head against the muscular chest.

"That's not near long enough," he told her huskily, his hand weaving in the short curls, pressing her to him.

"But, Sloan, how can you love me? I'm not pretty or rich or—"

"Stop," he interrupted her, almost angry again. "I love you, and I won't have you saying those things about yourself. When you first came, for all intents and purposes I was crippled. Then I was walking again, and you left. Everything should have been perfect, but I was more of a cripple without you."

"But I don't fit in—"

"The only thing that's going to stop you from arguing with me is kissing you."

She laughed and nuzzled his neck. "That might work," she said shakily, and raised her head to meet his descending mouth. Her lips parted under his, and the blood rushed through her veins. No longer did she question if Sloan's feelings were interwoven with a deep sense of appreciation. He loved her; she knew that now as intuitively as she had recognized her own feelings.

Possessively his hands slid over the womanly curves of her rib cage to cup the swelling fullness of her breasts. He shuddered and buried his face in her neck. "You'll marry me." It wasn't a question, but a statement of fact.

"Yes," she breathed in happily. "Yes."

"Children?"

"As many as you want."

"My, my, you're agreeable."

"All right, no more than ten."

He rubbed his chin along the top of her head. "You won't go away if I take a shower and change clothes, will you?"

Her arms curved around the broad expanse of his chest. "Are you kidding? You've given me enough reason to hang around for a lifetime."

Chuckling, he kissed the top of her nose. "Are you always going to be this stubborn?"

"You'll find out," she teased.

"I can hardly wait."

An hour later, their arms looped around each other's waist, they slowly sauntered down the flawless beach. Their bare feet made deep indentations in the sand, their footsteps punctuated by Sloan's cane.

A brisk breeze whipped a curl across Joy's face. Sloan tucked it around her ear and kissed her hard and deep.

"I love you," she told him shakily, her voice still affected by his kiss.

"I wondered how long it would take you to say it."

"I admitted it to myself a long time ago."

Above, a flock of seagulls circled and let out a loud squawk. Joy paused and shielded her eyes with her hand.

"Sloan," she whispered in disbelief. "It's L.J."

"Honey, there are a thousand birds out here that look exactly like him."

"He's up there. That's him," she cried, pointing him out for Sloan. Happiness trapped the oxygen in her lungs. "It's got to be him."

"Joy." Sloan arched both brows.

Her attention was directed to the flock of birds that flew down the beach. Only one stayed behind, landing a few feet away.

"It is him," she whispered.

"You didn't tell me I would be forced to fight off flocks of admirers," Sloan teased with a smile of intense satisfaction.

L.J. quirked his head as if to say he didn't have time to chat, spread his wings, and flew back to his friends.

"He just stopped by to say hello," Joy murmured happily.

"And I," Sloan whispered, pulling her into his arms, "have come to stay a lifetime."

* * * * *

Join #1 *New York Times* bestselling author

DEBBIE MACOMBER

for the *Dakota* trilogy, featuring
heartwarming stories about a second-chance
town with an unforgettable tale to tell!

Collect them all!

"[Readers are] certain to take to the *Dakota* series
as they would to cotton candy at a state fair."
—*Publishers Weekly*

Be sure to connect with us at:
Harlequin.com/Newsletters
Facebook.com/HarlequinBooks
Twitter.com/HarlequinBooks

www.MIRABooks.com

MDMDTRI0516R2

#1 *New York Times* bestselling author

DEBBIE MACOMBER

**returns with two beloved Manning family
tales of love and romance.**

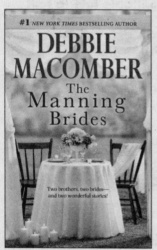

Rich Manning and Jamie Warren
have always been friends—and
nothing but friends. However,
that changes when she asks
him to father the child she so
desperately wants. Rich agrees—
if she'll marry him. Because
he thinks their *Marriage of
Inconvenience* could become a
real marriage instead.

His brother Paul, a grieving
widower with three small
children, turns to Leah Baker
for help and comfort. When
that comfort begins to grow
into something else, Paul
discovers that he wants *more* than
a *Stand-In Wife*!

Available now, wherever books are sold!

Be sure to connect with us at:
Harlequin.com/Newsletters
Facebook.com/HarlequinBooks
Twitter.com/HarlequinBooks

www.MIRABooks.com

MDM1860

#1 *New York Times* bestselling author

SHERRYL WOODS

returns with a *Sweet Magnolias* story where one woman's homecoming doesn't turn out quite as she had planned.

There's no place like home, especially if it's Serenity, South Carolina. For Annie Sullivan, though, the homecoming is bittersweet. She'd always envisioned a life there with her childhood best friend, Tyler Townsend. But Ty's betrayal has cost her the family and the future they'd once planned.

For Ty, losing Annie was heartbreaking. Still, he can't imagine life without the three-year-old son whose mother left him for Ty to raise. Ty wants it all—Annie, his child and the future he'd dreamed about—and he's back home in Serenity to fight for it. But getting Annie to forgive and forget may be the hardest challenge he's ever faced. With the stakes so high, this is one game he can't afford to lose.

Available now, wherever books are sold!

Be sure to connect with us at:
Harlequin.com/Newsletters
Facebook.com/HarlequinBooks
Twitter.com/HarlequinBooks

MIRA®

www.MIRABooks.com

MSHW1902R

#1 *New York Times* bestselling author

SHERRYL WOODS

concludes the *Perfect Destinies* saga with this beloved, sassy tale of revenge with an unexpected twist!

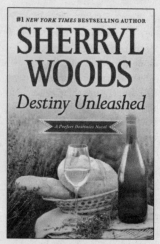

For twenty years Destiny Carlton has put family and duty ahead of her own hopes and dreams. Now, with the orphaned nephews she raised grown and married, it's time for the once free-spirited artist to reinvent herself yet again, this time as a savvy businesswoman out for revenge. Her target: William Harcourt, a man she once loved, a man who now seems hell-bent on destroying her family's business.

For William, going after Carlton Industries is a high-stakes gamble. He's gotten Destiny's attention, but he has also infuriated her family. Now they stand firmly between him and his real goal—winning Destiny's heart.

William has set the corporate game in motion, but suddenly he's playing by Destiny's rules. And when an unpredictable woman's fury has been unleashed, who knows what unexpected twists life might take?

Available now, wherever books are sold!

Be sure to connect with us at:

Harlequin.com/Newsletters

Facebook.com/HarlequinBooks

Twitter.com/HarlequinBooks

MIRA®

www.MIRABooks.com

MSHW1889

↶ LIFE IN ICICLE FALLS ↷

SHEILA ROBERTS

Home is where the love is...

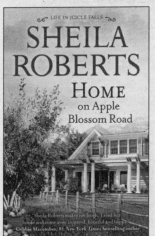

Colin Wright and Mia Blair grew up in Icicle Falls, but they left years ago—and not on good terms. Now Colin's grandmother Justine has died, and they've come home to honor this woman they both loved. That's when they get some unexpected news. They're about to inherit something. Jointly. They just have no idea what. It turns out that Justine's designed a treasure hunt for them, like the ones they enjoyed when they were kids and best friends.

On the trail of Justine's treasure, Colin and Mia follow a series of clues that take them down memory lane—ending up at the orchard on Apple Blossom Road. What will they find there? And what did Justine know that they didn't?

Available now, wherever books are sold!

Be sure to connect with us at:
Harlequin.com/Newsletters
Facebook.com/HarlequinBooks
Twitter.com/HarlequinBooks

MIRA®

www.MIRABooks.com

MSR1879R

#1 New York Times bestselling author

SUSAN WIGGS

returns to sun-drenched Bella Vista, where the land's bounty yields a rich harvest...and family secrets that have long been buried.

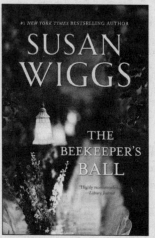

Isabel Johansen, a celebrated chef who grew up in the enchanting Sonoma town of Archangel, is transforming her childhood home into a destination cooking school—a unique place for other dreamers to come and learn the culinary arts. Bella Vista's rambling mission-style hacienda, with its working apple orchards, bountiful gardens and beehives, is the idyllic venue for Isabel's project...and the perfect place for her to forget the past.

But Isabel's carefully ordered plans begin to go awry when swaggering, war-torn journalist Cormac O'Neill arrives to dig up old history. He's always been better at exposing the lives of others than showing his own closely guarded heart, but the pleasures of small-town life and the searing sensuality of Isabel's kitchen coax him into revealing a few truths of his own.

Available now, wherever books are sold!

Be sure to connect with us at:

Harlequin.com/Newsletters

Facebook.com/HarlequinBooks

Twitter.com/HarlequinBooks

www.MIRABooks.com

MSW1900

Turn your love of reading into rewards you'll love with
Harlequin My Rewards

**Join for FREE today at
www.HarlequinMyRewards.com**

Earn **FREE BOOKS** of your choice.

Experience **EXCLUSIVE OFFERS** and contests.

Enjoy **BOOK RECOMMENDATIONS**
selected just for you.

PLUS! Sign up now
and get **500** points
right away!

Earn
FREE
REWARDS
Join
Today!
HarlequinMyRewards.com

MYR16R

DEBBIE MACOMBER

32988	OUT OF THE RAIN	___ $7.99	U.S.	___ $9.99	CAN.
32918	AN ENGAGEMENT IN SEATTLE	___ $7.99	U.S.	___ $9.99	CAN.
32828	ORCHARD VALLEY BRIDES	___ $7.99	U.S.	___ $9.99	CAN.
32798	ORCHARD VALLEY GROOMS	___ $7.99	U.S.	___ $9.99	CAN.
32783	THE MAN YOU'LL MARRY	___ $7.99	U.S.	___ $9.99	CAN.
31888	DAKOTA HOME	___ $7.99	U.S.	___ $9.99	CAN.
31883	DAKOTA BORN	___ $7.99	U.S.	___ $9.99	CAN.
31838	THE MANNING SISTERS	___ $7.99	U.S.	___ $9.99	CAN.
31819	TWENTY WISHES	___ $7.99	U.S.	___ $8.99	CAN.
31678	HOME IN SEATTLE	___ $7.99	U.S.	___ $8.99	CAN.
31645	TO LOVE AND PROTECT	___ $7.99	U.S.	___ $8.99	CAN.
31624	ON A CLEAR DAY	___ $7.99	U.S.	___ $8.99	CAN.
31598	NORTH TO ALASKA	___ $7.99	U.S.	___ $8.99	CAN.
31587	A MAN'S HEART	___ $7.99	U.S.	___ $8.99	CAN.
31580	MARRIAGE BETWEEN FRIENDS	___ $7.99	U.S.	___ $8.99	CAN.
31551	A REAL PRINCE	___ $7.99	U.S.	___ $8.99	CAN.
31535	PROMISE, TEXAS	___ $7.99	U.S.	___ $8.99	CAN.
31457	HEART OF TEXAS VOLUME 3	___ $7.99	U.S.	___ $8.99	CAN.
31441	HEART OF TEXAS VOLUME 2	___ $7.99	U.S.	___ $8.99	CAN.
31426	HEART OF TEXAS VOLUME 1	___ $7.99	U.S.	___ $9.99	CAN.
31413	LOVE IN PLAIN SIGHT	___ $7.99	U.S.	___ $9.99	CAN.
31395	GLAD TIDINGS	___ $7.99	U.S.	___ $9.99	CAN.
31357	I LEFT MY HEART	___ $7.99	U.S.	___ $9.99	CAN.
31325	A TURN IN THE ROAD	___ $7.99	U.S.	___ $9.99	CAN.

(limited quantities available)

TOTAL AMOUNT	$ _____
POSTAGE & HANDLING	$ _____
($1.00 for 1 book, 50¢ for each additional)	
APPLICABLE TAXES*	$ _____
TOTAL PAYABLE	$ _____

(check or money order—please do not send cash)

To order, complete this form and send it, along with a check or money order for the total above, payable to MIRA Books, to: **In the U.S.:** 3010 Walden Avenue, P.O. Box 9077, Buffalo, NY 14269-9077; **In Canada:** P.O. Box 636, Fort Erie, Ontario, L2A 5X3.

Name: _____

Address: _____ City: _____

State/Prov.: _____ Zip/Postal Code: _____

Account Number (if applicable): _____

075 CSAS

*New York residents remit applicable sales taxes.
*Canadian residents remit applicable GST and provincial taxes.

MIRA®

www.MIRABooks.com

MDM0716BL